Shroud Publishing Presents...

EPITAPHS

THE JOURNAL OF THE
NEW ENGLAND HORROR WRITERS

Edited by Tracy L. Carbone

SHROUD PUBLISHING
MILTON, NH

Shroud Publishing Presents ...

EPITAPHS

The Journal of the New England Horror Writers

First Edition

First Printing Nov. 2011
Copyright © 2011 NEHW
All Stories © their Respective Authors
All Rights Reserved

Editor: Tracy L. Carbone
Cover Art from an Original Relief Print, Book Design and Layout
by Danny Evarts
Line Editors: Stacey Longo & Danny Evarts

The text of this book was composed using Adobe Garamond Pro.
Display type was set in Bordeaux Roman.

ISBN: 978-0-9827275-9-1

The stories in this book are works of fiction.
People, places, events and situations are the product of the author's imagination.
Any resemblance to actual persons, living or dead, or historical events, is purely coincidental.

No part of this book may be reproduced, stored in a retrieval system, or transmitted by any means without the written permission of the author and publisher.

Shroud Publishing LLC
121 Mason Road
Milton, NH 03851
www.shroudmagazine.com

Acknowledgements

Thank you to Shroud Publishing and Timothy Deal for agreeing to publish, and being enthusiastic about, the NEHW's inaugural horror anthology.

To my counterparts on the New England Horror Writers Board for their input and story reading, with special thanks to Danny Evarts and Stacey Longo for their line edits and continual support throughout the process.

Also to the 250 plus members of the New England Horror Writers, an amazingly talented and growing group of like-minded horror folks. I am honored to have read your work.

To the contributors, I am thrilled to have my name attached to yours.

– Tracy L. Carbone
Editor

About the New England Horror Writers

Founded in 2001, New England Horror Writers (NEHW) provides peer support and networking, with a relaxed and social mindset, for authors of horror and dark fantasy in the New England area. NEHW also supports its writers' goals and promotes the work of its members.

NEHW is primarily a writers' organization, focusing on authors of horror and dark fiction in all mediums (novels, short stories, screenplays, poetry, etc.) in the New England area. We are also open to professional editors, illustrators, agents and publishers of horror and dark fiction.

NEHW activities include book signings and group panel discussions at conventions, as well as purely social gatherings. With members ranging from Maine to Connecticut, NEHW events take place in varying locations, making it easier for people to meet.

The NEHW Committee:

Tracy L. Carbone
Timothy P. Deal
Danny Evarts
Scott T. Goudsward
Jason Harris
Stacey Longo
Dan Keohane
T. J. May

newenglandhorror.org

Contents

Princes and Princesses, Kings and Queens   vii
An Introduction of Sorts by Peter Crowther

To Sleep, Perchance to Die   3
Jeffrey C. Pettengill

The Christopher Chair   10
Paul McMahon

A Case of the Quiets   22
Kurt Newton

Build-A-Zombie   28
Scott T. Goudsward

Not an Ulcer   32
John Goodrich

The Possessor Worm   42
B. Adrian White

Make a Choice   50
John M. McIlveen

The Death Room   68
Michael Allen Todd

Perfect Witness   69
Rick Hautala

Stony's Boneyard   83
Glenn Chadbourne & Holly Newstein

Kali's Promise   94
Trisha J. Wooldridge

Sequel DAVID BERNARD	*102*
Malfeasance DAVID NORTH-MARTINO	*106*
Private Beach STACEY LONGO	*116*
All Aboard CHRISTOPHER GOLDEN	*121*
Holiday House L. L. SOARES	*141*
Lines at a Wake STEVEN WITHROW	*154*
A Deeper Kind of Cold K. ALLEN WOOD	*155*
Alone P. GARDNER GOLDSMITH	*168*
Pandora's Box ROXANNE DENT	*170*
Chuck the Magic Man Says I Can MICHAEL ARRUDA	*178*
Burial Board T. T. ZUMA	*190*
Windblown Shutter JOHN GROVER	*194*
Cheryl Takes a Trip STEPHEN DORATO	*207*
Legend of the Wormley Farms PHILIP ROBERTS	*218*
The Church of Thunder and Lightning PETER N. DUDAR	*226*
CONTRIBUTORS	*237*

Princes and Princesses, Kings and Queens

An Introduction of Sorts by Peter Crowther

You can keep the whole wide world
I'm just happy with New England
(with apologies to Billy Bragg)

I've spent time in a lot of American states—good quality time in every single one ... great places and great people—but, you know ... I've always enjoyed myself most in New England. Why? I couldn't tell you. It's just the way it is.

Some folks say that the New England states are the closest in feel to England: maybe that's true, but I know that wasn't what I was looking for when I found it. I think I was looking for the American myth, and I reckon it's more likely to be found in New England and upstate New York than anyplace else.

About twenty years ago, I set about editing an anthology of stories by American writers who I felt used the place setting of their work almost as strongly as the characters in the tale.* They weren't all New England writers, but when I sat down to create the pitch letter (four pages, for crissakes!), I figured that was where my head was at.

---

* The anthology was titled *Heartlands*, and I had warm and positive responses—that I was okayed to use with prospective publishers—from the likes of Tobias Wolfe, Michael Bishop (his 'Blue Kansas Sky' was the eventual result), John Updike, Ed McBain, Joyce Carol Oates, Max Allan Collins, Barbara Kingsolver, Lawrence Block and several more. I sought help from the marvelous Marty Greenberg who thought it was a tremendous idea, and Marty immediately drafted in assistance from the William Morris agency, who thought the project would be snapped up in a flash. Alas, it wasn't to be.

Peter Crowther

I was already in love with Stephen King's Maine and Robert B. Parker's Boston, Archie and the gang's Riverdale (who knows where it is … it's probably in *Archie* creator John Goldwater's Mississippi, but for me it's pure Massachusetts), Ray Bradbury's Greentown (okay, the midwest but it's got Vermont in its soul), the poetic triptych of Walt Whitman, Robert Frost and Emily Dickinson, whose tragic couplet:

Parting is all we know of heaven,
And all we need of hell.

inspired me to write one of my own best-received stories ('All We Know of Heaven'), Ed McBain (whose Isola is a microcosm of every big American city—mainly New York but it feels like Boston to me), John Updike, Richard Ford and Elizabeth Hand (a Mississippian and a New Yorker respectively, though both now reside in Maine), Paul DiFilippo, Howard Phillips Lovecraft, Alice Hoffman, Edgar Allan Poe, Jack Kerouac, Lowry Pei ('Who?' you say … read *Family Resemblances*, a giant of a book), and my good friends Joe Hill and Christopher Golden.

There are more, of course—many more—and I'll think of them as soon as I've handed this piece across and it's printed up. But let's go with it the way it is or we'll never move forward.

I was commissioned by *New Musical Express*'s new music/arts magazine *Vox* to interview Stephen King way back in 1988, and Nicky and I spent the entire summer traveling our own version of William Least Heat-Moon's *Blue Highways* before winding up in Bangor, only to find that Steve had been called away to the *Pet Sematary* set. By this time, we'd seen enough to know we liked it (though the ocean around Bangor is even colder than here at the Yorkshire seaside) so, after a couple of days, we dawdled down from there and discovered Wells … plus, a few miles further south, Ogunquit. We've been back a couple of times, staying in Ogunquit and reading (and writing) on the beach, eating lobster rolls for lunch, and availing ourselves of the tremendous restaurants that line the streets. And once I get there, I just don't want to come home.

And that's because, when I am there, I feel like I'm home already. Just like I feel I'm at home in the pages of this formidable anthology.

But that's not to say the book you're holding is an easy read. It ain't. But then, if that's what you were looking for, you just plumb came to the wrong house. Right from the get-go, with Jeffrey Pettengill's 'To Sleep, Perchance to Die'—which if it were a song, would be pure garage and as raunchy as all get out—you know that you're going to come through a changed person, and Paul McMahon's quietly threatening 'The Christopher Chair' clinches it in spades.

I've done my fair share of poetry-writing so I know just how difficult it can be ... particularly when it's firmly within genre. Trisha Wooldridge's ambitious tone poem 'Kali's Promise,' Steven Withrow's short but hugely effective 'Lines at a Wake' and Kurt Newton's remarkable 'A Case of the Quiets' are each of them a pure joy, with Kurt's outing coming across as a blend of Roald Dahl and Shel Silverstein's songs (go re-listen to 'Sarah Cynthia Sylvia Stout,' who came to a terrible end when she doggedly refused to take the garbage out, and you'll see what I mean).

Do you ever think about dying? I mean, really? Do you ever stop what you're doing and imagine the year/month/day/hour/minute/second when it all stops ... when the heart stops pumping and you suddenly don't quite feel that hand that has been holding yours—stroking yours—with his/her face watching tearfully, telling you to hush, it's okay, it's okay to let go? Michael Todd has and his poem 'The Death Room' suggests he's thought about it often.

But that's not to say there are not some gentler moments, and the first of these comes in Scott Goudsward's lovely 'Build-a-Zombie,' which seems to me to be crying out for a kind of kids' book treatment complete with Glenn Chadbourne illustrations.

A good few years back now—maybe twenty—Jennifer Beale persuaded Ramsey Campbell to write something for her new novella line. The result—*Needing Ghosts*—was an absolute joy and, in my opinion, the piece set the tone for what has come to be Campbell's oeuvre ... a fractured humor coupled with a sense of truly surreal horror. And John Goodrich's 'Not An Ulcer' fits right in there, with generous overtones of Harlan Ellison's 'Shatterday' thrown in for good measure.

I'm a sucker for stories told in the form of an exchange of letters. One of my faves was, I believed, by Tom Monteleone though, having spent a frustrating (but nevertheless enjoyable) hour trying to find it amongst a couple thousand hardcover anthologies, I drew a blank. Thanks goodness then for Tracy Carbone, the editor of this fine tome, who reminded me that Tom's tale was titled 'Love Letters.' I just googled it and discovered the anthology in question is Rich Chizmar's *Cold Blood* and I've now found the volume. Hurrah! Well done, Tracy! Another one was a song by Dean Friedman, 'The Letter,' from his 1976 debut album, which came with this kickass couplet, written by an anxious back-home mom to her runaway child out there in the Big Wide World:

> *So what's it like to be on your own,*
> *a roaming vagabond, away from home,*
> *in search of some forgotten door?*

Now, B. Adrian White's Lovecraftian 'The Possessor Worm' isn't like either of those, but rather something from Hope Hodgson's *The House on the Borderland* ... a major gross-out that's impossible to forget. Great story.

Nicky and I had a great few days in Provincetown, culminating in a wonderful whale-watching boat ride, so John McIlveen's 'Make a Choice,' a super-dark riff on William Styron's novel, rang a lot of bells. I can see this as a TV movie, though it may be too heavy for studio execs to put their weight behind.

I first encountered Rick Hautala at a World Fantasy Convention—can't remember the city or the year (those gigs tend to spread into each other ... except for the New Orleans one, of course). But the first time I really met him was at Necon when I was a Guest of Honor. And boyoboy, ain't that the most 'fun' convention you ever saw? And ain't this tale from him ('Perfect Witness') just the saddest thing you ever read? Bravo, Rick.

Bravo, too, to Rick's wife, Holly Newstein, and Glenn Chadbourne for their superfine 'back from the dead' tale, 'Stony's Boneyard,' And it's so nice to find someone else who likes The Smithereens—that you, Holly or you, Glenn?

Elsewhere we have 'The Sequel,' David Bernard's harrowing riff on literary agents' percentages—something that's close to all of our hearts—and, in 'Malfeasance,' David North-Martino's solution to police interrogation.

And as for Stacey Longo's 'Private Beach,' well ... it should be part of a literary double-feature along with fellow New Englander Stephen King's 'The Raft.'

Chris Golden's 'All Aboard' is typically superb and gave me pause for thought. It wasn't just the pure mechanics of the tale—excellent though they are—but rather his choice of the train-time. Now this may sound dumb, but it's absolutely crucial (because, come on folks, things in stories do not happen by accident). Thus the 3:18 train is just more effective than, say, the 3:05 or the 3;26 or the 3:57. Don't ask me why—aside from the syllable count—it just is, and it matters hugely. As for the story itself, 'All Aboard' manages to mix poignancy with horror so that you don't know whether to stop reading or start weeping. Tremendous stuff. Tremendous, too, is Philip Roberts' 'Legend of Wormley Farms' which possesses a lyrical quality that almost takes it out of genre. Another writer to watch, methinks.

L. L. Soares' 'Holiday House' and K. Allen Woods' 'A Deeper Kind Of Cold' are cake mixtures lovingly blended in the literary kitchen … 'House' being a mix of nostalgia, ghosts and monsters (a sure-fire triptych in my view) while Woods' SF-cum-horror yarn is that rarity in that it makes you want to look away while you're actually reading it. This is Guignol at its Grandest!

The first page of Roxanne Dent's 'Pandora's Box' describes with stark brevity the three-minute destruction of a perfectly normal family, while P. Gardner Goldsmith's 'Alone'—which could almost have been a very dark *Twilight Zone* one-hander—should, by rights, have been possible only from a truly deranged mind and not from the eternally affable Gard. Mind you …

Don't go into the special room! Nah, they never listen do they … and Michael Arruda's character in 'Chuck the Magic Man Says I Can' is no exception. The shmuck. And in the end, we're glad he did.

T. T. Zuma is totally new to me, but his story 'Burial Board' packs a wallop that belies the author's lack of exposure. He's a man to watch. There's much to praise, too, in Stephen Dorato's 'Cheryl Takes A Trip,' not least that opening sentence. No, don't look at it now—see, you just couldn't wait could you!

John Grover's 'Windblown Shutter' introduces us to another attic (there are a few of them dotted around this book, which just goes to show you should have them boarded up without delay: nothing good can come down those stairs, believe me).

And finally, Peter Dudar's 'Church of Thunder and Lightning,' a monument to a spiteful god whose followers are, not surprisingly, a little on the strange side.

And there you have it. A veritable cornucopia of delights, some scary (one or two very scary indeed), some just strange, and a pleasing number possessing both whimsy and reflection in equal amounts. I'm thrilled to be a part of it—heck, I'm thrilled to have had the opportunity to read it!—so huge thanks to the Editor (with hearty congratulations on a job well done), and hearty congratulations, too, to the contributors: it's a mightily fine and headily varied (in content but not quality, the latter being uniformly high) tome. I've jotted some names down so that I may watch out for further scribblings.

Maybe I'll get to meet some of them in the flesh next time we're over in New England—I sure hope so. Until that time, let me paraphrase the wonderful John Irving with this sign-off:

> *Fare you well, you Princes and Princesses of Maine!*
> *You Kings and Queens of New England!*

Ayuh!

– Pete Crowther
Hornsea, England
Sunday, 11 September 2011

Shroud Publishing Presents...

EPITAPHS

THE JOURNAL OF THE NEW ENGLAND HORROR WRITERS

To Sleep, Perchance to Die

Jeffrey C. Pettengill

Evan Marchand lay on the bed as a skeletally thin lab technician attached sensors to his head. He started sweating as the confining oppressiveness of Lockwood General Hospital's Sleep Study Lab weighed on him. It was quickly becoming his least favorite place in the world. His chest tightened and it became harder for him to breathe. He wondered if the hell of staying in this cramped room for one night was worth the possibility of getting a good night's sleep for the rest of his life.

The technician took a piece of gauze and wiped perspiration from Evan's brow as he tried for a third time to affix a lead to his forehead. In a very reassuring tone he said, "I know it looks scary, but trust me, after the test is over and you get your new CPAP machine, you'll never have trouble sleeping again."

The man staring back at Evan Marchand from the dresser's mirror was barely recognizable. Despite the familiar ample jowls and triple chin, he saw a stranger. Dark circles surrounded dull-looking gray eyes. Perspiration was already matting his normally fluffy brown hair to his skull. A single bead ran down his forehead and dripped from the tip of his W. C. Fields-like nose.

"Boy, you look like hell," he told his reflection. "You need some serious sleep." He sighed. "There's nothing to be afraid of. It's a perfectly safe machine. People have been using them for years. Have you ever heard of anyone dying from a silly CPAP machine?" He paused, as if waiting for his mirror image to respond.

"No, of course not. If they weren't safe, they wouldn't be in use."

The rationality of those words struck him like a dead skunk in the middle of the road. They were pungent and made him want to get past them as quickly as possible. He couldn't get the sense of dread to leave him.

Continuing to look at himself in the mirror, he acknowledged the sleep apnea was definitely taking its toll. Not only was he dozing at his desk during the day, but the lack of sleep was making him look a lot older than his thirty-two years of age. Much older.

Turning, he looked at the machine sitting on the nightstand. More sweat streamed down his face at the thought of the mask over his nose. His thick knees trembled. Moving to the bed, he plopped down on its edge. It protested under his massive bulk as it did every night. By now, he was so used to the bed's complaints he no longer heard them.

The machine sat there, patiently awaiting him. It was a rounded square with four buttons just above a handle. One button was lit. The thing appeared to be bulging and ready to explode. Located on the machine's faceplate, along with the power and airflow ramp-up buttons, was the logo of Lockwood General Hospital. It stared at him like a menacing eye, seeming to follow his every movement in the room. One plastic hose connected it to a humidifier, which would keep the air he breathed moist. A second hose ran from the machine to a triangular plastic mask large enough to cover his nose.

He sighed, recalling how difficult the sleep study had been. His body quaked with the memory of how the confined feeling of the air mask intensified last time. He had not anticipated how it would heighten the claustrophobia the room had triggered. *How am I going to fight that thing when I go to bed*, he thought, shaking his head.

"Can I find the strength every night to put that mask on and keep it on?" he asked the silent machine. He closed his eyes. "It's too much work. Why couldn't they have had one of the newer machines with the nasal tubing? At least with that one I wouldn't feel so constricted."

Tears welled up in his eyes. *Why does everything have to be so difficult for me?*

His mouth was dry. It looked simple enough, unassuming, non-lethal, but it scared the crap out of him. Most people with sleep apnea would look at the mask and be overjoyed at the thought of the blissful slumber it promised to bring. But for Evan, the only thing going through his mind was suffocating in his own carbon dioxide.

With a shaky hand, he lifted the mask up. Examining it, he understood how it worked, but the knowledge didn't help. A wide elastic strap was attached in four places and would hold the unsettling object in place on his face. The plastic was hard and clear. Its triangular piece of rubber would surround his nose, creating the seal to keep the air in, giving it nowhere to go but through his nostrils and down his throat. The forced air would keep pressure on the loose soft tissue which sometimes fell over his windpipe preventing him from breathing as he slept. A T-shaped piece of plastic extended upward to rest against his forehead, giving the mask additional stability as he slept. Two more pieces of rubber kept the T-piece's hard plastic from biting into his brow.

His nerves shrieked as he brought the mask to his face. He closed his eyes, trying not to see the life-threatening plastic. But there was no getting away from the image. In his mind's eye, it became three times larger, looking large enough to engulf his entire head. His heart raced. Blood rushed through his ears, sounding like a crashing waterfall inside his head. His breathing grew more rapid as the fear forcibly took hold of him. He screwed his eyes more tightly shut against it, trying to keep it at bay.

Pressing the cool rubber to his overheated skin, a shiver danced down Evan's spine. His palms perspired as he held the mask in place and slipped the elastic straps over his head. The pressure on his face sent his already-raging nerves over the edge. They cried out for him to tear it off, to free him from its confines, to not suffocate him.

Evan inhaled.

Without the machine forcing air through the mask, breathing was difficult. The seal prevented him from drawing in a full breath through his nose. All that came through was the small amount of air he could pull in through the slit which allowed carbon dioxide to escape.

What if the machine shuts off while I'm sleeping? He wondered. *What if the power goes out? I'll suffocate.*

Panic surged again. He ripped the thing from his face and threw it to the floor. Sweat dripped into his eyes as he stared at the infernal contraption on his nightstand. Despite its innocuous light gray color, Evan saw it as a menacing lethal monster waiting to pounce on him, biding its time until he was asleep and unaware.

He shook his head. "There is no way I'm going to be able to do this without help."

The bed's frame creaked in relief as he stood and padded down the carpeted hall to the bathroom. There he got some water and a prescription sleep aid. He paused before popping the little helpers into his mouth and stared at himself in the mirror.

He was now paler than he had been when he'd seen his reflection earlier, nearly as white as a bed sheet. Sweat was pouring down his face in rivers.

Grabbing the hand towel, Evan wiped his face dry. He took the magic sleep inducers and gulped some water to get them down.

Not even the pills allowed him to get a sound night's sleep any more. He had given up on them months ago, but he hoped taking them tonight would relax him enough to put the mask on. Then he could let the machine to do its work and help him get the deep sleep he really needed.

As if to allay his concerns, Evan let out a loud yawn.

Looks like the pills are starting to work already. He filled his cup with fresh water and headed back to his room. "Better get this over with."

Stepping through the bedroom door and turning to place the cup on the nightstand beside the machine, Evan stopped. His jaw opened, then closed. His hand went limp. The glass of water fell to the thickly carpeted floor with a soft thud and splash.

There, sitting atop the CPAP machine, was the mask he had thrown on the floor. It was resting carefully balanced on the neatly coiled hose, giving the impression of a snake curled upon itself waiting for the right opportunity to strike out at its unsuspecting prey. The hospital logo was illuminated by the lit off button, giving it the appearance of an infernal red eye watching him. It made Evan feel even more like a helpless target.

"That's impossible," he stammered, trying to understand how the mask could be sitting on top of the machine. He yawned again. His eyes fluttered, attempting to close.

I must have picked it up on my way to the bathroom, he attempted to rationalize.

No, I couldn't have. I'd have remembered doing that. And why would I have placed it in such a neat display? I've never put anything neatly away.

Evan's mind grew fuzzy as the medication worked through his system. He couldn't think straight. He heard Morpheus's voice hypnotically calling him to the land of dreams. He so wanted to join him there. The pills' magic was working so strongly within him he teetered where he stood.

He toppled onto the bed.

What about the machine? he started to think. Unconsciousness swept over him like a wave over a drowning man.

Evan's dream self screamed in terror and sat up in bed.

He knew it was a dream because what he was seeing was not possible.

The CPAP's hose was poised, ready to strike. The mask wove back and forth like a snake's head, looking for the opening it needed.

Evan scrambled along the headboard to the far side of the king-sized bed.

The air coming out of the machine sounded like a serpent's hiss. And, like a cobra, the mask struck with incredible speed and accuracy.

The hose and mask lashed out at Evan, covering his nose. The elastic strap settled around his head, making the seal tight. Its T-shaped piece sliced through the soft rubber separating it from his forehead and into his flesh. Blood trickled down his brow.

Evan's hands scrambled to grab the mask and pull it off his face, but the strap and seal were too tight. It was as if they were fastened with superglue. His fingers couldn't grip on to either the strap or the mask. He jerked his head back to pull the hose free from the machine, but it just went taut, holding him firmly at its full length with no give.

Heart pounding like a timpani, he whipped his head back and forth. The strap constricted itself in response, tightening the pressure on his head. An image of the face-hugging creature from the *Alien* movies flashed through his mind. A fresh wave of panic surged through him in response. The scenes with them in it had always terrified him the most.

Climbing onto his knees, Evan gripped the hose with both hands and pulled with all his strength. His back arched and he groaned with the effort, but the hose would not pull free from the machine. The CPAP held its spot, as though it was nailed to the nightstand.

The sound of the machine's pumping changed, from a soft, soothing hum to a harsh, intense buzz. The air's intensity increased. The previously gentle pressure blowing into his lungs grew more forceful. It shocked Evan as he felt his lungs expand with the incoming air. The constant flow prevented him from fully exhaling the air already filling his lungs. It continued to pump into him nonstop. The pressure inside Evan's chest mounted.

Desperation seized him. Eyes bulged out of their sockets. He opened his mouth and tried to exhale. He needed to release the air inside of him. He managed to expel some of it, but it was rapidly replaced by the machine. Evan felt his lungs overflow like water running over the banks of a river, and still it sought more space to fill up.

For a dream this seems horribly real! Evan's mind screamed in panic. He struggled to exhale. *I need to wake up! This isn't real. It's only a dream!*

Digging his fingers into the flesh where the mask's rubber surrounded his nose, blood seeped out, staining the rubber and flowing into the corners of his open mouth. His fingers grew slick with the liquid and slid, losing their purchase on the mask.

The CPAP machine continued to buzz angrily on the nightstand as it pumped increasingly higher pressure air into Evan's body. His stomach began to expand as the air now passed down the esophagus. It was as if a balloon was growing inside him. In fact, it was like having two balloons inflated within his body. The pressure in his lungs was constant, not increasing, and not forcing his lungs beyond their already stretched-to-the-limit capacity, as the additional air found a new container to fill. His stomach stretched and swelled in reaction to the incoming air.

The ghastly hospital technician's words the morning after the test, when he was setting him up with the accursed machine, suddenly echoed in Evan's memory. "You won't have to worry about snoring again, fat boy," he said, his lips twisted into a feral leer, sinister black eyes taking in the full measure of Evan's bulk.

Inside, the pressure of his internal organs squishing each other increased. His heart struggled to beat against the heavier lungs.

With horrified eyes, Evan looked from his bloody hands to his stomach. It bulged even further outward than it normally did. It started in one spot, looking almost like a pimple growing before his eyes. Then it spread.

Evan finally understood what was happening and what was in store for him. He had watched Chinese chefs make Peking duck before. To separate the skin from the meat they'd use a bellows to force air into the body.

Evan's ears popped as his internal body pressure grew too much for the air around him and tried to offset itself. Then they popped again, and again, and again. It was similar to being in a rapidly ascending airplane, his ears popping to match each new level of elevation.

But it was doing nothing to stop the increasing air within his body. The next pop he heard, and felt, was not in his ears, but in his chest, and it was accompanied by a wave of intense pain. At first he wasn't sure what it was, but when the pressure against his heart and ribs started to lessen slightly, he had a horrifying idea of what had happened. One of his lungs had blown out, like an overinflated tire.

The air started to flow more freely, and faster. As it did, Evan saw more air pimples rising just underneath the surface of his skin. They multiplied with more rapidity to the point where they started combining into larger air bubbles, separating his skin from his body. The skin stretched and tightened as it expanded. The pain of his skin peeling free from the muscles was excruciating, but his mind didn't linger on it.

I feel like a freaking sausage casing being stuffed to the bursting point. Somebody, please stick a fork in me. I'm done.

Under the formidable pressure, Evan's heart stopped pumping.

His obese, overinflated body toppled forward across the bed. It rocked there gently.

Evan Marchand's CPAP machine stopped buzzing.

His sleep apnea was cured.

DEEP WITHIN THE BOWELS OF LOCKWOOD GENERAL HOSPITAL, where the Sleep Study Lab resided, the living skeleton of a man who operated the lab smiled. With a bony finger he depressed the console's button, disconnecting Evan Marchand's CPAP machine. In a sinister chuckle he muttered as he returned his focus to the overweight woman lying on the bed in the next room through the glass separating them. "Sleep well, fatso. Forever."

The Christopher Chair

Paul McMahon

I chew my thumbnail as Sheila walks out of the bedroom. Her legs are bony shadows within her nightdress, and her arms push against the cramped hallway walls for support. Her hair is flat and greasy, the hair of someone who's been sick. I wonder if Lazarus's hair looked that way when Jesus called him from the tomb.

I look away as she enters the kitchen. My gaze floats to the clean square of paint centered over the telephone table. Within it, an empty nail-hole peers back.

Sheila tugs free the chair across the table and sits down slowly, pleasurably, as someone will after standing all day. I cannot meet her eyes. I look at the grease spattered on the wall over the stove, the paint peeling off the window sill, the kidney-shaped water stain on the ceiling.

"The kitchen looks lovely," she says.

I try to meet her eyes and end up looking at my pocketknife between us on the table. Its blade is folded away. I wonder if I am going to Hell.

"What did you do?" she asks.

My gaze averts to the clean square of paint again, focuses on the nail hole as if the answer to Sheila's question can be found there. I tell her about pushing the antique wheelchair up the Torys' front walk the day after Mr. Tory destroyed his late wife's.

It's as good a starting point as any.

Despite my grip on the chair's handles, my hands trembled as I neared the Torys' front door. The house pulsed with an angry silence. Yesterday I'd arrived to Jules and Mr. Tory screaming at each other. I'd found Mr. Tory sprawled on his bedroom floor amid the wreckage of a disassembled wheelchair and bleeding from a three-inch gash in his right forearm. It needed stitches, but he'd refused to be taken to the hospital. I'd wrapped his arm the best I could.

I couldn't blame Mr. Tory for destroying that old chair. His wife had taken to it while still vibrant and beautiful after her brain tumor eclipsed her sense of balance. In the six months that followed, Mr. Tory had watched her shrivel to skeletal proportions while losing her memories and her ability to speak coherently. She'd finally died in the chair when the tumor swallowed her ability to breathe.

I worried that Mr. Tory would refuse this chair as well. He'd asked me to borrow it from the church for Mrs. Tory back when she first became ill, but old Father Morin feared the stories about its healing powers and refused to allow it off the church's property.

I pressed the Tory's doorbell.

"Get the door!" Mr. Tory bellowed.

"I *am*, Dad," Jules hollered back. The door opened a crack and Jules peered out. Whispered: "You got it."

"I got it," I said. Jules watched while I maneuvered the antique chair into the living room, then whistled under his breath.

"Ugly son of a bitch, ain't it?"

"Who's there?" Mr. Tory called from the back bedroom.

Jules ran his finger along the armrest. The chair was a gangly, high-backed thing, strung with wicker across the back, seat and footrests. More wicker was stretched over the wooden armrests. The back piece had the image of a walking staff woven into it with a slightly darker mesh.

"Jules! Who's there?"

"It's Pope," Jules shouted. He'd called me that since middle school even though I scrapped my dream of ordination after the accident that tore apart my family. "I appreciate this," Jules said. "Thought I was gonna have to carry him around the rest of his life."

"It wouldn't have to come to that," I said. Jules had a penchant for rushing to the extreme. One time Mr. Tory had asked him to trim a bush in front of the house.

Jules had worked for an hour trying to make it symmetrical, and managed to trim the thing all the way to its trunk. Then he'd cut that down as well. That explained why, as old as he was, Mr. Tory had been up on a ladder, trimming his own tree last year. He'd fallen and landed badly, snapped his spine just above the waist.

With his health insurance still in shambles after Mrs. Tory's lingering death, Jules had dug her old wheelchair out of storage. Mr. Tory used it grudgingly for two months before a routine colonoscopy revealed a polyp. Mr. Tory insisted the wheelchair had caused it. When Jules left the chair beside Mr. Tory's bed, he'd taken it apart.

"Do you want to bring it to him?"

Jules shook his head. "You do it. I need to get some stuff. Snacks for the game. You want anything?"

"No. Don't be long."

"Back before tip-off."

Jules sidestepped the chair and left without looking back. I waited until I heard his truck start, then pushed the antique chair down the hall.

Mr. Tory nearly wrenched his neck trying to see me from his bed. When he recognized the chair he seemed to stop breathing. "The Saint Christopher chair?" he whispered. I couldn't identify a single emotion in his tone and decided he must have too many for me to isolate just one. "Take it away. I don't want it."

I swallowed. "It was free. You can't afford more than that."

Mr. Tory's face tightened, but he offered no verbal response. The bandage around his right forearm showed only a small spot of blood. I congratulated myself on closing that cut. Then my eyes drifted to the spindly shapes of Mr. Tory's legs and I had to look away.

"I won't use it," Mr. Tory said.

"I'll help you," I said, but when I bent forward Mr. Tory swung at me.

"Get that goddamn chair out of here! Go get a cheap one at the Salvation Army that ain't got voodoo stories about it."

"You're worried about the stories?"

"People *died* in that chair, Robert."

"There's no proof of that."

"There's no proof they didn't, either."

I said nothing, but I didn't let my gaze drop. "You shouldn't have destroyed Mrs. Tory's wheelchair yesterday."

"Pris *died* in that piece of shit, and it was starting to kill me! I was healthy as a horse until I spent two months in that chair. Now I've got colon cancer."

"You don't have—"

"Yes, I do! I don't care what them idiot doctors call 'em, I call 'em *tumors*. And the only thing to do when you get the tumors is die. I want a chair no one died in."

"Any chair I find at the Salvation Army will be there because its owner died. You're going to convince yourself that any chair I bring you is making you sick."

Mr. Tory glared at me. A dark patch of whiskers shadowed the corner of his chin. He'd shaved without a mirror. "Years ago you told me you'd rather die than let someone else take care of you. Without a chair Jules will have to carry you around for the rest of your life. Is that what you want?" He narrowed his eyes at me, his breath heavy. After a long moment, his gaze finally dropped to the chair. "This chair will allow you to watch TV when you want, go to bed when you want, eat when you want. You'll even get to use the bathroom by yourself." I slapped the chair's seat. "*And* it's high enough that you'll be able to eat at the kitchen table."

Mr. Tory looked like a child trying to maintain the fleeting fury of a temper tantrum. Finally, his mouth slipped into a grin. "At least *this* chair will be easier to take apart."

"Your choice. But that would leave you at Jules' mercy for the rest of your life."

Mr. Tory gazed at the Christopher chair for a while. His expression softened, and he looked up at me. "What about the stories, Pope? Why's this been buried in the church attic all these years?"

I'd been trying to answer that question myself. On my way to St. Mary's this morning I'd convinced myself that legends of the chair's healing power were bogus. After the ex-canonization of St. Christopher people would naturally believe that icons in his name would stop working. Of course there would be the occasional story of one doing harm. It was human nature to exaggerate, after all.

"It's just a wheelchair," I said, finally. "God graces *people* with His gifts, not objects. Believing this chair has the power to heal is akin to worshipping the golden calf, isn't it?" The story of the woman healed by touching the hem of Jesus' robe flashed in my head, but I shoved it away. "Celtics tip-off in less than thirty minutes. I won't be coming to get you."

I angled the chair so Mr. Tory could climb in and locked the wheels. Then I went to the living room and turned on the TV. I left the volume low enough that Mr. Tory should be able to hear it but not make anything out, then I sat and listened for noises coming from the bedroom.

I've never been crazy about basketball, so I hoped that Jules would return quickly. A beer commercial showing blondes skiing in silver bikinis came on, and suddenly something Father Simmons said this morning brought me back to the attic of St. Mary's church.

"That's a weird design." Father Simmons stood in silhouette in the attic doorway, jangling his keys as he watched me push the chair toward him. He'd been assigned to St. Mary's after Father Morin collapsed of a heart attack while sorting through old boxes up here. Father Simmons was young, and it had taken a long while for the congregation to warm up to him. I, however, had helped him move in, and we'd struck up a pretty good friendship, being the same age. When I'd gone to him about borrowing the chair for Mr. Tory, I had expected the same refusal I'd gotten from Father Morin years ago. Father Simmons had surprised me, though. He'd grabbed the attic keys and insisted on coming up with me.

"That looks like a walking staff," Father Simmons said as I reached the doorway. He squatted and traced it with his finger. "What a curious design for a wheelchair."

"It's the symbol of Saint Christopher," I said.

Father Simmons smiled. "Not Saint anymore, I'm afraid. The only record of his existence is an unsubstantiated legend." Father Simmons stood and rubbed his hands together. "Christopher was a giant who made a living carrying people across a river." I was familiar with the story but didn't want to be rude, so I kept silent. "Legend goes that one day Christopher carried a child across, and the child grew heavier with every step. Once across, the child became Jesus and told Christopher to stop carrying the weight of the world on his shoulders. The church decreed that a single legend wasn't enough to prove Christopher's existence. So they ex-canonized him."

I forced a slow smile. "Fascinating."

"Hasn't affected what the faithful choose to believe, though. They can remove his sainthood, but they can't scrub his influence from our hearts and minds."

Something cracked in the bedroom, and I saw that more blondes were skiing on TV—only this time they were dressed properly as they were advertising Wachusett Mountain Ski Resort. It was a struggle not to leap off the couch to check on Mr. Tory, but I managed to sit through three more commercials. Then I heard a scrape, and the urge to check on him became too much. As I started to stand, Mr. Tory spoke.

"Not a word."

He was struggling to line the wheels up so he could pass through the living room door. The Christopher chair dwarfed his old, frail body. The back stretched six inches over Mr. Tory's head, and though its color was light it made Mr. Tory's skin look bloodless and dead. The armrests were wider than his arms, and his feet rested on the wicker footrests like dead animals.

He rolled the chair backward, then tried to straighten out enough to squeeze into the living room. He was succeeding in moving the chair, but only millimeters at a time. I watched him struggle for another minute before standing up. "Let me help you."

"Sit down! You wanted me to do this, you can just watch me and suffer. I hope it kills you."

Despite his surliness, I was proud of him.

He hadn't gotten the chair through the door by the time the game started, so he sat where he was with his fingers curled around the armrests. The spot of blood on his bandage was larger. He must have re-opened the cut climbing into the chair.

It started just after the Celtics' first basket. Mr. Tory's voice, a hoarse whisper, edged out the sound of the TV.

"I can move."

I turned my head, thinking he'd finally gotten the chair through the door, and my insides froze. His feet, immobile since he fell from that ladder, tapped on the dark wicker footrests.

"I can move," he said again. His face tightened as his right leg lifted completely off the footrest. He straightened it, and his knee gave a sharp pop. Holding it in the air, Mr. Tory pivoted his foot at the ankle. His spotless sock pulsed as he wriggled his toes.

"Holy shit," I whispered.

Mr. Tory brought his leg down and then executed the same movements with his left leg, just as precise, just as deliberate. I started to think that maybe the doctors had been wrong. Maybe Mr. Tory's spine *hadn't* been severed. Maybe it had only been pinched. Maybe he'd somehow freed it climbing into the chair. That had to be the explanation.

"How is this happening?" Mr. Tory asked. He stared at me, waiting for some kind of answer, but I could only shake my head. He started to giggle.

"Can you walk?" I asked.

"I can move!"

"Try to walk." I went and crouched in front of him, grabbed the front legs of the chair, and pulled it through the door. The next instant I flew backward and cracked my head against the coffee table. Mr. Tory laughed.

"I kicked you!" Mr. Tory sang. "I kicked you, I kicked you!"

If the chair could heal, why had it been locked up all this time? The question nagged at me as I rubbed the lump on my head.

"Can you walk?" I asked again.

Mr. Tory stopped laughing. A look of determination creased his expression. "Of course I can."

I stifled my own giggle as I climbed to my feet. I watched Mr. Tory slide forward. The chair rocked as he did, so he locked the wheels before turning his attention back to the task.

His pale, bony hands gripped the wicker armrests. Slowly, carefully, he slid his feet under the wicker footrests and folded them up out of his way, then he planted his feet on the living room rug. There was no sound to his movements, and yet each foot touched the floor with a resonant boom I felt in my chest.

"I wish I had a video camera," I whispered.

Mr. Tory's knuckles whitened. He stared at his feet as if mentally willing them the strength to hold his weight. Slowly, he started to lift himself from the chair.

A thin line of blood trickled out from under the bandage and traced a path along Mr. Tory's wrist. It curled around his hand as he rose, stopping against the wicker armrest just as Mr. Tory rose to his feet. He remained hunched over, his forearms trembling, his knuckles white as they gripped the armrests.

"You can do it," I whispered.

His pulled his left hand away from the chair, and for an instant his knees weakened. He stood that way, his right hand anchoring him to the chair in a bloody grip, for a long time. I was taking in a breath to offer more encouragement when Mr. Tory jerked his right hand away.

His legs crumbled, and I failed to catch him before his face thumped on the rug.

"Shit!"

"You almost had it," I said. I eased Mr. Tory onto his back, then placed my hand on his chest. His heart was racing dangerously.

"What the hell happened?"

"You almost had it," I said again. Then I saw his expression. Mr. Tory's gaze was angry, searing.

"My legs were *there*, Pope. And then they *weren't*."

"They haven't been used in months," I said. "They're weak. They couldn't handle the weight."

His expression grew sterner as he started at me. "I could feel them. I could feel the footrests and the air on my toes. Even through my socks." I nodded, unsure if he wanted me to say something, wondering what he wanted me to say. "When I let go of the chair I couldn't feel them anymore. They weren't there!"

"Can you move now?"

Mr. Tory closed his eyes and concentrated. His face was peaceful at first, determined but emotionless. As the seconds ticked by with no result, the corners of his mouth began to twitch and his eyebrows began to tighten.

"Okay, okay," I said. "That's enough." I rubbed my hand on his chest, trying to get him to relax, but he only tightened more. He groaned and his hands trembled with exertion. His legs didn't even twitch.

I lifted Mr. Tory's right hand. The bandage was bathed in blood. The stain on the rug might never come up.

"That's enough," I said. I squeezed his hand and he relaxed. "We've got to re-bandage this arm."

With some effort I got him back into the chair, then got the first aid kit and returned to remove yesterday's bandage. The gash was bleeding freely, but both ends of the cut were crusted and starting to heal.

"You really need this stitched up," I said.

"I can feel them again." Mr. Tory's eyes were intense, glaring at me, glaring through me.

"Your legs?"

"Yes my legs. What the hell do you think?"

"What—" I started, but he cut me off.

"It's this goddamn *chair*." I saw his eyes widen and realized he was building energy. I rolled backward, narrowly avoiding his kick. Jules' truck rumbled outside, and I hoped he'd get in here quickly.

"This is a healing?" Mr. Tory kicked at me, thrashed his legs in the air as if he were kicking in a swimming pool. "What kind of miracle is *this*? My legs work only when I'm sitting in a fucking wheelchair?"

"Your … um … spine," I desperately tried to retrieve my train of thought from when he'd first started moving—something about his spine being pinched?—but I couldn't think past Father Morin's words. *It turned evil.*

I struggled to my feet.

"Get out of my house."

"But—"

17

Mr. Tory's right arm came up now, pointed directly at me, and a drop of blood dripped onto the armrest. "Get out."

"But—"

Mr. Tory slammed his forearm on the armrest. "Get out! Get out! Get out!" Blood spattered as he hammered his arm on the armrest.

I backed away as Jules slammed the truck door outside. I froze when Mr. Tory started to stand once again. He looked like he was going to do it this time. His movement was sure and quick, and he even stepped forward with his left foot before he had completely released the chair—

—but the instant he did he collapsed.

He screamed when he landed, a sound swirling with rage and frustration. I stared at his scrawny legs splayed on the blood-stained rug and couldn't look away even when the door opened behind me.

Jules whispered: "What the hell?"

Mr. Tory pushed himself up with his left hand as I squeezed around Jules, whose "few snacks" consisted of a bulging grocery bag under each arm. "Take this goddamn chair with you!"

"WHAT HAPPENED THEN?"

I shake my head and realize I've fallen silent. I'm staring at the nail-hole in the wall, must have been the whole time I talked, but I don't remember seeing it. I wonder how long I've been silent.

"Bobby?" Sheila says. "What happened then?"

"I went back to the church to find more information on the chair. You want coffee or something?"

"Sure."

I busy myself setting up the coffee maker, noting with a twinge of disgust that I haven't cleaned it in a very long time.

"Did you find anything at the church?" Sheila asks.

"Nothing. There wasn't a record of the thing anywhere. Not even the date it was—" I almost say *banished* "—put away."

"What happened to Mr. Tory?"

"Jules brought him to the hospital. It took fourteen stitches to close his arm. The doctor showed them the X-rays of Mr. Tory's spine. Severed clean through." I smile as I remember Jules telling me about that hospital trip. "I still feel sorry for the doctor who told Mr. Tory he'd been dreaming."

The coffee maker gurgles, and I return to my place at the table. I fold my hands in front of me and wish this story was over. I wish there was no more to tell.

"Did Mr. Tory let you back in?"

Now, for the first time since Sheila walked out of her bedroom, I meet her eyes. They are soft and watery blue, the way I remember them from when she was a child. I swallow and glance over my shoulder at the coffee maker, which is still dripping. I take a deep breath, let it out slowly, and realize I'm staring at that nail-hole again.

"Three days later Jules left a message on the answering machine. Said he figured out how the chair worked."

I TOOK MY TIME TURNING OFF THE CAR, UNLATCHING MY SEAT BELT, climbing out and closing the door. My legs seemed to be filled with lead, and though I moved slowly I felt like I couldn't catch my breath. The silence inside the house seemed deeper than it had the day I'd brought the chair. I reached for the bell, but pulled my finger away before ringing it.

Jules hadn't said Mr. Tory was walking. He'd only said he'd discovered how the chair worked. Most likely the worst that would happen was Mr. Tory would kick me out again. I decided I could handle that. I pressed the doorbell.

It opened instantly, and Jules stuck his head out. His hair was mussed and there were dark circles under his eyes. A smear of dried blood flaked on the left side of his jaw.

"I did it, Pope," he said.

He swung the door open. I entered slowly, wanting to bolt for my car but lacking the determination to make my legs obey. My gaze darted to the spot on the rug where Mr. Tory had fallen. The bloodstain remained, far too dry to account for the smear on Jules' face.

"Okay, Dad," Jules called.

"Now?" Mr. Tory yelled from somewhere unseen. His voice sounded haggard and scratchy. I remembered how frail he'd looked sitting in that gangly chair.

"Now!"

"Wait," I said, but no one heard. My voice was powerless. Something scraped somewhere down the hall.

"What did you do?" I whispered, but my voice was ignored again.

Another scrape, and Mr. Tory giggled. That sound practically stopped my heart. I imagined a man much older than Mr. Tory shuffling up the hall with his last ounce of strength.

Another scrape, and Mr. Tory's foot appeared in the doorway. I thought he was wearing red socks.

His other foot scraped around the corner, dragged on the floor like he hadn't the strength to lift his leg, and this foot was red as well. It couldn't be socks because the red speckled his pajama bottoms.

"Blood gives it power," Jules whispered from behind me.

Mr. Tory stood in the doorway, his arms at his sides. He wore only pajama pants, and his pale skin glowed in violent contrast to the splashes of blood marring his chest. I wondered how his bare feet could have made those awful scraping sounds.

"I can walk, Pope," he said. He smiled a slow, dazed smile and spread his arms to clutch the sides of the doorjamb for support. Blood dripped from his forearms. As he lifted his leg to step into the living room the edges of his smile trembled, then his eyes fluttered and rolled upward.

I moved to catch him, but too late.

His face, from the nose up, slammed on the coffee table. Snapped his neck with a sound that cracked my soul.

Jules screamed, dropped, and yanked his father's bloody body into his arms in one fluid motion. Mr. Tory's back was a dark, scaly sheen of blood, but the contour was wrong. Instead of his muscles curling in to meet the spine, his back was flat. In the center, barely discernible beneath the blood, was the dark hint of a walking staff.

"THE CHAIR WORKED," SHEILA SAYS.

Her voice pulls me back, makes me aware of the nail hole once again. I remember the picture that used to hang there. Mom, Dad, Sheila and me grinning like fools at the rim of the Grand Canyon. Less than a year before the accident that killed Mom and Dad. Less than a year before Sheila became a quadriplegic.

"The chair worked, and you let me lie in there all this time."

I swallow, though I have no spit. "I was afraid of it," I say. I look into her eyes again. She is five years older than she was in that picture. Five years older, but smaller.

She lifts her coffee cup with her right arm, leaving a spot of blood on the dingy tablecloth. Within the sleeve of her nightdress, I catch a glimpse of the wicker I've taped there. I tore it off Mr. Tory's body before the police arrived.

"If you start to feel weak, cut your arm again," I say, sliding my pocket knife toward her. "Just a little. It only takes a drop or so."

She takes the knife gingerly, as if afraid of it. "What happened to Jules?" she asks.

Jules is in jail, awaiting arraignment on murder charges. He'd gone too far, as usual. He'd used too much blood, taped every piece of wicker to his father's flesh, cut him every place the wicker touched. But I can't tell her this without crying.

"Some other time," I say. "Some other time."

A Case of the Quiets

Kurt Newton

Always jabber-jawing,
fidgety-sitting,
nonsense singing,
sneaker kicking,
parent-driving up the walls
with gray hair streaking,
nerves near-breaking,
until one Christmas morning
the mysteriously tall and creepy
Uncle Lumpkin paid a visit,
bringing presents wrapped with string
and not much else,
the smallest one,
a shiny wooden box,
brought specially for you.

"Thank God you came,"
your parents thanked,
their hands no longer shaking.
Uncle Lumpkin merely grunted,
his eyes as dusty cold
as the old junk sitting
in his antique shop.
"What is it? What is it?"
your voice rose to shrieking,
as you tore at the string
in a frenzy of pulling,

A Case of the Quiets

until the string snapped
and you grabbed at the latch
and opened the box,
only to find
Uncle Lumpkin's gift was
a box full of nothing inside.

It was about then,
in the face of such a cruel hoax,
you threw the worst fit,
the most unrehearsed tantrum;
you screamed and you kicked
and you punched at the walls
in a delirious dervish
of falling and flailing,
and while you were sobbing
in the room corner dust,
to your parents
you heard Uncle Lumpkin say,
"Don't worry,
just place the box beside the boy's bed
and all that awful noise will just go away."
He laughed a laugh then,
a hideously insidiously
chuckle of sorts,
then wished Merry Christmas
and headed for the front door.

That night as you lay tossing
and turning in bed,
your mind furiously spinning
with worrisome dreams,
you heard your door creaking,
as if someone was creeping
into your room
to do something sneaky,
but you weren't quite sure
if the creaking wasn't just part

of the dream you were dreaming,
until the dream noises stopped
with the click of a latch
and you bolted upright,
and there on the floor
was Uncle Lumpkin's gift,
its lid opened wide
like some kind of mouth,
and you screamed
but nothing but silence came out,
and when you looked down
the wooden box shuddered once,
then snapped its lid shut.

After that
not a word,
not a squeak,
not a squawk,
try as you might
not a sound could be heard,
just the click of your tongue
as you tried to force air
past your lips to call out,
but the thing in your throat
that made all the sounds
was no longer there.
Your parents appeared
at your door just the same,
rushing in all concerned
about nightmares and fever;
your mom felt your forehead
while your dad hovered nearby,
and when you pointed to the floor
at the box at their feet
you discovered it was suddenly gone.

All the next day
your parents merely smiled

as you tugged
and you pulled
and hand-signaled your wants.
"Ah, the peace …"
"Ah, the quiet …"
"What a relief …"
"What silence …"
They each looked so happy
you wanted to scream,
so you threw another tantrum,
but after several minutes of
thumping and thrashing
and exorcism-like spasms,
you realized the effect it was having
just wasn't the same.

So you sat in the corner
and tried to think of a way
to get your voice back,
and the first thought you thought
was to find that odd box
Uncle Lumpkin brought
from his antique shop
and open it back up,
and once your voice was returned
to its rightful spot,
you just might turn the tables
on those who disabled
your voice in the first place
for the sake of their ears.

So while your parents were out
(which often they were)
you searched and you searched
in closets and cabinets
and crawl spaces that left
little room but to squirm,
until at last in the attic,

where lost things are kept,
you found it sitting atop
a much larger box
that looked the same as yours
only ten times the height
and ten times the width,
brought by the same Uncle
from the same antique shop
you were sure,
but for what purpose
was anyone's guess.

But first things first …
you grabbed your box
and unhooked its latch
and lifted its lid,
and in an instant it felt
as if your throat
had swallowed a pill
too big for itself,
and you shrieked with joy
at what your ears heard.
With your box now in hand
you began to plot your revenge,
but for some odd reason
unknown to you then,
you couldn't leave well enough alone.

There was something inside you
that just had to know
what was trapped inside
that much larger box,
a voice like a whisper,
like the voice of the wind,
like the voice of your mom
when you were sick with a fever
and lying in bed
and she sat by your side

until you were better again,
you heard that voice now
coming from within.
So you reached out
and without thinking
you lifted the lid,
and suddenly everything went black.

The voices now had breathing attached,
all crammed together
with arms and legs folded
like baby clothes stored
for generations to come.
"Why did you open the box?"
your parents asked,
and you could have asked the same question
but right now nothing mattered
but the footsteps heard
shuffling into the attic,
and a hideously,
insidiously familiar chuckle
that made the hair on your neck stand up,
"Ah, the peace …
Ah, the quiet …
No more complaining …
No more whining,"
you heard Uncle Lumpkin say
before he slid a lock through the latch
and snapped it up tight.

Build-A-Zombie

Scott T. Goudsward

Timmy stood in the aisle of the mall, oblivious to the crowds around him. He stared practically open-mouthed at the collection of horror action figures and T-shirts behind the store's window. Werewolves, vampires and mummies stared back through plastic eyes. He rubbed a gift card between his fingers and sighed. In the glass he caught his reflection, still tired from the birthday party the night before, brown hair with a bed-head lump on the side, red-rimmed brown eyes, and of course, the freckles.

"Why couldn't I get a gift card to a cool place like this?" Timmy slunk deeper into the mall, aware of and embarrassed by his destination. "Should have just gotten me something from the girls' department at the mega-mart." Timmy smoothed out his bed-head as he walked and stuffed the gift card in his pocket. He shuffled to the very end of the mall, walked around the food court and rode the escalators until he had to face the inevitable.

Timmy stopped outside the bright yellow entrance to the store, sighed and then pulled the card out of his pocket. He stepped into the store, waiting to be assaulted by over-cheery chubby women in yellow and pink uniforms. He held out the card to the first person he saw and turned his eyes to the floor.

"You're in the wrong store, honey."

"What now?"

"Next store over, this is The Bear Store." Timmy's eyes rose, with a trembling hand he took the card and backed out of the store. He looked at the print on the card and then at the store's sign and ran to the next store.

"Welcome," he said under his breath, "to Build-A-Zombie."

The store's entrance beckoned like a forbidden cave to a spelunker. The archway to the store was green, pus green with black and red smears. The floor tiles were stained and Timmy couldn't guess their original color. Half of the overhead lights blinked on and off.

"What do you want, kid?" came a voice from behind the counter.

"I got a gift card," Timmy stammered. "Good for one zombie." Images flashed through Timmy's brain of the horrific abomination he would create and then leave it around the house for his mother to see. She would scream at the stuffed doll every time she saw it. He stifled a laugh as a hand jutted out from the shadows and thrust a clipboard at him.

"Walk around, choose your parts, and fill out the form. Try to step over the puddles and sticky bits on the floor, you lose a shoe I'm not getting it back for you." Timmy nodded and headed past the counter, aware of the watching eyes on him. There was an octagonal structure in the middle of the store; machinery hummed and thumped from inside.

He shivered under harsh cold breezes from the air conditioning. The first aisle, against the wall, read "HEADS." Timmy took three steps into the aisle, then grinned a naughty little grin. The shelves were lined with heads, human heads, some with hair, some not. Some had eyes, others had only one, and a few even had eyes that hung by veins and muscles from their sockets.

He was torn between two heads, one obviously a man with long stringy hair, splotchy beard and an eye patch. The other could be a girl, he wasn't sure, the features were soft, like the head was asleep. Timmy checked off #4H on the clipboard and hurried to the torso aisle.

Timmy wanted his pirate-head-looking zombie to have a strong body. He stopped at one he liked. Maybe the guy who owned it worked with jackhammers or lifted weights. Then Timmy saw the female torsos. Ugly pirate face and girl body, he giggled. Then a thought crossed his mind. He reached a trembling hand toward a female's chest, closest he'd ever been to a booby. He went for a grab and pulled his hand back when he saw the unblinking eye of the security camera. Timmy continued to browse the torsos and thought for a moment, "How am I going to get this home?" He shrugged and marked off a body on the form. Legs and arms were appropriate to the torso; he tried to get matching colors so the zombie wasn't patchwork.

On his way back to the counter, his eyes stopped on a strong pair of legs, chewed to the bone from the ankle down. Tubes and wires were connected to the limbs; small charges induced slight twitches and movements he hadn't noticed. The tubes kept blood incoming and outgoing. He ran back to the torsos and stared until he saw the abdomen move on one. He stifled a scream and jumped back. His hand brushed against the structure in the middle. The hum was much louder and something inside sloshed around.

He dropped off the clipboard at the counter, and the shadowy figure came into focus. Fresh out of high school, greasy hair, dirty braces and face matted in acne. "Go wait someplace." He handed Timmy a buzzer with flashing lights. "I'll buzz you when it's time to stuff it. People like to do that." Timmy nodded and left the store. He found some napkins on a bench and wiped the crud from the bottom of his shoes. Time passed agonizingly slow; he checked his cell phone. Still twenty minutes before his ride came.

"Should I call Mom?" he muttered. "Let her know she needs to put a tarp in the back seat?" Timmy knew what zombies ate. He'd seen all the Romero movies. "Where do I buy human meat?" People near him stopped and gave him a look, like he had posed them the question. "Hello? Look what store I'm in front of?" The lady of the bunch screamed and ran out of the mall.

Through the dirty windows figures moved, two of them looked like they held something down on a table, the other two like they were sewing something together. A sign caught Timmy's eyes, it was smeared with redness, but the print was easy to read. "EVERYTHING YOU NEED TO SUSTAIN YOUR ZOMBIE SOLD HERE." The buzzer in his hand went off. Timmy let loose a high-pitched scream, then caught himself and ran into the store before anyone noticed—he hoped.

There was a body on a tarp on the floor, rope securing its arms and legs, but the head was free and it snapped at the clerks around it. "Follow us and mind the mouth. This one is bitey." The shirt of the beast was opened up and the empty chest cavity exposed. Rib spreaders kept the bones in place. They were headed toward the structure in the middle of the store; a strange dark hut that hummed and thumped.

The doorway to the hut was barely high enough for the clerks to get through. Timmy stuffed a hand into his mouth and gagged when he saw the source of the noise. A small walkway surrounded the inside. The clerks went to the left, and Timmy stopped dead.

In the center of the room was a large opaque tumbler. It reminded Timmy of a cement mixer, except he could see shadows of everything that sloshed around inside. Big chunks of meat and long slimy tendrils all mixed together with a dark fluid. The clerks laughed at him and how pale he'd suddenly gotten, so white his freckles seemed to glow like neon.

"Kid," one of them said. "You want to pull the handle? Time to stuff." A long tube jutted out from the side and had been maneuvered into the chest cavity. Timmy shook his head and the switch was thrown, entrails and organs slopped down the tube. Timmy watched, horrified, like watching a body taken out of a car wreck on the highway. When the zombie was full, the head lolled side to side and snapped again.

"You sure picked a hungry one, kid."

"It's my birthday present," Timmy said robotically, his hands clenching and unclenching.

The others gathered up the flaps of skin while they were sewn shut. "The guts don't matter, kid." Timmy went to look at his name badge but it was smeared with dried blood. "They seem to last longer with the organs and blood. Now, it's going to leak for the first few days, and it's going to smell. Give it a week and you'll be fine." Timmy nodded and backed out of the hut. "You need to keep it chained up and try to keep it from eating its own insides. Keep it someplace cool and dark, otherwise the stuff inside will spoil faster."

The four clerks dragged the tarp out of the doorway and dropped it near the counter. One of them handed Timmy a Chinese food takeout box filled with parts and bits.

"This will keep it fed for maybe a week. Don't overfeed it, either. It's like a big stupid dog. It will always want more. Now, per our license, we snipped the vocal chords so it can't growl or moan." He handed Timmy a bag stuffed with paperwork. "Everything you need to know about caring for your zombie. Leave the ropes till you get home." They waved to Timmy and slapped each other on the backs, headed to the break room.

Timmy stared at the bag, then the takeout box and then his zombie. He'd already decided to name him George. He took out his cell phone and pressed #3 on the speed dial and waited for his mother. "Wait 'til they get a load of this."

Not an Ulcer

John Goodrich

DUDLEY HATED TAKING THE BUS. IT WAS FULL OF NIGGERS, FAGGOTS, retards and worse. He tried to bury himself in his book, shutting out the press of degenerate humanity. What the hell was wrong with people that they had to yak on about what they'd seen on TV last night? Were their lives so empty? Couldn't they shut up for a minute? Dudley gave up trying to read and stared out the bus window. With the sun down, the city lights passed behind his reflection.

Late as usual, the bus dropped him off, and Dudley walked his slow way back to his apartment. He turned on the TV as soon as he got in the door. The babble helped push back at the empty silence.

He ate two packages of mac and cheese while flipping channels. When he was done, the remains of the evening stretched out before him. He tried to return to his book, but couldn't concentrate. After an hour of fidgeting, the idea of visiting the park seeped into his head. He turned the television back on to drown the thought. The park was poorly lit, some part of him reasoned. No one would know. Angry, Dudley poured himself a few fingers of Jim Beam, and confronted himself in the bedroom mirror.

"You don't need to go." The Dudley in the mirror looked him straight in the eye, not at all cowed by his authoritative tone. "You've been working hard. You're well above the monthly quota, and it's not even the twentieth."

Dudley-in-the-mirror wasn't impressed. There was something suspect about him, something soft, almost feminine. Dudley wiped at the mirror, hoping to change the image. His other self stubbornly remained the same. To dispel the illusion of weakness, he rolled up a sleeve and flexed his bicep. He could not form the rock-hard muscle he once had.

"You don't need this. This is the sort of bullshit that gave Cheryl an excuse to leave. It's a weakness, something we should have left behind long ago." But the man in the mirror didn't want to listen.

"Please," he whispered, wheedling now that command and anger hadn't worked. "Please, I don't want this." It was a lie. The hated part of him wanted it in a deep-down way that words couldn't touch.

A second shot of Jim Beam strengthened the rebellion. Dudley glared at the mirror, which had somehow gotten the better of him again. Fuming, he pulled out a cheap wallet without identification, and stuffed a fifty dollar bill into it.

He dropped his regular wallet on the table, along with all his change and key ring, keeping only the key to his apartment. He pulled on a dark overcoat, despite the summer night's warmth, and locked the apartment door behind him. Letting out a deep breath that was both of determination and longing, he walked out to meet the pretty man-boys who only came when the sun was down.

He returned some forty-five minutes later, furtive and out of breath. Tired but relaxed, he took a shower. His belly seemed larger than usual, the skin taut. He couldn't even see his toes over his distended gut. God he was fat. His mouth hardened into a disapproving line and he scrubbed himself harder.

Out of the shower, his skin pink and raw in places, he laid down on the empty flatness of his queen-sized bed. He pulled out another bottle of Jim Beam, which lived in a drawer next to his bed. Three swallows burned his mouth, and soothed the jagged edges of his bitter self-recrimination. He glanced toward the mirror, but the angle was wrong to catch a glimpse of the satisfied image that lived in it. Safely alone with his guilt, Dudley surrendered to unconsciousness.

On the bus the next morning, Dudley still felt weighted down. He was getting weaker, not stronger. He'd spent more than two hundred dollars at the park in the last three weeks. As he stewed over this thought, a great fat bulk, like a primeval mastodon, squeezed its ponderous mass down the aisle, brushing him as it passed. The bus swam around him as the reek of too many bodies engulfed him. Gasping for air, he pulled the cord and escaped the bus.

He regretted the move as soon as he put foot to pavement. He was fully five blocks from his office, which stood on the crown of a steep hill. Jogging turned the fat on his belly to lead before he had gone a single block. He really should get a gym membership, he thought, feeling his heart thunder in his chest. Not too long ago, he would have been able to run up this hill without breaking a sweat. Now, he was almost out of breath, and the hill seemed to get steeper.

He arrived at work at a quarter past eight, his button-down shirt plastered to his sweaty torso. The receptionist looked at him with slattern-eyed condescension.

"You're late—oh, you're sweating, Dudley. Are you okay?" She had the effrontery to use his first name, as if they were friends.

"I work harder than anyone in this office," he snapped. "You'd think I might get a little slack as to my time of arrival." She bowed under his verbal assault, and looked back at her computer screen.

"I just wanted to make sure you were all right." Her voice was meek.

"I had a *year* in *college*." His hiss was cutting. With nothing left to say, he stalked past her desk and onto the main floor of the call center, with its rows of grey cubicles. At work, there were no mirrors.

He sat down and booted up his computer. How could it only be Tuesday? He saw the day stretch out before him. Beyond that was the work week, and beyond that a month that was an endless hill of paperwork for him to roll the mighty stone up. This was what made him fat and unhappy, the endless grinding days to make no difference. Dudley Gerritson looked upon the mighty work ahead of him and despaired.

THE SUN HAD SET BY THE TIME HE LEFT THE OFFICE. THE TIDE OF paperwork had receded, and he'd made a few sales on top of that.

The commute home was strange. People were looking at him. His guts were ropy. He must have eaten something bad. Angry, he stomped into his apartment and picked a good boxing match on pay-per-view. Jim Beam helped him sleep.

On Wednesday morning he was sluggish. His stomach still bothered him. No longer leaden, his guts squirmed as if infested with maggots. Breakfast didn't help, and the nausea stayed with him through the trial that was his morning bus ride. He caught furtive glances from the loathed people on the bus. What was wrong with him? He checked himself in the bus windows. Hair neatly combed, tie on straight … but he didn't look good. His cheeks were hollow, his eyes sunken. How could he look so wasted when his belly was so large?

He spent the day in a state of heightened alertness, which he told himself was not fear. Drinking to get sleep was leaving its mark on him. What choice did he have? Without a few swallows of Jim Beam, he could toss and turn all night. His worries faded as he fell into the rhythm of his work day, calling people, convincing them they needed new windows, then filling out the paperwork for the sale. He stayed late, finishing up, dreading the bus ride and the silence of his apartment.

He survived the commute with little more than a feeling of disgust, until he came to his stop. Nausea roiled up as he waited for the door to open. As he doubled over to keep from puking, someone shoved him from behind, and he spilled out onto the sidewalk.

He hit the bottle hard, unable to shake his fear. Tension and whiskey made his head throb like his bloated and painful stomach. He felt disassociated and powerless, an ineffectual ghost in his own apartment. He slept fitfully, awake every few hours.

Thursday's ride home was a horror show. Crammed together like niggers in the triangle trade, the stench of pressed-together bodies was overwhelming. Dudley shrank away from the spic standing next to him. He closed his eyes and tried to wish it all away, but the stink was inescapable, and his flesh burned to touch that sensual, dusky skin. The bus lurched, throwing hot bodies together. He spent the rest of the ride with his fists clenched, breath hissing between his teeth. He arrived at his apartment bleary-eyed and exhausted.

He ordered a meat-lover's pizza for one, flipped channels while he ate, then shut the TV off. The comfort food did nothing to settle his rebellious stomach, and he could not get the feel of the Latin man off his skin. The clock said seven, too early to go to bed. He cleaned a little, then settled back in his reading chair. He couldn't concentrate, his mind always returning to that stolen touch on the bus. He threw his book down. What would he do for the next three hours? The answer he did not want came immediately. Setting his jaw, Dudley poured himself a whiskey and went to confront the bedroom mirror.

"I am not a faggot!" he screamed at his reflection, then clamped a hand over his mouth. He took a deep breath, dropped his hand, and began to reason with the Dudley in the mirror.

"I get that you're lonely." He knew his own tone of false sincerity. He had a lot of practice with it. "I get that. But isn't there something else we can do?"

"If wishing worked, you'd be paying women." Dudley's hand went over his mouth again. He never responded when he was lecturing himself. God, what was he coming to, arguing with his reflection? His paunch gurgled and roiled, echoing his turmoil.

"It's not just about me. Think of what this would do to Dad."

Harold Gerritson loomed tall and stern in his son's memory: distant and unsmiling, his perpetually disapproving mouth set in a hard line. Harold wanted a son who was wasn't a pussy, who could fight and drink and play sports like a man. He'd bought thirteen-year-old Dudley a subscription to *Hustler* to help him grow up right. And yet, when Dudley had gotten his lacrosse scholarship, it hadn't been good enough. He should have gotten one for football, and at a better university. Not that any Gerritson before Dudley had gone to college.

And if he'd been disappointed then, how could Dudley even contemplate something as shameful as … wanting men? The stern spectre of his father's unforgiving features was far too easy to imagine, even as Dudley admitted to himself that he couldn't remember the last time he'd called home. Had it been months? Nearly a year?

"It's your life, not Dad's."

"Shut up." Which side of the argument was he on? To cover, he took a swallow of whiskey, only thing that seemed able to settle his disaffected stomach.

"So what are we—am I going to do? I can't keep on like this." He eyed his reflection, daring it to come up with a reasonable solution.

"We could find a guy we don't have to pay—"

Dudley slammed a fist into the glass. Blood oozed from his knuckles, and a hundred fractured Dudleys stared jaggedly back at him. His eyes stung. God, he was so alone.

He staggered over to his first-aid kit. He splashed some Jim Beam on his knuckles as an antiseptic, and a took a few gulps as an anesthetic. Dudley felt like he was plucking the glass out of someone else's hand. Once he had wrapped the hand in gauze, he finished off the bottle, then stumbled into bed.

Something flapped and flowed its way into his dreams, a lean figure capering madly to an unrecognized, fantastical tune. The figure filled him with a terror built of hope and longing. He wanted to get close, although whether to join in the dance or murder the dancer he didn't know. And then it was gone, the haunting melody replaced by the dull shrill of his alarm clock.

Dudley didn't risk a look at his fractured bedroom mirror. Sleep hadn't refreshed him. A swallow of whiskey got him to the bus on time, but it didn't stay with him. By eleven, despair hovered over him like a personal thundercloud, and his belly was bloated to the point of bursting.

He couldn't leave. People judged him by his job and family. Dudley had already screwed up a marriage, he couldn't make a mess of his job. What would he be then? No better than one of those damned bums that whined and cadged change on the street corner.

Dudley could feel the panic rising in him as the hollow futility of his existence crashed in on him. He ran to the bathroom and locked the door behind him. Only then, with a solid door separating him from the unfeeling world, did he break down weeping on the cold tile floor. Long, uncontrolled minutes passed before he could stop.

He eventually stood, and for the first time that day, looked at himself in a mirror. Dudley-in-the-mirror's eyes were haunted, his hair unkempt, clothing disheveled. He already looked like one of the faggot bums that peddled useless shit on the street. The future unrolled itself before him, where he slept under a bridge and muttered to himself, collecting tin cans in a shopping cart so he could buy a two-dollar bottle of booze. But was that existence so different from this one? Wade through filth so he could reach the goal, the weekend or the bottle of booze? Both goals were illusory; the weekend and the alcohol were both gone too quickly to provide any lasting satisfaction.

From somewhere, he found the strength to claw back from the brink of despair. He could pick up the broken pieces of his life and turn them into something worth living. If he worked at it, he could make himself a worthwhile person. He would need to be strong—stronger than he had been. He would throw out the empty wallet, and move away from his apartment with easy access to the park. He looked his reflection in the eye. He would survive this. And the first thing he would do was get rid of his damned fat midsection. Maybe then his stomach would give him some peace.

Dudley's eyes were dry by the time he left the security of the bathroom, his movements stiff and uncomfortable.

His bitch of a boss was waiting at his cubicle, and Dudley knew he would get raked over the coals. Rebecca avoided all contact with her underlings, except to chew them out.

"Can I have a minute in my office?" she asked, sugarcoating the axe Dudley knew was about to fall. Panic pumped bile into his throat. The air was hot, his shirt collar too tight, but his hands were inexplicably cold, and he could feel himself beginning to sweat.

"Sure." He was in no condition to argue. Without another word, he lurched toward her office.

Panicked heat flashed through him when she closed the door behind them. He would not go quietly. No one had served the company longer or with more devotion than he had. Perspiration beaded on his forehead, and the office walls loomed close.

"Are you all right?" She asked it with quiet concern, and he stared at his feet, unable to gauge the strength of his response if he opened his mouth.

"Dudley?" she persisted.

"It hasn't been a good week." His tone was strangled. Trying to find anything but her lying brown eyes to look at, Dudley settled on watching the lines bounce across her computer screen.

"Your work has been slipping for the last couple of days, Dudley, and you're not looking healthy. Is there anything we can do for you? You're one of our best people, and this is unlike you. Do you need some time off?"

He tried not to laugh. She'd stab him in the back and fire him when he was away. It happened all the time. He thought about telling her to shove the entire company somewhere that he had no doubt was tight and cold. Instead, he said nothing.

"I know you're proud of your attendance record. But you've got so much vacation time built up that it shouldn't make any difference." Rebecca oozed cloying, insincere sympathy.

"No, that won't—" he started, but he felt something like a hand move in his belly. Nausea boiled up in him, and he leapt to his feet. He distantly heard Rebecca ask "Dudley? What's wrong?" He took three hesitant steps toward the door, before collapsing to his knees. All he could think was that he wanted to throw up outside her office if he could. Then, abruptly as it had started, the attack was gone. Dudley tasted bile.

"Look, you're obviously not having your best day." She dripped with saccharin kindness. "Tell you what, I'm going to send you home, but it won't count against your personal time, all right?"

Head buzzing, guts roiling, Dudley knew he would not make it through the rest of the day.

"If there's anything—" she began.

"No." He cut her off, unwilling to hear any more of her simpering lies. "I need a little time and some space, and I'd appreciate it if you didn't crowd me."

She held up her hands to show that she was leaving him alone, and he left her office without another word.

The bus ride was strange at noon. The harsh sunlight was not kind to the interior of the bus, nor ill-bred mob in it. At least there weren't many of them, and Dudley took a seat far away from everyone else.

He stared out the window at the passing city, trying to sort out his life. His stomach was bloated like a pregnancy, the skin taut as a drumhead. God, could it be cancer? Maybe it was something as simple as an ulcer. He worked too hard, and he'd gone through a divorce, and he was having those... feelings. No wonder his body was rebelling.

He rubbed his belly, hoping to calm it. Poor thing, so tied up in knots with his confusion. His fingers slipped into indentations. Dudley screamed and leapt up, tearing at his shirt. For a brief second, he could see the impression of a skull, pressed against the inside of his skin. It opened its mouth briefly, then pulled back. Screaming, Dudley fled the bus, nearly falling to the asphalt in his haste.

He sprinted into traffic, dodging cars as horns blared. He ran until he was out of breath and lost. What would he do if this wasn't just an ulcer? He was too young to get cancer. Lost and empty, Dudley wandered, cracked pavement moving beneath his feet, grubby and soot-streaked apartment buildings hemming in the sky. What was happening to him? Cancer didn't make skulls pop out of your belly.

Sodium streetlights made sickly pools of yellow light on the sidewalk when something kicked his gut from the inside. He rushed into an alley, looking for a garbage can to puke into. He only got a little way in, and then fell to his knees. The pain was excruciating, but he held on, crawling and holding his belly.

Dudley heaved like he had drunk bad tequila. What emerged was not vomit, but some sort of pinkish solid, as if his organs were coming up. Horrified, he tried to clench his mouth closed, but the purges were too violent to be stopped. Eventually, the agonizing heaving eased, and Dudley flopped onto his side, too surprised that he was alive to react to the outside world.

He lay, panting and exhausted, until he heard the uneven shuffle of bare feet on pavement. Dudley opened his eyes to see a tall figure capering in darkness not five feet from him. He stared at it with repulsed fascination until it turned, and he could see the raw, wet, bipedal thing, all ropy muscles and too-tight mottled red and yellow skin. Dudley did not want to look at the twisted limbs, or the horrifyingly familiar face.

In the midst of its dance, it caught him watching. It stopped, facing him full on. Dudley held his breath, not daring to move. The thing born of his vomit laughed a long, terrible while, then did a beautiful pirouette in the dark shadows of the alley.

"Hello at last, Dudley." The thing's speech was a burbling rasp, as if it were unused to speaking, or its bones had not yet hardened. There was something familiar about the voice.

The two stared at each other, and Dudley was the first to look away.

"What are you?"

"Don't you recognize me? You've seen me, even argued with me." It had a manic grin as it stooped to press its face near Dudley's. "I'm all the parts that you tried to strangle. I'm everything about yourself that you have rejected." The uncanny eyes bored into Dudley's. "There's a lot more to me than you thought, isn't there?"

Dudley felt his eyes grow hot. "Not really." His repressed self crouched over him, a rail-thin grotesque in a disgusting alley, wearing a filthy blanket like a cloak.

"We both have what we want." The thing cocked its head, birdlike. "I'm free, and you're rid of me."

It stood, and Dudley struggled to his knees. There was an emptiness in him, as if a weight had been lifted. A void that ached.

The creature—the other Dudley—surveyed the dark alley as if he were a prince exploring his new kingdom.

"I think I'll go dancing, maybe. Go out and have a good time. Find a man I can love."

"No! You can't!"

Dudley's hands were around his twisted double's throat, desperation loaning him the strength he needed to seal off his warped twin's air.

"You can't!" he shrieked, wrenching his other self's head around. "You aren't me!"

The grotesque fought back with surprising strength. Fingers fumbled at his face, but Dudley kept squeezing the scrawny throat. The creature grasped at his hands, and managed to loosen one. Dudley grabbed it by the ears and slammed its head into the brick wall. After the second blow, he could see red spatter. Fuelled by a savage loathing, the red stains only spurred him on. After several impacts, the thing went limp and slid bonelessly to the alley's filthy concrete.

He'd done it. He'd purged himself of everything he'd hated. Yet Dudley felt no sense of triumph. In fact, he didn't feel anything at all. No rage, no bitterness, no joy, as if he were just the empty, emotionless shell of himself. What had he done?

He gazed down at his twisted reflection, pitiable now in death. He knelt, and gathered the strange corpse in his arms, desperately wishing it back to life. But he didn't feel it. He didn't feel anything at all.

The Possessor Worm

B. Adrian White

From: Julius Susset Sent: Fri 09/30/11 1:01 PM
To: Dorothy Rust
Cc:
Subject: From the new place in Boston's fabulous North End

Hey Rusty, how's the traffic back there in sunny California? Sucks! I can't believe it took me so long to move out here. Boston is the most beautiful city in the world. Seriously, it has so much history compared to L.A. It's weird, there are buildings, like mine, that are older than the whole city of Los Angeles. And they are crammed in between these 21st century skyscrapers. The restaurants are epic. The clubs are buzzing with all sorts of pretty boys and girls.

Oh, and you know how L.A. spreads out and out like somebody spilled something? Well this city goes straight up like a shiny glass forest. And that makes the greater metropolitan area small enough that you can walk anywhere. Seriously, you can walk your dog along the Charles River and like, fifteen minutes later be across the city at Quincy Market eating clam chowder. Although I wouldn't recommend it, the clam chowder I mean. It's like someone dumped seafood into a little white bowl of snot. But anyway, you don't even need a car. It's fabulous.

You know how we kept thinking the deal on this building was too good to be true? Well it wasn't. It's just like the real estate papers said, a historic two story in the North End. The price was fucking criminal, Rusty. The realtor said the previous owners had abandoned the property after only two weeks. It belonged to a young couple. I guess the guy was some big executive at one of the financial firms on State Street. He shows up for his first day or two then nothing. They call, no answer. An admin or someone from the office stopped by and no one's home. Eventually, the firm called the police. All the furniture was still here but no young couple. Gone without a trace.

So, I come along and wham! Pay day. I got both floors and they threw the furniture into the deal. It's that darling New England traditional. All luxurious dark woods and leather.

Two floors can you believe it? Thank God for deadbeats.

If it makes you feel better it's cold and rainy a lot of the time.

Missing you,
Julius ☺

```
From:    Dorothy Rust          Sent: Fri 09/30/11 1:15 PM
To:      Julius Susset
Cc:
Subject: From the old place in L.A.'s not so fabulous
West Hollywood
```

Let me start by saying screw you. Okay, my envy fit has abated and I hope there are no hard feelings.

I just kept worrying something was wrong with the place. But no, you are just really lucky. Why don't I ever find deals like that? If you weren't my best friend I would hate you.

Have you been tripping since you got there? Yuri got me a really great batch of windowpane. I'll bring some when I come see you.

So where did they go, the couple I mean? Did you ever find out?

What does the new place look like? Did you find your camera? Can you e-mail me some pictures or what?

... Rusty ...

```
From:    Julius Susset         Sent: Fri 09/30/11 1:38 PM
To:      Dorothy Rust
Cc:
Subject: From the new place in Boston's fabulous North End
```

Are you kidding girlfriend, unpacking sounds a lot like work and with all my space, I don't know that I'll ever need to.

Since my camera is lost to sloth, I will have to give you the e-tour.

43

Ready? Right this way and watch your step. This glamorous field stone structure was built in 1636 as part of Crowley University of Metaphysical Study. I guess they opened two days after Harvard but they didn't do quite as well. Evidently the Puritans weren't as excited about studying magic as they were about studying the Bible. Go figure.

Really, I can't wait 'til I can give you a real tour. But for now. The place has two stories and a basement. I've only been down in the cellar once. It has a completely nasty vibe. It was wet and there were too many dark corners. And extra weird, I found out the house isn't on the city sewer system. There is a cistern buried somewhere underneath the house. There is a hatch in the darkest corner of the basement where I guess owners used to throw their garbage or the failed research or whatever. Now all the laundry water and crap and piss go down there.

Hey, how about we continue our tour? In order to ascend to the first floor, would you like to take the stairs or the elevator? Yes that's right, I said elevator. No kidding Rusty, there is one of those old-fashioned elevators with the accordion gates and it works. When we get off on the first floor we are struck by the wide open design where kitchen, living and dining areas are all contained under the gorgeous exposed beam ceiling that hangs thirteen feet over our heads. And windows from floor to ceiling with three full baths, one on the first floor and two on the second. Four, count them, four bedrooms upstairs.

Anyway, now that you are suitably jealous, I am going to sink back into my luscious leather sofa and watch some TV.

Lonely without you,
Julius ☺

```
From: Julius Susset          Sent: Mon 10/03/11 8:30 AM
To:   Dorothy Rust
Cc:
Subject: The new kid
```

I know you aren't up, unless you haven't gone to bed yet, but I start my new job today and had to talk to you about it. I'm really excited. I just know this one is going to be perfect. I can feel it.

Oh, and you will be happy to know that this deal of the century is not without its little problems after all. Something is wrong with the plumbing. It has been making all sorts of noises the last day or so. Also more good news, I think I heard a mouse in the toilet last night. There was something splashing around in the bowl. And this morning it was all clogged up. Looks like I am going to need a plumber or something.

Anyway, wish me luck.

Your bestest friend ever,
Julius ☺

```
From: Julius Susset          Sent: Tue 10/04/11 12:30 AM
To:   Dorothy Rust
Cc:
Subject: <no subject>
```

Rusty, you got to help me. Call 911 for me. I can't. It won't let me. It stops me.

```
From: Dorothy Rust           Sent: Tue 10/04/11 12:51 AM
To:   Julius Susset
Cc:
Subject: What's wrong?
```

Julius, what's wrong? Are you alright?

```
From: Julius Susset          Sent: Tue 10/04/11 12:57 AM
To:   Dorothy Rust
Cc:
Subject: <no subject>
```

It's inside me Rusty. I'm not sure what it is. It's like a worm only it's long and thick like a big snake. And it's inside me. It hurts.

I was sleeping and I woke up to use the toilet. It was waiting for me in the bowl. When I sat down, I heard a splash and felt the wet and cold. Then it was pushing inside me. I tried to stand up Rusty, I did, but it pulled me back down. It's so strong. And it slid inside me. It hurts Rusty. And it knows things about me. It knew when I tried to call 911. I think it heard me talking. It understood what I was saying. It told me to hang up and it hurt me inside till I did. I can feel it coiling and twisting in my guts. I need help. Please Rusty.

```
From: Dorothy Rust          Sent: Tue 10/04/11 1:03 AM
To:   Julius Susset
Cc:
Subject: Everything is okay
```

    Julius honey, slow down. Everything is going to be okay. When did you take it? It doesn't matter, you'll be down soon. Did you take a full tab? Listen, I want to call 911, but if you left it out in plain sight … The last thing you need is the po-po kicking in your door and finding a bunch of acid on your kitchen table you know? So, I am going to call you on the phone and I will talk you through this one. You haven't sent me your new number so please e-mail it. It's going to be okay. It always is right? I'll take care of you.

    … Rusty …

```
From: Julius Susset         Sent: Tue 10/04/11 1:09 AM
To:   Dorothy Rust
Cc:
Subject: <no subject>
```

    No, don't call. It will know if you call and it will dig something sharp into my guts. It will hear me talking to you and it will know that I am trying to get help. I don't think it knows that my fingers moving on the computer keys are sending messages. So please don't call, or it will kill me like it did the couple that used to live here. It told me what it did to them. It showed me in my head. How the man went to work and it waited in the water. Then the woman went to pee and it shot up inside of her, into her womb. It showed her stories too and hurt her. She tried to call 911, but it wouldn't let her. Then she was going to run outside to get help and it hurt her. It hurt her so bad she couldn't walk. She couldn't go out into the daylight.

    I think it's hurt by bright light. I think that sunlight would kill it if I could get it out of me.

    And when she tried to go outside for help it made her do terrible things to herself with a razor blade. Then the worm made the woman jump into that filthy septic hole in the basement.

    It got the man too when he went into the bathroom looking for his wife. He tried to fight it, but in the end it made him go down and throw himself into the dark stink-filled tank too.

So if you call, it will make me do the same thing Rusty. Please don't call. Send me e-mail. I just wish it would stop moving around in there.

```
From: Dorothy Rust           Sent: Tue 10/04/11 1:19 AM
To:   Julius Susset
Cc:
Subject: RE: Take it easy
```

Okay Julius, I am coming out to see you. I am getting a plane ticket and I am going to come ride this one out with you. And next time, you don't trip alone. Especially with new stuff from a new dealer in a new place. I am coming. You go to bed. Sleep if you can. I know it isn't likely but just see if you can. At least wrap yourself in blankets and get as comfortable and safe as you're able. You're safe you know. You are okay. It's just the acid talking honey. I will be there as soon as I can.

... Rusty ...

```
From: Dorothy Rust           Sent: Tue 10/04/11 3:07 AM
To:   Julius Susset
Cc:
Subject: I am at LAX
```

Julius, I am just about to get on the plane. It's a red-eye that should be in Logan at 7:30 your time. We board in five minutes. It's a non-stop and once you start working you can pay me back for the ticket. I am kidding.

I hope that you will be on your way down or all the way back to earth by the time I find your place. And you and I are going to talk about your tripping with new source acid when I get there. Julius, you just got to stay easy for a few more hours. Everything is fine.

... Rusty ...

```
From: Julius Susset          Sent: Tue 10/04/11 6:14 AM
To:   Dorothy Rust
Cc:
Subject: <no subject>
```

Don't come. Please get this before you come here. If you read this, stay away from the house. It's waiting for you. I'm so stupid. I should have known. It can show me pictures in my mind of course it knows what I'm thinking. I thought it could hear my voice like it said it heard the woman's voice. I should have known it was lying to me. It hates and it kills and it's smart. It knew what I was thinking when I was typing and it just let me believe it didn't. It needs you Rusty. It needs a woman. It's going to have babies and it needs a way to get them out of the house. The babies have to travel in a woman's uterus. They have to get out of the house Rusty. They can't all live in the tank, they will kill each other.

It tried to use the woman, but she started to cut it out of her with a razor knife. The worm didn't make her hurt herself. She was trying to keep it from escaping into the public sewer system. She ruined its plan when she grabbed the razor knife and started cutting. The worm knew it couldn't get outside, couldn't get the woman to a public toilet. Then it waited coiled around her ovaries and tubes till her husband came home.

She was on the floor and he ran to her and the worm struck out of the hole in her pelvis she had cut with the razor. It pushed into his mouth and down his throat into his stomach. And it made him throw her into the tank then it made him climb in behind her.

It's sleeping now but when it wakes up it will know what I am thinking. And it can reach into my mind and make me do what it wants me to do. It will know that I am going to stop it but this thing will force me to sit and wait for you. I'm not strong like you. I can't fight it. When it tells me to do something, I will do it. But I am not going to let it get you. It dies in sunlight Rusty. It burns up if you can get it into the bright morning sun. It didn't mean to show me that, but maybe it can't help letting me know what it thinks anymore than I can keep my thoughts from it. The woman had the right idea. If I can just be quick enough ...

I'm sorry for the mess Rusty. I wish I'd gotten the chance to see you one more time. I'll miss you.

```
From: Dorothy Rust           Sent: Sat 10/22/11 11:33 AM
To:   Angela Rust
Cc:
Subject: I am looking forward to your visit sister
```

Hi Angie,
I am so glad you're coming. I am having such a hard time. You remember

The Possessor Worm

Julius. You remember how sweet he was. How helpless. I should have gone with him you know? I should have stayed with him for a couple of weeks. Taken care of him. He never was any good at being alone.

God Angie, you should have seen it. When I got there ... I am having trouble sleeping. I keep seeing the whole scene when I close my eyes. I keep seeing him there in his bed with his laptop next to him and all that blood. The knife he used was still hanging out of his side. How do you do that Angie? How do you take a knife and slice your own stomach open? Everything was just lying there in his lap with cold morning sun slanting across him like some sort of insane Jean Francois Millet painting. The blood had dried and turned brown in his white sheets. I keep seeing all of it when I dream. The trip must have been so bad Angie; he cut himself open. He kept talking about something in his intestines or his stomach. I don't know. He tried to cut it out.

Well, I will see you soon and we can look at some pictures and drink some wine and have a lot of laughs huh?

Bye for now,

... Rusty ...

Wait, there's something else. Something I have to tell someone. I am going to write this to you and then you will delete it. Gone. Understood? This has to stay private because it doesn't make any sense and I don't want anyone thinking I've lost my mind. Okay?

There was a trail across the bed and onto the floor when I got there. It was brown and dry and flaky like road kill baked on a summer street. And at the end of the trail, on the floor there was a shape. A long curved shape that was the same dried brown mess. Like something had been there but had burned up in the sun. He said sunlight would kill it but that's not possible is it? And Angie, there was something else. It was at the end of the curving crusted shape. It was a small piece of bone that was barbed like a fish hook. It was just lying there gleaming white on that polished floor. But that's not possible because it was just a bad trip right? So you'll delete this e-mail won't you?

Make a Choice

John M. McIlveen

"I have to whiz," Christopher Seth said, squirming as if a particularly large flea were chewing his ass.

"That's not humanly possible," said Joseph Seth, eyeing him in the rearview mirror. Matthew, the other of the Seth twins, gave a quick eye roll and returned his attention to the drop-down video screen.

"It's a long ride, but worth it," Joseph explained. "You'll see."

Nestled in Provincetown Harbor, Mayflower Heights was about three miles from the tip of the Massachusetts panhandle, a butt-numbing one hundred and ten miles from Boston by highway, though merely fifty as the seagull flies. Christopher released an irritated groan. For him, it felt like cross-country by horse and buggy.

Julie Seth watched her son writhe. "I think he really has to go," she said. "Maybe we can make a quick stop."

"We stopped for him not fifteen minutes ago," Joseph practically whined. "There's no such thing as a *quick* stop."

"That's what happens when you get the short straw," Matthew said, holding his thumb and forefinger about an inch apart.

"That so?" Joseph asked, smirking.

"Yeah," Matthew said. "My pipeline's fine." He wrapped Christopher in a firm headlock.

"Get your peter-beaters off of me," Christopher said. He tried wrestling free, but Matthew lathered his forehead with an animated spittle-laden lap.

"Oh god … residual penis!" Christopher bellowed, wiping his forehead across the back of his father's headrest.

"They're not our children," said Julia. "Some kind of alien intervention occurred in utero fifteen years ago."

"Still up for two weeks of family bonding?" Joseph asked. He turned the Yukon into a Burger King and found an empty spot. Christopher was barreling for the entrance before they even stopped.

"Wouldn't trade it for the world," she assured him. "I still can't believe it's the same cottage!"

Five months earlier a flyer appeared on the community board where Julie worked. *FOR RENT: $1500 per week - Call Ed Henry - ext. 4147*, the ad read. The resolution was grainy, but she recognized the Mayflower Heights cottage immediately. Her grandparents had once owned it, and she spent most of her childhood summers there. Ed seemed pleased by the coincidence.

Matthew's head appeared over his father's right shoulder. "Can we get some food, dude?"

"Dude?"

"Dad doesn't rhyme with food, don't be ridiculous!" Matthew said. "Come on, I know you're aching to fossilize your arteries with fat-laden gobs of death served under the guise of meat and potatoes."

"Well, since you put it that way," said Joseph.

THE LINE WAS STAGGERING. JULIE SUGGESTED TRYING SOMEPLACE ELSE, but Christopher turned doleful brown eyes on her and with a philosopher's air, said, "Mother, would you truly deprive your own flesh and blood—not to mention twins of the highest order—the right to indulge in mass-processed, pre-formed, deep-fried onion rings?"

"Bacon double cheeseburgers," corrected Matthew.

"Onion rings."

"They give you ass rot," Matthew said.

Julie hushed them, appalled. "We're in public," she said under her breath.

"It's true. He could gag a crap-eating dog!"

"That's enough," Joseph said, mortified.

A deep, hearty laugh erupted from behind them causing them all to turn. Julie, not vertically blessed, felt like a child as she looked up to see the man's face. He was about six-foot-five, at least sixteen inches taller than her, and ruddily handsome with untamed shoulder length hair. He wore Levis and a sleeveless Ghillie shirt over a well-toned body. He smelled musky, herbal, and under it, earthy, yet thoroughly pleasing. Julie wanted to ask which cologne he wore, but considered her humiliation should he answer *none*.

"Hey, it's Braveheart," Matthew said, nudging Christopher.

"Bring me Wallace. Alive if possible, dead … just as good," said Christopher in a passable Scottish accent.

Joseph glared at his sons, paid for the meal and humbly led his family to an open table. Julie settled into one of the formed plastic chairs, bothered by how close they were mounted to the table.

"I'm too fat for these chairs," she said.

"Matronly," Joseph corrected.

Christopher grabbed a few fries from Matthew's carton as they doled out the food.

"Hey, scrotum, stop filching my fries!"

"Just a couple. I only have rings."

"That's the price you pay if you want to stink, you cesspool."

Julie rolled her eyes and Joseph grinned sheepishly.

The man who had been standing behind them in line laughed again with gusto. He seated himself at the neighboring table.

"Pardon my following you, but open tables are scarce," his voice poured rich and smooth like melted chocolate.

"Deep voice there, Darth," Matthew said.

"Twins, right?" He asked.

"He's my clone … asexual, though."

"Christopher!" scolded Julie.

"No offense," said the man, his smile genuine and disarming. "They have spirit. There's no foul in that."

"They have plenty of that," Joseph agreed.

"Where you headed?" he asked. Julie glanced at Joseph, and the stranger said, "I apologize, too many hours behind the wheel makes one eager for conversation."

"I hear that," Joseph agreed. "We've rented a cottage in P-town for two weeks, on Mayflower Heights."

"From Boston?" he asked.

"That obvious?" said Joseph.

"Mayflowah," Matthew said.

"Drive the cah to the bah, it ain't fah," added Christopher.

"You can take the boy out of Boston, but you can't take Boston out of the boy," the man offered his hand. "Name's Chris Tana. T-A-N-A. Most people call me Tana."

Joseph shook and said, "I'm Joseph, this is Julie, Matthew and Christopher."

"Pleased. Those are good Christian names," Tana said.

"Yes," said Julie. "Joseph's parents tease us for giving Jewish boys such blatantly Christian names."

Tana flashed another winning smile. "Well, be it Christian or Jewish, they are good, strong names." Matthew flexed like a comical bodybuilder.

"I'm heading that way myself. I was offered far too much money to do some stonework there," Tana said. He stood and lifted his tray.

"Hey, I bet you're a mason," said Matthew.

"Sometimes," said Tana with a wink. "Maybe we'll bump into each other."

They watched Tana leave without as much as a glance backwards.

"Odd," said Julie.

"Agreed," said Joseph.

"You see him snarf that Whopper?" asked Christopher.

"What do you make of him?" Joseph asked Julie.

"Easy on the eyes, in a Tarzan kind of way."

"Calm the juices, Jane. I didn't mean *that* way."

"That's disturbing," said Matthew.

"Oh, fine," she teased. "He seemed friendly, but maybe a little too smooth. You know, Crocodile Dundee meets Barry White; the voice doesn't fit the man."

Matthew said, "I think he was looking for a nice kosher Jewish boy with the same name as him for a little pickle smooching."

Christopher said, "Now that's disturbing."

THE SETHS SEEMED PERFECT.

Tana watched them exit the restaurant and climb into their Yukon. People were so damn easy, so willing to dole out information to complete, and yes, *dangerous* strangers. So unaware of how much they opened themselves up.

Joseph Seth backed within inches of Tana's Camry, a thoroughly nondescript 2006—exactly how he liked it—and turn right out of the parking lot.

He waited two minutes before taking off for his *new* destination ... Mayflower Heights.

Julie climbed out onto the short gravel driveway and stared mawkishly at the New Englander with its screened-in porch and white cedar shakes; so typical, yet, so unique. Thirty years and it looked unchanged from the sun-soaked days when she ran up these steps, anxious for Grammy's homemade chowder. The screened door's spring would thrum to its limits as Grandpa yelled, "Hold the door for Pete's sake!" Then it would slam shut with a resounding *crack!*

She hoped her sons would enjoy the beach as much as she had. "You're the ideal age for this," she told them. Her antics would seem pitiable on today's high-speed standards. Just the frantic pace of modern video games astonished her. The hand-eye coordination was dizzying, especially to someone who peaked when Pong and Pac-Man were state of the art. "I have so many stories to share from my childhood!" she gushed.

"Uh, I ... have to ... uh ... feed the llamas," Matthew said.

"Yes, definitely the llamas!" agreed Christopher. "Surely they're famished!"

"Okay you clowns," Joseph said. "Grab something besides yourselves."

Laden with luggage they made their way into the cottage. Nobody noticed the beige Camry parked two hundred feet away on route 6A.

For two days Tana watched, waiting.

Matthew and Christopher stumbled out of the little cottage shortly after six, Tuesday evening. They jogged away jostling each other, intent on the beach, shops, arcades, and a great deal of bikini appreciation. Julie and Joseph left shortly afterward, off for some selfish entertainment. Tana's gut told him that *now* was the best time, and his gut was uncanny.

Tana stayed well back. At six-five he didn't blend in very well, despite the thickening crowd near the heart of Provincetown. Tracking the boys was easy, since they stopped often to girl watch.

As daylight waned, the boys refocused on the shops and arcades, and soon entered a candy shop. Tana waited outside, pretending to mull over tacky, high-priced Cape Cod and Provincetown trinkets, and keeping his eye on the confection-seeking boys. They emerged, bags in hand, a long red strawberry whip hanging from Matthew's mouth. Tana stepped toward them, looking introspective.

"Hey, it's Braveheart dude," Matthew said, elbowing Christopher sharply.

Tana looked up and said, "Well, hello! I figured I'd see you again. How's your vacation?"

"Okay, so far," Christopher said.

"Great! How are your parents?"

Matthew said, "They're tickled pink. They'd get excited watching mold grow."

Tana laughed. "Well, there's no place quite like Provincetown, right? As long as they don't make the mistake most people do and invite all the relatives."

"Nope, just two weeks of us, the big bond-a-thon," Matthew said with an eye roll.

Bingo!

Tana smiled and said, "Don't underestimate family bonding; someday your life may depend on it."

The boys exchanged a silent glance.

"Stay safe," Tana said and waved. "Masons have to hit the sack early."

"Rock on," said Christopher. Matthew groaned.

"Bet on it," Tana said. He rounded the corner of the nearest side street and broke into a sprint.

CHRISTOPHER GAVE THE PINBALL MACHINE A SHARP THRUST ... a little too sharp. Tilt.

"Ha! I win, gerbil dick," Matthew yelled.

"Pus tooth," retorted Chris.

"Pus tooth?" Matthew asked. Christopher shrugged. A man in an orange vest veered past glancing at his watch, reminding Christopher of their curfew. He checked his cell phone and backhanded Matthew's bicep.

"What?"

"Shit! We gotta hyperspace, it's eleven-seventeen."

"We're screwed," Matthew said, taking off in a sprint.

"Wait!"

At nearly eleven-thirty, Matthew led the way up the porch stairs, flung open the screen door, and shot into the cottage. He came to an abrupt stop. Christopher collided with him, nearly sending both of them to the floor.

"What gives, you stooge?" Christopher complained, winded, fighting to maintain his balance. He saw why Matthew had stopped.

Chris Tana sat on the living room couch, appearing very at ease with his legs splayed before him. He scraped his nails with a wicked-looking switchblade that reflected flashes of light as he maneuvered it.

"You're late," said Tana. His voice was vibrant, emphatic, and too disturbingly friendly. "Not very responsible, are you?"

They watched Tana warily, alternating their gazes from his face to the switchblade.

"Where's our parents?" asked Christopher.

Tana served a blinding smile. "So serious," he pouted mockingly. "Lighten up, you'll get ulcers." He started at his fingernails again, and nonchalantly nodded. "Your parents are in there."

Christopher looked to the kitchen doorway. He moved cautiously forward, feeling far enough from Tana to chance a look. Matthew stuck behind him, his eyes locked on Tana, who remained focused on his nails.

Tana said, "Unfortunately, your parents are a little tied up at the moment."

Joseph and Julie Seth sat bound to chairs with duct tape; their mouths were taped as well. They faced the doorway where Christopher and Matthew stood, their backs to the counter. Julie stared at her sons, terror lighting her eyes. Joseph Seth appeared unconscious, slumped in his chair. Blood trickled from his left temple near his eye in a rivulet.

"Dad's going to have a headache," Tana said, inches behind them, making them jump. "Pardon me, I didn't mean to startle you." He moved past them so smoothly he seemed feline.

"What do you want?" Matthew's voice trembled. Tana seemed pleased.

"Just a little entertainment, but so we're on the same track, if either of you even try to run, mom and dad are dead. Boy Scout's promise." He raised three fingers and gave a quick nod.

"Have a seat," Tana said, motioning to two chairs facing Joseph and Julie from the opposite side of the kitchen.

Neither boy moved.

Tana reached behind his back. "Abracadabra, handgun!" He said, displaying the barrel of the gun the way Vanna displays $250 vowels. "This, I'm sure you bright young lads know from CSI or whatever other drivel you may watch, is a silencer. Ignore my requests, and I can become very convincing, and with no more sound than one of those silent farts you're so fond of."

Christopher and Matthew obediently sidled into the chairs. Tana grabbed a canvas duffle bag from beside the refrigerator and set it near the boys. He withdrew a roll of duct tape, squatted, and began taping Matthew's legs to the chair. Christopher looked at the top of Tana's head, contemplating driving his foot into the man's chin, but his leg betrayed his thoughts by twitching.

"Behind your knee is a very busy artery. If you try what you're thinking, I'll have you squirting like a gas pump. You can yell, but a bullet or a knife—your choice—is wonderful for silencing vocal chords. Do you want to take that chance?" He looked up. Christopher returned the stare as stoically as possible, but his chin quivered, divulging his fear. Tana winked and taped Matthew's hands and arms behind the chair, and then went to work binding Christopher. He backed their chairs against the wall, still facing their parents. He rounded the table in the center of the room, pulled something from his pocket and waved it under Joseph Seth's nose.

"Wake up, sunshine," Tana said. Joseph pulled away from the smelling salts, opening confused eyes. He looked from Tana, to Matthew, to Christopher, and to Julie. Finally comprehending, he yanked at his restraints, emitting angry, muffled protests. Tana placed the gun barrel squarely between Joseph's eyes, initializing a torrent of panicked, stifled cries from Julie.

"You should stop," he said to Joseph, and then repositioned the barrel on Julie's brow. "You're killing your family." Joseph immediately stopped his protests.

Returning the gun to the small of his back, he said, "Thank you. Now that I have your attention, I imagine you'd like to know what this is all about." The fear was so palpable he could almost smell it. He sat on the edge of the table; all eyes were glued to him. "You see, I get bored rather easily, so I invent new ways to entertain myself. You seem like a fun-loving family." All of the Seths started shifting eyes among each other.

Tana gave an embellished sigh. "Did I lose you already?" He stood straight and spread his arms, as if trying to share a simple point. "We are going to play a little game, a game called *Make a Choice*." Tana actually felt the tension rise. He stared intently at Joseph and Julia and raised two fingers, a mocking peace sign.

"I noticed two things when we met the other day. First, your sons, though not identical, are clearly twins. Second, you both love them very much, and *that* is what makes this game so much goddamned fun."

He walked to Matthew and Christopher, though his words were still directed at the parents. "This game takes about twelve hours to play. I would love it to take longer, but I'm a busy guy with other commitments and I must leave by noon tomorrow." He put a hand on Matthew's head. "And when I leave, either one of your sons," he paused and put his other hand on Christopher's head, "or both of your sons will be dead."

Julie started shaking her head frantically, tears welling from eyes ready to eject from their sockets. Joseph remained composed, but white hot hatred emanated from him. Tana was truly enjoying this.

"Wait! I'm not finished," he said raising a finger. "*This* is the important part. Whether one or both of your children die … is entirely up to you." He pointed to Julie and Joseph with both hands. "You get to … come on, say it with me … Make a Choice!"

"You're fucked, man," Matthew said bitterly.

Tana went nose-to-nose with Matthew. "Most certainly, though not *nearly* as fucked as you. But, let's not get off track. It's all very simple, Mr. and Mrs. Seth, you have twelve hours to decide which one of your sons die, or," he rose up and pointed to Matthew and Christopher, "they both die."

"You won't get away with it, they'll find you," Christopher said.

"Who'll find me?" Tana theatrically lowered his head as if waiting for a secret. "I'm flattered you think you're my first, but you're not by a long shot. But, I do think you'll be my best one yet."

Tana drew the shades. He moved to Julie, bent to her level and said, "The beautiful irony is, even if you don't decide who dies, you've still made a choice … both die."

Julie's eyes swam out of focus, rolled back, and she passed out. Beaming, Tana jumped up and pumped his fist. "I love when that happens!" He brought out the smelling salts and coaxed Julie back.

"For the next eleven hours you will all remain in the kitchen. This way you will have a good last look at your son … or sons. It's now twelve-oh-seven. I'm a generous guy, so you have until eleven-ten tomorrow morning. That's three free minutes." He laughed and left the room.

Matthew and Christopher hadn't muttered a word in nearly two hours. They were looking at her, desperation and profound fear holding her gaze, the same thing they must see in her eyes. How could that bastard even think of something so inhumane? The death of one would be the death of the other, at least in spirit, and the death of either would split her heart in two. Her sons, dear God! Julie's stomach clenched and her vision wavered, threatening unconsciousness again.

No! She had to remain strong for the boys. Why wasn't Joseph helping? Why wasn't he trying to save them? She turned to meet his eyes, and hated him for what she saw there.

Don't you dare give up, you fuck! She wanted to scream at him, hit him and tear that look out of his eyes. She glowered at him. You created them with me, Goddamn you! What about your vows? 'To love and protect.' You're not holding up your part of the deal. We need to be protected, not be the eleven o'clock news. Not reduced to something people shake their heads at, shocked, appalled, rapt, and think 'what a shame,' then go back to their tuna casseroles, whiskey sours, or cribbage games, maybe amused, definitely entertained, but mostly unaffected.

CHRISTOPHER NEEDED THE TOILET. HE SQUIRMED IN HIS CHAIR and looked at his parents, anguish etching his features. Joseph checked the clock and his nerves turned to ice. 2:27 a.m.! The minute hand seemed to move like the second hand.

"Hey!" Matthew yelled. "Hey, my brother needs the bathroom!"

Tana entered the kitchen, evidence of sleep clinging to his features. He looked at them one by one. His eyes stopped on Christopher. "How we doing, lad? You appear a bit uncomfortable."

Christopher locked his gaze on the floor.

"He needs the bathroom," Matthew said.

"I heard you," said Tana. "Your brother can talk."

"He's afraid."

"I want to hear it from him." Tana moved within inches of Christopher's bowed head. Joseph saw Christopher's body tense as if awaiting a blow.

"Do you need the bathroom, Christopher?" Tana asked.

"Please," he barely whispered.

"I think not. I'd have to release you and then bind you up again. Too much trouble." Tana checked his watch with embellished movements. "Besides, this won't take long. In slightly more than eight hours you may not have to worry about it any longer."

Matthew surprisingly shouted at Tana, "Fuck you, you dick!"

The backhand was rattlesnake quick. Tana's hand was back to his side before Joseph knew his son had been struck. Julie flew into a rage, struggling to free herself from the restraints. Anger also boiled within Joseph, but a backhand was the least of their worries. He would save his energy for the right moment; he needed to be ready if it presented itself. This prick was cool and aloof, but surely not flawless. Tana would slip eventually, somehow.

Matthew's cheek blossomed to a fiery glow that would darken and swell. His eyes brimmed, but Joseph knew, for Julia's sake, Matthew wouldn't allow himself to cry.

"What an impolite young man you are," Tana said. "If I were your parents, I wouldn't want a child as rude as you. In fact, I would think your disrespect should only simplify their decision." Tana looked smugly at Joseph, grabbed a fistful of Matthew's hair and gave him an openhanded slap to the face that sounded like a bullwhip.

It was a direct challenge that shook Joseph to the core, and made his quandary all too clear; Tana had castrated him, rendered him impotent. Tana could perform any perverse desire his putrid mind conjured up, and there wasn't a damned thing Joseph could do. Panic blazed a searing stream up the center of his back, over his shoulders, down past his buttocks and into his legs. Like a trapped animal, Joseph threw every iota of himself into his attack. The tape had to give under his fury. The bones and sinews of his arms and legs would shear through it. Joseph tipped, falling sideways until his head impacted the floor with a blinding flash and the tearing of claws at his temple.

He tasted blood, yet somehow remained conscious. He saw Tana's boots as they approached. He braced for the kick he knew was coming... but it never came.

Tana squatted on the floor near Joseph, displaying a satisfied smile. He said, as if confiding with a dear friend, "Bet that brought you back down to earth. I was wondering how thick, or thin, your resolve was." He lifted Joseph and his chair with minimal effort. "Don't be offended by the love taps I gave your son, but we need to know where we all stand in this little game."

Julie's tears flowed freely, carrying with them her dignity and spirit. As if reading Joseph's earlier thoughts, Tana walked over to Julie, put a giant hand behind her head, and pressed her face directly into his crotch and pumped his hips perversely against her. He looked at the three Seth men and said, "It appears that I'm winning."

"Get away from her, you fucking pig!" Christopher sobbed.

"Very noble, one point for Christopher," Tana said. He gave a final thrust and pulled away.

Joseph saw the dampness of Julie's tears on the man's crotch, and a dense blackness pushed through him, fueling his hatred and rage.

CHRISTOPHER FELT AS IF HIS BLADDER WOULD SPLIT. Twice he had cried out, only to hear a low chuckle from within the living room. It was 4:12 am, and for nearly two hours, his mother's gaze had remained locked on some indistinct point on the floor. His father's gaze drilled the living room doorway, a more definable focus, but just as unmoving as his mother's.

Another searing jolt ripped his abdomen and a spray of urine released. If he hadn't been taped to the chair, it would have doubled him over.

"Let it go, man. Stop torturing yourself," Matthew whispered. His face was unbalanced by an eggplant-colored swelling high on his left cheek.

"I can't," Christopher hissed between gritted teeth. Unable to withstand the pressure, it all let go with an anguished cry. Christopher sobbed as urine poured from him, flooding down his legs, over the chair, and onto the floor.

A victorious cheer rang from the living room. Tana emerged, a Cheshire Cat grin on his face. "Do I hear music? Tinkle, tinkle, tinkle," he sang, almost effeminately.

"Fuck you," Christopher croaked, humiliated.

"Flattered," Tana said and winked. "Maybe later."

"I'd figured you as a pedophile," Matthew challenged. "What's wrong, you miss your daddy's dick?"

Tana roared with laughter, genuinely amused. He said, "You can play, too. I'll even invite your parents to watch."

Joseph Seth drilled Tana with a look so disturbing and seething it appeared to pause their captor momentarily. Composing himself, Tana rhythmically tapped his foot in the puddle of urine on the floor.

"I smell weakness, which can't help your case much," he said. He rubbed his hand briskly over Christopher's head as if he were a favorite nephew. Christopher gnashed his teeth at him, trying for his hand, or perhaps a finger, just barely missing.

"Whoa, Cujo!" Tana said, pulling back. "Your parents should put you out of your misery. Isn't that what they do with rabid animals?" Tana turned to leave, but stopped. "What's that?" he said, pretending to hear something. He leaned to Christopher. "Did you say kill Matthew, not me?" He stood back up feigning concern. "Is that the kind of loyalty one should expect from a twin brother?" He shook his head and walked back to the living room. Christopher thought a little of the arrogance had left his step.

THE SOUNDS OF WASTE MANAGEMENT TOSSING GARBAGE CANS about woke Tana up. He looked at his watch, thought about the boys in the kitchen, and smiled. He had to give the little shits credit, they had gumption. The intensity of the urine smell in the kitchen surprised him. The Seths were all haggard-looking, gaunt with dead expressions.

"Hello kids!" he said merrily. "See, I gave you an extra eleven minutes, I'm a nice guy. Add the three extra minutes I gave you last night, that's fourteen, which happens to be the ages of our men of the hour." He clapped his hands like a game show host. "What a bunch of fuddy-duds. Well, the show must go on."

He turned to Julie and yanked the duct tape from her mouth. Julie cried out, and little beads of blood soon gathered between specks of adhesive residue.

"Ooh, that's going to leave a mark," Tana grimaced. He yanked the tape from Joseph, retrieved the roll from his duffle bag and taped Matthew and Christopher's mouths. Neither boy protested.

"Same rules apply. Any noises I don't like, you've chosen both boys, simple as that. Now, please enter our specially designed silent chamber behind door number one," he said, motioning to the first bedroom door. He dragged Joseph's chair into the bedroom, and then Julie's. "You have less than one hour to make your decision. You kids behave," he said, closing the door.

"Rot in hell," Julie said.

Tana smiled. "Too late," he said.

MATTHEW TURNED AWAY AS TANA EXITED THE BEDROOM. He considered begging for their lives, but knew it would please the perverse worm. Matthew had prayed throughout the night, looking for inspiration. He found none. Tana's heavy trod approached. Matthew refused to look at him, certain he was up to some cruel task, but Christopher's muffled grunt startled him. Matthew looked at his brother's disheartened face, and then at Tana.

"What?" Tana asked.

Another muffled question.

"Why?" asked Tana. Christopher nodded.

After mild deliberation, Tana said, "Why not? Nothing personal, I needed players, you met the criteria."

JULIE DIDN'T WANT TO THINK, FEEL OR HEAR, SHE JUST WANTED to shut down, to curl up and sleep, down in a deep, dark hole where nothing could get to her. She barely noticed when Tana moved them; she stared blankly at the floor and hadn't shifted her gaze since. Time, though so crucial, was irrelevant; there was no clock.

"We have to do something," Joseph said.

She said nothing. She wanted *silence*, but it evaded her. Tana was talking to her sons beyond the door, his voice sounding too normal.

"Julie, for Christ's sake!" Joseph hissed.

"He's lying," Julie said. "He'll kill us all."

"I had the same thought," Joseph admitted.

"We can identify him." Julie finally raised her eyes to meet Joseph's. "Do you think for a minute he'd let three of us go? We're not going anywhere."

"We have no other hope."

Julie wanted hurt him, to drive steel spikes through him. "Are you going to decide which one of our sons he … *murders?* Can *you* make that choice?" She asked. "I could never forgive you for choosing a son to die."

"I could never forgive you for letting both die," Joseph countered.

"It'd probably be better if neither lived."

"How can you say that?" Joseph asked desperately.

"How can you choose?" Julie hissed with so much disgust that Joseph pulled away. "Think of what that would do. Think of how he would feel."

"But …" Julie stopped his words with her eyes, knowing what he was going to say, *but he wouldn't feel it for long.*

"You bastard!" She sneered with so much acid her voice sizzled. "Five seconds of that kind of betrayal would be too long. I refuse to sentence either of my sons to death."

"Then they both die!" His eyes burned.

"I hate you!' Julie growled. She started crying uncontrollably. "I-hate-you-I-hate-you-I-hate-you!" She looked at her husband and saw a stranger, a sallow and repugnant parasite. He and Tana were the same, evil and contemptible, so willing to take the lives of her sons.

They sat in silence; neither knew how long.

"It'd have to be the emotionally weaker one. He wouldn't survive without the other one," Joseph said quietly.

Julie knew he meant softhearted Christopher. She couldn't believe he chose. She wanted to rip his heart out, yet inside she knew that poor, logical Joseph was on autopilot. He, the accountant, was taking tally and things weren't adding up. His eyes were dead, empty and hopeless; concentration camp eyes.

"No," Julie whispered.

"Knock-knock," Tana said. "Time's up!"

He dragged Julie and Joseph back into the kitchen. Terrified eyes exchanged looks all around. Matthew and Christopher, ashen and diminished, looked abandoned.

"I love you both," Julie said with a weak, cracking voice.

"Shh-shh," Tana moved to Julie's side with unbridled enthusiasm. "No time for sentiments, because, you know what time it is? That's right! It all comes down to this! The big finale! Final Jeopardy. Yes, it's time to *Make a Choice!*" Tana stood, arms spread and a huge Bob Barker smile on his face. The smile faded and he dropped his arms. "What deadbeats!" he said.

Joseph Seth said, "Let them go. If you have to kill someone, kill me."

Tana looked incredulous, as if Joseph were a child who had just been monstrously defiant. "I'm awed by your cowardice. You're not getting out of this that easily, Bucko! But, this suspense is a killer. So, speaking of killer, who did you choose?" he said, as if asking what flavor ice cream he liked.

Neither Joseph nor Julie spoke.

"Come on, out with it. We heard you talking. They're just *dying* to find out, if you'll excuse the pun."

Still, no one spoke.

Tana moved in front of the boys. A switchblade popped open and all four Seths jumped in unison.

"So, you chose both," Tana said.

"No!" Joseph shouted.

"Who?" Tana asked, sliding the blade softly down Matthew's arm.

No answer.

Julie was shaking, her chin quivering and her arms twitching as if on the verge of hypothermia.

"Who!" Tana hollered. "Ten seconds or they both take it in the throat!"

Joseph said something. Tana rushed to him and leaned close.

"What was that?" he asked.

"No," whined Julie.

Joseph stared at the refrigerator.

"Did you say Christopher?" Tana persisted. "Or was it Matthew?"

Nothing.

"Who?" Tana roared.

Joseph said something.

Tana jumped up, his arm raised skyward. "Christopher it is!" he said, as if awarding the winning bid.

Christopher and Matthew stared at their father, both wide-eyed.

Joseph dropped his head and wailed. Julie looked at her sons, shaking her head in denial ... in agony.

Tana extracted a small silver can and a rag from his duffle bag, folded the rag and poured the contents of the can onto it.

"Ether, if you hadn't already guessed," Tana explained. He placed the rag over Joseph's nose.

"What are you doing?" Joseph cried.

"Do you really want to watch?" Tana asked.

"He's going to kill us all," Julie said through anguished tears. "I told you!"

Within moments Joseph and Julie were slumped in their chairs.

JULIE AWOKE TO A SEARING PAIN IN HER TEMPLES AND AN AWFUL taste in her mouth. It was dark, but she could see the form near her. She sat up and looked at her arms as if they were a newly formed part of her body, felt ridges in her wrists where the tape had bound her, and then remembered.

She shook her husband fiercely. "Joseph! Oh god, the boys!"

Joseph sprung upright, looking around frantically. He cringed as the ether headache slammed him. "Wait!" he said. He held Julie back with a straightened arm. "Listen." There were voices from behind the closed door.

"It's the TV."

"Tana might still be here. I need a weapon. Anything!" Joseph whispered. He got up, quietly opened the closet door, grabbed the hanger rod from the supports and threw the loose hangers on the bed.

Joseph opened the bedroom door slowly. The hallway and kitchen beyond were dark, except for the telltale flashing of the television on the walls. Inching ahead, they turned the corner and peeked into the living room. Matthew and Christopher were slumped in their chairs, facing the television. It was impossible to tell if their eyes were opened or if their chests moved.

Joseph cautiously entered the room, taking everything in. "Watch behind us," he said. Another step and Matthew jerked to attention. Julie stood, unmoving, praying for a sign from Christopher.

"Tana gone?" Joseph asked. Matthew nodded and Christopher's leg twitched.

Alive! Julie rushed forward and touched their faces, their arms, raining kisses on them, but not totally believing. Joseph freed the boys and Julie undertook the painful task of removing the duct tape from their mouths as Joseph called the police.

HOURS AND COUNTLESS QUESTIONS LATER THE POLICE WERE coming up empty, and some even seemed skeptical, despite the bruise on Matthew's face and Julie's tape abrasion. No Chris Tanas existed in the database, plenty of Chris Tanners, but none matched the description. One officer noticed, with implied accusation, that Chris Tana was an anagram for *anarchist*, and *satanic* could also be derived from it. The Sergeant in charge felt it was no coincidence. Neither did Joseph.

The police showed a composite sketch to business owners, the few that recognized Tana only remembered his height and good nature. Joseph figured he wouldn't be found. Tana and his easy arrogance had probably spent years terrorizing people and melting into the woodwork.

The building inspector produced no pulled permits for masonry work, and no recent outdoor masonry work was evident anywhere in Provincetown.

Matthew and Christopher spoke little that evening, answering questions with little more than affirmative and negative grunts. Matthew maybe said five words to Joseph. Christopher, none at all.

With a little persuasion by the police chief, the Seths were roomed at the Anchor Inn Beach House, even with the summer crowd. The cottage was cordoned off as evidence, not that anyone wished to go back.

ALONE IN THEIR HOTEL ROOM, THE SETHS SAT IN NEAR SILENCE. Very few words were uttered. They all knew what the others were feeling, words were worthless.

They got out of it alive. It turned out positively, considering all that happened, Joseph figured, yet he was constantly aware of their eyes on him, especially Christopher's, averting when he looked back.

An officer knocked on the door, startling them. He said, "The Sergeant has more questions. He'd like you at the police station at 9:00 am."

"Just me, or all of us?" Joseph asked.

"Your choice," said the cop.

Christopher laughed.

It was not a good sound.

The Death Room

Michael Allen Todd

If walls could speak, I pray, dear tell,
That the Death Room would convey a tale of Hell,
Of fading breaths and morphine highs,
Of groans of pain and long goodbyes …

On surface, it seems ever so quaint,
Ruffled curtains adorn windows with safe white paint,
But beyond that veneer a darkness lies,
Capturing echoes of suffering and deathly cries.

I shun the place, but it's ever so close,
Filled with memories of torment and shades of ghosts,
All my childhood lost in a sea of sighs,
With nary a word from God to explain just why.

Some days I detest Him and His infernal ways,
His lack of communication and our numbered days,
His indifference to man and our lonely plight,
We are abandoned, alone, to tread the night.

So the Death Room waits patiently for me to reside,
Knowing full well that I can't ever hide,
For inevitable is Death's long icy grasp,
And ere long one breath shall be my last …

Hopeless to escape, and deaf to my tears,
I am left alone here to rot in my fears,
For no matter how I run, *or what I may do,*
Some day the Death Room will lay claim to me too.

Perfect Witness

Rick Hautala

> " ... *see, see! dead Henry's wounds*
> *Open their congealed mouths and bleed afresh.*"
> –Richard III, I. ii. 55-56.

I'M CONFUSED, REALLY CONFUSED.

I can see bright lights all around me.

Too bright.

I know there are people nearby, too.

Sometimes it sounds like there's a whole crowd, milling around somewhere in the outer darkness behind the blinding lights. A faceless, nameless mass of people, like an audience, unseen, but I sense their presence behind the glare of stage lights.

At other times, or maybe at the same time, I can tell there are a few of them—maybe three or four people—standing close to me.

I think they're doing things to me, but I can't feel anything.

I don't know where I am or what's happening to me.

Can anyone tell me?

I try to move my arms and head, but my whole body feels like it's a lump of damp, senseless clay. There's no sensation in my legs. Absolutely none.

Not even the sensation of pain.

Nothing.

It's almost like my body doesn't exist.

What the hell's happening to me?

I don't remember a thing, not since …

When was it?
Earlier tonight?

Yes. Now I remember ... I was walking back from the Wild Horse Theater to my apartment on Irving Street, in Cambridge, when a man—hell, no! He wasn't a man. He was just a kid, for Christ's sake, stopped me and demanded I give him my wallet and cell phone.

At first I started to reach for them, but in an instant, I decided not to hand it over so easily. I think I might have tried to put up a fight and get away front him.

Is that what happened?

"We have to administer the rest of the drug very slowly. I have no idea if he will experience any pain, but I don't want to risk losing him again."

Hey! ... Who said that? ... Who's there?

It's a woman's voice, but no one answers me.

Did I speak out loud?

Probably not.

I strain to open my eyes, but I have this weird sort of dull sensation that they're already wide open. I keep trying see better, but the light is so bright it stings my eyes. I'm trying to adjust to it, but I can't.

At least there's pain.

Thank God for that!

If there wasn't any pain, I might think I was paralyzed or ... or dead.

At least I know I'm alive.

Just barely.

It's weird how those gray shapes keep drifting around in front of me, floating by like ... like there are people, milling around me.

I wish I knew who they were.

I wish I knew where I was.

I want to know what's happening, but my body is still totally numb.

"Mr. Thurmond, I hope you keep that camera running. If this works, I don't want to miss a single second of it."

Miss any of *what*?
Who said that?
Where the hell are you?

In the distance, I can hear other voices, buzzing like the droning hum of a wasp's nest. I can't make out anything anyone is saying. It still reminds me of the indistinct chatter of a crowd, talking softly in the dark in expectation of a show that's about to begin.

Come on!
Somebody!
Please!
Say something!
Talk to me!
Why can't I see you?

I can't feel a thing, but I'm positive, now, that they are doing something to me.
What the fuck are you doing to me?
Oh, shit!
Wait a second.
I think I know what's happening. I remember, now. I started to fight with that kid, and I think he might have—
Shit, *yes*. He had a gun!
I've been shot!
I'm wounded.
I must be dying!
Oh, God, I'm afraid that might be what's happening!
I remember clearly, now; that he had a gun aimed straight at me. He was standing close, and I made a grab for his wrist, hoping to push the gun away, but there was an explosion of light.

Funny.

I don't remember hearing anything. There was no loud blast. And no pain. Just a burst of intense white light, and a dull feeling like someone had punched me in the gut, and then … then …

… nothing …

So that's it.

I've been shot!

I must be lying on the sidewalk where I fell.

Am I bleeding to death?

Why can't I feel anything? Even that faint whisper of pain is gone now.

These people … maybe they're paramedics … and the others … They must be the crowd that's gathered around to watch.

To watch me die!

Shit, that's it!

I'm dying … on the street.

They're trying to save my life, but I'm dying anyway!

Oh, Jesus! … Oh, shit!

I don't want to die!

"You have to remember, your honor, that this is the first time we've attempted to do something like this. The medical technology has only been tried in test cases. We have to proceed with caution."

That was a woman's voice again, but why did she say "your honor"?

What the hell is she talking about? Is she a doctor or something? And who's she calling "your honor"?

Hey, wait a second …

I think she's the one doing something to me. For a moment, there, I could almost feel my body again … at least a little bit. There's something hard underneath me. Must be concrete. I must still be lying on the sidewalk? It feels that way, but it also feels as though my knees are bent.

Maybe this is how I hit the ground after the shot.

"Given these rather unusual circumstances, do you gentlemen agree that we can dispense with the usual formality of swearing in the witness?"

Swearing in?
What witness?
What the hell are they talking about?
Jesus Christ, stop talking nonsense and do something to save my fucking life!

Even as I think this, I can feel a warm current of sensation rushing through my body. The heavy, lumpish feeling in my chest is starting to loosen up, and I think—yes! I can feel a dull throb of pins and needles spreading into my arms and legs. The center of my chest feels like it's on fire.

I can't tell if I'm turning my head or merely shifting my eyes back and forth, but when I look around, the light becomes more diffused. The figures leaning over me—I think I can count three of them now—are still indistinct. They're surrounded by faint halos of light that ripple with deep blues and purples like colors I've never seen before!

It's beautiful, but—

Oh Jesus, I'm *really* scared!

"I object, your honor. I think this entire experiment is nothing more than a ... a charade ... a mockery of justice. Considering that we are taping this, I respectfully ask that we sequester the jury so they won't have to observe this ... this macabre spectacle."

That was a man speaking, and I try like hell to figure out what he's talking about, but I'm so swept up by the gushing, burning sensation of feeling as it spreads through my body that I can't concentrate on anything anyone is saying.

I imagine my body is an ice-bound river, and warm spring winds and the steady tug of flowing water underneath the ice are finally breaking apart the hammer-lock grip of the frozen surface.

I'm dizzy with a heady rush of euphoria as my vision clears even more, and I can see that I am not lying in the street, bleeding to death.

I'm in a room.

And I'm sitting up in a chair.

My hands are clamped to the chair arms in a viselike grip. I know, even if I wanted to, I wouldn't be able to move them. Across my chest, I can feel the tight pull of a restraint that makes it difficult—no, impossible for me to breathe. It's the strap that's keeping me erect in the chair, not my own strength.

When I try to open my mouth and run my tongue over my lips, there is no feeling whatsoever. It's as if my face has been shot full of Novocaine.

"Objection overruled, Mr. Applegate. While I grant that this is a most unique situation, I'll reserve judgment as to whether or not the evidence we receive is or it not admissible."

As my vision continues to resolve, I try to look around. Off to one side, I see the source of light—a high bank of windows through which bars of iridescent blue light are streaming. The light shimmers in slow, sinuous waves that maddeningly flicker through the colors of the spectrum. Everything appears to be watery and insubstantial. Halos of rainbow light surround everything.

Arrayed against the wall, below the windows, are numerous dark shapes.

People, I realize.

They appear to be frozen in place, as immobile as mannequins.

I try to blink my eyes, and it seems to take forever for the rough, sandpaper feeling to scrape across my eyeballs. I am startled when I rotate my head slowly to my left and see the dim silhouette of someone standing close beside me. The nimbus of light surrounding him—at least now I can see this is a man—masks his features as he leans close to me. I get a faint whiff of something stale, almost rotten, and that makes my stomach growl.

"Can you hear me, Mr. Sinclair?"

I want to answer him—I truly do, but when I try to clear my throat and take a deep breath, I have no sensation whatsoever of breathing. My chest feels like it's encased in iron bands. When I lean forward, the restraint presses into my chest, but—surprisingly—I feel no pain. The indistinct features of the man's face loom closer to me, resolving like a slowly developing photograph out of the shimmering haze. I see a terrifying, cartoon face with a wide, smiling mouth frozen in the center of a white balloon, and two dark, dimensionless balls that have to be his eyes.

When he speaks again, repeating his question, his lips move in flabby, rubbery twitches that are not at all in synch with his words.

"Do you understand what I'm saying to you, Mr. Sinclair?"

Again, I try to take a breath to speak, but the best I can manage is a slight nod of my head. I have no idea if I really moved. There is no pain, but the bones in my neck feel dry and splintering. If I move even the least bit, I fear my spine will snap like a piece of rotten wood.

I try to focus on this man's face and am surprised to notice that I feel no need to blink my eyes. I can't move them. The lids are frozen wide open as though I am permanently terrified.

Which I am.

I stare blankly forward, hoping my vision will resolve so I can turn my head and see who is talking to me.

"Can you see my hand, Mr. Sinclair?"

Something that looks like a huge, black crow flying across a stormy sky flashes in front of my face. It goes by so fast I can't possibly turn my head to track it.

"I would ask, Mr. Charles, that you not push him quite so hard."

There's that woman's voice again, speaking from somewhere off to my right. She's trying to make it sound like she's in control, but I detect a frantic edge of worry in her voice. When I try to turn my head to look at her, the total lack of sensation makes it feel as though my eyeballs are detached and rolling around inside my head, completely out of control.

"I understand, Dr. Murphy, but you indicated that we might not have very much time when he is even semiconscious. I repeat, Mr. Sinclair, can you see my hand. How many fingers am I holding up in front of you?"

Again the black crow flaps its way across my vision.

This time, I see two blurry lines, like fence posts, pointing straight up.

Two.

I think the word, but there is no way I can say it out loud. As much as I strain to speak, I can't feel the vocal cords in my throat. They might as well be cut. I'm disembodied … floating in a hazy, gray soup of vague lights, shadows, and sounds.

"I could administer a small amount more, your honor, but in my opinion, we've already pushed this to a dangerous level."

"I respectfully submit that this is a complete waste of the court and the jury's valuable time, your honor. My client and I request that you strike all references to this shameful incident … this mockery of justice from the record and that we proceed in a customary manner."

"Again, Mr. Applegate, your objection is noted and overruled. Please. Proceed with your line of questioning, Mr. Charles."

While this exchange is going on, I am only half listening because I am struggling to make my throat work. It's like trying to flex the muscles of an arm that's been amputated.

There's nothing there—not even the lack of sensation.

… nothing …

After a few moments of struggle, I feel another, stronger gush of warmth that's centered in my chest. The heat radiates outward like a glowing coal being fanned by a gentle breath. My throat tenses. The tendons and muscles are as stiff as bars of rusty iron. I can feel a faint thrumming that brings with it an agonizing jolt of pain.

"… two …"

In a sudden, nauseating rush, my vision resolves more clearly, and I see where I am.

To my right is a tall, oak-paneled desk behind which, high above me, sits a man dressed in a dark robe. The few wisps of gray hair he has are combed straight back from his wide, pale forehead. His face is crisscrossed by thin, red lines of exploded capillaries, particularly on his nose. Drinker's tattoos, I used to call them.

I'm surprised I can see such detail now.

Beside me, to my left, stands a man wearing a fancy three-piece suit of dark blue. His necktie is a design of squares with dark circles—like eyes—in the center. It looks amazingly three dimensional against the blinding white glare of his shirt. He is leaning forward with both hands on the arms of the chair in which I sit.

In front of me, a little to my right, stands a rather attractive, dark-haired woman. She is wearing a white laboratory smock. It swells out due to her ample breasts. She has a syringe in one hand, and I can see a needle and the plastic tube of an IV feed that has been taped to my exposed left forearm, which is strapped to the other arm of the chair.

Perhaps the most shocking thing I notice is the color of my own skin. It's not just pasty white; it's gray and looks exactly like the senseless, immobile clay I imagine it is.

"Very good, Mr. Sinclair. Two. That is correct," the man in the three-piece suit says, smiling broadly as he leans even closer to me. "I'm holding up two fingers."

His features don't look quite so cartoonish anymore, but they are still horrifyingly animated as a smile spreads across his wide face. His teeth are big and flat, and I am gripped by the sudden fear that he is going to lunge forward and bite me.

"I know it must be terribly difficult for you to speak, Mr. Sinclair," he says, "but if you please, could you indicate with either a sound or a motion of your hand that you understand what I'm saying?" He glances over his shoulder. "Is this acceptable to you, your honor?"

As I stare at him, the rippling halo of light that surrounds his head gradually blends from vibrant blues and purples to deep, fiery reds and oranges that shift across his features like flickering flames.

Unaccountably, I feel the cold hollow stirrings of hunger.

Yes ... hunger!

"My name is Raymond Charles, Mr. Sinclair. I'm the lawyer representing you in this case."

I want to ask him exactly what case that might be, but I'm fairly certain that it has something to do with the night I was mugged and tried to fight back. I realize that I must have been wounded, and I wonder if I have been in a coma all this time and am just now coming out of it.

There must have been some serious brain damage.

"You may remember that, on the seventeenth of December, you were accosted on your way home from work by a young man. Do you recall that incident?"

"... yes ..."

It takes every bit of effort I can muster to say that single word, which reverberates like the heavy clang of metal in my ears.

"Mr. Sinclair, I am informed that we don't have much time, so I must get directly to the point. I have to ask you, do you think you would recognize your assailant if he were to be presented to you?"

I turn away from Mr. Charles, sensing that the painful stirrings of hunger inside me intensify when I look at the glowing curtains of red light that surround his face. The fleshy folds of his skin fairly vibrate with energy and life. I try to concentrate on remembering exactly what happened that night—when?

How long ago?

It could have been days or weeks, or it could have been several months or even years. The memory is so distant, I have no way of knowing. The image of my attacker's face swirls in my mind like a face looking up at me from underwater.

Dark hair shifting in heavy, oily curls swirls around his face.

Eyes dark and liquid, slide nervously back and forth.

Thin, tight, almost bloodless lips are pursed, and the pale skin above his upper lip is marked by the faint wisp of a mustache. His skin looks greasy and pimply, but it is what I see inside those eyes that I remember most clearly.

Fear …

Fear and silent desperation.

"… yes …"

Even as I say the word, this boy's face materializes in front of me. It, too, is surrounded by a sparkling sheet of red light, and the gnawing hunger churning inside me intensifies until it becomes excruciatingly painful.

Hunger is the only pain I know.

The woman, apparently a doctor or nurse, says something to the man who has identified himself as my lawyer, but her words are lost to me as I stare again into that boy's dark, desperate eyes.

"Is this the man who attacked you, Mr. Sinclair?"

I hear the words, but they mean nothing to me.

The gnawing hunger growling like a disease inside my gut is more demanding. I am distantly aware that my mouth has dropped open … my teeth are grinding back and forth as I strain forward, but the strap across my chest holds me in place. I try to raise my arms, but they, too, are firmly held in place by restraints.

"… yes …"

"I object, your honor," a voice suddenly yells, sounding like a sudden clap of thunder.

"Overruled."

"I ask you again, Mr. Sinclair, and if you can, I would like you to speak a bit louder for the sake of the jury. Is the man standing in front of you the same man who accosted you on Irving Street on the night of December seventeenth and, at gun point, demanded that you give him your wallet and cell phone?"

"Objection. Leading the witness."

"… yes …"

"If it pleases the court, I would like it noted for the record that Mr. Sinclair has identified the defendant, Mr. Leroy Peterson."

"So noted."

"Objection, we haven't established the credibility of this witness."

"Overruled. Who better to identify his assailant, Mr. Applegate, than the murder victim himself?"

"Your honor, I think we're losing him."

When the woman speaks this time, even through the boiling pain of my overwhelming hunger, I recognize the edge of panic in her voice.

All around me, explosions of shadow and light blend and swirl in an insane riot of color and sound. I am dazzled, confused, and the only clear thought I carry through this confusion is that I am hungry …

So hungry!

"Your honor, I realize this is a rather unusual request, but I would beg the court's indulgence to allow me to ask if Mr. Peterson would please step forward and touch Mr. Sinclair on the hand."

"I object! This has gone on long enough. It's well past the point of morbid curiosity."

"May the court ask, Mr. Charles, exactly why you are making such an unusual request?"

"I beg your indulgence, your honor, but it is an ancient tradition that, if a corpse is touched by his murderer, the wounds which were inflicted by that individual will begin to bleed again."

A corpse?
Bleed?
What the hell is he talking about?
I'm not a corpse!

Voices explode around me, but I am so consumed by hunger and the numbing fear that embraces me that I don't understand a single word. Stark terror squeezes me with mounting pressure that soon becomes intolerable.

"I object! This is patently absurd! Why, this is a … this is a medieval superstition we're talking about, not modern jurisprudence. Your Honor, I would like to request that these entire proceedings be declared a mistrial, and that the—"

"Please calm yourself, Mr. Applegate. In light of this rather unusual situation, which is certainly something *I've* never experienced before, either, please instruct your client to do as Mr. Charles has requested."

"I will not!"

"You will, or I'll find you in contempt of court."

Every fiber of my being is charged with tingling jolts of electricity. The raging urge to eat, to kill, to rip into the throbbing, living flesh so close to me is overpowering. It fills me with a spiraling insanity, but there is nothing I can do. I thrash wildly against the restraints. My head reverberates with a loud, crashing sound that I soon realize are my teeth gnashing. Hot, sour saliva floods my mouth and the back of my throat, and then—through it all—I feel something else.

A touch … like a pin prick …

On the back of my hand.

It sizzles and crackles, but for only an instant. Then dark, rolling clouds churning with thick clots of ropy gray and black descend across my vision. All colors fade, and once again I am clutched by the sensation of being frozen into immobility. My muscles go rigid. My bones feel like iron spikes.

Something touches the back of my hand for less than a second, and then a dull leaden sensation seeps through my body like poison.

Oh, my God! Look!" a voice suddenly cries out. "He's … he's bleeding!"

I am so lost in my own internal agony that I can't distinguish whose voice it is.

I no longer care. It sounds so impossibly faraway I would cry … if I could.

"It's true! The stomach wound is bleeding again!"

"But that's impossible," someone else says. It might be the judge, or it might be the man who claims to be my lawyer.

"A corpse can't bleed!"

I am past caring as darkening waves engulf me, pulling me under with powerful , irresistible surges.

All of my senses dim.

The last thing I hear before everything resolves into pitch black nothingness again is a faint, echoing voice.

"Thank you, Dr. Murphy. That will be all for now. You may return Mr. Sinclair to the morgue now."

"Perfect Witness" ©1995 Rick Hautala.
Originally published in *Fear Itself*, Warner Books, 1995.

Stony's Boneyard

Glenn Chadbourne & Holly Newstein

Stony Tilton winced as the fresh line below his left shoulder blade took a sharp turn south. The tattoo gun buzzed like a wasp against his skin, and the line progressed down toward his middle back. Bonnie had been working on his back for almost an hour, and when the needle trolled through a patch of skin that she had recently detailed, he jumped.

He turned and shot Bonnie a pained glance over his shoulder, but she only grinned.

"Jesus! You diggin' a ditch back there? Son of a bitch feels like ground beef!"

"Don't be such a pussy," Bonnie replied. "You know the rules—no sniveling." She paused to examine her work. *Better to get the outline down right the first time, bold and clear,* she thought. Tiny threads of blood traced the new work and began to bead up on the fresh ink. She wiped them off with antiseptic soap, then leveled the gun, pressed the foot pedal, and the needle bit into Stony's shoulder again. Stony hissed this time, spraying a little spittle into the air.

"All right, that's enough." His voice rasped a little. "Fuckin' needle feels like a sixty-prong hay rake." He stretched his arms and climbed out of the antique barber's chair that served as Bonnie's work station. Bonnie had picked the chair up at a yard sale shortly after she opened her tattoo parlor. It was perfect for the shop because it weighed a ton, so it was steady and didn't move around, plus she could twirl clients around in the chair to get to tough-to-reach areas.

Besides, barbers were the original tattoo artists. If anyone ever doubted Bonnie's word on that, she would point to the old Norman Rockwell print she'd framed and hung in the shop. A sailor was sitting in a barber's chair, and the barber was tattooing another woman's name on his arm, right below the preceding ten or twelve that had been crossed out.

"Your history lesson for the day," she would say, and their eyes would go wide. "If Norman-freakin'-Rockwell painted it, it must be true, eh?"

Stony stood up stiffly and cracked his neck with both hands.

"We can finish up next Monday," he said.

"It's your dime," she replied. She put the tattoo gun down on the cluttered worktable next to the chair and peeled off her latex gloves. There was a crumpled pack of Marlboros next to the line of ink cups, and she picked it up and shook out a cigarette. She lit it and puffed deeply, sending two jets of smoke streaming from her nostrils.

"Want a shot for the road?" she asked.

"Why break tradition?" He was still stretching, flexing his painful shoulders.

Bonnie took his arm and turned his back to her.

"Let's take a look here. You're a walking billboard for me, y'know."

She rolled back on her stool and regarded Stony's back with pride. It was damn near finished now. A dozen gravestones, all carefully placed within an intricately drawn cemetery that took up his entire back. Each stone had its own little plot, carpeted with grass and fallen leaves. A lone oak tree with spidery limbs was centered in the middle of the cemetery. An oversized, glowing jack-o'-lantern lolled against the roots. Bonnie was particularly proud of that jack-o'-lantern—it had been her idea, and Stony had agreed. Its leering carved face stared out at the world from eyes that Bonnie's ink magic had made nearly incandescent.

A dilapidated old stone wall was stitched along the cemetery's border, tying it all together, and there was an ornate wrought-iron gate at the entrance that read "Stony's Boneyard" in flowing antique script. A few crows flew eternally in the sky above the cemetery along with a small clutter of leaves. It was her best work, and both of them knew it.

"So … how's it look?"

"See for yourself," she said. She handed him a large hand mirror, and he walked to the full-length mirror in a corner of the shop. He looked at the tattoo for some time, the hand mirror glinting in the late-afternoon light as he turned it to get different views.

"Damn, you're good. You're a sadistic bitch, but you are good. Don't let anyone tell you different," he said, staring at the reflection of his well-inked back. The tattoo had begun simply enough—years ago, Stony's mother had died. He'd been unable at the time to afford a headstone, but he did have enough money to memorialize her in his own skin. He had come to Bonnie's shop, and she inked a headstone on his back finer than the real one he'd bought a few years later. As the people who mattered to Stony passed on over the ensuing years, he would come to Bonnie to have another headstone added to his back. The tree and the stone wall and the jack-o'-lantern were details added as the tattoo grew. Eventually the tattoo spread over Stony's wide shoulders and down to his waist, and his living "boneyard" became a local legend. If you were interested in seeing the tattoo, all you had to do was show up at the Shamrock Tavern on Friday or Saturday night, and for the price of a beer and a shot, Stony would remove his shirt, and you'd get your own personal viewing.

Bonnie began adding a blank headstone whenever Stony came in.

"That way, all you have to do is come in for the name," she had said. But as the tattoo grew, becoming more elaborate, she knew it was more than just names. For him, the cemetery was about respect, about remembering, and about love. He loved and missed everyone inscribed on his back—for good and bad. They had filled his life once, and now they were gone.

She also knew that more than an artist/client relationship existed between them, but neither of them ever pursued it. The tattoo was intimate enough.

As if he had read her thoughts, Stony spoke.

"Tell me," he said, as much to himself as to Bonnie, "Why was it we never did the nasty?"

"Because I like you, you old goat," she retorted. She chuckled and stubbed out her cigarette in the overflowing ashtray.

"Oh yeah, that's it. I forgot for a minute. Where you stashing your jug these days?"

"In the medicine chest, behind the bandages."

Stony opened the cabinet and pulled out a fifth of Jim Beam. From the top shelf he took down two shot glasses etched with tiny skulls. A halo was over one skull, while the other had horns sprouting from its brow. He'd given her the glasses on her last birthday.

"You know," she said, "you're all filled up. There's no more room there. I couldn't fit another stone in there if I tried."

Stony smiled. It was a faraway smile, almost sweet—an expression Bonnie had never seen on his weathered face before.

"Well, babe, I'm thinkin' that's okay. I'm plumb out of friends now." He filled the glasses, and they clinked them together.

"There's always me," she said. "And hey, when are you taking me for a ride on that old bike of yours? It's about time."

"How 'bout tomorrow?" Stony tipped back his head and threw down his shot.

"You be here," she said.

BONNIE AWOKE EARLY TO THE SOUND OF THE TELEVISION JUST AS she'd fallen asleep to it the night before. The perky newscaster reading the morning's litany of global death and disaster irritated Bonnie so much that she couldn't doze off to sleep again. Out of habit, she reached for her cigarettes on the nightstand, but her hand froze in midair.

"A Brunswick man was killed last night in a motorcycle accident near the Cook's Corner Mall." The woman stared earnestly into the camera. "Fifty-three-year-old Robert Tilton was struck by a car and pronounced dead at the scene. The driver, a local juvenile, is charged with underage drinking and vehicular manslaughter. His name is being withheld at this time. For more on this story, let's go to Ann Collins …"

Bonnie fumbled for the remote and turned off the television. She listened to the early morning quiet with the same attention she'd given the TV a few moments ago. Presently a robin sang. Traffic droned by on Maine Street. The neighbor kids were playing in their yards; their voices piping on the breeze that lofted Bonnie's bedroom curtains. Life was going on. But not Stony.

For a few minutes she lay still in the bed, feeling nothing but emptiness.

Then, like a spring storm, the tears began. Slowly at first, trickling hot and slow over her cheeks and down into her hair, and then coming faster and faster, her chest heaving with violent sobs that tore from her gut. She curled tightly into a ball, hugging her knees and rocking in her bed as grief engulfed her.

BONNIE SAT AT A TABLE IN THE SHAMROCK TAVERN, WAITING for Robby to bring her a beer. She fidgeted in the black dress she'd bought ten pounds ago and had worn to Stony's funeral today. The dress cinched her hips too tightly and rode up her thighs too far. She wished she'd gone home and changed first.

Stony had been right about one thing—he was plumb out of friends. There had been maybe a dozen people at Kinney's Funeral Parlor. The plain, inexpensive casket was closed in mute testimony to the extent of Stony's injuries. Bonnie found out that the kid who'd hit him was drunk out of his mind, seventeen years old and didn't even remember the accident. He'd hit Stony broadside at about sixty, reducing the bike to a pile of scrap metal and sending Stony flying twenty-five feet to land on the macadam. Then the kid freaked out and lost control of the car and ended up running over Stony's head. As usual, Stony hadn't been wearing a helmet.

Bonnie looked down at the shiny maple lid of the casket and shuddered.

She recognized an aunt, a cousin, a few of Stony's coworkers from Bath Iron Works. There was a funeral wreath commemorating his twenty-five years of service at BIW. Bonnie had thought it was longer than that. A minister she didn't know said the usual things, and then it was over. She declined to go to the cemetery, and walked over to the tavern where a few mutual acquaintances had gathered for a send-off.

Bonnie knew that she was the only one there at Shamrock's for Stony's sake. The rest were there mainly because they were regulars and Stony's passing was merely an excuse to toss down a few extra shots. All the people who really mattered to Stony had long since preceded him out to the Whispering Pines Cemetery, each listed in order of their own passing along the contours of Stony's shoulders and spine.

Everyone but her.

She sighed and tugged at her skirt.

Robby returned to the table holding two long-necked brown bottles in his right hand. He gave one to her and sat down.

"How was it?"

"It was a funeral. Seen one, seen 'em all."

"I can't deal with fucking funerals." Robby took a swig. "Never even went to my old man's. Left that up to my sisters." He shrugged. The light from the big window at the front of the bar reflected off his shaved head. He had a long beard that he'd braided into two twirling cords beneath his chin. And he was a true devotee of Bonnie's ink—his body was covered with tribal designs from neck to ankles. He looked slightly unreal, like a character in a video game. Or that guy from Moby-Dick.

"Well, aren't you the dutiful son," she said, a bit more coldly than she'd intended.

"Hey, my Pop was a son of a bitch anyhow. He rained nothing but shit on me for thirty years," he replied, and shrugged. Then he leaned across the table.

"You got any pot?"

Bonnie smiled. Stony had referred to joints as "little doctors" because they wore white coats and fixed your head.

"Not me."

More familiar faces made their way to the corner where Bonnie and Robby sat. In time, shots of Jim Beam appeared, a memorial tribute to Stony. They reminisced about Stony and discussed the funeral, and then gradually the conversation drifted to other matters. Bonnie had tattooed almost everyone there, to a greater or lesser extent, and her most recent work was examined as sleeves were rolled up and shirts unbuttoned. The question of joints came up again, and the guys eventually retired behind the dumpster in the parking lot.

Bonnie walked down to her shop, but she didn't open for business. Instead, she made her way to the medicine chest and pulled out the bottle of Beam she'd shared with Stony on his last day on earth. She poured herself a shot, and as she lifted it to her lips, she heard the unmistakable, soft sound of clinking glasses echo in the empty room.

"I really, really liked you, you old bastard,' she whispered, and drained the glass.

She spent the rest of the day in her closed shop, wiping down equipment, sterilizing tubes and needles, ordering supplies and doing some bookwork. She took comfort in the familiarity of her shop and the dullness of the routine. It kept her from thinking too much.

She came home at eight. She walked through the kitchen, not stopping to think about dinner. She went to her room and yanked off her dress, leaving it in a heap on the floor as she pulled on a comfortable oversized T-shirt. She flopped down on her bed without turning on the television, and sleep overcame her moments later.

THE NEXT MORNING, BONNIE WAS SITTING ON THE FRONT STEPS OF her shop, drinking a cup of coffee in the warm sunshine. A distant radio played "Behind the Wall of Sleep" by the Smithereens. Bonnie found herself singing softly:

... and I lie in bed and think of her

Sometimes I even weep
When I dream of her behind the wall of sleep.

The air smelled like fresh dirt and growing grass, and the sun beamed down on Bonnie's shoulders and her long, glossy brown hair. The sky was a clear sapphire blue, the birds were chirping and calling, making a perfect cacophony of song, and the breeze blew warm from the south. She gathered her hair into a twist and lifted it up off her neck, letting the breeze tickle her skin.

"Perfect day for a ride," she said out loud.

The throaty, familiar sound of a Harley echoed along the street and drew closer. The bike came to a gliding halt in front of the steps and Stony got off.

"Sorry I'm late," he said.

He was younger, somehow. A long coil of blonde, not gray, hair had come loose from its leather tieback and fell across his shoulder. His blue eyes, the color of the sky, sparkled like sun on the water. He looked about twenty-five—ten years younger than Bonnie. He was wearing a T-shirt that read "I Told the Bitch to Hang On"—with two ragged holes torn in the sides.

"Great shirt," she said, as if Stony returned from the dead every day.

A million questions fought their way into her conscious mind, but she deliberately ignored them. She didn't want to know. She didn't care. He promised, dammit!

He winked and motioned toward the back of his bike. She got up and walked down the steps. She climbed on and put her arms around him as he kicked the Harley into gear. They rolled down Maine Street toward the back roads and the open spaces. Bonnie's hair jigged behind her in a tangled cloud as they gained speed, and she grinned so wide she thought her face might split.

Stony reached down and patted her thigh with a big leather-gloved mitt. He glanced back and saw her grinning.

"You know how much I love you, man?" he shouted into the wind. Then he laughed and gunned the throttle.

The ride seemed to go on and on, forever and ever, amen. Bonnie cleared her mind of anything ugly—the bills, the shop, all the shoulds and oughts and most of all, how the hell she could possibly be roaring up the road on a dead man's bike—and let it all blow away in the early-summer winds. Euphoria surged in her blood, pulsing with the throb of the engine. She was fused with Stony and his motorcycle, welded into a fabric of metal and flesh and peace and happiness. It would come to an end soon enough, but right now it just didn't get any better than this, and she had Stony to thank for it; she owed him, even if the feeling only lasted for a few moments. She leaned her cheek against the warm cottony curves of his back and held him tight, filled with the joy of the moment.

They continued along at a ferocious clip, passing everything on the road, drinking in a vivid patchwork of fields and trees gone green and yellow and pink with new life—until the sun dipped behind a cloud, and Stony slowed down.

Bonnie knew at once that the ride was over. *I'm the balloon girl, and someone's come along with a big sharp pin*, she thought with a pang.

Stony craned his neck to face her.

"Sorry, babe, but I can't go much further. There's rules."

Bonnie said nothing, but her spirits fell even lower. Stony's face had aged, and he was fifty-three years old again. Lines cut deeply into his cheeks and around his mouth. His long hair had gone gray and thin, and his eyes were set within a net of wrinkles now. But they were still blue, and they still sparkled.

"Good ride, though, huh?"

"The best," she answered, her voice husky with emotion.

"And I guess you know where we're really headed ... where we're finishing up."

She nodded.

The road narrowed now, and tangled woods followed them along either side. Spring had turned to autumn in less than a mile, and the trees were gnarled and black, their bare limbs snatching at a slate-gray sky. After another half-mile, they topped a rise and rolled slowly along beside a broken stone wall. On the left side of the road was an old graveyard. Stony killed the bike's engine, and they rolled to a stop at the entrance.

The place was run-down and dilapidated. Witchgrass and long tangles of vines had taken over the entire lawn, and the stones all seemed to poke up at twisted angles. They leaned awkwardly from stumps choked with muck and leaves. More than a few were ruined, cracked in half.

Bonnie's eyes narrowed, then widened in recognition. "Christ!" she gasped.

"'Bout time you figured it out," Stony replied. "I always did peg you for brainy."

They got off the bike and walked into the cemetery, stepping high over the squealing chain. A light drizzle began to fall, and Bonnie shivered and wrapped her arms tightly around herself. They walked on, going deeper and deeper into the cemetery, moving toward the highest point. There was a lone tree at the crest of the hill—an old oak, with spidery limbs. A jack-o'-lantern rested against the roots of the tree, grinning in fiery red and yellow. Bonnie bent down and ran her hand over its curved orange surface. Instead of feeling smooth and cool and hard, as she expected it to, it was warm and rubbery and yielding—like human flesh.

A crow cawed, and Bonnie started at the sound. She stared at the headstones, remembering how she had lettered each one, the tattoo gun pressing against the living skin of Stony's back, the rasping sound of his curses when she dug a little too deep. Stony touched her arm, and she turned and looked at him.

He smiled.

He had changed again, and she understood why they had kept his casket closed at the funeral. Yet Bonnie found herself giggling.

"You look like Wile E. Coyote," she said, eyeing the perfect tire imprint on his split forehead.

"Yeah, real funny," he replied. "But hey, I can see the humor." His shattered mouth curved into a crazy toothless grin. Bonnie looked away, her giggle becoming a sob.

Along the crest of the hill, a line of people appeared. They were little more than scarecrows; their ragged, rotted clothing fluttered as the wind passed through it. One of them stepped forward.

"Time's wasting," he said. His voice was little more than a throaty groan. "We should be moving along."

The others came closer, surrounding them; long lengths of matted hair hanging from their half-bare skulls. A fringe of pointed ribs poked through one man's side, and he brushed at them with a wizened, skeletal hand. Some—the ones who had been dead the longest—were nearly fleshless, their clothing in tatters, the wind whistling through their empty eye sockets. Bonnie stared at the dried-up creatures, hitching forward like zombies, and recognized them. They were all Stony's friends—the ones who had gone before him, the ones with their headstones on his back.

She suddenly knew what he wanted her to do, and her fingers closed on an oversized tattoo gun.

"I need to get moving, babe," Stony said, and patted a blank stone which had magically appeared next to her. She knelt before the stone and lifted the gun. It buzzed to life and she pressed the tip against the headstone, which was made of warm flesh instead of cold granite. Stony leaned on the curved top of the stone, watching her work.

She carefully inked:
Robert "Stony" Tilton
FLY FREE

Stony knelt beside her and patted the top of her head.

"You're the only one who could do this for me, y'know. And not because you're a great artist." She looked up into his face, and he smiled. "You could do it because you're a friend of mine." His smile widened. Her eyes filled with tears, and for a moment Stony's face blurred before her, looking whole and young again. He leaned down, putting his face close to hers, and for a moment she thought he was going to kiss her.

"A real friend," he said softly into her ear. "Just like these assholes here." The corpses began to chuckle, their heads nodding in unison. Bonnie let go a whoop of laughter that seemed to come up from her toes. It took with it all the grief and sorrow that had filled her.

The corpses turned and began walking away from them, toward a line of motorcycles that had appeared along the ridge, their chrome gleaming in the fading light. Stony helped Bonnie to her feet, and then joined the shambling procession. Bonnie stood and watched, fascinated, as they all straddled their bikes. The sound of twelve Harleys sputtering and coughing to life reverberated through Stony's Boneyard, and the bikes filed out toward the open road beyond.

As he came to the gate, Stony turned back to Bonnie and lifted his big, gloved hand in a thumbs-up gesture. Then he disappeared.

Bonnie stared at the gate until the rising wind, bitter cold, cut through her like a knife and made her eyes sting. She blinked and looked up at the sky, which was darkening quickly. Without Stony beside her, she was suddenly afraid. She began to run toward the gate. As she ran, she could feel the sky above pressing down on her, and the ground beneath her pounding feet shook and shuddered, nearly throwing her down. But she kept her balance, and crouched low as she ran to keep herself steady.

She didn't look at anything directly—her focus was on the rusty chain at the gate—but it seemed to her as if everything was blurring and becoming indistinct.

Just keep running, she thought. *Run, and don't fall down.*

She was only a few strides away from the gate when her hair whipped out in front of her as a giant gust of wind nearly lifted her off her feet. At the same time, the ground heaved up as if to throw her forward. She dove for the chain and went over, tumbling in the dirt and leaves until she rolled to the side of the road that had fronted Stony's Boneyard. She leaped to her feet and looked, her eyes wide with wonder.

The blazing afternoon sunshine dazzled her after the darkening gloom of the cemetery. Noise rushed back in upon her—birds, the drone of a far-off lawn mower. She blinked in the sunshine, feeling the light and the life all around her.

She turned to look behind her. She saw a cemetery, shaded with tall pines, granite headstones marking each grave site. Down the path, in a patch of sunlight, was a freshly-turned grave. Wilted flowers were scattered on the dirt, their limp petals fluttering like rags.

A white painted sign by the gate read: WHISPERING PINES MEMORIAL PARK.

"You were always good on your word, Stony," she whispered.

Then she turned away and began walking back home.

Kali's Promise

Trisha J. Wooldridge

God never answered;
why should this be different?

Blue-black, leggy, pointed tongue
        dagger fingernails
the Goddess stood.

Just a thing from the Internet
        A spell
A thing she thought as useless
        as CCD and newspaper classifieds
            of Ave Marias
            Saint Anthony
            Saint Francis
            Saint Theresa, little flower
            and Sweet Baby Jesus

Blue-black, leggy, pointed tongue
        dagger fingernails
Kali waited.

Hate rose up.
        Hate and pain and sadness
        Nothing to lose
Her mind must already be gone
        to see a Goddess of revenge in her living room.

Blue-black, leggy, pointed tongue
        dagger fingernails

the Goddess asked:
>WHY DID YOU CALL ME?

And she answered.
>Revenge, blood ... I want him to hurt as much as I do!
>He deserved this, not me.
>I want to tear his body
>>to shreds
>>smaller than the pieces
>>he left
>>of my heart
>>and self-respect.
>>I want him to Hurt!

The Dark, sharp-tongued, sharp-fingered Goddess replied:
>AND WHAT WOULD YOU GIVE ME FOR
>YOUR REVENGE?

She paused.
Eyes closed, lips sneered,
>hand pressed on the baby-swollen belly,
>she offered up:
>This! This! Take the child, do what you will!
>So that he knows so well my pain!

Kali scoffed:
>WHAT DO I WANT
>WITH THAT
>WHICH YOU WOULD PAY TO GET RID OF?
>IT IS NO SACRIFICE.

Tears froze
>stood still
upon mortal cheeks.

Fist clenched
Jaw clenched
Stomach clenched
>as if to squeeze out the parasite
>that started
>this whole mess.

Then, me! Take my life.
Shed my blood upon your altar!
That his runs in rivers.

Kali laughed:
> WHAT DO I WANT
> WITH WHAT
> YOU NO LONGER VALUE?
> IT IS NO SACRIFICE.

Blue-black, leggy, pointed tongue
> dagger fingernails
the Goddess waited
> and watched.

The woman fell to her knees
> tears burning cold upon her flesh
Still not moving.

Old stories said
> the gods were not patient.
What, then, what?
She offered:
> Tell me what you want for this and I will give it.

She forgot that gods were unfair.
A foolish mistake
> all things considered in her current state.

Kali smiled.
Blue-black, leggy, pointed tongue
> dagger fingernails
the Goddess smiled
> and said:
> I WANT YOUR VENGEANCE.
> I WANT YOUR HATE.
> I WANT IT ALL.
> GIVE IT TO ME
>> AND HIS BLOOD WILL RUN LIKE RIVERS
> I WILL BREAK HIS HEART

>   HIS WILL
>   HIS PRIDE
>   AND HE WILL FALL AND BEG FOR MERCY
>   A HUNDRED THOUSAND TIMES OVER.
>   AND FIND NONE.

The woman answered: Yes!
> It is yours, all of it.
> Do exactly as you promise
> and it is yours!

Kali replied: SO BE IT.
> COME MIDNIGHT I FULFILL MY PROMISE.
> NOW, I TAKE YOUR SACRIFICE.

Blue-black, leggy, pointed tongue
> Kali reached her pointed fingernails
> into the woman's chest.
> Blood ran like rivers
> stained her shirt

but she felt no pain.

The Goddess reached into the woman's heart
> and removed
>> the hate
>> the vengeance
>> the pain

And left the woman sleeping.

The woman awoke
> time 10:30

and wondered at the peculiar dream
until she saw the blood.

She tore her shirt
> to reveal
>> no scars.

But her heart pounded so!

She forgave him.

        Benediction
        Absolution
        Grace
        and Freedom!

Her heart said:
    No!
    Hurry, before it's too late!

The woman ran
    barefoot
    torn shirt
    tear-stained
    to the T-Station two blocks away
and bought a ticket.
One-way
    all she could afford
    without her purse
    only pocket change.

So late.
The woman stepped the hallowed dance
    of anxiety
    impatience.
The commuter rail took
        soooooooo
                daaaaaaaamnnn
                        looooooooong
She ran the rest of the way.

Time 11:50

Out of breath,
    she knocked,
    she rang,
    he answered:
What the fuck?
    he yelled
Are you doing here?
At this hour?

I came, she breathed
    I came ...
    to warn ...

What? he yelled
    Spit it out! A paternity suit?
    Call my lawyer!

No! Wait!
    she cried.
    Too late.

Dagger fingernails
    reached
    around
dug into his stomach.

Blood ran rivers
    down his shirt
    over his trousers
    dripping waterfalls down the doorstep.

Blue-black, leggy, pointed tongue
    dagger fingernails dragged
    the shocked-silent man
    still alive
    to his living room
    where
the Goddess eagerly waited.

I AM PLEASED YOU CAME TO SEE.

No! Wait!
    The woman ran
    hit an invisible web
    held her tight
    like mother's arms
    so she could see.

Blood ran rivers
    stained the carpet.

His eyes bulged, grew bigger
and bigger
until they exploded
milky, egg-white dripping from his sockets
but she knew he could still see.

Please!

Said Kali:
WE HAVE A COVENANT.
I WILL NOT BREAK MY PROMISE
NO MATTER WHAT.
SO IT BE.

A hundred thousand invisible razors
tore off the man's clothes
and then his skin
Kali turned his head
crammed her pointed tongue
down his throat
Kissed
and shredded his throat
mouth
lips
Long limbs twisted around his body
pulling, tugging
until muscles
and tendons
tore
away
to bone.

The man screamed
a hundred thousand murdered cries
of babes
raped women
abandoned mothers
rotted souls
and died.

Kali's Promise

Kali kissed him again
    gentle
      on the forehead
like a mother.

A wave of daggered fingernails
    shredded the web
      holding the woman
who fell.

Blue-black, leggy, pointed tongue
    daggered fingernails
the Goddess
kissed her too
    before disappearing.

The woman crawled
    to the kitchen
    for a knife.
She held it to her wrist
    her throat
    her heart
but couldn't.

Kali took that too
    as promised … everything.

The woman lay
    in a puddle of tears
    too shallow for drowning
where the officers found her
    with the murder weapon
    covered in his blood.

Blue-black, leggy, pointed tongue
    daggered fingernails
the Goddess laughed.

Sequel

David Bernard

I WAS JUST ABOUT TO START MY RESEARCH WHEN THE PHONE RANG. Normally when I'm about to start working, I'll let it go to the answering machine, but I was expecting a call from my new literary agent. One of the great advantages of currently having the best-selling horror novel in America is that the stink of money makes the publisher pay attention to the cash cow. And Harry may have been new at being my agent, but he was an old hand at fawning over his two-legged revenue streams.

I sighed to myself and grabbed the phone. "Hello, Harry." Harry had a set routine, and caller ID had not altered his routine. "It's me, Harry. How's America's favorite gore-meister?"

"I don't know, Harry. I'll ask Stephen King next time I see him." Harry asked the same question every time and I answered it the same way every time. I suspect Harry used the verbal foreplay to justify his percentage.

I looked out the window at a hawk soaring over the Manuxet River. I decided to forego the niceties before Harry completely killed my creative mood. "Harry, *Blood Keeper* is a best seller and I love that fact. But it's only one book and if my soon-to-be ex-wife has her way, I don't know if I'll see another royalty check before the bank decides I can't pay the mortgage on this farm."

I heard him light a wooden match on his thumb and start a cigar. That was a good sign. "That's why I'm calling. You've lived in Massachusetts for five years, correct?"

Yes," I said, beginning to feel the vein in my forehead start to throb. I looked out the window again and decided it wasn't a hawk, it was an eagle. "We've been over this, Melissa and I bought this farm five years ago, but I married Melissa in California. My former agent felt that getting married in a community property state gave Melissa a claim for half the royalties in spite of the prenup agreement."

He exhaled into the phone. Nobody borrowed Harry's phone without a hazmat suit. "Well, I bounced it off the legal department and they say Dean was whistling Dixie. Massachusetts divorce law applies. They're not divorce law specialists, but they say you're fine at first glance. Under Mass. law, you should get about two-thirds of the assets as the higher wage earner. And that's not factoring in that Melissa ran off with Dean—she committed adultery and took off. A judge is going to take that into consideration."

I smiled. Harry wasn't telling me anything I hadn't known. "Yes, my lawyer can't locate them to serve the divorce papers, so I'm suing for divorce by abandonment and hoping for a default settlement. I still think there's something fishy—Dean was a lot of things, but greed was his most endearing trait. I can't imagine he'd walk away from his percentage of *Blood Keeper*."

I could imagine Harry squinting at his notes. If it had percentages or dollar signs, Harry could remember every detail. Everything else was a little hit or miss. "We'll take his percentage out of the checks and put it in a trust fund. When he reappears, it'll be sitting there waiting for him. When he asks for his fees, we'll have the boys in legal take it to a judge and have him declared in breach of contract. If he doesn't show up in a couple of years, you have him declared legally dead. Either way, you get his 15% back."

"Harry, you've made my day. Now I feel like I can get back to actually writing something instead of this business crap. And although I'm sure he'll show up when the money runs out, I love the idea of having Dean declared dead."

Harry was not a fan of horror or my odd sense of humor. "Listen, as much as I hate to interrupt your really creepy musings, the VP wants to know how your next book is doing and when can he have a rough concept to start the marketing people thinking?"

I paused. "Well, I haven't got the specifics in place quite yet, but it will be about a serial killer with an overdeveloped sense of irony. He tortures his victims, but he kills them by removing a body part that he finds appropriately humorous. So, when he kills a drunk, he cuts out the liver, when he kills a model, he skins her alive."

The silence on the other end was because Harry really didn't like anything about horror but the commission.

I patiently tried to explain. "It's an experiment in seeing how far black humor can go before it de-evolves back into true horror."

Harry was now out of his comfort zone and we both knew it. "That sounds like something the marketing department would come up with."

"So give it to them as a head start. I should have a finished draft in a few days," I said, looking at the clock.

"Well, get back to work." It was getting close to Harry's lunch time and the bartender would worry if he was late.

"That's the plan. Thanks, Harry." I hung up the phone. Time and Harry's 15% waited for no man.

I strolled over to the gurney where the backstabbing excuse for my former literary agent lay bound and gagged. The little beads of sweat were beginning to mess up his expensive coif, and the fear in his eyes was great enough to overwhelm the Botox treatments. Dean was beginning to suspect that I was not pleased with being cuckolded and I assume that the gag was the only thing preventing the weasel from begging for his life.

"Dean, old buddy, I'd thank you in the foreword for the inspiration you're about to provide, but technically, I haven't seen you since you ran off with Melissa, so that would be awkward to explain. So, please excuse the slight—it's nothing personal."

"Frankly, I'm having trouble with this part. You see, the concept requires something ironic to be removed surgically, and since we both know you don't have a heart, that kills my first choice, so to speak."

Dean didn't seem to notice the clever pun, but then again, he did seem somewhat distracted by the shiny row of surgical instruments on the tray near his head.

"Dean, old pal, I'm stymied. My second choice would be to castrate you, since that's what got you into this mess. But that's only ironic to me. It doesn't scream 'agent' like it should to my adoring readers. I mean, Melissa was easy—she broke my heart." I stepped aside to give Dean a clear view of the jar holding the exorcised part of my dear, late wife.

Dean's eyes widened far beyond what I'm sure his plastic surgeon would recommend and a muffled shriek managed to work itself out through the gag. That was useful— I jotted down a note to include that part as Dean began to thrash beneath his restraints. Of course, it would do him no good; the restraints were designed to hold a far stronger, albeit equally involuntary, participant in my anesthesia-free "literary research."

I'm not sure if the sweat rolling down his ashen face was getting into his eyes or if he was weeping, it would be a moot point momentarily. He would be weeping, and shrieking, and begging for a quick death that would not be coming.

I looked out the window, savoring the muffled noises. I was beginning to think it wasn't a hawk or an eagle, but rather a buzzard. That meant I needed to bury Melissa deeper. I'd fix that in a few days when I was finished with Dean.

"Dean old buddy, please consider this your official termination notice. You have however inspired me. As my literary agent, you're entitled to 15% of *Blood Keeper*. But, since you violated my trust, I'm going to reclaim that commission."

Fear clouded comprehension in his eyes, and unless I missed my guess, the king of power lunches was in the process of soiling himself.

"Dean, here's a fascinating little factoid. The body mass of a man of average weight and height such as yourself is composed of, among other things, 12% fat, 45% muscle, and more importantly, 15% skeleton."

Dean suddenly realized how I was going get my 15%, and the muffled mewling sounds were truly impressive. I just hoped I could translate the glorious noises into appropriate prose.

I picked up a bone saw.

Malfeasance

David North-Martino

"You can't torture suspects and get away with it," Assistant District Attorney Kathleen Brennan said. She rose out of her seat, her face flushing to the same hue as the cherry wood table that stood between her and the detective and his lawyer. She hated how her pale skin so easily revealed her anger. In her line of work showing emotion could be perceived as a weakness, especially for a woman.

"Would you rather have a dead little girl?" Detective George Drake asked. He was calm on the exterior, but she could sense his anger raging behind his eyes.

"George, please," Drake's lawyer said. "You're not helping. Let me handle this."

The lawyer turned back to Kathleen. "Please sit. Let's talk about this rationally."

Kathleen eased back into her seat carefully, keeping her expression cool and her back straight to convey authority.

"My client would like to plead down. He'll do a hundred hours of community service and you won't contest his full reinstatement."

"And why would I do that, Mr. Kort?" Kathleen asked, unable to will away her exasperated expression.

"You're looking at a hero to this city, Ms. Brennan," Ronald Kort said, peering over his reading glasses.

"Some hero. Detective Drake's tactics got the kidnapper acquitted. He's out on the street and he may very well do this to someone else's child."

"It was the only way I could get him to talk," Drake said. Now she could see his anger and exasperation. "He wanted me to torture him. He wanted to corrupt me. And if I didn't enhance my interrogation that little girl would have suffocated. You would have thanked me for doing this if it had been your daughter. I can guarantee it."

"Don't bring my daughter into this," Kathleen said, feeling her temples throbbing.

Edward Fagan had done something beyond horrible, but she was convinced that Drake didn't have to become a monster to stop him. And as for her daughter, she had learned to compartmentalize her professional decisions from her personal life. It was the only way she could get the job done and survive with her sanity. And that's just what she did. Tucked his comment away deep in her brain where it wouldn't sway her in any way.

"You've protected one little girl, and while that's certainly admirable, you've left the rest of the city unsafe."

"If he does something again you won't have to worry. When I find him, I'll kill the bastard."

Kort waved him off and then turned back to Kathleen.

"You're right," he said, giving her an affected smile. "Fagan's rights were violated and he was acquitted. He might do it again. Then again, he might not. Either way, the police know who he is now and will have an easier time tracking him if he does try something else."

"That's not good enough, and even if it were I would never agree to let Detective Drake return to his duties."

"Your boss is up for re-election. Think about it. How do you think the voters will react to Detective Drake's imprisonment?"

She didn't need to think about it. An hour later her boss gave her the answer. The perpetrator was free and now so was the man who had tortured him. Despite her efforts, the city wasn't any safer.

DARKNESS ENVELOPED HER CAR AS WELL AS HER MIND AS SHE DROVE the dimly lit streets in her Volvo. Her childhood fear of the dark returned, coupled with the fear of the very real human monsters that lurked in the shadows of society: next-door neighbor serial killers, radicalized suicide bombers, and pedophile priests. She wondered how she was able to get out of bed in the morning or leave work at night. How could anybody? But she felt she got the worst of it.

Her job was not unlike that of an aboriginal shaman putting rocks in his mouth as he drew out disease, allowing the sickness to be absorbed by the stones, and spitting them out so that the pathology didn't infect his body.

The big difference between her and a shaman was that she didn't have a conduit stone to transfer the disease. Instead, she absorbed the evil, one case at a time, until she had been ravaged by the seediness of humanity.

Sometimes Kathleen wondered why she held on to her ADA position. She could easily suck it up and go to work at her father's firm. She had shunned that advantage, wanting to make it on her own, and also wanting to make a difference. Instead, she had found that corruption and politics kept her from acting her conscience.

If she wanted to throw her values away, which she felt she was doing anyway, she could take her father's example and defend all the worthless scum in the world and not rely on his support, and she had to think about her daughter. An ADA's salary wouldn't pay for private school.

After her marriage ended with Rodney, she had reluctantly taken her father's handouts. After she learned of the affair, she wouldn't accept Rodney's money, even child support. She didn't want anything to do with him.

A brightly lit sign that read *Brenton Luxury Apartments* stood out against the darkness, the only place in the whole city where she truly felt safe.

The underground garage stood preternaturally quiet. As soon as she pressed the key fob and heard the reassuring chirp she hurried through the expansive parking area, comforted by the security cameras that watched for danger 24/7. The only sound now: the echoing clack of her heels on concrete.

Living here was like living in isolation. She rarely ran into her neighbors. She didn't mind that. After dealing with people all day the last thing she wanted to do when she came home was deal with more people.

The elevator brought her smoothly to her floor. She walked out, took a left, and headed for her apartment door. It would be good to see Vanessa, find out how her day had been. The late hours the job required made her feel less like a mother and more like a ghost that flittered in and out of her daughter's life. Her housekeeper had become almost a substitute parent, keeping Vanessa from becoming an upscale latchkey kid while her mother was out trying to keep the streets safe.

Kathleen rummaged in her purse for her smart card. Finding it, she waved the small plastic device in front of the electric eye. The access light turned from red to green and she heard the click of the mechanism as it unlocked. She opened the door.

No light shone in the apartment. Something wasn't right.

"Vanessa? Mrs. Perez?" Kathleen called out. She thought she heard someone, a muffled sound. She hesitated. Should she go in or run down to the security desk? If Vanessa was hurt time was of the essence. Her fingers ran across the cool surface of the inside wall, finding the plastic switch, depressing it, lighting the apartment.

Mrs. Perez lay on the carpet, bound with rope, her eyes filled with tears, the sound of her voice muffled by a gag.

Ohmygodohmygodohmygodohmygod!

Kathleen couldn't think. Things like this weren't supposed to happen here. They had security, and lights, and alarms.

Kathleen ran to her, falling to her knees. She pulled the gag out of Mrs. Perez's mouth and drew it down over her chin until it went slack and lay like a kerchief over her throat.

"Where's Vanessa? Who did this?" Panic made her eyes bulge and her mouth dry.

Mrs. Perez babbled in Spanish, trying to wrap her mouth around words between her sobs.

"I can't understand you. I need English." Panic turned to anger. "English! What happened? Where's Vanessa?"

"Oh Jesus! Ms. Kathleen. He took her! He took Vanessa!"

TIME SLOWED, EXPANDED AND CONTRACTED SIMULTANEOUSLY, leaving Kathleen feeling disassociated from her body and her actions. She barely remembered untying Mrs. Perez or dialing 911. Lethargy set in, as if helplessness were a drug that circulated in her blood. How long she had to wait for the police she did not know. Mrs. Perez tried to comfort her, but Kathleen could offer none in return.

The uniformed division arrived, asked questions, probed and prodded the apartment. She could vaguely register Mrs. Perez's answers to their questions. A man had come up to deliver a package; she'd opened the door and he'd forced his way in. Kathleen knew the rest of the story.

While Kathleen fretted, the police set up a command center in her apartment. An hour went by, maybe two. While they waited, the officer in charge tried to soothe her with reassurances that they would find her daughter.

One cop, a burly fellow who looked like he spent most of his off time in the gym, walked in holding a manila envelope. The officer in charge opened it, looked inside, and then poured out a DVD into his hands.

The supervisor approached her.

"One of my officers found this during a sweep outside the building," he said. "I think it was left for you."

She nodded. He walked over to her entertainment center, turned on the plasma and her Blu-Ray player, put the disk in, and pressed play on the remote.

What she saw brought her to hysterics.

The shaky handheld video showed her sweet, beautiful Vanessa, wrists bound, in some type of a wooden trunk. The trunk was small enough that Vanessa had to remain in the fetal position to fit inside. The image made her think of how her daughter might have looked inside her womb.

Her daughter was scared. Oh God, she was scared. He set the camera down on an unseen table or shelf then walked over and closed the lid of the trunk while Vanessa writhed inside, her protests muted by a gag.

With uncaring aggression he pounded nails into the lid, trapping her daughter inside. The image Kathleen had of a womb changed horrifically into a coffin. The jarring bang of each hammer hit threatened Kathleen's sanity.

Once he had sealed the lid, he put the hammer on the earthen floor of what must have been an unfinished cellar. He pushed the trunk across the floor and then down into a freshly dug hole. Grabbing a shovel that had been hidden out of camera range, he shoveled dirt over the makeshift coffin.

Kathleen doubled over then, fell to her knees and vomited on her rug. Racking sobs making it difficult to breathe. She was barely aware of the two officers who bent down to assist her. She looked up to see the horrible man staring directly into the camera, directly at her. Edward Fagan. The man Detective Drake had let get away.

"She has twenty-four hours," Fagan said into the camera.

Kathleen dug her fingers into the rug and screamed, screams turning to sobs. She felt a slight pinch as a paramedic gave her a sedative. The room and everyone and everything in it turned to soft-focus, a humming in her ears blotting out all sound, and then everything switched to blackness.

KATHLEEN AWOKE GENTLY. BLURRED VISION SLOWLY FOCUSED. The police were still in her apartment and she was lying on her leather couch. She sat up too quickly and felt blood rush to her head.

"Easy," a paramedic said, guiding her back down with a soft touch of his hands on her shoulders.

Everything came rushing back: Edward Fagan, her daughter, the womb-turned-coffin, but she couldn't feel the same pain as before the sedative. It was as if a barrier had been erected or a distance created that blunted her emotions and sanded down the rough edges of her nerves.

"Did you find her?" she asked. "Did you find Vanessa?"

"You passed out as I was giving you the sedative. You've only been out about thirty minutes," the paramedic reassured her. "You want to try and relax. Let the police do their job."

She sat up more slowly this time, determined to keep herself from getting too excited. She had to be strong for Vanessa's sake. Then she recognized a man across the room. *Drake!* Even the sedative couldn't hold down the rage brought on by the sight of that man.

Kathleen raised herself off the couch, slowly propping herself up with one hand on the armrest, gently pushing away the helping hands of the paramedic. Her head throbbed and she put the other hand over her forehead, the way a drunk might after an all-night bender. She slowly shuffled over to Drake, who was standing by the door talking to another officer.

"Drake, what are you doing here?" She didn't wait for his answer. "I don't want you here or anywhere near my daughter."

"I know that," Drake said, turning away from the other officer. "You were right. I made a mistake and now you and your daughter are paying for it. Let me make this right. I know Fagan, Kathleen. He wants to be found. If he didn't, he wouldn't have given us such a short time frame."

Kathleen nodded her head, acquiesced. The fire Drake sparked inside her had blazed intensely, but now had all but burnt out. She just wanted her daughter back.

"If I know Fagan, I'm going to find him tonight. I need you to clear your apartment. Stay here alone and wait for my phone call."

"What are you planning, Drake?" she asked.

"You don't want to know," he said. "You're not going to like it."

Before she could protest, Drake started barking orders to the cops in her apartment, leaving her more confused and panicked than before.

As the cops exited, the paramedic placed three tranquilizer capsules in her hand.

"I'm not supposed to do this," he said, his voice hushed. "Just take one when needed. If you take them all it will knock you for a loop."

Only minutes after the paramedic and the rest of the officers departed, the helplessness set in, and she had to go back to the couch and sit down. She didn't know if she could rely on Drake, but she had no other option. There was nothing left to do but worry. There was nothing left to do but wait.

AN HOUR LATER THE DOOR INTERCOM BUZZED.
"Yes?" Kathleen asked, depressing the answer button.
"Kathleen?" She recognized the voice. "It's me, Rodney."
She closed her eyes and let out a deep sigh. Rodney was the last person she wanted to see. But Vanessa was his daughter too, and she couldn't deny him. She buzzed him in.
Five minutes later she let Rodney into her apartment and found herself embracing him despite herself. They cried together, maybe as much for their broken relationship as for their lost daughter. In moments like this it was easy to forget past pain and hard not to wish that things could go back to the way they had been.
He looked nice in his khaki pants and blue dress shirt, and the subtle hint of cologne he wore stayed with her even after the embrace.
"Do you need a drink?"
"I could use one."
The phone rang, making her jump, a surge of adrenaline eating away at the barrier the sedative had erected. She answered.
"I need you to meet me," Drake said.
"Rodney's here."
"Who?"
"My ex-husband."
"Find a way to get rid of him. If you ever want to see your daughter again, you better come alone."
He rattled off an address. Kathleen committed it to memory.
The line went dead.
"Okay, thank you, Detective," Kathleen said.
"Who was that?"
"Detective Drake. He just wanted to check in on me. No word yet," Kathleen said, hoping Rodney couldn't tell she was lying.
She had to think quickly. There was no way Rodney would let her go

alone. Truthfully, she didn't want to go by herself. Something felt very wrong about that, like Drake was up to something sinister. His request that she come alone sounded a lot like a threat. She wasn't sure she could trust a man who could so easily cause pain to another human being. But she had to get her daughter back.

"Let me get us those drinks," Kathleen said.

She entered the kitchen, took out two scotch glasses from a cabinet and some ice from the freezer. Here she was, doing what only played out in soap operas and spy novels.

She broke open each of the three tranquilizer capsules and poured the powder into Rodney's glass. This was absolute madness. A couple cubes of ice, a splash of single-malt whiskey, and a swirl with a stirrer and she had, what they might call in Chinese restaurants, a Suffering Bastard.

She watched, her lips dry, as he took a sip. He pursed his lips and swallowed. She held her breath.

"Wow. It's been awhile. I'm not used to the taste of straight Scotch."

She let out a breath and gave him a smile that she felt might be too bright, too straining.

"Bottoms up," she said.

Kathleen didn't have to wait long. As they continued their conversation she could see beads of sweat erupt on his forehead, his eyes glazed and then cleared, only to glaze again.

"I'm suddenly feeling very strange," Rodney said. Then he looked at her and she could see recognition in his eyes.

"Did you put something in my drink?" He lurched at her, trying to grab her wrist. She jumped back, off the couch, and walked slowly backwards. "You little bitch. Why would you do this?"

"It's just a tranquilizer, Rodney," she said. "I need to meet the detective alone. Everything's going to be okay."

But she wasn't sure that things were really going to be okay or if they'd be okay ever again. Rodney fell back on the couch, holding his head. Kathleen turned and ran for the door, leaving the safety of her apartment behind.

By force of will, Kathleen kept her speed to the posted limit. She didn't need to get pulled over by the police. Rodney had delayed her long enough and time was ticking away. If she were ever going to see her daughter alive she would have to get to her soon.

Following her GPS, she navigated her Volvo onto a dark street in a run-down part of town. The directions led her to what looked like an old abandoned factory building.

She pulled into the parking area, empty except for Drake's Dodge Charger. She checked her mirrors to make sure no one was skulking around and then took a deep breath and let it out, trying to steady her nerves.

Drake met her at the front entrance.

"Follow me," he said.

She did as he instructed, walking behind him as he led her down a dimly lit hall. The place wasn't so abandoned after all.

"I have a friend who lets me use this place from time to time, no questions asked," Drake explained, as if he could read her mind.

The building was in disarray, the furniture and equipment covered in a layer of dust. Kathleen didn't want to know what Drake's friend used this place for.

He brought her to a staircase and they descended into the basement.

"Where's my daughter?" Kathleen asked.

"We don't have her yet. But soon."

They came to a door. Drake glanced back as if to appraise her readiness. Then he opened the door and they walked inside.

Kathleen gasped when she saw Edward Fagan strapped to what looked like an old-fashioned dentist's chair that had been bolted to the floor in the middle of the room. He didn't look scared. He looked smug.

A rage came upon her, guttural, instinctual, the rage of any mother trying to protect her young. She felt an urge to kill him, a tug of war between her civilized nature and ancient bloodlust.

Drake brought a tray to a rolling table a few feet away from the trapped monster. Sharp tools waited: metal dental picks, pliers, a bone saw, and a scalpel.

"He won't give up the information easily," Drake said.

Kathleen regained her senses.

"Are you going to torture him?" Kathleen asked, aghast.

"No. I'm not," he said as he put the tray down with a metallic clank.

Kathleen breathed a sigh of relief, felt her pulse slowing back to normal.

"You are," Drake said.

"What?"

"He won't give me any more information. He's already turned me into a monster. Now he wants to do the same to you."

"Your principles for your daughter's life," Fagan said, and then laughed.

"Just make sure you don't make the same mistake I made," Drake said quietly to Kathleen.

With that Drake walked past her and to the door. Kathleen looked back at him, unable to process what had just happened.

"The clock is ticking. If you don't get this done soon we may never get your daughter back alive," Drake said, and then left the room, left her alone with her own racing thoughts and a madman tied to a chair.

"Where is my daughter?"

Fagan just smiled at her.

"Tell me!" Her voice sounded guttural in her ears, barely human.

"I don't think you have it in you to get the information from me," Fagan said, eyes bright with anticipation. "I wonder if you'll even try."

There was nothing left to say. She didn't have time to wait. She swallowed her anger and let her mind go numb.

Kathleen walked to the tray and picked up the scalpel.

Private Beach

Stacey Longo

Tom and Shanna walked right past the NO TRESPASSING sign. She was carrying the blanket; he had a bag of fried chicken from a fast food joint and a bottle of champagne. It was a solemn night for Tom; he was going to tell Shanna how he felt, that while he wasn't ready to marry her *yet*, he certainly felt that he would marry her *someday*, and he had a tiny diamond ring with sapphire chips in the band to prove the seriousness of his intent. He was the one that suggested an evening picnic on the beach.

Tom and Shanna had been a couple since his senior year of college, when they'd met in biology class and found themselves lab partners. He was struggling to pass the course. Shanna, two years younger, excelled in science, and had tutored him through the class. They'd been partners ever since, and over the past two years, he'd only cheated on her once; something she'd never found out and he'd never shared, but he was proud of himself just the same. Only cheating on a girl once was a personal best for him, and was all the proof he needed that Shanna was the girl he was meant to marry. Someday.

They had about forty-five minutes of daylight before the sun set over the water, and he intended to make the most of the romantic setting. They trudged over the dune, passing the sparse tufts of razor-like grass, agreeing without speaking to head toward a flattened semicircle of sand next to a large, blackened log of driftwood. The wind tugged at the blanket as Shanna tried to smooth it down; she found a rock and a plank of wood, left over from a bonfire, to secure the corners.

"Take a walk?" she asked, smiling at Tom with her emerald green eyes, and he felt his jeans tug uncomfortably for a moment. He nodded, and they latched hands, strolling down the beach.

It was low tide; there was a line of seaweed and debris that the ocean had rejected tracing a path down the sand. The wind was warm, but agitated—Tom had to blink repeatedly to keep grains of sand out of his eyes. "Watch your step!" Shanna yelped, sidestepping an opaque glob with tendrils. "Here's another one!" she squealed, moving in closer to Tom, as if she needed him to protect her from the dead jellyfish. They meandered on, walking closely, Shanna occasionally stopping to examine a shell or pretty stone.

"What's with all the dead jellyfish?" Tom complained, stepping squarely on a gelatinous mass. He was grateful to be wearing his sneakers. He was pretty sure that jellyfish could still sting, even when dead, and he didn't want to experience that ever again. He'd been stung by a jellyfish when he was fourteen, vacationing in Pensacola with his folks, and the pain he'd felt then, ten years ago, was still easy for him to recall to this very day. He'd wound up in the hospital, feverish and unable to breathe, and although the doctors had told him there was a chance he'd grow out of his allergy to sea jelly venom, he'd never tested that theory. His chest tightened at the sight of the lifeless orbs that littered the beach like raindrops. "Maybe we should head back to the blanket," he said with a nervous laugh.

Shanna bobbed her blonde head in agreement, and they turned around. "Maybe it's mating season or something," Tom commented, and Shanna shrugged.

"Could be. Or it's a lemming-like mass jelly suicide?," she offered, weaving her way around the jellyfish bodies. "Although it doesn't seem as bad back this way."

This was true. Tom noticed there were fewer bodies back toward the section of beach where they'd tacked down their blanket. Had it been this way when they'd started their walk? Tom wasn't sure, but he was glad. The jellyfish bodies were starting to make him lose his appetite, and he didn't want an air of squeamishness to affect the heartfelt vow of affection he had planned for later on.

Tom and Shanna made it back to their picnic spot quickly. Their dinner and champagne were still sitting on the blue-checkered cotton blanket, waiting for their return. "Look at the sand! It looks like a Zen garden," Shanna said softly. The sand was rippled like circles on a pond; Tom hadn't noticed when they'd first spread out the blanket, but admittedly, he'd been admiring the way Shanna's black jeans hugged her backside.

"Yeah, neat," Tom grunted, sitting down and opening up the bag of chicken. "Let's eat—I'm starving!"

Shanna swatted at his arm, but settled in next to him on the blanket.

They ate quietly, hungrily; Tom occasionally paused to offer a smile at his girl. She was beautiful, even when confronted with the messy task of eating chicken on the beach; she dabbed at her mouth delicately with a napkin between bites, which made Tom's heart skip a beat. If it weren't for his college loans, and his new job, and the upcoming real estate license exam that he had to study for, he'd marry her right now. But Shanna still had a semester left of college, and had no idea what she wanted to do for a career; best to wait until they were both more settled and secure. Shanna stopped for a moment, looking at him curiously.

"You sure are deep in thought. What's on your mind?" Tom winked at her, wiping his hands on his jeans. Now was as good a time as any to bring out the ring and make his promise to her.

"Shanna, I ..." he stumbled over the words. Breathing deeply, he tried again. "I wanted to talk to you tonight. I was hoping—hoping—listen, maybe you should ditch the chicken bones." Shanna had the bones from her dinner carefully cradled in a napkin in her hands.

"What should I do with them? I don't want to litter," she grinned, and blushed slightly.

"Toss them over the dune like I did," he frowned, but she shook her head.

"I can't throw that far, you know that. I'll just bury them in the sand, I guess." Shanna shifted over to the side of the blanket and started digging. When she had a hole big enough and deep enough to dispose of her bones, she slid her hand in with the chicken remains. "Oh!" she gasped, and tried to pull back. Her hand remained in the sand. "Tom, help! I can't get my hand out! Something's got me!"

Tom leaned forward. Dusk was starting to fall, but he could see that her left arm was buried in the beach up to her elbow.

"Are you trying to be cute or something?" He snickered nervously, unsure of what kind of game she was playing. Was she making fun of him?

"Tom!" Shanna screamed, and her whole body seemed to lurch forward into the sand. He scrambled to get up and help her, but it was too late: he watched, horrified, as her head, then her torso, and lastly her legs disappeared in one fell swoop into the beach. The sand shifted, resettling; the meditative ripples reappeared on the surface.

"What the hell was that? Shanna?" Tom's mind was racing over what he'd just seen. His girlfriend had just nosedived under the sand, and not so much as a handprint remained. Quicksand? He'd never heard of quicksand yanking someone in and smoothing itself out like he'd just witnessed this sand do.

There had to be something under the beach, he decided. Some sort of —worm, or giant vole—had just sucked his girlfriend down into its lair.

Tom laughed; it was a high-pitched, manic screech that did not sound like him at all. He kneeled down next to the spot where Shanna had disappeared and started scooping, looking for any sign of her—her shoe, her leg, some sort of proof that she'd really just been there. He pawed at the sand frantically, and then he felt it.

A tug. And it wasn't from a giant worm or sand-tunneling vole. It was the sand itself, sliding around his wrist, pulling gently at first, then more firmly, furiously; Tom ripped his hand away quickly, and not without a little force. The surface of the beach leveled out, settling back in to rippled circles.

Tom looked around frantically. The whole beach, he had to consider, could be like this. The path through the dunes back to the car was about a yard away. His heart sank as he realized that the parking lot where his Jeep now sat was nothing more than packed sand; he wouldn't be any safer in his SUV than he was on this thin blanket. He looked down the beach. In the fading sunlight, he looked for the jellyfish carcasses that had mottled their path when he and Shanna had strolled down the shore earlier. He couldn't see any now. He assumed that the beach had swallowed them up as well.

Tom felt a hot tear escape from the corner of his eye; he was going to die here, suffocated by the sand, he was sure of it. If he even made it to the car without being pulled in to the beach, he would have to act pretty quickly to drive the Jeep out of the lot before the whole vehicle was gulped down into the earth. His car was known to be temperamental on the best of days; one false start and he and the car would be history. He stared at the waves that mocked him from the ocean, lapping at the shore. His romantic night was history. He should have proposed, he thought, chastising himself. Why was he thinking they should wait? Life was short. He should have grabbed on to the chance to marry Shanna while he could, instead of his convoluted plan to "promise" her to marry her "someday"—it sounded lame even to him now, he realized, scowling. He watched the seaweed floating on the waves, winking in and out of sight, mocking him. He was an idiot. And now Shanna was gone, before he could even tell her how stupid he was, how much he loved her …

There was something about the seaweed that distracted Tom from his self-flagellation. It floated in toward him, and then pulled away with the tide again.

It floated. Just like Tom would, if he could make it to the sea. He could make a dive for the ocean, and pull his feet up off of the sand, and float to freedom. He'd seen breakwater rocks a little way down, and even now, lights were shining in the seaside mansions that abutted the beach. If he could make it to the water, and swim to the rocks, he could walk his way to safety without stepping once on the dunes that waited to consume him.

Tom breathed deeply, trying to steady his nerves. It was just a short sprint to the ocean. He thought he could make it. Had to believe there was a chance. He pulled off his sneakers and tossed them off the blanket. He counted one, two, three—his sneakers were sucked down with a quick 'bloop!" into the sand. Three full seconds. Tom was pretty sure he could make it to the sea in three seconds. Maybe four.

He couldn't stay on the blanket for one more moment, he realized in terror. There was nothing to stop the beach from pulling him down where he stood; as if in response to his train of thought, he felt the ground shift beneath him. *Here goes nothing*, he gulped, and tore away from the blanket toward the darkening ocean. He felt the sand tug at his feet as he ran, lungs burning. His steps became more difficult as he got closer; the sand was pulling hard now, making it seem like Tom was running through mud; he yanked his feet free, diving into the waves headfirst. The water was cool, but not unpleasant; his body warmed up quickly as he swam out further, trying to increase the depth between himself and the seabed below. He started to cry in earnest now, in relief; he had beaten the beach, the crazy, carnivorous stretch of sand that even now he thought he could hear roaring in frustration over his escape.

He looked around while treading water, and spotted the black silhouette of the breakwater rocks to his right. The moon shone brightly now, picking up the phosphorescence on the waves. Tom blinked. The phosphorescence was below the surface, as well, lighting up orb upon orb of drifting jellyfish, lazily swimming through the undertow. He realized his arms were ablaze, and wondered how many tentacles he'd brushed in his frenzied swim to escape the sand; even now, he felt the sting of jellyfish tendrils on his calves as his legs flailed below the surface. He couldn't stay here among this school of jellies. He kicked out toward the rocks in a frenzied crawl stroke, even as his chest started to seize.

All Aboard

Christopher Golden

That dreadful autumn, Sarah Cooper woke nearly every night in the small hours of the morning and lay in the dark, back toward her husband, the memory of their dead son filling the space between them.

During the day the tension did not weigh so heavily. Sarah and Paul wandered the house only dimly aware of one another, ghosts haunting their own marriage. Resentment and blame hung in the air like static building before a thunderstorm. Sarah knew that she ought to try to comfort her husband, but Paul did not seek her out, nor did she look for solace in his arms. Cruel and capricious happenstance had taken Jonah from them—a bacterial infection, a spiked fever, an ambulance too slow to arrive—but they had to hold someone responsible, and each found fault with the other, and guilt in the mirror.

They couldn't stay in this house much longer. Sarah would never survive it. Fifty-seven Brook Street existed now as a museum of sorrow. Jonah had bounced on the sofa, bumped his head on the coffee table, marched his walker across the kitchen tiles as a baby, and slept in his parents' bed almost as many nights as his own. The toys had all been packed away, but his room remained with its books and stuffed polar bear and the dinosaur border that ran along the top of the bedroom walls. Sarah kept that door closed, but could not bring herself to take down the pictures in the living room and the downstairs hall and from the bureau in her bedroom. Her hairbrush had brushed Jonah's hair. His Spider-Man cup hid at the back of a kitchen cabinet, waiting to be remembered; waiting to remind her.

How did Paul stand it? Sarah didn't know. They avoided the conversation most of the time. That seemed even worse because it felt like they were trying to pretend Jonah had never been there—that they did not grieve.

But Paul made an effort to talk around the absence of their son, just as he usually avoided meeting her eyes.

By October, they spoke only when absolutely necessary.

When Sarah found the fuzzy Scooby-Doo costume she had bought Jonah over the summer, unable to resist even though Halloween had been months away, she crushed it against her chest and wept into the costume, brown fabric soaking up her tears. Then she put it in a box of Jonah's things that she planned to donate to the Salvation Army. She never mentioned it to Paul, and as Halloween approached, he never asked.

In the second week of October, she woke in the night with only the glow of a distant streetlamp filtering through the window. It must have been two or three o'clock in the morning. After so many weeks of such awakenings, she knew sleep would not be in any hurry to return so she lay and listened to Paul's rhythmic breathing.

The gulf between them had grown over the weeks since Jonah's death, expanding a little at bedtime every night. They hadn't had sex in all that time, though there had been times in the small hours of the morning when she had needed so badly to be held, to be touched, to be loved. But night after night they lay back to back, shoulder and neck muscles bunched with tension and expectation, and they edged further away, widening the gap between them.

A glow of moonlight draped across the shadows of their bedroom and the gauzy curtains billowed with the crisp autumn breeze. Sarah lay on her side and stared at the windows, at the curtains, and at nothing. The windows rattled with powerful gusts—the weather changing, winter drawing nearer—and she heard the skittering of dry leaves across the driveway and the front walk.

Then, off in the distance, the lonely whistle of a train.

Sarah had heard the sound every night for nearly two weeks. At first it had been barely audible, so that she had trouble determining its origin. Each night it seemed to become louder, though of course the train tracks couldn't be any nearer. In all the years she had lived in Dunston, she could not recall ever having heard the sound before, never mind seen a train. It must, she told herself, only run late at night when the town slept, when only insomniacs and grieving mothers might hear it.

She listened as the whistle faded and felt a terrible longing, wished she were on board that train, bound for destinations unknown.

When her tears came, she let them slide down to dampen her pillow.

Her husband did not stir, but Sarah was not surprised. Paul had long since stopped being stirred by her tears, even in the light of day.

She slid nearer the edge of the bed and watched the moonlight and the billowing curtains and listened to the shush of the autumn leaves blowing across the lawn. In time, sleep would claim her again, tears drying on her face.

Sarah would hear the whistle of the train in her dreams, where she held her tiny son in her arms and rocked him, singing him softly to sleep on the way to his own extinguished dreams.

THE NEW OFFICES OF STERLING SOFTWARE HAD BEEN BUILT JUST AT the edge of town, near a narrow metal bridge across the Kenyon River. Window glass winked in the morning light as Sarah drove over the bridge, her travel mug rattling in the cup holder on the dash, spurting up a dollop of coffee.

The Kenyon River meandered southward under the bridge. In the spring it roared, but in autumn it remained a gentle whisper. She followed the road northeast on the other side, coming around a corner, all the while keeping the Sterling building in sight. It stood at the top of a hill that had been transformed into a mini-industrial park, complete with a Comfort Inn and a T.G.I. Friday's restaurant. Sarah barely saw any of those buildings. In truth, she barely saw the road or the rich, harvest-hued foliage of the trees around her. Her focus was on driving to work, and she could do that with her mind on autopilot.

The dashboard clock read 9:12. Late again, and she felt badly about it. A tremor of discontent passed through her. Exhausted, she'd rushed to get ready, and the mirror had reflected both her tiredness—in the dark crescents beneath her eyes—and her haphazard attempt at fixing her hair and putting on makeup. *Get your life together, Sarah. You're dropping the ball.* But the advice sounded hollow. She couldn't convince herself that any of it mattered. Work. Sleep. Face. Life.

The car jittered over train tracks, causing her coffee to burble again.

Sarah frowned and tapped the brake, slowing down and glancing in her rearview mirror. She'd been over those tracks twice a day every day for more than a year, ever since Sterling had moved to the new location. There were no railroad crossing signs, no flashing lights, nothing.

Another few minutes won't matter.

She put the car in reverse and backed up, checking to make sure no other cars were approaching. At the tracks she braked again, pausing to peer both ways along the line. Grass grew up between the wooden ties. The rails themselves were dark with rust. In either direction the tracks curved away into trees and undergrowth that had begun to encroach over the years.

Sarah shook her head. No trains on this line. Not for years.

As she drove on, she could not help but glance at the mirror. The memory of the whistle from the late-night train lingered, and led her to thoughts of Jonah and her dreams.

No. Work.

If she thought about Jonah, she would be useless at work. They had been more than kind, had offered her as much time as she needed to mourn. When Sarah had announced, after six weeks, that she was ready to return to her receptionist position, the office manager—Ellie Poole—had asked if she was *really ready*. Sarah had thought it a foolish question. How could she ever be ready to go to work, to put her loss behind her?

But at home all that awaited her was the museum of sorrow, the constant reminders. Her coworkers' sympathy made work little better, but at least she could find distraction there.

Sarah found a parking spot near the front of the building and climbed out. Dropping her keys, she swore as she bent to retrieve them, then slammed the door. With her purse over her shoulder and her coffee in hand, she hurried up the walk to the front doors. Inside the glass and chrome lobby, Martin stood at his security post, one earbud of his iPod in place and the other hanging loose. When he looked up and saw her, his face blossomed into a warm smile. The young guard seemed to be the only one at Sterling who could be genuinely happy to see her without his warmth devolving into pity.

"Morning, Sarah."

"Hi, Martin."

Behind the reception desk, a secretary named Laura Rossi gave her a grim look. Ellie had obviously shanghaied her to substitute until Sarah showed up, and the wide-bottomed, curly-haired woman did not bother trying to hide her displeasure. Sarah was almost glad that Laura didn't tiptoe around her.

"Let me guess—car trouble?"

"I'm sorry, Laura. The last time, I swear."

The woman got up from the reception desk and sighed, rolling her eyes, but she waved the apology away as though Sarah's tardiness was no big deal.

"It's fine. Martin's good company."

Martin grinned broadly. "I was serenading her."

Sarah managed a thin smile. Martin liked to sing, but softly, mostly to himself. She never minded, but she suspected that someone as generally uptight as Laura would be driven to near madness by the man's musical mutterings.

The phone began to ring. Laura shot it a dark look, then turned her back and went through the door into the main offices. Sarah hurried over and picked up.

"Sterling Software. Can you hold, please?" She put on her headset, then took the caller off hold and transferred him to the northeastern sales manager.

"Some people can't seem to figure out how to use an electronic directory," Martin said.

Sarah nodded, but broke into a yawn.

"Don't do that," Martin protested, yawning in reply. "It's contagious. No fair."

"Sorry, just didn't get nearly enough sleep last night."

"Pretty much every night, isn't it?"

His face and voice were kind. The question wasn't an intrusion. Martin never intruded on her grief. If she didn't want to answer, he would not mind. But Sarah found him warm and easy to talk to.

"I fall asleep all right," she said, pushing her hair away from her face to meet his gaze. "But I wake up in the middle of the night and then it takes me an hour or so to drift off again. It's weird what you hear at night, though, y'know?"

Martin removed the earbud and held the cord in his hand. "I do. The quietest noise seems much louder in the middle of the night."

"Yes!" Sarah said. "During the day I can't even hear the clock ticking, but at night it's so loud. And now I hear the train every night. I almost listen for it."

The security guard gave a soft laugh and a shake of his head. "Now you're just fooling with me. That's not nice, Sarah."

She stared at him. "What do you mean?"

"Come on. The Three-Eighteen? I'm not falling for that old story. Didn't believe it when my grandmother told it, either."

A tractor trailer growled as it pulled into the parking lot and continued around past the building, headed for the loading dock in back. It distracted them both for a moment. When Sarah looked back at Martin, he was studying her curiously. She sat forward in her chair.

"What's the Three-Eighteen?"

His eyes became narrow slits in his dark face a moment and then widened with sudden realization. "You didn't grow up around here, did you? I forget sometimes."

Sarah shook her head. "Nope. My family comes from upstate New York. I moved here with my father when I was thirteen."

"Right, right. You've told me. Sorry. He worked at the mill, right?"

"Worked and died there," she said. "So what's this train thing?"

"Just a local ghost story. Most towns have a house all the kids think is haunted and I'm guessing we do, too. But the story that always gave me the creeps was about the Three-Eighteen. My grandmother used to talk about it and the counselors at camp used to tell it around the fire, along with the ones about Hatchet Mary and the Hook and that kind of thing."

Sarah frowned. "So, it's a ghost train?"

"That's the story. Passes by every night at 3:18 a.m. 'Carrying the ghosts of the ones folks can't let go of,' my Gram used to say. And it's only those folks, and people near dying themselves, who can …"

The words trailed off.

Breathless, Sarah stared at him. "Who can what?"

Martin gave her a sheepish grin. "Who can hear it. That's how all those old stories go, y'know? Supposed to creep us all out. That way if you hear a train whistle after dark or something that even sounds like one, you're supposed to think it's the Three-Eighteen come to collect you."

She dropped her gaze and stared at the marble tile beneath her chair.

"Sarah?"

His voice made her flinch. She looked up. "I hear the whistle every night."

Martin laughed and came over to her desk. He splayed one strong hand on the counter where people laid out their ID to be allowed inside.

"Sarah, come on. It's just a story. Whatever you're hearing, it's something else. Got to be some late-night road work, smoke venting from the damn sneaker factory or something. But it's not a train, and it sure as hell ain't the Three-Eighteen."

She took a long breath and let it out with a small, self-deprecating laugh. Of course Martin was right. Sarah felt nauseous just thinking about the few moments she'd spent seriously considering the campfire tale as truth. Every town had local folklore.

"You okay?" Martin prodded. His wide eyes were full of concern. "I shouldn't even have mentioned it, but you brought up the train whistle and I just figured you were teasing me. This isn't the kind of thing you ought to be thinking about."

"I'm okay," she promised. How to explain the numbness inside and the gulf between herself and her husband? How to explain that the word 'okay' had entirely lost its meaning for her? Paul had always liked grim novels about the destruction of human society or the ecosystem or worse; he called it post-apocalyptic fiction. But Sarah was living a post-apocalyptic life. People who hadn't been through it couldn't possibly understand.

"You sure? It's only that you never seem like you're all here, if you don't mind my saying. Ellie Poole's been bitching about you coming in late and, well, looking kind of run-down."

Sarah couldn't believe it. Ellie, who'd been so nice, was sniping behind her back after what she'd been through?

"Bitch," she whispered, glancing around at the doors that led into the main offices, just in case the bitch in question might walk in and overhear her. "Am I in trouble, Martin?"

"Not that I've heard. I'd have told you. But that could change."

Sarah nodded. Of course it could change. The second Ellie figured that Sarah had had enough time to mourn Jonah's death that she couldn't file a wrongful termination law suit, the witch would come gunning for her.

With a sigh, Sarah sipped from her cooling coffee. "Guess this is the last late morning for me."

A Mercedes slid through the parking lot and into a space. Martin put the single earbud back in place. He and Sarah both watched as a man stepped out of the Mercedes and started for the front door.

"Y'know, if sleep's the issue, you oughta get your doc to prescribe something," Martin said. "I took that one with the butterfly once. You know, the one in the TV ad. Worked like a charm."

Sarah straightened her top and smoothed her skirt, trying to look as professional as she could in spite of her state of mind. As the dark-suited man from the Mercedes opened the door, she glanced at Martin.

"I tried pills. They just make me more tired in the morning," she said.

Then she smiled at the visitor. "Good morning, sir. How can I help you?"

The man spoke and she barely listened, her thoughts still on Martin's suggestion. Sleeping pills would have been such a blessing, a respite from restless nights. But the few times she had taken them, they had interfered with her dreaming. And her dreams were the only time she could be with Jonah.

Nothing mattered more than that, including her job. Ellie Poole could go to Hell.

"Have you ever heard of the Three-Eighteen?"

Paul looked up from his plate—he'd made them a risotto that had once been a favorite for both of them, but now tasted bland to Sarah. Everything tasted bland to her now.

"You mean that old story about the ghost train?"

"Yes."

He shrugged. Even his indifference had sharp edges, cutting her with disdain. "Sure. When I was a kid we'd all talk about it. Go out to the tracks. One time I camped out down there all night with Jimmy Pryce—remember Jimmy?"

Sarah shook her head. She didn't. Paul was two years older than she was. She'd only been in high school with him for his senior year and then he'd graduated. But he'd lost touch with most of his old friends over the years. Whoever this Jimmy Pryce was, he hadn't sent them a card or flowers when Jonah died. The parade of faces at the funeral were a blur to her—she couldn't remember who had been there or not—but the cards and flowers she recalled perfectly.

"No? Jimmy thought you were pretty hot when you transferred in from New York." He smiled, and perhaps for a moment there was a glimmer of hope and life in his eyes, of happier times. It dimmed, as it always would, forever after.

"Anyway, we camped out down by the tracks one night. Spent the whole time scaring the crap out of each other with flashlights and telling ghost stories. When you're a kid you believe that stuff, deep down, even though you've gotta act like you're too mature to believe it, and too tough to be scared by it."

Sarah pretended to smile; a kind of peace offering. Then she went back to the flavorless risotto with Paul studying her closely. Their conversations had been infrequent in the past few weeks, and often tense. They talked around and above things and never addressed what lurked below.

Jonah would never hear the story of the Three-Eighteen. He would never camp out by the train tracks and tell ghost stories, never go trick-or-treating or have a friend like Jimmy Pryce, whose antics he would look back on fondly when fatherhood and dreaded maturity came along and the hard climb toward forty had begun.

Forty. At thirty-two, Sarah felt ancient. Sometimes she thought about what it would be like to be truly old and abandoned, stashed in some nursing home, all her passions diminished or taken away, waiting for it all to end. Waiting to die. This didn't feel much different.

"Why do you ask?"

The tone of the question, the awkwardness in his voice, put a chill between them. It should've had the opposite effect. Here he was, trying to have a civil conversation about something more than the weather or perfunctory work-related trivia, but it felt so forced that Sarah only tensed up further.

"No reason. I heard someone talking about it today and was surprised I'd never heard it before."

"You were thirteen by the time you moved here. Probably too old for ghost stories."

Again she forced a smile.

Paul took another bite of risotto and they descended into the sort of funereal silence to which they had become hideously accustomed.

Jonah had had his father's eyes.

Sarah managed a few more bites and then endured several minutes more at the table before allowing herself to rise and bring her dish to the sink. "I'll clean up later. I've been wanting a bath all day."

She'd been taking a great many baths of late. Paul had remarked on it only once, two weeks earlier, and she had told him tersely that she needed the alone time. He'd had no response for that. Once she might have confided in him, told him what she really did during those long evening baths with the radio playing up on the shelf—that sometimes she touched herself and tried to remember what it was like to be alive and in love and full of lust, and sometimes she used the edge of a razor blade or her tiny scissors to scratch and lightly cut her flesh, trying to discover if she had the courage to cut deeper and let herself bleed.

Either way, whether searching for passion or pain, she cried. With the water hot and steam rising, sometimes she even pretended to herself that there were no tears.

HER EYES SNAPPED OPEN AND SHE INHALED SHARPLY. SOMETHING had woken her tonight. It took a moment for her mind to make sense of the thumping bass coming from a car passing by at the end of the street. God, that was loud. Some kind of post-modern blues-funk like Amy Winehouse, and it wasn't drifting off the way it should have been. The car had stopped for some reason.

Rubbing her eyes, Sarah slipped from beneath the covers and went to the window. She pulled the curtain aside and tried to peer out into the dark toward the end of the street. Not much breeze, but the night pulsed with the beat of that song. There came a laugh, the slam of a door, and then the car roared away. Some kind of mischief going on down there—the kind of thing she and Paul might have gotten up to, once upon a time.

Paul had left the window open wide and Sarah backed away and hugged herself tightly, shuddering. Even without a breeze, the night was cold. The weather had shifted again, but New England was always like that.

With a frown, she realized she had been unconsciously rubbing the bandage on her forearm. She had gotten a bit carried away with the scissors in the bathtub tonight. *That's one way to look at it,* she thought, sleep still clouding her mind. Her arm ached where she'd cut it, and she hoped it had not become infected. If Paul noticed, that would be difficult to explain. Of course that was an enormous 'if.' He barely saw her any more. She might as well be made of glass—a window where a woman used to be.

The clock ticked loudly on the nightstand. Once they had kept a baby monitor there and the sound of Jonah turning restlessly had kept her alert. But now there was only the clock and the soft breathing of the automaton who had taken the place of her husband.

Sarah watched Paul sleeping. He had mastered the emotionless mask that he wore during the day, but could not control his unconscious mind. His features were tight with sorrow and consternation. His dreams brought him the nightmares he spent the days attempting to evade.

Beyond him, the clock on the nightstand read 2:13 a.m. Sarah blinked and stared at it and the display clicked over to 2:14. She turned toward the window. The gauzy curtain seemed like a veil now, but though she could not see as far as the Kenyon River from here, she did not want to look out across the town toward the river.

She climbed back into bed, sliding deep beneath the covers. On her side, she pressed her eyes closed and slid one hand under her pillow, an exaggerated pantomime, as though she could fool her body into thinking it was capable of falling right back to sleep. But experience had taught her better.

For fifteen or twenty minutes she lay there, stubbornly persistent.

When she surrendered to the inevitability of her insomnia, she opened her eyes at last and glanced around at the moonlit glow of her bedroom. Paul breathed softly beside her.

Sarah wanted to scream. If only her sleeplessness could have been made incarnate, turned into something she could kick and punch and claw. But it could not be fought. Especially tonight. Just as she had been pretending to herself that it would be possible to simply fall back to sleep, she had also avoided acknowledging the conversation she and Martin had in the foyer of Sterling Software that morning.

Again she glanced at the clock. 2:37, and Paul still sleeping, so peacefully.

Sarah slid from bed and grabbed her blue jeans, pulled them on. She'd been sleeping in a light blue T-shirt she sometimes wore to the gym and didn't bother with a bra, just pulling a fuzzy red sweater on over it. With another glance at Paul, she took a pair of socks from the drawer in her nightstand and went quietly downstairs.

She paused only once, while tying her sneakers, to wonder what exactly she hoped to accomplish. Her chest tightened with anticipation, a kind of giddy excitement that might have been hysteria. Then she went out the front door and pulled it quietly closed behind her. Her own car was parked inside the garage and the automatic door opener made a lot of noise, so she took Paul's Cherokee.

As she pulled out of the driveway, her hands were trembling. She didn't click the headlights on until she reached the end of the street and turned on to the main road. The dashboard lights cast an industrial gloom inside the car and the radio played low as she drove away from home, following the same course she took on her way to work.

The clock on the dash read 2:49.

Sarah hit the gas and the car lurched forward, speeding up. She couldn't be late.

She traveled as though she herself were a dream, gliding through the sleeping town in the small hours when night seemed darkest. Nothing else moved but the wind. In that surreal landscape, anything seemed possible.

At 3:11, her headlights picked out the old bridge over the Kenyon River. Sarah slowed as the car shuddered across the bridge, black water rushing past below. When she hit the pavement on the far side, she turned left and gunned it, tires squealing. All through the drive she'd managed a kind of Zen calm, complete with steady breathing and quick but even pulse. The sound of the tires broke her focus. Her face flushed with heat and she felt her heart pounding in her chest as she sped along the road that curved beside the river.

Without a railroad crossing sign or any other warning, she came up on the abandoned tracks too fast to stop. She rocketed over the tracks before hitting the brakes and skidding to a halt on the shoulder of the road.

3:14.

Sarah killed the engine and just sat there for a few seconds, hands on the steering wheel, listening to the car cool and tick and settle. If she gripped the wheel hard enough, her hands wouldn't shake. She felt her throat closing and her eyes brimming and she bit down on her lip.

Go home. Stupid girl. There's nothing for you out here.

Of course there wasn't. Why had she really come here? What did she expect, racing across town in the middle of the night, chasing ghosts? *You're losing it, kid*, she thought, grinning in the dark enclosure of the car. *Just losing it.*

But that was bullshit, too. She'd lost it the day Jonah died, and never gotten it back. Trying to pretend otherwise had been her sole occupation ever since.

With a shaky laugh she took the keys from the ignition and popped the door. The night wind gusted, whipping her hair across her face, crisp with the rich scent of autumn. From somewhere there came the smell of a wood-burning stove, carried on the breeze, and it made her realize that she was not the only one awake tonight. Not alone in the dark.

She slipped the keys into her pocket and shut the car door, then started walking toward the tracks. How many minutes left? Just a couple. Sarah stepped onto the tracks and looked in both directions. The moonlight only dispersed so many shadows, but enough to see that nothing about the tracks had changed. They were overgrown and unused, nearly buried in some places.

Closing her eyes, she raised her arms, imagining the 3:18 coming. Would it pass right through her, or run her down? Or might it, instead, pick her up and carry her away? Her eyes snapped open and she crumbled inward, wrapping her arms around herself. With a deep breath she stepped off of the tracks, beginning to rub her thumb across the bandage on her wrist where she'd cut too deeply. Last night she'd almost been brave enough to join Jonah.

A long minute passed, and then another. Sarah glanced back and forth along the tracks, and then put her face in her hands, aware of how seriously she had deluded herself … of just how lost she had become.

Then she heard the whistle. It came softly a first, a distant, mournful cry. She caught her breath. It was the same sound she had heard night after night as she lay in bed, unable to sleep. Sarah pulled her hands away from her face. Still barely able to breathe, she turned to the left, staring along the tracks.

The whistle sounded again, moving closer, so much louder. Louder than she'd ever heard it.

"Oh my God," she whispered, shaking.

Unblinking, she stared along those tracks, but there was no sign of any train. She stood just at the edge, where the metal rail was sunk into the pavement. The whistle came again, this time so close that she winced at the sound. She could see nothing, but now she could hear the chugging of the train.

Mouth agape, Sarah took a step back.

The whistle blew, and the scream was so loud she covered her ears. Then the wind struck her, the hot blast of air displaced by the passing locomotive. Eyes wide, she stared at the place where it ought to have been, but saw only the road on the other side of the tracks and the trees on the riverbank beyond.

And maybe something else. The night air seemed to ripple, to have texture, just a hint of substance. Sarah glimpsed a face through a window. She blinked and other faces flashed by in the zoetrope flicker of passenger car windows. They streaked across the darkness in the space of seconds. Still there was no train, nothing but the night and echoes and the chuff and clank of a machine she could not see.

One of the faces was Jonah's.

A blink, only. There and gone in the fraction of a moment. The strength of her hope and grief could have summoned his image. But Sarah knew. She'd seen him.

"My baby," she said. And then she cried. "My baby!"

She fell to her knees beside the tracks as the wind from the passing train diminished and then subsided entirely, and the whistle grew distant. After a while she crawled forward and put her fingers on the old rail. The metal was so cold. Sarah lay down there in the road for a while, body across the tracks. A car might have come and run her down. The thought occurred to her, but she thought that wouldn't have been so bad.

Sometime before four o'clock, she staggered back to the Jeep.

Paul let her sleep in. By the time Sarah rolled out of bed on Saturday, it was after ten o'clock. She took her time showering and getting dressed, then went downstairs and had a glass of orange juice. It had been a dreamless sleep, and when she'd woken it had taken her a minute or so for the mist to clear from her mind. When the events of the previous night came back to her, Sarah felt herself suffused with a profound contentment. Her soul had been empty for so long, but now it began to fill up again.

Jonah was gone from this house—from the world, even. But he was not out of reach.

The front door was open. Sarah went out onto the steps and saw Paul raking leaves in jeans and a New England Patriots sweatshirt. He looked so much like the old Paul, the one who'd loved her before he started hating himself. If only she could have stepped down onto the grass and by doing so enter the time before Jonah, when he would have welcomed an embrace on the lawn, when Paul had been playful and his eyes bright with possibility.

"Good morning," she said.

Her husband looked up. For a moment he smiled, as though he'd forgotten all the loss and resentment, but then she saw it draw like a veil across his face. The illusion shattered.

"Morning, sleepyhead," he said. Sarah appreciated the effort to be cordial. "You must've been up all night."

"Pretty much. After I woke up, around two, I couldn't get back to sleep until it started to get light."

He leaned on his rake, real concern in his eyes. "Honey, I'm sorry. You sure you don't want to start taking those pills?"

Sarah smiled. "It's Saturday. No law against sleeping in. Listen, I was thinking I'd make some chicken salad with the leftovers from last night. Some onions and celery. Sound good for lunch?"

"Yeah," Paul replied, still studying her. "Sounds great."

She still loved him, and she pitied him, and she hated him, just a little. Sarah did not really blame Paul for what happened to Jonah—that had been nobody's fault. But she wished that they could have found solace in each other. If only he could find some kind of peace in himself, he could stop pretending his heart had not been torn apart. He could have held her and cried, let her feel it was all right to cry with him.

But that time was past.

AFTER LUNCH, SHE TOLD PAUL SHE HAD SOME ERRANDS TO RUN, and went to the cemetery. The leaves eddied on the breeze and rustled in whispers along the grass, red and yellow and orange. She parked her car on a narrow, paved path that separated the modern part of the cemetery from the earliest graves, which dated back to before the Civil War.

Sarah got out of the car and shut the door. Quiet and peaceful, the cemetery seemed beautiful to her. The sky hung bright blue above the rolling lawns and the trees full of autumn colors. Some of the crypts were marble and others granite, while a handful of the older graves were marked by statues of angels.

She took a deep breath and started across the lawn. Tree roots bulged under the soil like raised veins. Sarah brushed a hand against an old oak as she passed. On her way to Jonah's grave she made a small detour, stopping by the granite block that marked her parents' resting place. Her mother had been killed in a car accident when Sarah was very young, leaving her father to raise her. He'd been her whole world, until Jonah came along.

The family name—her maiden name—was engraved on the front in large letters. KOSKOV. On the back, both of her parents were listed, with their dates of birth and death.

Eli Josef Koskov

Teresa Annalise Koskov

Sarah ran her fingers across the engraved letters. "Hi, Daddy." She kissed the tips of her fingers and touched them to his first name.

Three rows further along she came to another. The cut of the stone differed, and instead of granite it had been fashioned of a blue-tinted marble. This one said COOPER. Sarah didn't walk around to the back. She had stared too long, too often, at the letters that spelled out her son's name.

She sat on the grass just to one side of the grave and sang to him the songs she had always soothed him with when he had trouble falling asleep. Billy Joel's "Lullaby." Harry Connick's "Recipe for Love." Melissa Etheridge's "Baby, You Can Sleep While I Drive."

Sarah had visited Jonah without her husband many times. But that afternoon was the first time she did not cry.

AFTER DINNER—A CHICKEN CACCIATORE PAUL HAD PUT TOGETHER while she was out—Sarah cleaned the house. It started with the dishes, but afterward she could not stop herself. Compelled to continue, she moved into the living room and dining room, then upstairs into the bedroom to wash the bathroom and put away a week's worth of laundry that had lingered, folded, in baskets. Paul watched television on the sofa the whole time, calling to her every half hour or so to come and sit with him, to relax.

Sarah couldn't relax. She could barely stand still.

At bedtime, she slid beneath the sheets, bathed in the blue, flickering light of the television. Paul liked to have the news on while he fell asleep. He took comfort in the chatter, the monotonous drone of the voices. Sarah tried to tune them out. The news held no interest for her; it was nothing but a parade of tragedy. When Paul touched her hip, she thought he might want to make love. The idea startled her; it had been so long. But he only looked into her eyes.

"You all right?"

The question made her want to laugh and scream in equal proportion. Hadn't they both agreed that it was the most foolish question anyone ever asked someone who'd suffered a terrible loss? Of course she wasn't all right.

"Just tired," she said.

"Hope you get some real sleep tonight."

"Me, too."

But his eyelids were heavy. Already, Paul was drifting off, and Sarah didn't know if he'd even heard her.

As soon as he had slipped into a deep enough sleep, she got up again. The clock on the nightstand read 11:49. Pulling the covers up to make sure he wouldn't feel any draft, she left the bedroom. For an hour or so, she sat in Jonah's bed, surrounded by his things, holding a plush raccoon that had been his favorite—it had come with the name Sticky Fingers, but Jonah had mispronounced it as "Tikki," and afterward they had never referred to it any other way. She held Tikki close, rubbing it under her chin.

Sometime before one o'clock she went back into her room and changed into jeans and a sweatshirt. She'd never taken off her socks. After a visit to the bathroom, she carried Tikki downstairs and turned on the television, volume down so low she could barely hear it. Not that it mattered—she'd put on Cartoon Network and it was the visuals, not the sounds, that comforted her. Jonah loved any cartoon, no matter how old or how lame the animation. They had often curled up together and Sarah had stolen catnaps while Jonah watched. Tonight, Tikki watched with her, but there was no chance of Sarah falling asleep.

At two o'clock she set Tikki on the coffee table and turned off the TV.

She laced up her sneakers and went out to the driveway. She'd left her own car out of the garage this afternoon. It didn't seem fair, somehow, to take Paul's Cherokee.

THE RAZOR CUT DEEP. BLOOD SLID OUT OVER THE PALMS OF HER hands, filling the lines first and then dripping from her fingers. In the chilly October night, the cuts felt like burns, yet she shuddered as she dropped the razor to the tracks.

Sarah grimaced, a strange satisfaction filling her. She let her arms dangle at her sides as she knelt on a wooden railroad tie, right in the middle of the tracks. She had half an hour or so before the 3:18 was due, so she had chosen a spot away from the road. On the off chance that a car came by, she didn't want to get run over. What terrible irony that would have been.

She let her head loll back and she stared at the stars. If she closed her eyes, she thought she might have been able to fall asleep. What lovely irony. It felt as if she'd been holding her breath ever since Jonah's death, and tonight, at last, she could exhale.

So she waited, and she bled. As the minutes ticked past she began to grow colder, not just on her skin but down deep in her bones. Her eyes fluttered.

It might have been that she closed them for a while.

The whistle startled her. Sarah blinked and caught her breath, staring along the tracks, searching for some sign of the train. That mournful cry came again, much closer than she would have thought. A terrible ache filled her and she felt weak from the loss of blood. Her body's instinct was to rise, to get out of the way, but that sluggishness gave her a moment to consider, and instead she stayed just where she was, content to wait in the path of the 3:18.

She stared down the tracks, narrowing her eyes. A light had appeared in the darkness. The more she focused, the more distinct it became, until Sarah realized that tonight, circumstances had changed.

The 3:18 was coming, and she could see it. The shape of the train hurtled toward her, just a hint of steam blurring the night above the engine. The sound filled the night, then—the whistle, the clank of metal, the chuffing effort of the furnace.

She smiled and her eyes moistened with tears.

The noise grew and the train hurtled closer, a phantom engine, only an intangible silhouette. But it was real. She had not imagined the whistle or the wind, and she swore to herself that she had not imagined Jonah.

Elated, she held her hands up as though to embrace the 3:18. What would happen when it struck her, or passed through her, Sarah could not be sure. But she knew what she wanted, what she had prayed for as she opened up her wrists. The cuts had started to scab, but raising her hands tore them open again and trickles of blood ran down the insides of her arms.

She thought of what it had felt like to hold Jonah against her, to rock him to sleep, to watch him at peace.

Her breathing came in short gasps. She closed her eyes and threw her arms out wider.

The train hissed loudly and a blast of cold air struck her, blowing back her hair. She heard the screech of its brakes and opened her eyes to find the enormous locomotive slowing to a halt. With a kind of gasp, it came to a stop twenty feet away. Sarah stared at the 3:18. In the darkness it looked almost real, but she could see right through it.

An icy ripple went through her. A ghost. So close.

But then the truth of what was happening rushed in and she felt the smile blossom on her face, so wide that it hurt. Weak as she was, she staggered to her feet. She slipped in her own blood and nearly fell, but she ran for the train.

"Jonah," she whispered, under her breath. "I'm here, baby boy."

Sarah rushed alongside the first car, looking through the gauzy windows. Images floated within, faces that loomed up from a gray nothing beyond the glass. Some of them seemed to be in pain, while others only looked lost, their eyes vacant. The transparent figure of a little girl gazed out at Sarah with hope in her eyes. Sarah shook her head and ran on. She did not want to linger on any of those faces.

The second car gave her no answers and so she moved on to the third, wondering if she should have tried the other side of the train—wondering how long she had before the train began to move again and whether she should just try to get on board. Had enough of her blood been left behind on the tracks for that?

After the third car, she began to panic. Sarah ran.

"Jonah!" she called. "Where are you, sweetie?"

Halfway along the fourth car, she staggered to a halt. One hand fluttered to her mouth, smearing blood on her face. She laughed into her hand.

Jonah waved to her from the window. Then he retreated, as though getting up from his seat.

Sarah ran to the door at the end of the car. She could see through it to the trees on the other side and the river beyond, but the train itself had substance. It pulsed and gave off a strange luminescence, which might only have been the influence of the moon. The 3:18 was a ghost in and of itself, ridden by phantoms. But Sarah had not forgotten the story that had first brought her here. Near death herself, she could see it well enough.

Now she reached toward the handle beside the door, expecting her fingers to pass through the misty nothing of that specter. Instead, her bloody hand gripped cold metal.

"Oh, my God," she whispered. "Thank you."

She put a foot on the metal step below the door, and hoisted herself up into the open door at the rear of the car. Immediately, the train hissed and lurched, slowly starting forward once more. She could hear the clack of the rails and the breeze as it began to depart.

Sarah looked up and saw Jonah standing in front of her, on the platform at the back of the car. His precious face was just as she remembered, open and smiling, eyes full of love. Jonah reached for her. A shadowed figure loomed behind him, but she paid the other ghost no mind as she put out her arms to her son.

Strong hands snatched him backward, lifted him up and away from her.

"No!" Sarah cried.

The ghostly figure coalesced from the shadows, and she saw the face of the man who held Jonah.

"Daddy?"

He held Jonah against his chest. The boy wrapped his arms around his grandfather's neck, clinging to him, resting in that embrace.

Sarah's father stared at her, his eyes somehow more real than the rest of him, peering out at her from the gray realm of spirits.

"Stop holding on to us, honey. We're fine. The only thing that hurts us now is you not living the life we can never have. We'll see you again, when it's time."

Turning Jonah away from her, he reached out with his free hand—a gossamer thing, translucent and floating, a bit of nothing and shadow—and touched her face. He gave her a wistful smile, and then he shoved her.

Sarah tried to reach out and grab hold of the door frame, but her fingers passed through it like smoke.

She fell backward from the slowly moving train, hit the ground and rolled. By the time she looked up, she could hear it picking up speed, could feel the breeze of its passing, but she couldn't see it any more.

The 3:18 had come and gone.

Sarah stared at the place where it had been until even the most distant whistle had disappeared, and all she had left was the memory of it. Somehow she knew that she would never hear the whistle of the 3:18 again.

For what seemed an eternity, she sat and waited to die. And when she did not die, she held her hands up in front of her face and looked at her wrists. The right still bled, though not much, and the other had begun to close already. Blood clotted and dried and crusted over. She had not cut deeply enough.

Sarah screamed, enraged that she still lived.

And then she cried.

So lonely, but alive.

In time she rose, weak and disoriented from blood loss, and followed the train tracks until she found her car. She managed to open the door and slid behind the wheel. Sarah wrapped her jacket tightly around her wrists, tangling herself up to stop any further bleeding, but could do no more. Unconsciousness claimed her.

Some time later, with the sky beginning to lighten in the east, her eyes fluttered open. Her cell phone had been in her jacket pocket, and it was ringing. Freeing one hand, she managed to retrieve it.

Paul.

Sarah opened the phone and fumbled it to her ear.

"Hello?"

"Oh, God," he said, "you had me so scared."

"I miss Jonah," she mumbled.

He cried then, for the first time in a very long time, and Sarah knew that they had both bid farewell to ghosts that night.

"All Aboard" ©2007 Christopher Golden.
Originally published in *Five Strokes to Midnight*, Haunted Pelican Press, 2007.

Holiday House

L. L. Soares

Bright red and green banners proclaiming *Merry Christmas* hung from the walls, and a fully decorated Christmas tree took up a full corner of the room, even though it was the middle of July. Hundreds of Christmas cards, most of them yellowed with age, covered at least two of the walls like wallpaper.

Another room was full of Halloween decorations. Yet other rooms were shrines to Easter and New Year's. And there was a birthday room.

Marybeth didn't really notice them anymore. They were just normal rooms now. She had no desire to put anything away. Time was eating its own tail, and by the time she really thought about it, the holidays would be back, and their corresponding rooms would be current again.

Besides, the truth of the matter was Marybeth was too old to care any more.

She walked past the Christmas room on her way to the kitchen. Once there, she sat down at the kitchen table, the white linoleum stained with yellow spots, and poured herself some cereal. It was always the same, corn flakes. There was a time when she'd buy certain brands, but these days it was the generic brand the supermarket put out. They all tasted the same anyway.

On the other side of the wall, in Genevieve's room, Marybeth's sister was having sex with William Lansing. He came over every Monday, Wednesday and Friday morning, even though he was supposed to be happily married. Marybeth could hear their sounds, like always. They certainly didn't take any pains to be discreet. But the noises didn't bother her that much anymore. There were days, though, when Marybeth wished she had a William Lansing of her own.

And there was something else about William. He was Genevieve's link with the outside world. Someone who actually came over of his own volition. Something this house was starting to lack. *Visitors.* Genevieve had William, but he was only over a few hours a week, all added up, and had a life of his own. However, Marybeth had no contact of her own with the world outside. No one came to see *her*. It hurt the most late at night, when she couldn't sleep. She hardly ever slept anymore.

While there weren't many visitors from outside, Marybeth did get the occasional visitor from *inside* the house. Ghosts, she supposed they were. There was no other name for them. On rare occasions, they wandered the halls, and seemed harmless enough. She was sure that her mind wasn't playing tricks on her, that the apparitions were real. But they never spoke, and they certainly never offered even a hint of intimacy.

"Hiya, Marybeth," a masculine voice said from behind her, and it was good old William Lansing, patting down his silver hair and tucking his shirt in his trousers as he walked through the kitchen to the back door. "I hope you're finding this morning to be a lovely one."

"It's good enough, I suppose," Marybeth said, forcing a smile. She prided herself on the fact that she still had all her own teeth.

William nodded and kept on walking. He had a real estate business not fifteen minutes away by car. In fact, the first time he'd come here was to try to convince her and Genevieve to sell the estate, but once he'd realized that would never happen, he seemed content to make do with Genevieve's affections. At least his visits here weren't a total loss, and if anyone asked, he probably just told them that he was wearing the old Walecock sisters down with his salesman's charm.

He was gone and the screen door slammed behind him. It was only a few minutes later when Genevieve came out, still in her nightgown, her hair like white flames. "What's for breakfast, Marybeth dear?"

"The same as there is for every breakfast. Cereal. I hope that's to your liking."

"It'll have to be," she said, and sat down at the other end of the table. "I hope we weren't too loud this morning."

They were always too loud. It was quite clear they enjoyed putting on a show for lonely old Marybeth, acting like sex-crazed kids again. At first she resented it, but she'd since gotten used to it, and even found a vicarious thrill in the ritual.

"No, you were just loud enough," Marybeth said, suppressing a smirk. "We're almost out of milk."

"I'll have to call the market. I hope they send that nice new delivery boy again."

"I'm surprised you haven't seduced him, too," Marybeth said.

"I'm trying," Genevieve said with a wink. "Some things take time."

They both smiled at that, on the verge of laughing, but not quite getting there.

"Are you going to go outside today?" Genevieve asked. "We haven't been out to the beach in ages."

"I don't know," Marybeth said. "I wasn't planning on it. I like it better inside."

"But it's so hot in here. At least there's a breeze outside today."

"Maybe. It's been a long time since I left the house."

"All the more reason to come with me, silly."

"Let me think about it."

Marybeth thought about the strange blue beach down at the end of the dirt road that ran alongside their house. She hadn't seen it in nearly a year and it might be nice to go take a look again. For old time's sake.

Marybeth hadn't even noticed that Genevieve had left the room again. She was on the phone, placing an order for groceries. Marybeth could hear her in her bedroom, saying, "milk, eggs, apples." It went on for a while and just sounded more and more like a mantra until Genevieve stopped talking and hung up the phone.

"Marybeth?" she said, coming back into the kitchen. "I told them not to rush. They'll have someone bring the groceries over later in the afternoon. In the meantime, how about that walk?"

"So soon?" Marybeth asked.

"No time like the present, sister dear," Genevieve said. "And I see you're already dressed. Just give me a little bit of time to get ready, and we'll be off."

"Okay," Marybeth said, not sure now if she really wanted to go, but not wanting to put up a fight so early in the morning.

"Fine," Genevieve said, and went back into her bedroom to get her clothes, and then she walked back through the kitchen and down to the hall that led to the big bathroom they shared. The one with both a bathtub and a shower. There was another, smaller bathroom upstairs that had just a shower stall, but they never seemed to use that one these days. In fact, they rarely had any reason to use the upper floors at all.

Marybeth finished eating and rinsed her bowl in the sink.

She wandered into the Christmas room again. The multicolored lights on the artificial tree always seemed to calm her. She felt like she'd gone back in time to some Christmas morning of her youth.

"Look at me, lost in the past," Marybeth muttered to herself. "I'm turning into Miss Havisham."

She had to laugh at that. It had been such a long while since she'd last read Dickens. She sat on the chair across from the tree and started to nod off by the time Genevieve came looking for her.

"Are you ready?" Genevieve asked, poking her head in.

Marybeth's eyes shot open. Had she really fallen asleep so quickly? "Yes, of course."

"You always come here, to this room," Genevieve said, looking around at the lights and the banners and the layers of old cards on the walls. "I always know where to find you."

"I like it here," Marybeth said.

"Time to get some air."

Marybeth got up out of the chair, and could already hear Genevieve going through the kitchen to the back door. There was a six year difference in their ages, but it felt like a millennium now, as Marybeth got to her feet and started walking. *My God*, she thought. *It's like the tortoise and the hare around here. And I've become a tortoise without even realizing it.*

When she got out on to the back porch, Genevieve locked the back door, even though people rarely came out this way anymore. It was a force of habit more than anything else. Then she came up beside Marybeth and took her hand. "I've got you," she said.

There was a pathway behind the house, out to the beach, that only they knew about. It wouldn't do to wander along the dirt road everyone else used. Walking along their special path always made Marybeth feel like they were children again, off to have a summer adventure. Going over to the beach seemed so wonderful then. Like having a tea party on the moon.

"It never ceases to amaze me," Marybeth said, staring out over the expanse of blue clay. She squeezed her sister's hand. "I bet there's no one else in the world who has a beach like this behind their house."

"It's a *particularly* bright blue today," Genevieve said. And they both looked at each other and smiled. They were just outside the perimeter of the beach, and they immediately took off their shoes and stepped onto the clay with bare feet. It was soft and pliable.

Marybeth swore she could feel the sole of her foot tingling as she walked forward toward the water. The only sounds were the crashing of the waves against the rocks, and the occasional cry of a seagull.

"I don't know why it's been so long since we last came here," Marybeth said.

"I come here a lot more than you do," Genevieve said. "You just don't seem to be interested anymore. But I'm glad you agreed to come with me today."

"Me, too," Marybeth said.

They held hands as they walked across the clay beach. They walked far enough into the water to cover their ankles.

"Remember when Mama used to pack a lunch and we'd come out here? There were people who used to come out to the beach then. And afterwards Mama would complain about the clay. How it got all over everything."

"I remember," Genevieve said.

Turning back from the water, scanning the length of the beach, Marybeth noticed some odd holes dug in the clay. They seemed to be far apart, but there was a kind of pattern to them. They were quite large, big enough to be graves.

Marybeth remembered a story their father used to tell them, about "bottle people" who lived under the clay, sleeping there like subterranean insects waiting to emerge with the spring. She knew it was just a story, but looking at the holes, she felt strangely uncomfortable.

"I wonder what caused those big holes?" Genevieve said, talking loudly to be heard above the sounds of the surf.

"I have no idea," Marybeth said.

On the way back to the house, Marybeth noticed that someone had spray-painted words across the wall of what remained of the old gardener's quarters. She hadn't noticed the graffiti before. It read *Salvation is Obsolete*.

"What a bizarre thing to write," Marybeth commented, pointing it out to her sister. Genevieve pretended not to notice.

The house was coming up ahead. It was so big it even towered over the trees. There were so many rooms, there was no way they could occupy all of it. Even if they turned each room into every holiday imaginable, incorporating the holidays of all the different religions, and even minor holidays like Arbor Day or Groundhog Day, it seemed that there would still be plenty of rooms left over. As it was, most of them were unused, their doors pulled shut, more lost in time than even the holiday rooms.

The Walecock Estate, Marybeth thought, looking up at their grand old home. What a great place this was once, a historical place. Their parents had thrown spectacular parties here, and everyone important had come, even some celebrities of the time. Their grandparents had done the same. There was a rumor that Samuel Clemens, Mark Twain himself, had once slept in this very house, during a lecture tour of New England long ago.

Now it was a mausoleum. Marybeth could see the paint was chipping and some of the windows were cracked. It was in need of restoration. Too bad the money wasn't available for such extravagances. Their savings weren't what they used to be, and getting the roof replaced two years before had taken up a good chunk of the money that was left.

"All the memories here," Genevieve said, noticing that her sister seemed lost in thought. "It's amazing all the things that have happened here, in our very home. It's hard to believe it was all real."

"Yes," Marybeth said. "That's what I was thinking exactly."

"Sometimes I wish we could throw a big party here, like the old times," Genevieve said. "Like when we were children. Dancing and music and wonderful food. No one has even stepped into the ballroom in ages."

"That's because nobody ever comes here anymore," Marybeth said. "It's sad."

"William comes here," Genevieve said. "And the delivery boys." She meant it as a kind of joke, but she could tell Marybeth didn't understand, or wasn't listening again. "Yes, you're right," she quickly added. "It's not the same. The time for balls and dancing is long gone."

"THE GROCERIES SHOULD BE HERE SOON," GENEVIEVE SAID, looking at the wall clock. "We were gone a good two hours."

"It's the longest walk I've been on in ages," Marybeth said. "I think the air did me some good, but now I'm exhausted."

"Go sit down and catch your breath," Genevieve said. "I'll put the kettle on."

"Okay."

Marybeth wandered back to the Christmas room again and sat down in her favorite chair. It was then that she heard the humming. It came and went constantly throughout the day, every day. She was so used to it now that most days she didn't even hear it. And she'd long since stopped wondering what was causing it.

There were some days, though, when the humming seemed to give way to the voices. She hadn't heard them in awhile, and Marybeth had never told her sister about them. She didn't want to sound that dotty. It was something better kept to herself.

Marybeth let the humming lull her to sleep, until she was awakened by the kettle's whistle. Soon after, Genevieve came into the room, holding out a teacup. "Here you go."

"Thank you."

"Do you ever think this room is a sad place?" Genevieve asked, staring at the tree and its multicolored lights. There were plenty of boxes of replacement lights packed away in the closet, in case any of them burned out.

"No, not at all. It's the exact opposite of sad."

"Not for me. It reminds me of all those Christmases we had without Daddy."

"You still miss him, even now."

"Of course, don't you?"

"Yes," Marybeth said, taking a sip of tea. It was just the way she liked it. "I miss both of them. But it's been a long time now. The pain isn't as much as it once was."

"You're right," Genevieve said. "But it never really goes away, does it?"

Marybeth had to think about that one. It had been such a long time since their parents had lived here. And their father had died young, only forty-three when he had the heart attack. Mama had lived for two decades after that, but she'd always been sickly.

Now, it seemed like she and Genevieve had lived here on their own forever. Their memories of their childhood and their parents almost seemed like someone else's life.

Genevieve looked like she was in a trance, staring at the Christmas lights, and Marybeth took the moment to look at her face. She'd been beautiful once, the most beautiful girl Marybeth had ever known. There was enough of that left so that it wasn't totally gone, despite her age. Sure, her hair had gone white, and there were a few wrinkles here and there around her eyes. But for the most part she was still the same beautiful girl that Marybeth had envied when they were young.

Genevieve had never lacked for suitors and had been married twice. But neither marriage had lasted longer than a year. And she'd always come back here. To be with her sister again.

They'd both been adrift in thought when they were brought back to the real world by the sound of someone knocking at the back door.

The doorbell mustn't be working again, Marybeth thought. We'll have to get that fixed. Without a word, Genevieve left to go see who it was.

MARYBETH MUST HAVE NODDED OFF AGAIN. IT WAS WARM IN THE Christmas room.

She wondered how much time had passed since Genevieve went to answer the door, and forced herself up and on her feet. Marybeth went out to the kitchen.

There were bags of groceries on the table, still unpacked. And the door to Genevieve's bedroom was closed. She could hear sounds from there. Familiar sounds. Perhaps Genevieve had finally seduced the delivery boy, after all. Or maybe it was William, come back for a rare mid-day quickie.

How I envy her, Marybeth thought as she started unpacking the bags and putting things away. *She never had any problems getting the boys. They came looking for her in droves. It was like she had some magic power I was never privy to.*

Marybeth thought back on her life. She'd spent it all here. In this house. Never marrying, never going away. After their mother died, she rarely left the house at all. She didn't often feel like a prisoner, though, unless she thought about it too much.

She realized that the blue beach was the most exotic locale she'd ever been to.

It was then that the sounds from Genevieve's bedroom changed. What had sounded like the sounds of lovemaking changed to shouts and the sound of crying.

Marybeth went to the bedroom door and listened, trying to hear what it was all about. William must have returned and they were having some kind of lover's squabble. Except it really didn't sound like William's voice. It was younger. Stronger.

Angrier.

As she stood there, ear close to the door, Genevieve screamed and then went silent.

"Oh my God," Marybeth said softly to herself, torn between trying to open the door and help her sister, and fleeing the house entirely. Instead, she found herself frozen there, listening to the sounds of someone scurrying about behind the door.

The only phone in the house was in Genevieve's room. There hadn't been a phone call for Marybeth in years.

She finally got her feet to move again.

"Where do you keep the money?"

She was in the Christmas room again, nestled in her chair. Somehow, she'd thought he couldn't reach her there. That somehow she really had escaped into the past.

She stared up at him as he approached. The delivery boy from the market. Genevieve still called him "the new boy," but he'd been here at least a dozen times, and had always seemed so quiet and well behaved. Not a dangerous boy at all. But here he was. There was something different about him now. His eyes were wild and there were bloodstains on his shirt.

"Didn't you fucking hear me?" he asked. "Where do you keep the money, you old cunt?"

She tried to get her tongue to work. "The bank," she said.

"No, the other lady, she said you had some here," he told her. "Lots of it. But she wouldn't tell me where it is."

"No," Marybeth said. "We don't keep any here."

"You're lying," the boy informed her. Well, *she* thought of him as a boy, but he had to be in his mid-twenties. At what point did they really stop being boys and become men? The process seemed to take longer these days.

Despite his handsome face and the fire in his eyes, there also seemed to be something lacking there. Like he was missing something that would have made his mind complete.

What was this talk about money in the house? Marybeth wondered. What story had Genevieve told him to get him into her bed?

"Get up," he said, and she saw the knife then. She'd been so intent on his face that she hadn't even noticed it until now. "Get up now and show me where the money is."

Marybeth started to cry, because as soon as she saw the knife she knew she was completely alone in the world.

In the corner, behind the Christmas tree, she could have sworn she saw one of the ghosts peeking out at her with large, concerned eyes. A girl with a perpetually dirty face. Marybeth had seen her before, had even tried to talk to her, but the girl was very shy and certainly could be of no help to her now.

The delivery boy was close enough to touch her now, and his free hand grabbed her arm, just above the wrist, where it rested on the arm of her chair.

"I said get up!" he shouted, and pulled hard on her arm. She let out a cry as she was jerked out of the chair and to her feet. It happened so suddenly, she almost lost her balance.

He held her hand then, and it reminded her of the walk she'd taken earlier in the day with Genevieve, when they too had held hands. And now she was gone; she was sure of it. Perhaps it was her ghost Marybeth had seen behind the Christmas tree. Maybe it had been the ghost of Genevieve when she had been a child, if such a thing made sense. But it probably didn't. Besides, could someone become a ghost so quickly? And she'd seen that girl a few times before, when Genevieve was still alive.

"I'm not going to ask you again," he said.

The humming returned now, if it had ever truly gone, and it was louder than before. It sounded like a voice in her head. Between the humming and the boy touching her, she wanted so badly to scream, to shout her head off, but she didn't. She tried her best to remain calm, even though she knew that chances were good she'd be dead soon, too.

"In the basement," she said, repeating what she thought the voice in her head was saying. "We keep the money in the basement."

"Show me how to get down there," the boy said, pulling her along.

The house was very old, and Marybeth knew there were hidden mazes behind the walls. A whole other house nobody knew about. She'd explored some of it as a child, finding passageways completely by accident. But she'd stopped exploring ages ago. It didn't matter anymore. They didn't use most of the rooms that were in plain sight, why look for more?

She knew the basement was much of the same. That there were hidden rooms down there as well. Passageways that led to places she'd never investigated. Perhaps if she could get him down there, she could stall for time.

But time wouldn't help her. It would just prolong the inevitable. He wasn't going to leave without his money, and there wasn't any money in the house to give him. What little remained of their legacy was in the bank. Unlike the stereotype of batty old women, they'd been as practical as possible to make what they had last. No hidden loot under the mattresses. There was some jewelry, but it was mostly Genevieve's and he would have found that while searching her room.

Marybeth had no hope of overpowering him. And no one would hear her screams. Not in this house in the middle of nowhere. Even William Lansing wasn't due back until Wednesday.

"Is this it?" he asked her when she stopped walking. He made sure she saw the knife again.

"Yes," she said, pulling the bolt aside and opening the door that led downstairs. She flicked the light switch on the wall as they went below. It wasn't as bright as she remembered, and she made sure to watch her steps as she descended.

"An old house like this. You must have tons of hiding places."

"Yes," she said, knowing nothing she could say would save her.

She glanced at his shirt, at her sister's blood. He noticed her eyes. "Keep going," he told her.

At the bottom of the stairs, they found themselves in an enormous room in the shape of a hexagon. Marybeth remembered once that her father had said the shape of the room was a kind of trap to catch "bottle people." He only said it once, and it had no real meaning at the time. She wondered why she thought of that now.

"So," the man said, squeezing her arm tighter and raising the knife toward her throat. "Where's the money?"

The humming surrounded them now. Marybeth had heard it on the way down the stairs, but it was louder now than it had ever been before. And with it came the voices. She could hear them clearer now, talking in unison, but she could not decipher the language they spoke.

There were doors along the walls, doors without knobs, and she was going to point to one of them, to get him to go looking, and take him and his knife away from her, when one of the doors opened of its own accord and something approached them from the far wall. It was large and glowing and it moved strangely. At first she thought it was another ghost, but she could tell that this one seemed solid. It was large and translucent, with a white light that glowed from within, and it hovered over the floor like a balloon. Its small, almost human head rolled atop its frame, with darting eyes. She instantly thought of the "bottle people" her father used to talk about so very long ago. But this looked more like some kind of jellyfish than a bottle.

As it got closer, Marybeth noticed there were blue smudges on it, which had to be clay from the beach beyond the house. This thing must have come from *out there*. There must have been a passageway somewhere along the far wall that led outside.

Its features were hard to decipher. They came to her in flashes, like a series of snapshots, and it was impossible for her to take it all in at one time, and something about that hurt her eyes.

The boy dropped his knife. There were tears streaming down his cheeks, and then he suddenly seemed very far away. The glowing thing stopped perhaps a yard away, but did not touch them.

The man released her hand and dropped to his knees. He began to sob. Marybeth was surprised to hear him howl with sadness.

There was movement inside the creature's belly. Faces.

Her mother was there. Her father, too. And the nameless ghosts Marybeth had seen wandering the rooms of the house. The shy girl who had been hiding behind the Christmas tree upstairs, and the other ones. The ones who never spoke to her, but knew they were being observed. All of them pulsated within the translucent skin, as if the thing were a bottle for souls.

Genevieve was there too. Marybeth saw her now, peeking out from behind the others. There was a confused look on her face. Perhaps her death had been too recent for her to fully assimilate it yet.

She looked down at the wailing man. He was pounding on the floor with his fists, and then he just collapsed, sprawled across the basement floor, unmoving. She knew if she looked at the creature's stomach again, she would see him there now, too. But she could not bring herself to look.

She was afraid she would be next, but the thing did not advance on her. In fact, she could hear it as it slowly moved away. And then the humming stopped. Marybeth reached out for the staircase behind her and her hand closed upon the railing. She turned and made her way up the stairs as quickly as she could.

At the top she closed the door and pulled the bolt to lock it. Her breathing was labored. She was much too old for this much excitement and she feared her heart would fail her. But it didn't.

She had no idea what she had seen downstairs, but she knew it had something to do with the holes on the beach she'd noticed earlier, and she knew that it was not yet time for whatever that being had been to claim *her*. She had some time left. Time to get her things in order.

Marybeth went into her sister's room. The boy had torn the room apart looking for his precious money. It took her a few minutes to find the phone, but when she did, she dialed 9-1-1.

She could not bear to look directly at Genevieve where she lay on the floor, across from the bed. But she saw her blood on the sheets.

"This is Marybeth Walecock. A delivery man has killed my sister trying to rob us."

The police told her to stay where she was. That someone would be coming shortly.

Marybeth sat on the edge of her sister's bed and covered her eyes. Wishing herself away. Anywhere else.

Not even the Christmas room could comfort her this time.

Lines at a Wake

Steven Withrow

The first one knew the body as a baby.
She'd cradled him a quarter of his size.
A circumspect and disconcerted lady,
She couldn't trust the wisdom of her eyes.

The second mourner held a beaded rosary
Dead-gripped in her fist, a whispered prayer
Fumbled on her lips, her stance a pose she
Used to test the grief-encumbered air.

Paraded, close like cattle, past the casket,
The third an uncle, fourth a high school friend.
The fifth dropped her donation in a basket
Before she met his parents at the end.

The sixth pretended permanent confusion.
His, the most unnerving pose of all.
No one saw him enter, pale illusion
Who gaped down at his powdered face
                    Like a white wax doll.

A Deeper Kind of Cold

K. Allen Wood

Logan Ash drifted along a desolate road.

Formless swirls of gray and white cocooned him, as if he were in a state of transformation, waiting to be reborn. He could see nothing more, smell nothing still. He was aware of little more than the inexorable feeling of moving forward, always forward, and the low, steady hum that vibrated through his body—a body which he could only sense the presence of, like some phantom lurking in the shadows. Faint metallic pings echoed through the veil that shrouded him. Voices faded in and out, quiet but distinct, and always just out of reach.

So he continued to drift, moved by the invisible hands that guided him ...

Stacy could see Earth from here—at least, she thought she could.

It didn't matter.

She stared at the blue planet, barely larger than a speck of dust at this distance, and prayed. For strength, for love, for Logan. But most of all, she prayed for forgiveness. She longed to be home and be done with this ordeal. She wanted her life back, to feel whole again, to be free from the shame of her indiscretions.

"How is he?" Stacy asked, turning from the window.

Dr. Rona looked up from the handheld Patient Health Viewer he'd been scrutinizing. His graying hair caught the light and shimmered like an electric crown. Worry lines creased his forehead, but as their eyes met his features softened.

"Better," he said. "According to our systems, the infection is no longer present. There are some abnormal readings which we've not seen before—"

He held up a hand when Stacy opened her mouth to speak. "But I'm confident it's nothing to worry about. I think we'll be able to start the first step of Reversal soon."

Stacy moved to his side, breathing in the subtle mint of his aftershave.

He tapped the PHV screen twice and brought up Logan's neurological activity chart. "See here," he said, pointing to a series of spikes and waves. "Another day or two and these will all be back to normal."

Normal, Stacy thought. She didn't know what normal was anymore, not since the day Aaron died.

She and Logan were young then, both probably too apathetic to the bigger world around them. After high school, Logan had begun an apprenticeship as a spatial architect. He struggled with the responsibility, at first. He loved the *idea* of being an architect, and would grow to love it fully in the months following, but in many regards, back then, Logan was little more than a boy struggling to fill out a man's skin. Stacy, on the other hand, knew what she wanted: a family, to love and be loved unconditionally. When she got pregnant with Aaron, she ran from her mundane life as a nursing student as fast as she could and began planning the life she'd always desired, with Logan and the miracle that grew inside her.

But there were complications with the pregnancy. Logan's apprenticeship had only provided low-tier medical insurance, which didn't include coverage for what was referred to as "Old World Fetal Stabilization." Few women went through natural childbirth these days, opting instead for their children to be created in laboratories, a precise pick-and-choose meshing of the mother's and father's best DNA. Natural childbirth was considered risky, even dangerous, thus was expensive to cover, and they couldn't afford it, not on Logan's meager wages as an apprentice.

And then, late one night, six months into her pregnancy, Stacy's dreams were whisked away in a trickle of blood that ran down her leg and slowly pooled at her feet.

It had been seven years since that tragedy, seven years since Logan distanced himself from everyone and everything but his work. He did well for himself in those years, became one of the finest spatial architects around. Well respected by his peers, envied by many more.

And for what? Stacy thought.

Stacy had been on this medi-station for four months, living out of an overflowing suitcase that said more about where she was going than where she'd come from. She wandered the stark-white halls, nearly every nurse and doctor too busy to tend to her needs. She ate with the maintenance staff. Some nights she spent time with Dr. Rona. He treated her kindly, offered strength and comfort when she felt weak and empty inside, though it never helped. She was powerless and utterly alone.

Light years from home.

No friends or family to lean on.

And the husband she barely knew anymore in a coma.

Soon, though, Logan would wake, and things would change—for the better, she hoped.

Back to normal.

Despite the comfortable temperature of Logan's room, she always found it to be cold. A deeper kind of cold, one that crept into her bones and chilled her heart.

"So in another day or two," she said, "you'll bring him out from his coma?"

"Precisely," Dr. Rona said. "We'll first remove the electrodes from his brain, then patch the holes in his skull. Then we'll begin the slow reversal process. A simple procedure, really. Your worry is understandable, but unnecessary."

But she *had* to worry. She told herself it was for the right reasons, yet feared it had less to do with Logan's health and more to do with things of the heart.

Two weeks into recovery, Logan had shown signs of serious infection. Dr. Rona and his staff performed emergency cryosurgery to destroy the infected tissue—essentially killing Logan in the process. His body from the neck down was then encased in a plasti-cast and put on a low-level freeze. To keep the infection from spreading to his brain, his head had been quarantined from the rest of his body; surgically severed at the jugular by a cryogenic shunt, and kept alive in a sterile, hermetically-sealed Life System.

It reminded Stacy of those freak show exhibits from the Old World traveling circuses she'd read about as a child—*Be Amazed! Be Astounded! Come See the World's Only Living Head!*

Stacy looked at her husband and tried to remember the man she married. He looked so different now, so *unreal*, and every day he seemed to further morph into a stranger, a man that stirred vague memories of a time just beyond her grasp. It was like watching an old photo of a loved one wither under the relentless glare of the sun.

"How long will he remain like that?"

"Tough to say for sure," Dr. Rona said, the aged timbre of his voice as relaxing as a delicate, mellow wine. "Depends on a number of factors, really;

but I would expect him to be good as new in a few weeks."

He flicked off the PHV, and gave her a reassuring squeeze on the shoulder. "In a few days, he'll be awake, and you'll be able to speak with him for a short period each day."

She nodded. "Thank you."

"My pleasure," the doctor said. "But our time here is up for today. Logan needs his rest. He may be in a coma, but his subconscious knows we're here; the longer there's silence, the quicker the recovery."

Stacy clutched the doctor's lingering hand, grateful for the caring gesture, and stared into her husband's gaunt, jaundice-yellow face. Fighting back tears, she whispered, "I love you."

Echoing through the mist, Logan caught wisps of strange noises, fragments of familiar but ultimately meaningless words. These things, insignificant alone, were pieces to a bigger mystery, he knew.

But the idea that he was dead and trapped in some sort of purgatory weighed heavy on his thoughts. He wasn't afraid. Merely curious, compelled to move forward, one hushed moment at a time.

As the whites and grays danced and curled before him, the burning sensation returned. It had plagued him for days (or weeks, or months, maybe years; he wasn't sure), surrounding him as if the world beyond the white-gray walls were about to burst into flames.

Flames.

The word gnawed at him.

Ahead, the light shifted, the mist brightened. A dark figure lurked in the distance, an indistinct shadow illuminated by brilliant white. Fear grabbed hold of Logan's insides and twisted.

It struck him, then, that he was on the verge of revelation, a prelude to something bigger, what he'd wanted all along, yet ...

He was excited and, at the same time, fearful.

But there was no turning back. No matter what warnings this roiling storm of emotions wrought, some unrelenting force thrust him forward. Faster, faster, and faster still. He was helpless.

The mist embraced him; the white blinded him.

Then he heard a word that shattered it all.

A Deeper Kind of Cold

"Logan?"

Dr. Rona stood outside the unit that housed Logan's severed head. The doctor wore long gloves veined with golden circuitry and tiny colored wires that looked like worms slithering across his forearms. The prophetic perversity of this moment would strike Stacy in the days to come.

Consulting a large monitor that showed a three-dimensional cross-scan of Logan's brain, the doctor said, "here we go, Logan ... that's it, focus on the light."

The room's main lighting had been dimmed, casting everything in a dull silver-gray. Logan's eyelids flickered as he tried to adjust his eyes to the relative brightness, which would appear near-blinding to him after so many months in darkness.

With the fluidity of a classical painter, Dr. Rona worked the robotic arms inside the Life System.

"Logan," he said, his voice melodic, soothing. "Can you hear me? There you go, keep them open. Good, good. Very good."

Stacy watched from the observation deck above the operating room. The distance—and the separation created by the large viewing window—made her feel like an angel watching a man—her Lazarus, perhaps—rise from the dead. She openly cried for the first time in weeks, shunning the pretense of appearing strong, and gave herself fully to her emotions.

"Your husband was lucky," Dr. Rona had said when she first arrived. Stacy found it an odd choice of words given that the explosion had caused minor burning over most of Logan's body and severe swelling of the brain, but she was grateful Logan had survived, despite the turmoil and anger churning within her heart.

Logan was one of an elite class of creators, small gods in their own right, the hands and brains behind some of the galaxy's finest cities and stations. She understood the Architects' influence and importance throughout the course of history, but still she had slowly come to resent—and become jealous of—his love affair with his work. "It's my *job*," he'd say when she protested. "I have to go." But he didn't have to. He *chose* to. Chose to leave her, alone.

For seven years, she had been living her life for him, waiting, dreaming of the day he'd return and declare that he was home for good, and she was afraid he'd been living his life—and had nearly sacrificed it—for his work.

Part of her hated him for that.

She pushed the negative thoughts away. Logan was alive. That's all that mattered. The days of being alone were over. Soon she would return to a normal existence. A wife with her husband. Lovers. Best friends.

Happiness.

She would waste no more time dwelling on the past. It was time to move on, time to be strong.

She wiped away her tears.

THE COMPUTERIZED VOICE THAT TRANSLATED LOGAN'S VOCAL patterns unnerved her.

"I'm telling you," it said in mock-Logan, "something is wrong. I can feel it, Stacy. This burning sensation, it's just … constant."

Logan's lips moved just enough so that the herky-jerky movement matched the words, though barely. Before her sat a freak show caricature of the man she'd kissed goodbye six months earlier when he'd left on the assignment that had nearly cost him his life—and hers with it. She shivered at the sight of him, blamed it on the cool temperature of the room, and on more than one occasion found herself looking away when he spoke.

"Stop." She held up her hand, shook her head in frustration. "We've been over this. You *can't* feel your body! It's just fear. Nothing more. Dr. Rona says it's common for patients to feel a detachment from—"

"I know what the brilliant doctor says. I've been in a coma; it could be the memory of my burns; phantom pain until they turn off Brain Support. I get it."

"No, you don't."

"Dammit, Stacy, listen to me. Something is wrong."

Logan's eyes were still a vibrant blue-green, like emeralds catching shafts of moonlight, and his stare penetrated her with such power that, for a moment, she hadn't the strength to look away.

"Maybe you're right," she said. She'd heard stories of people coming out of deep comas or traumatic incidents, of being brought back from the realm of death, and bringing something back with them, something evil. Crazy thoughts, she knew, but no crazier than Logan's. *Tit for tat*, her mother would say.

Ever perceptive, Logan must have sensed her despair—or perhaps he saw it scrawled across her face like a suicide note—and changed his approach. "Listen, Stacy, I'm not crazy. I know I must seem nuts right now, but I'm telling you, something is not right. You have to believe me."

"You should get your rest," she said. "Tomorrow is a big day. I'll be back in the morning."

"Stacy, please."

She got up from the chair and turned away, gently running her fingers down the length of the rough plasti-cast. The exit door slid open, releasing a soft exhale of compressed air. Stacy stepped through without looking back.

Dr. Rona shuffled about the operating room in crisp white scrubs, checking monitors, scanning the digital readouts from the PHV that detailed every aspect of Logan's medical history, from birth to this very moment.

The doctor nodded. "Okay, Logan, we're going to slowly draw down the external current going to your brain. It should be painless, but the lowered current may make you feel a little sleepy. Don't fight it. Okay?"

"Okay."

"Good," the doctor said, his voice strangely flat, melancholy. "Once that's done, we'll remove the cast. By then your body temperature should be at normal levels. Then we'll do the thermo-reconnect and bring your organs fully out of stasis."

"Doctor," Logan said, "what if something goes wrong?"

"Like I've told Mrs. Ash," he said, glancing up at Stacy, who was watching from the observation deck above, "there's nothing to worry about at this point. The danger is long gone. In a week or two you'll be on a ship, heading home." He bowed his head for a moment. "Now, are you ready?"

"I hope so."

As the current was lowered, pressure built in his head. His nostrils and throat felt as if they were swelling, as if he were about to suffocate; warm tears trickled down his cheeks. Panic raced through him like wildfire, and then ... it was over.

Logan opened his eyes and blinked away the tears.

"Still with us, I see." The good doctor consulted his handheld device. He nodded. "Temperature is good. I'll now remove the cast."

He lifted a surgical laser out of its cradle. "You might see a little smoke. Don't be alarmed."

The doctor aimed the laser, pressed a button, and a beam of bright blue shot from its tip. Wisps of steam briefly rose from the frosty shunt.

Dr. Rona walked around Logan's sealed body, the laser burning through the cast's thick molding.

Logan wondered what it would be like to really *feel* again, to taste and smell and touch, to feel the dirt of a hard day's work under his fingernails, to kiss and make love to his beautiful wife. To feel alive again.

Standing to Logan's right, Dr. Rona cocked his head like a curious cat. He clicked off the laser and kneeled beside the cast.

"What is it?" Logan asked, growing concerned when the doctor remained out of view. Fear slowly crept back in, stretching, reaching, like dusk-spawned shadows portending doom.

When Dr. Rona reappeared, his normal, confident demeanor was gone.

"I'm not sure it's anything just yet. Where I made the laser incision—there seems to be some fluid seeping out of the cast."

"Fluid? Like what, urine?"

"No, no—" he paused, massaging his left temple with his fingertip "—at least, I don't think so. The cast absorbs and draws most bodily discharge through the bottom and into the waste system. That's how it's designed. But you were in stasis, so there should be no fluid."

"Then what is it? Come on, doc, what the hell is going on?" Logan's dread had returned tenfold.

The doctor's eyes widened, he took a quick step back and nearly knocked over a piece of machinery that looked like a giant metal spider. Dr. Rona let go of the laser-pen, and its taut wire snapped it back across the room where it pinged off a stainless steel cabinet. "Wait here," he said, and hurried out of the room.

Wait here? What an asshole.

Logan looked up at Stacy. She stood rigid, both hands pressed against her mouth, their weight pulling her cheeks down into an elderly sag, making it look as if she were a wax statue slowly melting in the sun.

Stacy screamed from behind the glass, turned, and ran from the observation room. A moment later, a dark shade slowly descended over the window like a massive eyelid.

"Hey ... Stacy." *What the hell is going on?* "Goddammit. Stacy."

Dr. Rona returned with Tony, a male nurse Logan had spoken with a few times. Next to the fatherly doctor, he looked to have been chiseled and groomed for assignment as an enforcer at one of the prison colonies in the outer reaches. They both stood in the doorway, staring at the ground by the plasti-cast.

"What's wrong?" Logan asked again. They ignored him.

Tony took a long, circuitous walk around the table Logan's body lay upon. "I've never seen anything like it," he said. "You?"

Dr. Rona shook his head.

"What is it?" Logan asked. "Good God. What the hell is going on?"

Dr. Rona glanced at Logan and quickly looked away. "We best get it over with. We'll find out soon enough." Tony nodded, and both men stepped closer to the cast. Tony gripped it up by the neck; the doctor grabbed the opposite end.

On three, they lifted.

A macabre sucking sound filled the room as they struggled to lift the top half of the pressurized cast free. The nurse gasped and wrenched his arms away as a roiling liquid mass exploded over the sides.

The top of the plasti-cast slammed down onto the table as Tony lurched backward, slipped, and fell to the ground. Viscous, red-brown liquid splattered against the protective shield that enclosed Logan's head. It descended in thick lines, like sweet syrup from a sugar maple—if its syrup had *things* living in it.

Tony began to scream.

Dr. Rona, still holding on to his end of the cast, lost control of it, stumbled forward with its momentum, and collided with the table. The cast hit the floor and the doctor's arms sank into the clotted fluid which filled the half of the cast that still lay on the table.

Logan watched in horror as the liquid quivered and crashed into the sides like waves breaking against a seawall. Long wormlike creatures squirmed and twisted within.

The doctor shrieked and spasmodically flailed his arms as if they were aflame. Chunks of skin and flesh battered the plexi-plated wall of Logan's prison-come-sanctuary. Spatter marks pocked the doctor's face; blood dribbled then flowed profusely from fissures in his skin that widened like burn holes. He stumbled around the room, upturning a large machine with many attachments and hoses, knocking over small metal tables covered in myriad medical instruments, shattering glass cabinets and scattering their contents.

Logan stared in shock as the doctor literally seemed to be disappearing before his eyes—piece by bloody piece.

Tony struggled to his feet, a discordant, watery gurgling escaping through a hole in his neck. His face—one eyeball dangling loose of its socket like a pendulous omen, a hole in the right cheek revealing a mouthful of writhing worms—was unrecognizable. His skin was covered in patches of shiny, bubbling blood. Bone-white worms wriggled across his body, slithering in and out of holes in the flesh, between strands of exposed muscle.

Rising to his full height, like a nightmare creature ascending from the depths of Hell, he lurched forward. He reached out and grabbed hold of the plasti-cast for balance. He stood there for a moment, breathing heavy, blood and bits of flesh falling away. He groaned, his body shivering violently. A tooth fell from his mouth and clinked onto the metal table.

He shuddered one final time, his body rigid, and crumbled to the ground, taking the table and its contents with him.

"Dear God," Logan said. Even the computer seemed to whisper the words. Where his body had once been, where his body should still *be*, was now nothing but empty space.

Someone screamed from beyond the room. Stacy, he wondered. He silently begged her to stay away.

Logan shifted his eyes. Dr. Rona stood a few feet away. He was hunched over, one arm holding his stomach, the other pointing at Logan accusingly. Blood dripped from it like rain over a clogged gutter.

Shuffling forward like a zombie, the doctor groaned, his breathing quick and labored. His muscles quivered with each step, and a small, fiery swath of skin pulsed on his forehead. Splotches of red darkened his once-white scrubs, spreading out like acidic rust. One eye was just an empty hole that appeared to sparkle from the inside as the voracious worms feasted on glistening flesh. The doctor's other eye stared intently at the machines keeping Logan alive.

Logan knew what he meant to do.

But then Dr. Rona's body twitched, his blood-blackened neck rippled and swelled like a cancerous lung taking its final breath. He turned toward the door, and exhaled one final word.

The doctor stiffened and threw back his head as if in rapture. His body convulsed once and collapsed to the ground in a shimmering red heap.

Silence filled the room.

Logan's mind, which to his amazement—and complete, ineffable horror—was nearly *all* of him, went silent as well. No one came to him, but he knew they were watching from the cameras. They'd have seen everything, and Logan imagined they'd stay away until either he or those things died. Whichever came first.

After a time, he wasn't sure how long, Logan became aware of the slow, meditative rotation of the medi-station—his own design—as it floated in space. The hiss of the respirator and dull beeping of the blood infuser were the only sounds he heard.

He called out once.

No one came.

As the minutes ticked by, Logan's eyelids grew heavy, weariness overcoming his fears. Exhaustion closed in and dragged him down into darkness.

When Logan woke, he found himself in a different room. The bright white and shining cold steel of the ICU had been replaced by a soft baby blue.

The room reminded him of the spare bedroom he and Stacy had prepared for Aaron, before the miscarriage.

In the years since that tragedy, so much had changed. It seemed like a lifetime ago. Stacy's love had grown fierce after Aaron's death, overbearing in her need to live the perfect life and never lose the things she held so dear, to atone for the death of her unborn child. She struggled under the weight of that guilt, and never spoke Aaron's name again. Logan, in response to Stacy's change, or perhaps his own need for atonement, found comfort in the mind-numbing monotony of his work.

In the wake of Aaron's passing, he and Stacy had slowly died a little as well.

The door across the room opened, and Stacy entered, her head haloed by the light from the hallway beyond. The door slid closed behind her.

She'd been crying. Dark circles shadowed her eyes like the tattoos of a barroom brawl. He wasn't sure what to say. He wanted to hold her close (an impossibility, he knew) and tell her everything would be all right, that he was sorry, that he'd been wrong.

But seeing her standing there, her eyes haunted, her face painted with a broad stroke of pale anguish, triggered something in Logan's mind. He saw flashes of what had happened in the operating room—the blood, the gore, the worms.

"I had hoped it was all a dream," he said.

She laughed, but it was a cold, barren laugh, devoid of mirth. "A dream," she said. She stood there for a moment, eyes rimmed with tears, then turned away and crossed the room, out of Logan's view.

Logan watched the minutes pass on the clock above the door to the room, the second hand in sync with the hissing of the respirator.

"Charles—Dr. Rona—is dead," she said after a time, her voice little more than a whisper. "And Tony."

He said nothing, couldn't find the words.

"Parasites, they said. Acidic worms, like nothing they've ever seen. Inside the cast the whole time, and they just multiplied and multiplied, and then—"

"Feasted." Logan finished the sentence for her. The word came out unbidden, powerful, as if his subconscious had thrown it away in disgust. It stung. His body had been eaten alive. He could barely comprehend the thought.

"Feasted," she whispered.

"I'm sorry," he said. It was all he could say, and he wasn't even sure to whom he was saying it.

"No, Logan. I'm sorry."

Stacy appeared before him again, trembling and shaking her head. She stared *at* his eyes, not into them. She wasn't seeing him, if she was seeing anything at all.

"I wanted so much," she said, tears streaming down her cheeks, "and you destroyed it all."

"Stacy, I'm sorry. We'll be home soon. Just you and me, like you always wanted. Everything will be okay."

Stacy's eyes widened. A look of profound terror crossed her face like a storm cloud blotting out the sun. "Stop it! Just stop it. This is crazy. It's not okay, Logan. Nothing is *okay*."

"I don't understand."

She chuckled. "You're right, you don't understand. We can't—you can't—live like … like *this*." She gestured toward him as if offended by his presence. "I'm sorry. I just … I can't do it. I waited and I waited, but you never came home, Logan. You never did."

Stacy had once told him that she never believed in love at first sight—until she met him. Now that didn't seem to matter. Logan had lost his body, not his brain, not the part that holds the true heart and soul of a person. But Stacy's version of the perfect life no longer included Logan Ash.

Remembering Dr. Rona's final moments, his final word—*Stacy*—Logan wondered if she'd made up her mind long before he came out of his coma.

Stacy closed her eyes. "I'm sorry, Logan. This isn't how it's supposed to be."

"Stacy, listen. Everything will be fine—"

"Fine! *Fine?* You have no fucking body!" She took a few steps back. "Do you have any idea what that even means?"

His thoughts reeled. The ferocity in her voice, the anger bordering on hatred, cut deep. "There are doctors that can find me a donor body. It happens all the time. I'll be good as new."

Stacy turned, and bolted for the door.

"We can do this," Logan pleaded.

STACY HAD TRIED TO SEE HERSELF IN LOGAN'S ONCE-BEAUTIFUL eyes, but she could only see his pain. Or had she witnessed her own pain, her own guilt reflected back at her? She cursed herself for not being strong. She thought she had loved him enough, through sickness and in health. The thought almost made her laugh, and she was ashamed that she smiled a mocking, sardonic smile. After the shameful things she'd done, the desires she'd given in to since first arriving, she hadn't thought it possible to find more self-hatred within her. But there it was, eating her alive. Tragically poetic.

But this was too much for her. It was too much for anyone. It would never—*could* never—be the same, for either of them. She had tried endlessly to reason out what had happened to make things go so wrong, but she could not be certain.

The room was dark now, its baby blue a deeper shade of midnight. Logan slept. She let out a feeble whimper, moved to the prison that condemned her husband, and lightly kissed its cold surface.

"I wanted so much for us, Logan."

Stacy tried to convince herself she was being merciful, that her actions weren't done out of spite. But she wasn't sure she believed any of it.

She took a deep breath, then reached over and switched off the Life System.

Logan's eyes slowly opened. He smiled. "Stacy," he said, before his face went cold with recognition.

She looked away, unable to look into his eyes, not until there was no pain left in them, not until he was at peace. Until she was at peace.

The computer relayed his final word: "Love."

Stacy switched the Life System back on.

"Love," she said, and walked away.

Alone

P. Gardner Goldsmith

He was alone.

The soft, ratty recliner embraced him like a diseased paramour, its tattered and decomposing arms wrapping around him as if in a love embrace. The beer moved automatically to his lips, flat and bitter. The last of the lot. The last beer he'd been able to find. It had been sitting in his clutch for an hour, warm as soup, foul as brine, but he held it nonetheless, as if tenaciously gripping a vestige of himself.

His fingers and palms ached, not from the intensity of his rictus hold on the drink, but from the hammering, the staccato blows against the spikes, driving them deep into the two-by-fours, slamming the beams against the frames of the doors and windows. The drywall wouldn't do. He had needed wood. They would be coming for him eventually, and he knew that plasterboard wouldn't hold.

His wife and daughter were decaying in the other room, what was left of their bodies swelling and turning to rot. Soon, the flesh would be falling off their bones, their skeletal frames exposed—the essence of their lives, lost for all time.

But it was better than the alternative.

He wanted to take them out before they began to stink, before the acrid perfume of their bodies seeped throughout the house to permeate everything, and before that foul, noxious stench could drown his memories of what had been. It would get into the carpets, into the chairs; it would invade the curtains that were going yellow and dusty behind the lattices of pine he had nailed to the frames. But he couldn't take them outside. He had to live with the smell, with the reality ...

That he was the last man alive.

It was strange how one's mind dealt with horror. True horror. The fear he had felt had moved in on him with stealth. First, it had manifested itself as a nagging, irritating sense of disquiet, an indefinable *something* that bugged him a tiny bit each day. Things outside were different, the people were different. It wasn't a pleasant place to be any more. It had changed.

They had changed.

And as the burden of the days accumulated, the realization became more defined.

Something was happening. They were becoming something *else*.

Sitting here now, at the end of everything, it seemed almost humorous how innocent he had been. How he had missed everything for so long, overlooked the changes until it was too late. Upon finally opening his eyes to reality, he saw that it was all around him. Within weeks, the world was inside out. It was over.

He never imagined people could turn into such unspeakable creatures.

There had been so many—friends and coworkers, neighbors and passers-by. He'd seen it happen to each of them. He could think about it all again, but now their names seemed irrelevant, their faces a blur, and the inhuman sounds of their voices merely part of a horrific fugue. Perhaps that was how the mind defended itself during fights for one's life, by pulling away from the details, creating protective abstractions, overlooking the closest, deepest terrors in favor of a larger picture, a picture of survival.

Even the images of his wife and child had become part of it.

Was this how it was to end? Humanity's last haggard breaths taken in a state of near oblivion?

Perhaps. But even now he held on, out of sheer strength of will and adherence to principle. He was the last human, the only one who could remember how it had been. As the world closed in, he would fight it. He had seen what had happened to them, and was not going to let it happen to him. He would resist. He would be himself to the last, and in the end, he would die a *man*.

He heard the thick buzzing of a large, heavy fly.

They were coming. He knew.

And he was waiting. Waiting …

Outside, the traffic flowed freely along a hot and shimmering road.

Pandora's Box

Roxanne Dent

It was Friday evening when the murderer crashed through the big picture window at 21 Oak Street and slaughtered the Landry family. Steve and his wife, Wendy, were watching reruns of *Law and Order*, but there was no law and order in their home. They didn't even have time to scream before they were torn apart. Their heads were ripped off and rolled along the new Persian carpet, scattering blood all over the walls and furniture.

Upstairs, sixteen-year-old Kimi stopped texting her boyfriend and ran onto the landing, wondering if she was going to have to call the cops. Judging by the sound of the crashing furniture and glass breaking, her parents were really going at it this time. It took just one glance before she ran screaming back into her room and locked the door.

Ten-year-old Connor was playing drums along with the video game "Rock Band" in the basement, a set of state-of-the-art earphones in his ears. The commotion upstairs was muted, and he turned up the volume to drown out the rest. He hated it when his parents fought.

Kimi's bedroom door was ripped off its hinges in the middle of a hysterical 911 call and she was savagely attacked. Her clothes were torn off, her breasts bitten and her right arm pulled out of its socket before she was dragged into the hall and tossed over the railing. Mercifully, she broke her neck in the fall and lay still on the polished wood floor. In death, her blue eyes remained wide with terror as the blood pooled under her.

Connor decided he needed a Coke. Removing his earphones, it was quiet. He ran upstairs. When he opened the basement door he stepped in blood. Everywhere he looked was smashed furniture, blood and body parts. Horrified, he stood frozen in shock.

The killer leaped down from the second story landing three feet from Connor, his back to him. Connor had no time to escape through the rear door, so he dashed back downstairs where he hid, shaking, behind the boiler.

The killer found him. Grabbing one of Connor's bloody red sneakers, he yanked him out of his hiding place. Lifting the boy up with one hand, he dangled him in front of him. Freaked out, Connor stabbed him in his bloodshot eyes with his thumbs and screamed at the top of his lungs, hoping the noise would alert the neighbors.

His screams ended abruptly as the murderer's lips pulled back in a vicious snarl and he bashed Connor's head against the boiler, tossing his limp body across the room. It bounced against the beige wall and Connor lay still, his brains oozing out onto the cement floor.

The whole grisly incident took less than three minutes, but even though the police arrived on the scene a few seconds later, the murderer had already vanished, leaving the back door wide open.

ALEXA WEST WAITED UNTIL HER HUSBAND JOHN STEPPED INTO the shower before she got out of bed. She pulled on sneakers, a black velvet sweatsuit and white turtleneck. Giving her shiny, shoulder-length honey bob a quick brush, she entered the kitchen, flipped on the television and made a pot of strong coffee. Removing two mugs she sat down, taking a sip, and waited for John to join her.

The news was depressing, as usual. She frowned as a picture of Steve and Wendy Landry came on. The newscaster was subdued and tried unsuccessfully to hide his horror.

"Last night, the police responded to a 911 call at the Landry residence at 21 Oak Street, only to find the entire family: Steve, his wife Wendy, their sixteen-year-old daughter, Kimi, and their ten-year-old son, Connor, brutally slaughtered. At this time, there doesn't seem to be a motive for the savage crime."

Alexa shuddered and turned off the television as she heard John come downstairs.

Six-foot-six, broad-shouldered and muscular, John wore a pair of faded jeans, an open plaid work shirt and lace-up work boots. Around his neck was a short steel chain with a chipped St. Christopher medal. He looked surprised to see her up so early.

John never shaved on the weekends, and he already had the beginnings of a beard. His shaggy black hair needed shaping, but even after three years of marriage he aroused her despite his unkempt appearance.

Alexa had never liked rough blue-collar types, but right from the start they had chemistry. She'd had a lot of lovers before John, but none more passionate. She felt a jolt of fear as his hazel eyes failed to meet hers as he accepted the mug of coffee she handed him. They sipped in silence for a few seconds.

"Sorry I was so late. I needed to finish up on the Morales project."

Deciding to come straight to the point, Alexa steeled herself. "Are you having an affair?"

John looked at her in surprise and then smiled, amused as he leaned over and stroked her cheek.

"When I have a wife who looks like you without makeup at six a.m.? Not likely."

Alexa shivered and moved out of his reach on the pretext of refilling her mug. John could always get to her physically.

Three months ago, John had limped out of a taxi late one night covered in cuts and bruises with a particularly deep gash on his leg. He said he'd been involved in a four-car pileup just outside of Boston and taken to the emergency room at Mass General. She recalled his shock.

"What a zoo," John had muttered as he'd taken a long swig of the ice cold beer Alexa had handed him. "The guy next to me was all sliced up, the blood pumping out of him. He was having some kind of seizure, screaming about how he had to get home. He ripped the IV right out of his arm. That's how I got so much blood all over me."

"It sounds like a nightmare, but at least you're all right."

"Yeah, it was pretty weird though. Wherever his blood touched an open wound, it burned like hell."

"My God! He could have had a blood disease. What did the doctors say?"

"Don't worry, the doctors tested him. He didn't have hepatitis or HIV or anything."

"Thank god," Alexa had murmured.

"It took massive amounts of drugs and ten guys to knock that freak out," John had added, "and I heard later when the drugs wore off he disappeared. Just took off, although how he could walk by himself beats me. After all that blood loss, I didn't think he'd make it through the night."

"Poor pumpkin," Alexa had murmured, kissing John's black and blues.

That night John had slept in her arms like a baby. In the morning, he'd woken her up and they'd had one of the most erotic lovemaking sessions of their lives. But from that night on, their marriage had begun to crumble.

The pattern was always the same. John romanced her with love notes, intimate, candle-lit dinners, gifts, and lots of sex. A few weeks later he began to withdraw, working into the wee hours and disappearing for two or three days. She couldn't take it anymore. She had to know.

The phone rang. John was already reaching out for it. He turned his back to her.

"Hi. Yeah. I'll see you in a bit. I know. I'll be there."

John hung the phone up and faced Alexa. He was nervous, edgy.

"Work?" Alexa asked dryly.

John put his arms around her, pulling her resisting body close. "There is no one else. I swear it. You have to trust me."

"Why?"

John stared down into her violet eyes. "You said you'd take me for richer or poorer, in sickness and in health. Remember?"

Alexa wriggled out of his embrace. "Don't play me, John. I'm not stupid. If it's not an affair, then what the hell are you doing when you go missing for days at a time?"

John hedged. "I can't go into it now. After I get home tonight, we'll have a long talk. I promise."

"When you return at dawn?"

"You don't understand."

"Who was that on the phone?" Alexa demanded.

John put his empty mug down and couldn't meet her eyes. "An old friend from college."

Alexa knew he was lying.

"I ran into Sam Parker last night when I picked up some chinese at Kim Chou's across from work. We reconnected. He needs help with plans he has for an inner-city community center. He could send a lot of business my way."

"Great! I'd like to meet him."

"No. I mean," he said as Alexa glared at him, "you'd be bored. We'll probably talk shop or exchange embarrassing stories about our college days. Dumb stuff." He put his mug in the sink and started to leave.

"Where are you going? It's six thirty."

"I have a few errands to run. I think Sam wants to camp out under the stars like we used to, drink a few brewskies and relive the good old days. If it leads to a contract, why not?"

Alexa got in his face. "Are you gay?"

"What!" John was shocked. "Come on, you know I'm not gay."

"Okay, so you're not gay and you're not having an affair with another woman. I still want to know where you go when you're MIA."

"I'm running late. Sam and I are going to meet for breakfast and plan the day. I swear I'll make it up to you tonight."

Alexa gritted her teeth, but she had her own plan, and it called for using her head instead of bashing his in. She would play nice. She forced herself to smile. "Tonight is the last time I'll be so understanding. When you get back I want the truth."

John took her hands and kissed them. "You won't regret it." Relieved, he didn't notice the steely glint in Alexa's violet eyes. "There are some things, Lexi, that are so incredible, so amazing it blows your mind."

"Really!"

John pulled Alexa to him and kissed her in that intense way he had that made her knees go weak. She felt him harden against her and her own body betrayed her with an answering response. He reluctantly released her with a groan. His gray eyes were almost black. He smiled and kissed her on the nose.

"Tonight I'll come clean, even if it freaks you out," he added with a laugh.

Alexa waited until she heard his SUV take off before she ran outside and jumped into her black Lexus. "This time, Mister, I'm going to see for myself what you're up to," she muttered.

ALEXA FOLLOWED BEHIND JOHN AT A DISCREET DISTANCE FOR TWO hours. She put in her sad music disks and sang along with "Time to Say Goodbye," and "The Last Words You Said," by Sarah Brightman, sobbing through most of them.

She almost missed John as he turned off the highway and drove five more minutes before pulling into the driveway of a black and white ranch.

Alexa wiped away the last of her tears with one sleeve as she parked in the next-door neighbor's driveway under the trees.

A pretty blonde in faded jeans and cowboy boots, her long, straight hair pulled back into a high ponytail, exited the house and joined him a few seconds later. They kissed, and even though it was chaste for John, Alexa felt her stomach churn and her face flush with anger. Her acrylic red nails dug into the leather steering wheel cover. Sam was Samantha. Alexa screamed in the car as she pounded the steering wheel with her fists. "Lying, cheating rat!"

Fueled by rage and determined to catch them in the act, Alexa continued to follow them as they entered New Hampshire. An hour later they stopped at a diner. Alexa waited in the parking lot, far enough away so John wouldn't spot the car. Not that he was interested in anything except his companion. She could see them as they sat at a window talking and laughing. At that moment, she hated him.

When John came wandering back at the crack of dawn he'd be in for a big surprise. The locks would be changed and she'd serve him with divorce papers.

But first, she'd get proof of his infidelity and hire one of those shark lawyers. Oh yes, John would rue the day he played Alexa for a fool.

After an hour and a half, John and Sam returned to the SUV. Their next destination was an hour away, down dirt roads and halfway up a steep hill to a small cabin in the woods.

Alexa's initial bravado began to crumble and she felt a wave of depression. Her husband was having an affair. Humiliated and feeling sorry for herself, Alexa almost abandoned the chase. But something deep inside screamed for revenge.

She recalled how hurt she felt when she was twelve and discovered her father was a player. Her mother's pathetic advice still infuriated her. "Sometimes it's best to close your eyes and not ask too many questions." Well, she wasn't her freaking mother, she thought grimly.

It was almost three in the afternoon. Alexa watched resentfully as the chimney started to emit smoke. The lovebirds had built a fire. They probably had a bearskin rug, too, she thought bitterly.

When the couple went to the SUV to unload some beer, it was all Alexa could do not to leap out of the car and confront them. She bit her lip. She'd wait until she could catch them without their clothes on.

Popping open the glove compartment, she tossed out gum wrappers, coins and maps and pulled out the Canon Mark IV camera John had given her last Christmas.

To her surprise, a few minutes later a green Ford truck drove up and two people stepped out. They were greeted warmly at the door by John and Sam. Fifteen minutes later, another couple drove up.

Alexa frowned. What was going on? The guests were bringing sodas and chips and casserole dishes. It was a goddamned party.

There was no way John could explain this, she thought furiously. He was leading a double life, socializing with people she'd never met. Maybe Sam didn't even know he was married. For all she knew John had a dozen wives. She'd seen it once on *America's Most Wanted*.

She felt a stabbing pain in the back of her eyes announcing the beginning of a migraine. Alexa closed her eyes and breathed deeply, but the headache only increased in intensity. She knew she had to do something quickly or she'd be sick in a minute.

Opening her eyes, she desperately dug in to her Jimmy Choo hobo purse, looking for relief. Pulling out a blue pill that had bits of tissue stuck to it, she ripped off the tissue and gulped the pill down with the few drops of warm Aquafina she'd forgotten to toss. She could afford to sleep for a few hours.

When she woke up she would sneak up and snap the damaging photos she intended to use in the divorce. She leaned back, lowered her seat, and was asleep in minutes.

Five hours later Alexa awoke, slightly groggy. It was midnight. The light of a full moon illuminated the cabin and the surrounding area. There was no sign of life. The cabin looked dark. She wondered why. All the cars were still there. Midnight was too early to stop partying on a Saturday night.

Alexa got out of the car, carrying the camera, and carefully made her way down to the cabin by walking in the damp grass so she wouldn't make any noise. It was deadly quiet.

In the distance she heard an owl. She tried to peer into one of the windows to see what was going on, but the curtains were drawn. She thought she heard thumps, moans and grunts. It sounded like sex. Could they be having an orgy?

Alexa's hand trembled as she turned the handle and the door soundlessly opened. She stepped inside and raised the camera, ready to snap pictures of John and Sam in the middle of a sex party.

Instead, she stood there, unable to take in what she was looking at. The light of the moon was enough for her to see it was much worse than she ever envisioned. She lowered the camera, her mouth open in horror.

Before her were couples in various stages of morphing into werewolves, their bodies half changed, their clothes ripped and torn, their teeth long and very sharp, their ears pointed and furry. They stared at her with narrow, red eyes, howling in rage as the flash went off. She dropped the camera in shock and ran for her life.

The wolves surrounded Alexa before she reached her car. A large male jumped on top of her, knocking her to the ground. He sunk his powerful canine teeth into her neck and ripped the flesh off. As the blood poured out, Alexa screamed, struggling to break free, but the enormous creature pinned her to the ground with his sharp talons as the others circled in for the kill. She felt their coarse fur press against her flesh.

The large wolf sniffed her hair. Alexa felt something strike her cheek and in a moment of shock, recognized the chipped St. Christopher's medal dangling from the wolf's wide neck.

A fleeting memory struggled for recognition deep in the wolf's red eyes before another werewolf bit through Alexa's right foot, snapping the bone. She screamed in agony as the fleeting recognition was replaced with the ferocious hunger of a wild beast. Alexa's screams mingled with the howls of the werewolves as their huge salivating jaws bit into her stomach and ripped her intestines out.

Chuck the Magic Man Says I Can

Michael Arruda

DEE WASN'T A VIOLENT GIRL, BUT JAMMING A PICK-AXE INTO Shirley's head would have suited her just fine.

"I don't want you going into that room, understand?" Aunt Shirley said. "Don't you roll your eyes at me, young lady!"

"I wasn't rolling my eyes," Dee lied. She turned her back on Shirley and gave her the finger.

"Aunt" Shirley wasn't even her real aunt. She and "Uncle" Trevor were simply friends of her parents who owned a great big farmhouse in the boonies of New Hampshire. Big deal! Just because they had space enough for two teenage girls, and because Trevor and her dad were such good friends, they got to spend weeks on end at the farmhouse while her mom and dad enjoyed some "honey-honey" time (whatever the hell *that* was—the things her mom said sometimes) in Europe or wherever the hell they wanted to go without their daughters. The bottom line: her parents were out seeing the world and she was stuck with Shirley, the Nazi witch from Hell.

It wasn't like they weren't old enough to be on their own. She was 14, and Fay was 17, but her parents preferred that they had adult supervision, or as her mom liked to say, "adult company." Adult company was fine, but did it have to be Shitty Shirley? Trevor was okay. She didn't have any problems with him. He was a real person after all. But Shirley—somewhere in her family tree she had a relative named Satan.

"It's locked so you can't go in there anyway," Aunt Shirley said.

Why she couldn't just drop the subject, Dee didn't know.

"I just want you two girls to know the room is off limits."

"Sure, no problem, Aunt Shirley. We won't go in there," Fay said, forever the peacemaker.

"Thank you, Fay. You're a good girl," Shirley said.

Dee hardened her face until she felt like Humphrey Bogart. She had no use for boring old black and white movies, but recently she had sat down with her dad and taken in *Casablanca*. She had actually liked it. She especially liked Bogart. She liked the way he took orders from no one. He did what he wanted when he wanted, and he didn't let anyone get in his way. He also looked out for himself. He stuck his neck out for nobody, she remembered him saying in the movie.

Bogart would have slapped Shirley across the face hard. Dee wished she could slap her aunt's face. Hard.

"It's your uncle's private place," Shirley said.

Was she still talking about that damn room?

"His refuge from the world," Shirley went on. "Ever since he started working the third shift, he's become protective of his private space. It's less the shift and more his new boss. He really gets to him."

No, Dee thought. *You get to him. How did he ever marry you in the first place? He's so laid back and normal, and you're a beast, the Queen Mother from Hell.*

Dee waited until Fay had fallen asleep on the recliner in the living room, her copy of Dostoyevsky's *The Idiot* open and resting on her chest. She didn't know how her sister could fall asleep in the middle of the day, especially here. The farmhouse was as bright as a bomb blast and just as pleasant. There were huge windows everywhere, filling the place with sunshine. You'd think with light like this the place would be cheery and full of happiness, but nope, it was as cold as a coffin, further proof that dear old Aunt Shirley was a witch. The bright light combined with the white snow on the ground outside practically blinded Dee and made her eyes water.

Winter vacation and she was stuck here. She should have been off skiing.

"We'll do the family trip next vacation," her mom had said.

Gee, thanks. Not that she was ungrateful, but she had a life, too, and didn't her opinion count for something? She had told her parents time and time again her feelings about Shirley, but it didn't seem to matter. Here she was again.

The Castle of Death. It was up to her to liven things up.

She stood at the bottom of the stairs. At the top waiting for her was *the room that thou shall not enterest*.

"Well, Aunt Shirley, I'm going to enter it just to piss you off." Dee climbed the stairs.

Smack dab in front of her was *the* room, her uncle's private playroom, or whatever the hell it was.

Funny, Dee hadn't thought before of invading Trevor's privacy. That wouldn't be cool. She was doing it only to spite Shirley. So, she thought, she'd just go inside the room for the sake of saying she did. She wouldn't snoop or look at any private stuff Trevor might have in there. Oh, maybe she would, if it looked interesting. For some reason, she didn't think Trevor would mind.

Dee grabbed the doorknob. It was locked, just like Shirley had said. Lucky for her, this wouldn't be a problem.

Dee reached inside the right pocket of her sweatshirt and pulled out the key she had bought from Chuck the Magic Man.

Chuck the Magic Man, now there's a name she hadn't said lately. She hadn't been into his store to buy anything in months, not since her mom had taken away her allowance, just because she refused to do her homework. Big deal. Parents!

Chuck owned the tiny downtown comics and collectibles shop she liked to visit, Chuck the Magic Man's Magic Shoppe. It was one of those stores that was about as big as her bathroom yet had enough stuff in it to fill a supermarket. She loved going in there. It smelled like bubble gum and pipe tobacco—cherry pipe tobacco, to be exact.

She liked Chuck. There weren't a whole lot of adults Dee enjoyed being around, but Chuck was one of them. Trevor was another.

Chuck liked her too. He always sold her things real cheap, like the key.

"Opens all locks," he had told her, and it was no lie because Chuck never lied to her. Everything he had told her about his products had been true, like the deck of cards that contained directions for 40 tricks, all of them easy to perform with foolproof results. She had never been one for card tricks, but with this deck, she fooled everybody, and it *was* easy.

Chuck would smile at her with his long curly brown hair and chipped front tooth. He wasn't a particularly good looking man, but he always smelled good, like soap and cologne, and he looked clean. He reminded her of that pirate from those movies, Captain Jack Sparrow, only he was older.

But Dee's favorite thing about Chuck was his attitude.

"You can do anything you want," he'd tell her. "As long as you put your mind to it."

And then he'd add, "Just study hard and do well in school so you can go off to college and get a good job. Don't be like me, stuck working in a store like this."

"But I'd love to work here!" She'd tell him. "I love this store!"

"Why would you want to work here? Set higher goals for yourself. Remember, *you can do anything you want.*"

He said that to her so much that she found herself saying it at home.

"I can *too* do that! Chuck the Magic Man says I can!"

She truly believed her parents had grown to hate the name, Chuck the Magic Man. Oh well. Too bad for them! She inserted the key into the lock and turned it.

Click!

"Thanks, Chuck!" she said silently.

She guided the door open with her left hand, and it opened silently, without even a creak.

She slipped inside the door, closed it again, and locked it, shutting Shirley and the rest of the world out. Dee was safe.

She turned around and saw the coffin.

She momentarily lost her breath and jumped backwards, bumping the door with a thud, which was the last thing she wanted to do.

There was no mistaking that it was a coffin. She had been to her share of funerals. Her parents had lots of old relatives, and more than a few had had their batteries run dry. She knew what a coffin looked like.

The question in her mind right now was, what was it doing here in the middle of her uncle's private room?

Her first thought was that he was a vampire, and she only thought this because of all those damn teenage vampire romance books her friends continually read. What crap! She had read Stephen King's *Salem's Lot*, against her mother's wishes (of course!) because her mom said she was too young, but she loved it, just as her sister Fay had said she would. Dee had perused the pages of more than a few of those vampire romances, and they were pure fluff compared to King's book. Anyway, Uncle Trevor a vampire was the most ridiculous thought she had ever had, and she quickly dismissed it.

So, why was there a coffin here? Perhaps this wasn't Uncle Trevor's room at all. Perhaps this room simply housed Aunt Shirley's dirty little secret. That made more sense to Dee. Shirley was keeping a dead body in the house. Whose dead body was it, and why was Shirley keeping it locked away in a bedroom all its own?

She didn't know about the second question, but she knew how to answer the first.

But did she have the guts? Yeah, she did.

She prided herself on the fact that she didn't frighten easily. In fact, she didn't frighten at all. Her dad could bring Fay to tears just with a stern look, a silent expression, but with Dee, his icy stares accomplished nothing. He could shout, rant, and stamp his foot, all to no effect. Dee would simply sit there with that hardened expression on her face. It was in her constitution, she guessed, in her blood. She was, in the words of her mom, "one tough cookie."

She chewed the inside of her cheek, a nervous habit she had yet to shake. Okay, maybe it wasn't going to be as easy as she first thought.

She looked around the room. There was very little furniture other than the coffin. There was an end table to her right with a lamp on it, and a chair next to the table that looked like a king's chair with its thick fancy legs, as if it belonged in a castle, the Castle of Death.

To her left, she saw an antique dresser of some kind with thin curvy legs that reminded her of the crests of ocean waves. It had tons of tiny drawers, each equipped with a tiny knob. Dee had seen a dresser like this before, in her grandmother's spare room, except her grandmother's had a mirror. This one didn't.

Behind her and to her left was a sliding door which was open just a crack. She peeked inside and saw men's clothes hanging from a rack. It was a closet. It smelled of moth balls.

She covered her nose and realized she was still holding Chuck the Magic Man's key. She shoved it back into her sweatshirt pocket and wrapped her arms around herself. It was cold inside the room, much colder than the rest of the house. She spied a heating vent in the floor. Strangely, it was closed shut.

Shirley wants the heat off in this room. A dead body roasting in a warm room would probably smell bad, Dee thought to herself. *There's a body in that coffin.*

The time had come for her to find out once and for all.

She felt along the edge of the coffin, probing with her fingers for a natural spot to lift. She didn't find any, so she decided to simply grab the lid and lift.

It gave way. She opened it quickly, saw a body, and stopped. She groaned inadvertently, swallowed, chewed the inside of her cheek like a squirrel gnawing on an acorn, and then—she lifted some more, until it was all the way open and she could see clearly the body lying in state in front of her was indeed her Uncle Trevor.

"Oh my God!" she whispered to herself.

She stepped back and covered her face with her hands. She wasn't about to scream, but she wanted to make sure not even a peep escaped her lips.

She rubbed her chin while she thought. It was Uncle Trevor all right, and he was dead. His flesh was a sickening shade of blue, and he wasn't breathing. She suddenly wanted to cry. She loved Uncle Trevor, but she didn't do crying. She simply sniffed instead, as if she had a slight cold coming on.

When she sniffed, she caught a whiff of a slightly putrid odor, like body odor mixed with wet clothing. It wasn't quite as bad as her dad's sweaty socks, but it wasn't pleasant by any means. This smell told her that Trevor had been dead a while, which made no sense to her since she had seen him alive the day before. Did dead bodies stink that quickly?

A wave of anger overcame her. Was this what it was all about? Trevor had died, and Shirley didn't want to tell them? Was it possible that Shirley was this cold-hearted, that she could actually cover up her husband's death like this? Dee easily saw Shirley as the demonic bitch that she was, but this was really out there.

Plus it made no sense. What was Shirley planning to do? Wait the remaining five days of their stay before doing anything?

Dee studied her uncle's face. His eyes were closed tight, as were his lips. His hands were clasped together resting on his belly, as if he were enjoying an afternoon nap. He wasn't wearing any shoes, just socks, which was no surprise since no one wore shoes in Shirley's house.

She looked back at his face. There was a slight gap between his top and bottom eyelashes that hadn't been there before. But how could that be? He was dead.

Yet, as she watched his face, she saw his eyes slowly, slowly open. She clenched the edge of the coffin tightly. His eyes were blank, at first, as if they were blind. Then he blinked— yes, the dead body of her uncle lying in front of her actually blinked—and his pupils turned gradually towards her until he looked directly at her.

It took him a moment, it seemed, to recognize her. Once he did, the blank expression left his face. A look of fear replaced it.

Dee didn't say a word. Neither did Trevor. They remained that way for a short while, motionless, eyes locked, mouths silent.

Something touched Dee's hand. Trevor's hands were still clasped over his belly. She looked down. A large brown cockroach had scurried onto the back of her right hand, and there it had stopped, as if it too were staring into Trevor's eyes.

Dee didn't have a problem with bugs. Fay would scream if she saw a spider, but Dee picked up spiders, roaches, worms, you name it. She even handled bees. They didn't bother her.

She reached over with her left hand and picked up the roach. She wasn't sure why. She held it in between her left index finger and thumb, in front of her face, examining it curiously. She looked back at Trevor. He was examining the bug as well. His lips parted, revealing his teeth. A pair of fangs protruded prominently from his mouth.

"No ... way," Dee thought.

She felt the cockroach in between her fingers, struggling to get away. She watched Trevor's face closely. As he continued to eye the roach in between her fingers, drool dripped from his lips.

"Do you want this?" she asked, jiggling her hand, shaking the bug.

Trevor's lips slowly parted into a devilish grin.

Dee extended her hand towards Trevor's face and dangled the roach above his mouth. His eyes widened. She dropped the roach, and it landed on his lips. He snapped at it and sucked it inside his mouth. Keeping his lips closed tightly together, he chewed the bug as if he were eating a crunchy cookie and swallowed.

There was almost a look of embarrassment on his face, as if he were ashamed that Dee had discovered his secret, but Dee's stone cold expression, which showed neither fear nor disgust, seemed to reassure him, and his face relaxed.

"It's okay," she said. "I won't tell."

And she wouldn't. She liked Trevor. Had it been Shirley in the coffin, she would have been pounding that wooden stake into her chest like there was no tomorrow.

DEE LAY AWAKE IN THE HARD UNCOMFORTABLE BED. The accommodations were always the same, ironing board mattresses, sandpaper sheets, starch stiff blankets tucked in tight, and pillows as soft as tires. She didn't sleep much at Shirley's.

The room was dark. The only light came from the window, from the glowing moon hovering in the night sky. Its pale rays cut across the room and fell upon Dee's legs. She lay outside the covers because underneath she felt trapped, pinned in a cocoon spun by Shirley. She hated that feeling. She needed to be free.

The bedroom door was shut, and no light seeped in from the hall beyond it. The old-fashioned clock on the wall tick-tocked loudly. It was the only sound she heard until the floor creaked.

Trevor stood by the foot of her bed.

The door hadn't opened. Even though she couldn't see it clearly in the low light, she knew it hadn't opened because it squeaked. She would have heard it. It was the dead of winter. Though the shade was up, the window was closed. How Trevor could have got into the room she had no idea.

She chewed the inside of her cheek. She said nothing.

Trevor stood above her head, towering over her as she lay in bed. He looked her in the eye, and she looked right back. His face seemed full of curiosity, as if he were wondering what it was that made her tick, as if he were trying to understand her lack of emotion.

It's simple, really, she thought. *I do what I want when I want, and as long as I'm true to myself, there's nothing you can do about it. Chuck the Magic Man says so.*

She wondered if Trevor could read minds. She didn't think so, because he still wore the same curious expression on his face. She wasn't going to make it easy for him either. She hit him with her best icy glare.

He raised his right hand and brought it towards Dee's face, as if he were going to stroke her cheek. She noticed he held something in his hand. In between his index finger and thumb, he held a cockroach, its little legs kicking and flailing. Trevor's blue lips parted, and he smiled, exposing his fangs ever so slightly. He looked at the roach and then back at her, as if to say, "You like?"

Dee gritted her teeth and swallowed. She knew what he wanted her to do. She had swallowed a goldfish once. This would be easier. She nodded.

Trevor waited, as if to make sure Dee understood. Then he gently placed the roach on her lips.

It quickly scurried from her mouth up the side of her nose towards her forehead. Just as fast, Dee grabbed the insect, pulling it off her face. Trevor's expression went sour. His face filled with anxiety, as if he feared she were about to ruin the moment, but she didn't toss the bug onto the floor. Instead, she calmly lowered it to just above her lips. She opened her mouth wide and dropped the roach inside.

She closed her mouth and chewed, slowly, methodically, as if she were savoring each and every bite, as if nothing she had ever eaten had tasted this good. The reality was far from it. The roach tasted horribly bitter, like blood mixed with dirt. She tried to make things better by imagining she was eating sunflower seeds. After several seconds, the taste of blood in her mouth became less nauseating, and she didn't have to pretend any longer that she was enjoying the experience. The coppery taste grew on her, as she rolled around the bits and pieces now mixed with her saliva inside her mouth, touching each morsel with her tongue, pausing to play with it against her teeth.

"Mmm," she moaned slowly.

Trevor trembled ever so slightly, and he wiped drool from his lips.

Slowly, she swallowed.

"Mmm," she moaned again. "That was good."

She suddenly felt exposed, as if she were lying naked in front of him.

He smiled at her gently and said, "It's okay. I won't tell."

SHIRLEY SCURRIED THIS WAY AND THAT ABOUT THE HOUSE, IN A TIFF. "He said this wouldn't happen!"

Dee sat in the living room playing her latest game on her PSP, occasionally looking up and watching Shirley with amusement. Had Trevor dribbled some blood on her precious rug, Dee smirked?

"Your sister's feeling sick today," Shirley said. "You keep that video contraption on low so the noise doesn't disturb her, you hear?"

Sick? That was the first Dee had heard of it.

Dee knocked on the bedroom door. Fay lay in bed, the covers pulled up to her chin.

"Shirley said you're sick?" Dee asked.

Fay nodded and coughed. "I feel awful. I think it's the flu."

Fay did look unbearably pale. Dee touched her sister's forehead. It was icy cold.

"You don't feel feverish," Dee said.

"I don't know about that. I've got the chills," Fay said. She sneezed and turned her head, so that she wouldn't sneeze on her sister.

Dee saw two tiny puncture wounds on her sister's throat.

She retreated to the basement. She wanted to be alone, to think. She looked ahead of her, at Trevor's tool bench, covered with hammers, saws, screwdrivers, and files. Gathering dust in the corner next to the bench sat several flimsy wooden chairs. It would be easy to break them apart, to take one of those wooden chair legs and sharpen it to a point.

She looked down at the floor.

A roach crossed the cement terrain.

There was only one person in the entire world who Dee felt understood her completely, and who she loved unconditionally, and that was her sister, Fay. She meant the world to Dee, and Dee would do anything to protect her.

Dee looked down at the roach on the floor. She stomped on it with her foot, and crushed it, crushed it until it was an unrecognizable blotch of bloody bits and pieces.

DEE STOOD IN FRONT OF THE COFFIN.

She placed the hammer and stake she had crafted from the wooden chair leg under her right arm pit and squeezed them tight, holding them there, while with both her hands she pushed open the coffin lid. It was heavy at first, but once more it opened rather easily, with that slight creak.

She huffed in frustration. The coffin was empty.

Did he know? Did Trevor know she was coming after him? Could he read minds? She never remembered any of the vampires she had come across in books and movies possessing the ability to read minds.

She heard a low rumbling sound, and she remembered the closet with the sliding door. She looked up to see Trevor step from the closet. He hadn't read her mind, because he looked surprised to see her.

Dee felt a sudden draft of cold air blowing from the closet, and it smelled musty, like a basement. She bet there was a secret passageway from the closet to the basement. She bet there were other secret passageways too, which would explain how Trevor had gotten in and out of her bedroom without using the door or window.

Trevor pointed to the hammer and stake.

"Why?" he asked.

"You bit my sister," Dee said. "Now you have to pay."

"Would you rather it had been you?" Trevor asked.

"For your sake, it should have been me," Dee said, without missing a beat.

The door to the room burst open, and Shirley turned on a light.

"What's going on, here? Trevor, what are you doing?" she asked, her face full of horror, as if she had caught her husband in bed with another woman.

"Shirley, help me!" Dee said.

"Help *you*? You little bitch! Why on earth would I help you?" Shirley said. She turned to her husband. "Kill her."

Trevor shook his head.

"What do you mean, no?" Shirley said. "You have no choice. You think she's going to keep her mouth shut about you? Think again! With that trap of hers she'll tell the whole world. You have to kill her! If you don't, I will."

Dee couldn't believe what she was hearing. Shirley was a royal bitch, but a murderer? She fought to keep her wits about her. She had to think fast.

"You'll never get away with killing me," Dee said. "Trevor, it makes no sense for me to die. I'm young. But Shirley over there, if she died, no one would suspect a thing. She's old! If you're going to kill anyone, kill her."

"Why you little tramp!" Shirley said. "Trevor won't kill me. He needs me. I keep him safe. And before you get any ideas, old man, about listening to your little slut here, you just remember who keeps your coffin protected all day. You think she's going to move in here and take care of you? Keep dreaming!"

What Dee said next came out of her mouth so fast she had trouble believing she was saying it. "Maybe I will take care of Trevor. Maybe I'm sick of my parents and want to move away from them. Maybe I want to move in here. Maybe I can satisfy Trevor in ways in which you haven't even thought of, Shirley! You called me a tramp! Well, you're right! I'll do things with Trevor that you don't even know exist! Kill her, Trevor! Kill her! I'm yours if you kill her! Feel my body in your arms right now!"

She ran to him, and he wrapped his arms around her.

"I feel good, don't I, Trevor?" Dee said. "Kill her, Trevor, and I'm yours! Do it!"

"Don't be stupid, Trevor," Shirley said, trying to sound confident. But she didn't sound confident. She sounded scared.

"Feel me," Dee said. "Kill her."

Trevor let go of Dee, and she no sooner had taken a deep breath when she was suddenly witnessing the unthinkable: Trevor grabbing Shirley by the neck and ripping her head from her shoulders.

Dee screamed.

And then she pulled herself together.

"Trevor, get me a mop!"

For the next hour Dee operated on pure adrenaline, cleaning the floor, wrapping Shirley's headless body and her head in a plastic tarp Trevor had retrieved from his basement work area. And when it was over, when the wood floor had been scrubbed so that only a hint of red remained, she took Trevor by the hand.

"I promise I'll take good care of you, Uncle Trevor. The best care ever! I'll tell my parents I want to stay here for the rest of the school year, that I want to enroll in that private school down the road you and my dad are always talking about. That'll keep me here for the next four years, and after that, we'll figure something out. You just rest now. I'll take good care of you."

Trevor reached for her shirt. She brushed his hand away.

"Not now. I'm too upset. Tomorrow. I promise," she said. "I'll be worth the wait, believe me. I'm going to take such good care of you, such really good care."

DEE OPENED THE COFFIN AND WATCHED AS THE BRIGHT SUNLIGHT from the large window bore down upon Trevor's sleeping body. It smoked at first and then sizzled and caught fire. Trevor opened his eyes but didn't seem to see her. He looked at his own body ablaze, and screamed in terror for about ten seconds before the flames consumed him.

When he had been reduced to ash, Dee slammed the lid shut.

DEE PRESSED SPEED DIAL ON HER CELL PHONE.

"Hello, Mom? It's Dee. Mom, don't panic or be upset, but I have bad news to tell you. Fay and I are fine. It's not us. What? Yes, Fay was sick, but she's better now. I helped her get better. But listen, mom, it's not us. It's Aunt Shirley and Uncle Trevor. Something horrible has happened. Something truly horrible. I don't even know if I can tell you."

Dee felt Chuck the Magic Man's key in her pocket. She squeezed it tight. "There was a fire."

She listened as her mother spoke to her in soothing tones, asking for more information, before requesting that she speak with Fay. As Dee handed the phone to her older sister, she thought again about her chances of getting away with this. She had had her doubts, but now, as she squeezed that key tight, she heard Chuck the Magic Man's voice, even felt his breath on her skin.

"Did you put your mind to it?" she heard him ask.

"Yes."

"Then you can do it," Chuck said.

And she knew then she could.

Burial Board

T. T. Zuma

WITH A START, TURNER RAPIDLY RAISED HIS CHIN. HAD HIS EARS caught the tail end of a groan?

Struggling to keep his eyes open, Turner swung his head in a wide arc, surveying the loft in an attempt to locate the origin of the sound. As the fog in his mind receded, he cursed silently, taking himself to task for falling asleep. *Did I dream it*, he wondered? The sound was slight, distant. The barn could be settling, he reasoned, or maybe it was a sudden wind gust.

Turner shook his upper body, hoping to chase away the fatigue and the bite of the cold. He sat motionless in his chair and listened. After a moment he was confident the sound was of no consequence and his eyes settled on his wife's body and the burial board to which she had been bound. As he gazed upon her, his mind wandered.

Though Mary rested on it now, it was not the first time the burial board had been employed. He had come by the board just one week shy of Christmas in 1818. They had not celebrated the holidays that year, nor since. Turner had acquired the board when the milk sickness claimed Nancy, his eight-year-old daughter.

He recalled his wife's concern when Nancy began to appear weak and listless. Then the poor girl stopped voiding, resulting in painful stomachaches and the loss of her appetite. Soon after, her breath was so bad it was a struggle just to get close enough to tend to her. At that point, Turner went to town and fetched the doctor. The news was devastating.

The doctor told them that Nancy had The Slows, a disease that came with drinking milk from tainted cows feeding on white snakeroot. The doctor wondered why Nancy was the only one affected by the disease and Turner explained that he and Mary did not drink cow's milk; they preferred goat's milk, but since their daughter enjoyed cow's milk they would sometimes trade off with the neighbors. The doctor had prescribed Castoris to help Nancy regain some strength, and sarsaparilla for her constipation and stomach problems, but he could prescribe no cure. Days later they had learned that their neighbors had succumbed to the disease. It was no more than a week after the doctor's visit when Nancy passed. Mary took her death hard, as did Turner.

Winter that year had come not only early, but cruelly. The snow was already knee-high, and the air so cold that the lakes and ponds had long frozen over. They would have to wait until spring to bury their daughter. The decision was made to place her in the barn, up in the loft, until the first thaw when they could give her a proper burial. Mary had insisted that Nancy be placed on a Christian burial board. Though he argued against it as their money was tight, he finally let her have her head.

Early in the morning, only three days after Nancy's passing, Turner removed the contents from their coin jar and placed it in his purse. He had no idea how much a burial board would cost, but he suspected that the meager contents of the jar wouldn't be enough to purchase a proper one. Unsure of what was to come, he saddled his mount and began the long and arduous journey into town. It had taken half a day when he had brought the doctor to his home, so he allowed himself that much time plus a little extra to find a board. Through no fault of his own, he soon discovered that he had miscalculated badly. The storm hit when he was halfway to town.

Between the high winds and blinding snow, Turner knew trouble had found him. He had lost his bearings in the whiteout and his horse protested its every step. He thought about turning back, but he had no idea in which direction to turn. He dismounted and grabbed the horse's reins; he needed to find shelter soon.

Though he'd thought about it often over the last two years, he still had no idea how he had found his way to the shack.

It had appeared out of nowhere. The simple fact was that he had walked right into it, striking his head against one of its side walls. Using his hands to follow the wall, he turned two corners until he came to a door. Turner pushed at it and was surprised at how easily it opened. He led his horse through the doorway and, once inside, he slammed it shut. He fell to the floor with his back sliding against the door and stayed there until he could catch his breath. After a few moments, he realized there was enough dim light coming from two windows on the opposite wall to study his surroundings.

Spying a lantern hanging from a peg, he lifted himself up off the floor and removed it. He noticed a box of matches on a shelf beside it so he removed his gloves and set the lantern to burning. What he saw in the shack confused him. Not only was it larger than he imagined, but it looked to be a gathering place of sorts.

Near the center of the room there were a series of chairs placed in an odd, circle-like configuration, around what Turner took to be a crude altar. The altar was a simple affair consisting of a long, thick, ebony plank set on a pair of stone pillars. Turner placed the lantern directly above the altar and realized a small cross had been carved through the center of the plank. Though Turner was not a religious man, he was however a practical one. He came to the conclusion quickly that he had found the burial board for his daughter.

Outdoors, the storm raged for a few hours longer, and then, as abruptly as it had began, it quit. Turner prepared for his trip back home. After first leading his horse out of the shack, he removed the plank from the pillars and secured one end of a rope around its length. He left the contents of his purse on one of the pillars and then carried the plank outdoors. Turner then tied the other end of the rope to his horse's saddle. Unsure of his location, he took a chance on a direction to travel. His choice served him well. He quickly found some landmarks and made it home, with the board dragging behind him, just as the sun was setting. That night, he and Mary placed their daughter in the loft and strapped her to the board.

Later that evening, Mary had the worst nightmares that Turner could ever recall her having. When she woke, all she could remember of her dreams was a groaning noise. She told him that it sounded like dry wood straining before it broke. Still in a daze and not quite awake, she had insisted on checking the barn and then dashed out of the house. Soon after, Turner heard her screams.

He rushed to the loft, where he found Mary weeping hysterically over the burial board. Pushing her aside, he saw the board was empty, their daughter's body missing. The two straps he had used to tie her down were still secured to the board and whole. The loft appeared to be undisturbed and there were no signs of torn clothing or body parts. Checking the outside of the barn, the only tracks in the snow he noticed were theirs. It was as if her body had simply vanished. His wife was never the same after that night. With her mental health declining over the past two years, Turner was not shocked—in fact, he felt relief—when he awoke this morning, the second anniversary of their daughter's death, to find Mary hanging from a beam in front of the fireplace.

Now here he sat in the loft, conducting a vigil over his wife's body, repeatedly recalling the circumstances that had brought him here. Finally, he wept. When his tears were exhausted and he thought sleep was warranted, he heard it. The groaning. It was subtle and intermittent, but it was there. It reminded Turner of the sound of a lake in late March when its surface was cracking, just before ice-out, when the thaw began; he knew something powerful was happening out there, warning him away, even if he couldn't see it.

The volume and frequency of the groaning increased. When he realized the sound was coming from the burial board, his spine stiffened. Staring at the board, his eyes grew wide. The board had begun to move.

While the center of the board was firmly planted on the floor, its ends were vibrating, as though straining to lift themselves. The volume of the groaning increased, it was almost deafening, and the pain in his ears became so severe that Turner thought they might be bleeding. Mary's body began to jerk wildly, mimicking the motions of the board. Her head and feet were struggling to rise, but the straps that had secured her to the plank held tightly. Turner could only stare in disbelief when, after a series of violent tugs, the middle section of her body began a jerky descent into the board. The two ends of her body strained against the straps. Finally, they forcibly slipped through the restraints and were pulled toward one another rapidly, forcing her upper body and legs into a V shape as they followed the rest of her down into the board. The sounds of bones splintering joined the cacophony of groaning when her knees were violently thrust against her skull. The impact caused her head to turn toward him and her eyes were now opened. Though they were milky and devoid of life, he felt certain they followed him as the remainder of her body was pulled down into the board.

Turner's paralysis broke. He rushed from the chair and stood above the burial board. He saw no trace of his wife's body. Bewildered and frightened, he trained his eyes on the board, hoping to find some cause as to what had taken her. Shuddering, he let out a whimper when he noticed that the small cross that had been carved through the middle of the board had changed. It had enlarged, and gained an airy substance. It was dark, even blacker than the ebony of the board. And its depth was unnatural. He went down on one knee, lowering his head until it was merely inches above the board, and then he peered into the center of the cross.

And when he felt the pull, he didn't even have enough time to wonder if it would hurt.

Windblown Shutter

John Grover

Click-clack, click-clack. The sound woke Shane from his sleep. Click-clack. He recognized that sound. It frightened him more ways than he could count. He didn't want to get out of bed, but he knew he had to. He knew it was the only way to learn the truth. Click-clack. Shane pushed his covers aside. Rain pattered hard on the roof. Lightning lit up the room in flashes—toys strewn about the floor, adored stuffed animals discarded for the night, coloring books stacked precariously.

Shane left his room and saw the attic stairs down the end of the quiet hall. Not another soul stirred. A green nightlight in the bathroom helped illuminate his path. The wind howled, somber, lonesome. He reached the attic stairs and placed his hands on the banister.

He made his way up, step by step, and heard the rain grow louder as he reached the attic's threshold. He froze, searching for his courage, knees buckling, body trembling. Damp palms made his grip slip. Finally he pushed himself to move and poked his head up into the attic. Click-clack. Click-clack.

Across the attic, dead ahead of him, sat a small open window. The wind caught its shutter, knocking it against the house—click clack. The wind moaned through the room and swayed the hanging light in the center of the ceiling. Shane followed the light with his gaze as shadows danced around him, setting eyes on a strange figure standing with its back to him. A plastic butcher's apron covered the figure from head to toe, and atop its head thick shaggy hair cascaded over broad shoulders. The figure lifted a cleaver with its right hand; the stained blade glinted in the light.

Shane wanted to scream but nothing came out. Instead, his mouth hung agape as the cleaver went down on a wooden table again and again, chopping in rhythm with the shutter, click-clack, click-clack. Shane's legs nearly gave out as he looked at the table and to the left of the figure spotted a woman's face … his mother's. The room spun suddenly and his vision blurred as the sensation of falling seized him.

A scream shattered the quiet of the house as Shane woke, bathed in sweat. His bedroom door swung open and his Aunt Marie hurried into the room. He sat up the moment he saw her and pushed his soaked sheets away. Another flash of lightning illuminated his aunt's concerned face.

"It's all right, honey." She went to his side, sat on the edge of the bed and took him into her arms. "Another dream?"

He nodded.

"They're getting worse. Maybe I should take you to a doctor."

"No doctors," he said. "I need the dreams. I have to see it."

"Sweetie, these nightmares aren't good for you. You've been through a lot. You lost your mom. You might want to talk to someone."

"I don't need to talk to someone. I need to see who did it. I need to see it, see it all."

"You can't see, Shane. It's a dream."

"I did see. I was there when she was killed. I would have seen who did it if I hadn't fallen down the stairs."

Shane ran his hand over his head; the scars from the stitches were still there after all these years. They itched, never letting him forget the night of his mother's murder. The night he went up to the attic, the shutter, the cleaver, before the fall that almost took his life. That night was lost in his nightmares, bits and pieces of it floated around his subconscious, perhaps never to be unlocked.

"Okay honey," his aunt soothed. "Do you want some water?"

"No, that's okay."

"All right. Call me if you need me."

He nodded and hugged her tight. He watched her head out of the room. She pulled the door behind her, leaving it slightly ajar. Shane waited a few moments then climbed out of bed. He slipped over to the door on his tiptoes and crouched at the opening.

The stairway banister stood in his line of sight as he listened to the voices of his aunt and Uncle Roy rise.

"That's the third one this week," Roy said, slight concern in his voice.

"I know, poor thing. I just wish I could do something."

"You're doing so much already. I really appreciate it."

"Where is his father? How could he do this to his son? Everyone knows that …"

"Don't start that again, Marie. My brother didn't do it. He couldn't. He loved her with all his heart."

"Then why did he vanish? Why hasn't he come forward?"

"We don't know that he can. He disappeared. What if whoever killed Gillian killed him too?"

"Then where is his body? Why would he leave her in the attic room but take *him* away?"

"I don't know. It was a maniac and they don't follow any logic."

Tears welled in Shane's eyes. The same arguments, same resentment, always. He turned from the door and went to his bedroom window. "Dad, where are you?"

CLICK-CLACK, CLICK-CLACK. SHANE POKED HIS HEAD THROUGH the attic's doorway. The light swayed. Click-clack. The cleaver swung. Click-clack. The shutter bounced off the house. Shane locked eyes on his mother's face. The cleaver went down on her for the third time and her face turned toward him suddenly. Her eyes popped open. *Run.*

He turned and looked up, the killer stopped hacking, shifted, and looked over his shoulder slowly. Just before Shane could see the face the room spun, he lost his grip and tumbled backward down the stairs.

Shane's eyes popped open, his eyes were sore, he'd been crying in his sleep all night. He panted so hard his chest hurt. After a few moments he calmed himself down. He was glad he didn't call out or scream this time. He loved Aunt Marie dearly but she didn't understand. She wanted it to go away, take away his pain, his memory. He didn't want that. He wanted to feel all of it; he never wanted the memories to go away, the memories of her. He never wanted his mother to go away. It was his connection to that night. It was his only way to find out what happened and why. He missed her so much. He missed home and how warm it was there, how it smelled, how it looked.

He listened for a moment and figured the household was still asleep. Shane wondered if he'd ever sleep like that. Wondered if the man wearing the apron and wielding the cleaver would always haunt his dreams, always stalk him and his mother. Was there ever an escape? Shane thought there was. The solution came to him at last. It had always been there, waiting.

He couldn't wait to tell his Aunt Marie.

"**Aunt Marie, I want to go back to my old house.**" Shane blurted it out the next morning on the drive to school. She almost hit the brakes but managed to keep driving.

"I don't think that's a good idea, sweetie."

"It will help me remember. I'm sure of it."

"Or it will just make things worse."

"I haven't been back there since the day it happened."

"That place only holds painful memories. What if it put you over the edge? There's no telling what might happen if you go there. It's too risky."

"I need to. Please, Aunt Marie. Please. I know you and Uncle Roy still have the keys. I need to see it again. The dreams are only getting worse. Please."

She didn't answer him. Marie pulled the car over. Doubt wore plainly on her face. She inhaled then turned to Shane. "I'll talk to Roy."

"You guys have to let me go. It's my house." His eyes welled.

His heart pounded inside his chest. An image of his house tried to form in the recesses of his mind but it was difficult. His mind buried it, tried to convince him that all he knew was his Uncle Roy and Aunt Marie's home. It wasn't true. He needed to know he was not that crazy kid locked away in his uncle's home, the damaged secret of the neighborhood. He had a history. It didn't just belong to his Uncle Roy … it belonged to him.

"All right," Marie uttered. "All right."

"Thank you."

"**I don't like it,**" **Roy said. "I think it's a bad idea."**

Shane watched from the top of the stairs, behind the banister again. He stared down at his uncle's auburn hair, hair the same color as his father's, and soaked in every word.

"He's insisting," Marie replied. "He thinks it might help with his issues. I might agree with him."

"Oh really? And are you a doctor or a psychiatrist?"

"No. That's not what I'm saying. If he believes it will work then maybe we should …"

"Whatever," Roy cut her off. "Fine. Do what you want. You're responsible for whatever happens anyway."

"God Roy, he's your flesh and blood. Don't you care?"

"I didn't want kids. Never did. You knew that when you married me. We just got stuck with this one."

"He's your brother's child."

"That's right, not mine. I don't even know him."

"You could have. Maybe if you gave him an ounce of attention or went to his side just once after one of his nightmares. No, I'm the one who's there when he wakes almost every night. He saw someone butcher his mother, Roy. You could at least pretend to be sympathetic."

"This conversation is over. Don't tell me how to feel about someone I barely know. Don't tell me how to feel about my brother and his wife. You know nothing about us, any of us. I don't need to explain any of this to you. Like you said, he's my flesh and blood—not yours."

"Then don't worry, Roy, I'll try to keep him from ending up in an institution. This is ridiculous." Marie stormed out of her chair.

Shane saw shadows shift on the walls and heard pattering footsteps. He bolted back into his room and to his bed.

"Shane!" His aunt's voice bellowed to the second floor. "Get on your coat, we're going."

THE FAMILY HOME NO LONGER HELD WARMTH AND SECURITY. It looked ominous to him now—vacant, lonesome, soulless. Windows were dark eyes. Front door a yawning maw. It stood empty. Lifeless, without laughter, without noise, without movement. Roy refused to put it up for sale. Instead, he let it languish, alone.

Shane didn't know why, but when he took his first step onto the front porch he reached out for his Aunt Marie's hand. She took it willingly.

Marie slid the key into the front door and unlocked the house. She eased the heavy wooden door with its deadbolts open and allowed Shane entry.

He stepped in and inhaled the musty scent first, then the first smells of memory hit him: his mom's peppermint tea from the kitchen, the sage-scented candles in the dining room, the smell of paint drying in a sewing room—she never could decide which color she wanted it to be. It hit him in one giant wave, threatening to overwhelm him, send him crashing to the floor in a puddle of pain and misery, but he held steadfast.

He let go of Marie's hand when he reached the stairs to the second floor and the family bedrooms. Above, his mother and father's master bedroom waited, as well as his own bedroom, a room he hadn't set foot in for years, a bed whose cold sheets longed for his warm form. Shane turned and looked up at Marie. He could tell she was nervous, although she'd never even been here. She swallowed and rubbed her hands on her pants. A look of distress hung on her face.

He felt it, too. His pulse raced. His throat went dry. He felt a bond with her and understood she probably dreaded going any further. He smiled then. "It's okay; I want to go the rest of the way alone."

"Are you sure, honey?"

"Yes, I'm sure." He saw relief wash over her.

Shane walked up, step by step, until he reached the hallway. The bedrooms lined the wall ahead of him, with a bathroom across from them. Everything looked the same. He stepped into his bedroom, examined it briefly and stepped back out. He turned to his right and there it was.

The attic door at the end of the hall was still open, the stairs extended firmly to the hallway floor just as he remembered. The sight of it filled him with unease. His hands trembled. Sweat drooled down his face in beads. Despite his apprehension, he started toward the stairs.

Above, the attic threshold was a patch of darkness. Shane steadied himself on the stairs, holding on to each rung as ascended. His head reached the doorway and with some hesitation he pushed himself through.

The attic was a large unfinished room, unchanged. Even the infamous table remained, centered in front of the window. Milky light streamed into the room. Cobwebs draped the corners like tattered tapestries. Dust, undisturbed, blanketed the wooden floor. The air was heavy. It smelled of rotting flowers. Through the dust, he noticed dark stains on the floor, mostly under the worktable. Obviously they were unable to obliterate it from the wood. The room welcomed him home with open gnarled arms beneath a blanket of oppression.

Click-clack. He heard it suddenly. Softly first then rising, rousing his fear. Click-clack. Shane looked at the window but did not see the shutter moving. Click-clack, click-clack, click-clack. In his peripheral vision he saw something in the corner of the room. He focused, noticing a figure crouching there with its back to him, obscured in the shadow and milky light. Shane froze, rooted to the spot.

Shane. A voice called from the figure, above the clatter of a shutter that wasn't moving. It was his mother's voice. *Shane.* It was all she could say to him. The figure stretched ... a shadowy leg shifted, an arm reached. Fingers scratched on the wall. Shane wanted to run. His legs refused to move. He wanted to scream. He lost his voice.

The figure crawled out of the corner and turned. He gazed upon the face of his mother—gaunt, pale, grief-stricken eyes. Her mouth gaped, lips moved but no sound came out. Her mouth stretched but still nothing. Shane noticed the frustration in her face and the tears rolling down her cheeks. She shook her head and pointed to the table in the center of the room.

He turned to look at the table but saw nothing. He didn't understand her but she continued to point a quivering finger at the table and shake her head. His gaze traced every inch of the table but still nothing called out to him. The light above the table began to swing, just like that night, and suddenly the room spun.

The room sailed around him and he lost his balance, collapsing. When Shane opened his eyes the room was alive again. The wind howled outside, the shutter banged against the window. The light above the table glowed. He lifted his head to see the man with the plastic butcher's apron bringing his cleaver down on the table, again and again. His mother's lifeless body lay prone on the table, rivers of her blood poured onto the floor. The cleaver slammed down again; the shutter banged click-clack!

The man stopped his hacking, his scraggly hair shimmied in the damp wind; it was obvious to Shane now that it was a wig. The killer turned slowly and looked over his shoulder. The eyes ... he knew those eyes. Shane almost screamed when he stared right at them, dead into them. They were his father's. The man's entire face was exposed now, the cleft chin, the shape of the mouth. Despite the paint around his eyes and the attempt to alter his appearance ... there was no doubt. It was his ...

"Shane! Shane wake up." Aunt Marie's voice shattered the daylight nightmare. He woke in her arms. "You were screaming ... you were screaming for your ..."

"Father!" Shane burst into tears, uncontrollable; a tidal wave held back far too long now broke. "It was my father! My father. I saw his face ... I ... saw ... his face!"

Marie held him for the longest time. Finally he stopped crying and quiet came over the room. "Come," she whispered to him. "Let's get out of here. This room isn't good for you."

Shane nodded his agreement and climbed to his feet. They left the house together.

When they returned home, Shane went immediately to his room and shut the door. For hours he sat on his bed and thought. Confused, hurt, enraged, he sat silently and felt every bit of it in all of its agonizing glory.

A knock resounded on his door. He turned sore eyes toward it. "Not now, Aunt Marie."

"It's me buddy, Roy."

"Uncle Roy? You can come in, I guess."

"Marie told me what happened."

"Did she make you come up here?"

"No, I wanted to come. See if you needed anything." Roy sat on the bed beside him. He lifted his hand as if to put it on Shane's shoulder but reconsidered.

"Thanks. I'm okay."

"Are you sure?"

Shane turned to him and gave him the once-over. An awkward silence hung between them. "Why would he do it, Uncle Roy? Why would Dad kill Mom?"

"I don't know."

"It can't be true." Shane looked at Roy again. He knew it had been a long time since he saw his father but his uncle looked a lot like him. Almost eerily so. Same hair color. Same cleft chin. He hadn't realized it before … but the more he stared …

"I know it seems unbelievable but I think it might be the only explanation. Your father vanished right after they found your mother. No one knows what happened to him. I don't want to believe it either buddy, but your Aunt Marie said you saw it in your dreams. Said you saw his face plain as day."

"I did." Shane lowered his voice. Something about Roy unsettled him suddenly. Discomfort washed through him. There were slight differences in his dad and Roy, but not much. Shane decided not to say any more. Gooseflesh rose on his arms. He looked away from his uncle. "I feel really tired. I think I just want to lie down and try to sleep."

"Okay, you call us if you need anything." Roy got off the bed and crossed the room to the door. He locked his hand around the knob and looked back at Shane. "Now maybe those nightmares of yours will finally stop." He smiled and pulled the door shut behind him.

"Doubt it," Shane said under his breath.

Shane dragged himself downstairs. He reached the bottom and saw his Aunt Marie chopping vegetables at the kitchen sink. The water drooled from the faucet in a steady stream into a colander. Shane scuffed through the hall and glided into the kitchen. He sidled up to her.

"Where's Uncle Roy?"

"I'm so forgetful. He ran to the store for me to get the main course for tonight's dinner."

Shane fidgeted. "Aunt Marie, why does Uncle Roy look so much like my father?"

"They're twins, honey. I never met your father but I've seen pictures of both of them together. Didn't you ever notice before?"

"Twins? I guess I didn't know what that meant before … I was too young. Uncle Roy never visited. I never really knew him. Back then he had a beard; he dressed differently in the pictures I saw. I never really saw them together."

"Wow, so you really have no real memories of Roy and your dad. Well, it's amazing how much they look alike with Roy's beard gone. I bet people could barely tell them apart. I wonder if their mother used to dress them alike?" Marie chuckled as she chopped.

The blade of her knife struck the cutting board again and again rhythmically. Shane placed his hands over his ears. She stopped, ceasing the sound. She stared at the knife, examined it as if the sound was something familiar to her.

She looked down at Shane and his eyes met hers. "What's this all about?"

"I don't know. I feel like something isn't right." He walked away from her and started back upstairs.

"Shane, wait."

Shane didn't respond. He just kept walking.

"Shane!"

Marie stopped at the top of the stairs and went no further. She saw him vanish into his bedroom and shut the door. She thought of following then reconsidered. She started back downstairs but stopped dead. Click-clack.

The sound halted her like an atomic bomb. Her gaze followed it to the attic door in the hall's ceiling. Click-clack. She walked the length of the hall and stopped beneath the door. Click-clack. Her hands trembled, although she didn't know why. She reached for the small cord dangling from the door and yanked with both hands.

The attic door came down and a set of stairs unfolded. Marie climbed into the attic and spotted the window across the room. The shutter was off its latch and the wind caught it. It banged off the side of the house and the window frame over and over. She headed for it immediately and tried to catch it.

Outside the horizon became gray, and a strange glow caught her attention. Marie gazed into the backyard. In its center the old opening to the yard's septic tank glowed. Marie latched the shutter and closed it tight. She climbed out of the attic and went to Shane's room. She peeked in and saw he was fast asleep.

She shut his door and slipped back down stairs. Forgetting the meal prep, she went out to the backyard and to the old septic tank. She bent to her knees and removed board after board until she reached a round metal cover. It was cold and heavy. She pried it open with all of her strength. A stink rose out of the earth. Marie winced but pushed on, placing her hand into the muck and waste. Her fingers brushed against something with an edge. She latched onto it and pulled.

In her hands she held the remains of a cleaver. Its handle was gone, only the blade remained, cracked and covered in rust. She gasped for air, heart slamming against her chest. She stared at the cleaver blade, speechless. Her world began to spin. The sky shifted and darkness fell over her. A sensation of falling enveloped her.

"AUNT MARIE, AUNT MARIE." SHANE SHOOK HER WITH BOTH HANDS. He stared at the cleaver on the ground, his terror growing.

Her eyes popped open. Her face was white. "Shane ..." Her voice was a whisper.

"He's coming," he said. "Roy's driving down the street. I can feel it."

"Say nothing," she told him. "I'll come get you tonight after he's asleep. Pretend like everything is the same. Oh God ... if he finds out. Dear God."

"Aunt Marie, you're shaking."

"I know, sweetie, I know." She dropped the cleaver back into the waste and hugged Shane tight.

They covered up the septic tank together and headed back into the house. Roy's car pulled into the driveway moments later.

In the dead of night Marie woke him. Relief washed over Shane when he opened his eyes. He felt as if he'd been waiting forever for her to come and get him. She put her finger to her lips. "We're leaving," she whispered. "We'll go to a hotel and in the morning we'll go to the police."

Shane hugged her and pushed his bedding away. He put on one of his jackets and took his aunt's hand. They headed for the door.

Roy appeared in the threshold. He drew his arm back and punched Marie across the chin. She went down hard. He shoved Shane out of the way and grabbed the writhing Marie by her hair. "Look at you two bonding. You both just had to keep nosing around. You just couldn't let the past be the past." He hit her head up against the bedroom wall and she went unconscious. "I'll deal with you later."

Shane made a run for it but Roy caught him with strong arms. He hauled his nephew up and took him downstairs.

Roy drove across town, Shane tied down in the back seat. "Your mother was going to tell your father. I told her it wasn't a good idea but she wouldn't listen. I loved her, ya know, but she was going to tell him about us, about her being pregnant with my kid. I told her I didn't want kids. Just like I've always told everyone. Why doesn't anyone listen? I never wanted kids, just like I didn't want you, Shane. I thought we'd get along fine, but now I see we can't. I didn't want to do this but what choice do I have now?"

Mom. The word flashed in Shane's head. *I'll see you soon.*

The car came to a stop and Shane looked up through the window. It was his old house. Roy shut off the car and got out. He opened the back door and ripped the boy from the car. "It's so sad, Shane," Roy said, carrying him to the front door. "Sad that you never got over your mother's murder. You were always so depressed, and when your Aunt Marie left us, you were so devastated, losing your only other mother figure, you returned to your old home and killed yourself."

Roy kicked in the front door. He dragged Shane, kicking and struggling, all the way to the top floor. The tape over his mouth was holding strong. Roy spotted the attic with its door open and its stairs down and headed toward it. "Makes it easy." He pulled Shane up to the attic room.

Shane felt the cold air hit his entire body the moment Roy pulled him in and threw him down on the floor. He tried and tried but couldn't wiggle out of the cords tied around him. He thought of his mother, of his Aunt Marie, and accepted what came next. It was all he could do. Hope slipped away. His spirit shattered. The only person in the world who was ever there for him wasn't even his own flesh and blood. He hoped to see his Aunt Marie in the other life.

"It didn't have to be this way, Shane. I wouldn't have touched a hair on your head. You weren't supposed to wake that night and you sure as hell weren't supposed to recognize me. You were so young, you barely knew me. She had to take you back here. I told her not to. You can blame Aunt Marie, Shane. And your damn father. If he hadn't come back from his business trip a day early I could have finished ... ah ... to hell with it all. Let's put this all to bed. Eh, Shane?"

When Shane saw Roy pull the cleaver from beneath his jacket he shut his eyes. He waited, winced, and tightened his muscles; waited for the end, but it didn't come. He heard a grunt suddenly and opened his eyes. He saw his uncle's twin put Roy in a chokehold and drag him away from Shane.

"Dad!" Shane cried as the twin brothers struggled. Shane's father easily overwhelmed Roy, having surprised him. Roy's face drained of all color, the shock and horror on his face was indescribable. Shane's father held Roy tightly, grimaced and pried the cleaver out of his hand. He brought it swiftly across Roy's throat and opened it wide. Crimson poured out of him until he twitched, trembled and went limp. Shane's father let Roy slump to the floor.

Shane lit up, his eyes widened. "Dad! Oh my God ... Dad. Where have you been?" His father came to his side and untied him. They hugged for as long as Shane could muster. "Dad, I've waited for you for so long."

"I love you Shane," his father said.

The sound of footsteps resounded downstairs. Shane turned his attention to someone climbing up the attic stairs. Seconds later, two police officers burst into the room.

"Freeze!" One of them called.

"It's okay," Shane said, "My Dad is—"

Shane looked around but there was no sign of his father.

"It's okay," the other officer said. "It's over." He went over to Shane. "We've been watching your uncle for years. We always suspected him."

Shane stared at the lifeless body of his uncle. He looked down at the cords that once bound him. "Dad ..." he murmured.

"It's okay son," the officer said. "You had to defend yourself. Let's get you to a hospital."

Shane curled the covers over him. He felt his Aunt Marie in the doorway, watching over him. He waited for her to close the door then he sat up. He smiled, thinking of his father. He knew he would finally sleep without the nightmare haunting him relentlessly. He was sure of it. He settled back down and closed his eyes.

Click-clack, click-clack. Shane bolted up. His eyes filled with tears. He threw the covers off his body and jumped out of bed. The bedroom door seemed hundreds of miles away, but he made his way to it anyway.

The hall looked surreal. The nightlight inside the bathroom flickered. He spotted the attic door and, unable to take his eyes off of it, made a straight line to it. Shane reached up and pulled the stairs down. Rung by rung he climbed, holding on to the banister with sweaty palms, his heart slammed inside his chest, both legs buckled. He reached the attic's threshold, poked his head through and peered in …

Cheryl Takes a Trip

Stephen Dorato

When she saw her body in the doorway to the bathroom, Cheryl Ziser knew the trip to Bermuda was off.

Her first reaction was not fear, or even confusion, but anger. She had always meant to go to Bermuda, damn it, had said she would be there by the time she was thirty-five. Really, it wasn't an amazing goal, not like mountain climbing or writing a symphony; Bermuda was only an hour's flight away. Her mother sent her specials clipped from the Sunday newspaper every few weeks, but for one reason or another, she never went.

I never had time, Cheryl thought.

She certainly didn't now.

Cheryl had finally called the ticket agency just two weeks ago (it seemed so *easy*, she couldn't believe she'd put it off for so long), and the tickets had come the following Friday, in the mailbox sandwiched between *Cosmopolitan* and *TV Guide*.

She could see the tickets now, in her line of sight only a few degrees from where her body lay, still in the very center of her kitchen table. It was much easier to look at them. They rested there, where they had been since the moment she opened the envelope, the focus of microwave dinners and Special K breakfasts. She remembered being careful not to set her teacup on top of them. Remembered leafing through the different slips, reading departure and arrival times and baggage claim stubs, until she had memorized everything.

Saturday, 9:45 a.m. departure. Just four days away.

And now, seeing herself on the floor, motionless and empty the way Cheryl *knew* death looked, she felt sick and more than a little confused. What had she been doing, just a minute ago, just before she saw the body? She couldn't remember.

When she reached out to touch the body, her hand met no resistance; she felt only a slight queasy feeling that vanished as soon as she took her hand away. The floor, however, was solid enough when she touched it.

She did not consider that this was a trick for a moment. She was dead. At least it had been painless—she assumed, since she could not remember having died.

What had happened? She remembered coming home from work, having supper—after that, nothing. Cheryl wore her usual Tuesday work clothes, but the body on the floor was naked and gleamed wetly, fresh from the bath. She could see the steam rise from its skin, but could feel no heat.

She didn't want to look at the body anymore.

"Oh God," she said, just to hear herself. Her voice was shaky but real. "What now?"

I'm dead, she thought. What do I do now?

IN THE MORNING, CHERYL KNEW NO MORE ABOUT *WHAT TO DO*. When nothing happened—no trumpets sounded from heaven, no demons from Hell came to collect her—she knew she had to leave the apartment. Even that was a trial; it took the better part of an hour just to force herself to walk through the door.

This is just an experiment, she told herself. I can always go back.

Cheryl spent the day walking through town, making her experiments. She spoke to strangers—sometimes screamed at them, hammered at them with fists that made no contact—and was unseen. She took an elevator (apparently substantial enough to lift her) to a restaurant at the top of the Prudential Center, where she sat with people as they ate their lunches and dinners, listening to their conversations and making bold, incisive observations on their shortcomings. None were heard. She entered a Catholic church in the morning, after wandering the streets of Boston the entire night, and sat in a pew waiting for a priest, a parishioner—for God—to notice her.

Nothing.

At the end of the second day she stepped off the platform at Boylston Station, into the path of an oncoming train, just to make something *happen*—but the train passed right through her. The sensation was not a pleasant one.

The apartment seemed unchanged, each time she returned; the body

CHERYL TAKES A TRIP

still lay in the bathroom doorway. The answering machine blinked with messages she could never play back.

Being invisible was frustrating, but being alone was much worse. Cheryl spent more and more time in the city.

Finally she went to see her mother—a long walk that took her most of her third day.

When she stepped through the door, her mother was on the phone, talking to the shrill next-door neighbor who was her mother's best friend whenever there was no one else to talk to. She could talk to anybody at all for hours at a stretch, even an answering machine: active participation was not required.

"And I tell her, Cheryl, you should *go*. Last month I even gave her fifty dollars toward it, she still doesn't go. Like she doesn't have enough—a hundred weeks of sick time built up!"

She felt two things, then: the familiarity of the scene, her mother's voice, this kitchen, the grain of this table; and utterly wrong, knowing she could never again sit at this table.

Go.

The word burned in her mind. Why not? She might be dead, but she could still feel the air, the warm sunlight, the ground under her feet.

She walked the dark streets for hours, glad to be finally safe here, when she realized she had to go. Back home, she reread the tickets—she could not touch them, only read the flight number and departure time on the outside of the packet—and found she still remembered everything.

Saturday.

She spent the rest of the night watching the clock on top of the Expo Center, waiting for the right time to come. It was just after eight now.

Tomorrow, in just over twelve hours, the plane would leave.

And Cheryl would be on it.

CHERYL HAD NO PROBLEM GETTING ON BOARD. BY THIS TIME her invisibility was old hat; she walked unnoticed past the security guards, through the metal detector, and onto the plane (where she was forced to step *through* the people in front of her, who would otherwise never have moved out of her way).

Her seat was on the wing—Cheryl had never flown before and had been so excited to get a window seat—but five minutes before takeoff some kid took the seat, sitting right on top of Cheryl. Her whole body tingled sickeningly and she moved to the seat beside him. She wished for some more substantial ghostly power, but none came.

At least the little brat was quiet as the plane took off. Cheryl leaned over him to look, feeling a tingling in her stomach: ghost butterflies. I'm *going*, she thought.

The flight took no time at all. Cheryl watched while others got their in-flight snack and complimentary beverage. At least she didn't need to use the bathroom. Soon they were descending, and though she was nervous, Cheryl felt none of the sensations the other passengers felt. Overall, the trip had been incredibly dull.

As they landed, Cheryl got to her feet and walked to the front of the plane. She still had to pass through more than one person, but then she was out and walking through the terminal—smaller, but much like the one at Logan Airport.

Standing at the edge of the runway, looking out at the clear water, the first thing she felt was loneliness. It made sense, she knew, but she had not thought about it till now.

She knew why she had never come to Bermuda. An obvious reason, one she'd hidden from herself for too many years.

Because she had never had anyone she wanted to go *with*.

You didn't go to a romantic island alone. That was pathetic. You went with a lover, a fiancé, a husband. Cheryl had nobody.

She sat on the tarmac, listening to the planes, for a long time.

"Well, hello there," a voice said behind her.

At first she ignored it—but turned around when she realized there was no shadow beside her.

He was older than she'd expected by his voice, maybe early forties, but solid and strong, with thick dark hair and an incredibly amused expression.

An angel?

"Hiya," he said. "How about I show you the island?"

FOR THE FIRST TWO HOURS, HE SMILED AND REFUSED TO ANSWER her questions whenever she asked. "There's plenty of time for that. See the sparkle of sunlight on the water? See that school of fish?" Cheryl found it nearly impossible to concentrate on what he was showing her: water, sand, fish, big deal. She wanted to talk. The heat did not touch her, thankfully, since she was still—and might always be—dressed in her Tuesday clothes.

Cheryl Takes A Trip

Once or twice, Eddie (at least he'd told her his name) pointed out some of the Walking Dead. He said, smiling when he said it, "They're just people, like us. Only they've been around so long, they're kind of *past* talking."

"How long?"

"Got me," Eddie said. "People been here fifty, a hundred years, they'll still talk to me. Not the Dead, though."

Only one of the Dead reacted at all to them: a woman with a young face and long, white hair. Her eyes, gray and clear, looked right through Cheryl—then focused on her for an instant. The woman nodded, and Cheryl nodded back.

Eddie kept walking.

"Wait. I want to ask her something."

"Cheryl," he said, serious for once, "that Dead, she won't talk to you. She won't. They nod, they smile. But I spent weeks just trying to get one of them to talk. They won't."

She agreed, angry. Absurdly, she thought of her mother, two hundred miles away. Would they ever be able to speak again? Or perhaps by the time their paths crossed, years from now, Cheryl would have changed into one of the Dead—earlier than the rest. A zombie prodigy. Did the Dead care that they were dead?

Tension bloomed in her chest, and Cheryl pressed her hands to her heart. She felt nothing at all.

Great, she thought. I'm one of the Neurotic Dead. Original.

"Look at the flying fish," Eddie suggested.

NONE OF THE SUNBATHERS NOTICED AS THEY STEPPED SOUNDLESSLY across blankets, leaving tracks which existed only in Cheryl's mind.

"I want to show you something," Eddie said coyly. When he pulled her into the water, Cheryl resisted. "We have to go under for this. It's okay." She let him guide her. It was strange underwater, feeling a phantom of pressure but nothing real. After a moment, Cheryl relaxed. There was no need to breathe. They walked across the bottom of the ocean, over rough coral. Schools of fish swam by, through Cheryl; the fish did not sense the ghosts among them.

Finally they came up into Eddie's treasure: a secret place, he called it. An underwater cavern, edged by rows of razor-sharp pink coral teeth set too close for a diver to enter. The cavern was nestled under the side of the coast, too hidden and too mundane for much exploring.

"This is my place. I've never taken anybody else here."

She smiled, and they sat in silence. Every time she closed her eyes she saw the Dead woman.

"Talk to me, Eddie. I've been with you all afternoon, and I don't know anything about you."

Eddie shrugged. "Does it matter so much? Now?"

"Yes. Say it anyway."

"Okay. I—my wife and I were on our honeymoon—my second honeymoon, my second marriage. My first ... well, I'll tell you about it sometime." He laughed. Nervously. "This was, oh, seven years or so ago."

"Anyway, I'm having a great time but my chest keeps bothering me. My wife tells me it's indigestion. Two hours later I feel my arm go numb, have a heart attack, *wham*, right in bed next to her. I sure showed her. Two days later she flies off with the body, leaves me stranded. That's the last time I see her. She's probably with someone else now."

"No—"

"We're *dead*, it doesn't matter. I hope she's with somebody else."

"Did you ever try to leave? To see her again?"

"No. I never figured I could, really. Certain things—like floors, the ground, we have this understanding. I don't pass through them. I don't know why. Other things, people, cars, moving things, it doesn't work that way. I figured I'd be sitting on the runway, and the plane would take off without me."

"Good thing it works. You'd never have met me."

"I knew you were different. Never saw anybody sit on a runway before."

"Oh, I always do that." Seven years. Cheryl thought of those three days walking through Boston. "You must be lonely."

Eddie just shrugged.

"Is there a God, Eddie?"

He shrugged. "I've been here seven years. The only thing I can say is: Got me, kiddo. If there is, I haven't seen him."

That night, as they lay in the darkness of the beach, listening to the ocean, Cheryl thought she heard a sound—the snarl of some wild animal in the surf. She sat up and listened, and the sound grew, seemed to come from everywhere around her. They were alone, but it didn't help. Cheryl huddled close to Eddie, feeling cold and afraid, knowing there was nothing that could really cover her, not really sure what she was afraid of.

Cheryl Takes A Trip

For a while, Cheryl was able to make herself forget the dream—if that's what it was—and to pretend this was just a vacation. It didn't last long. As they walked, cars and pedestrians pushing right through them, it felt wrong.

"Check this out," Eddie said. "Roses."

He pointed to an entire courtyard full of roses. Cheryl smiled, but it made her sad. Roses like the ones outside her apartment window, the ones that bloomed every year even though she never tended them.

"Eddie, where are all the people?"

"Who?" he asked, confused.

"All the dead people." Cheryl automatically reached out to touch one of the flowers, but her hand passed through it; with that queasy sensation, she felt a memory of her apartment. Her body, which she had left in that apartment. They'd have found the body by now.

"People die every day. And the Dead don't go away; they stay just the way they are, year after year. There should be hundreds—*thousands*—of dead people here."

"Crowd control?"

"No jokes. Really."

"I don't know."

Maybe there is a God, Cheryl thought. And maybe this is Hell. The really good people go to heaven, and the dull, pathetic people—like me and Eddie and the Dead—just get forgotten.

It seemed too cruel to think about.

She walked into the middle of the street, wanting someone to shout or honk at her; watched as cars passed through her. She looked through the crowd for someone who looked back, who noticed her.

Eddie followed.

"Go away, Eddie," she said, not sure why. His touch on her shoulder made her uneasy. "I need to be alone," she told him, and turned away.

When she looked back, he was gone.

A week later—Eddie still gone—Cheryl spotted the white-haired Dead woman.

"Talk to me," she said.

Nothing. The woman didn't break stride. Cheryl walked beside her a long time, repeating herself, before the woman would even stop. Finally

213

she grabbed the woman's arm and looked into her eyes.

"Why do you want me to talk to you?"

The sound of the woman's voice took her by surprise, deeper than she expected but somehow familiar. Like an older, wearier echo of Cheryl's voice.

"Where are all the people? All the dead people?"

That was all she could say. At first, no response, as Cheryl looked into those eyes, waiting for some shift or understanding.

"There's no one else here."

Cheryl shook her head. "You're here. Eddie's here. Where are the rest?"

"No one."

"Don't you know Eddie?"

"No," she said. "I know only you." And then she was gone, back inside that dead empty place in her eyes.

Weeks passed. Cheryl was alone. The few times she went there, Eddie's secret place was empty. It was hard to believe that anybody—even a ghost—had ever been here.

We never touch anything, she thought.

Once, as she watched the planes lift off from the airport, she considered leaving Bermuda. Where else could she go? Florida, Chicago, certainly. Germany, England, Russia?

Could she go back home?

Suddenly she felt as if she had been here a hundred years, that there was no place *but* Bermuda anymore. These planes went nowhere; beyond that horizon was nothing at all.

Where did she want to go?

Heaven, Cheryl thought. Or Hell. Just someplace.

That night she dreamed.

She had not thought it possible to dream, especially since she did not sleep—at least, she had no need of sleep. Sometimes she seemed to go somewhere else, somewhere inside herself, to not-be for a while. It should have frightened her, but didn't. Staring out at the waves at low tide, mounted one on top of another like tiny stairs, she drifted off, if not into sleep, at least into something like it, that place of no-thought.

She lay on the bathroom floor, the cold tile against her back, the hard ridge of the doorway against her spine. She could not move, only stare straight ahead, up at the ceiling. She was embarrassed that anyone should find her like this—

The tickets were on the table, twenty feet away; beside them was a tourists' brochure she'd leafed through a hundred times, and again that same night. She remembered the phrases telling of hidden groves and pink-sand beaches. She knew every word. She felt as if her soul were made up of those words. Her mind was ink, thick and black.

She heard the growl again, only this time it wasn't an animal; it was a chanting inside her chest, her head. *Little Cheryl, pathetic Cheryl, too terrible to go to Bermuda.* She didn't deserve to go. Little nothing woman, not worth talking to, certainly not worth loving, not worth *anything*, even her mother's voice seemed to hold some secret coil of contempt and weariness for her. Had she just imagined it? No, she had even seen it in the eyes of strangers. And what would Bermuda be? A place with tanned, paired strangers, all ignoring Cheryl as she had let the whole world ignore her, and—

For a moment, in the dream, she remembered dying. Just for a moment.

AND THEN SHE WAS BACK ON THE BEACH, WIDE-EYED, SEEING THE ocean, birds chase each other across the surf. There were no people here now.

Except Eddie. Eddie, who knew so little, but he was there, standing in front of her.

She needed him.

"You're here—thank God," she said, still not sure if there was a God.

"You have to go back."

"No."

Eddie nodded, smiled. It was suddenly hard to look at him. And then, just as sudden, he wasn't there anymore. "I'm not here," he said.

"What do you mean you're not here?"

No—her own voice, her own thoughts: I mean, *I'm* not here.
Her voice.

I'm not here, Cheryl thought. Where am I?

Hell, maybe. Heaven. Nowhere.

A clear realization, then, an image of herself as the Dead woman, those empty eyes her own.

Suddenly the beach—the hell, heaven, the nowhere—was gone.

STILL IN DARKNESS, YEARS, HOURS, AN INSTANT LATER—THINKING:
In the bathtub.

Where it had happened.

Where she had killed herself.

She remembered it now. The ceiling had been the last thing she saw: the ceiling, the television, her shallow breathing, the rich sweet smell from the water.

What she had done to herself, in the bathroom, was something she couldn't face even now. Ridiculous, now that she was dead, wasn't it? It didn't even *matter* now—but all that she could think of was the bath water, the mess. It had taken an incredibly long time, longer than the books made it seem.

Just before she had passed out, she had thought of the tickets, of her mother—thought *God no, I don't really want to die.* She had gotten out of the tub. Even doing that had taken a long time, too long, too much effort. Just to make it to the doorway, where the shock of the cold from an open window knocked her down.

I should have stayed in the tub, she thought, I just made more of a mess.

She sat there now, a pathetic monstrosity surrounded by her own lifeblood and cold water she couldn't feel, and knew she would never go to Bermuda, never be anywhere but right here, in the cold dark nowhere forever.

Bermuda came back to Cheryl, a ripple. She saw it all with the clarity of a photograph. That field of roses: the roses outside her window multiplied. Eddie: bits of her father and other men she'd known. None of it real.

Only real in Cheryl's world, the world she had created for herself a moment after her death, or in that last moment of life. A Bermuda shaped from pamphlets, dreams, bits of her apartment.

She would cry, if she had the strength to move—

Open your eyes.

It was her voice, but firm and patient, like calm instinct. She almost refused, afraid, but then her eyes were open—and it was not the same as before.

Color. The same dull apartment she had lived in for years, flooded with light from the window—even though she still saw a crescent of moon, knew it was nighttime, saw the darkness.

She got to her feet with a single step, effortlessly, and when she opened her mouth to speak, a sound–not like words really, more like a note–escaped.

Go out there.

Cheryl Takes A Trip

Her voice, again. Not English, not even a sentence, but a single clear note which carried that meaning inside.

As she passed the table, she glanced down at the tickets which meant nothing now, the letters all gibberish. Then she looked down at herself and saw that she was something different too. Not human, not anymore. Her legs, clusters of light and black filament, did not touch the floor.

She heard another note, far away, a call that she didn't understand, confused her. The fear came back, just for an instant. And then that new reflex inside her took over, that new certainty, and she answered it, and with the answering moved herself out of the apartment, halfway across the world to answer the note, leaving the ghost of fear like something it was, a residue of death and life.

And felt herself, like a grain of sand on a beach, a drop of water in an ocean, surrounded by the others.

Legend of the Wormley Farms

Philip Roberts

In the midst of summer, when the fiery sun turned the sky crimson at dusk and the insects began their songs, Clifford Firth often ended his days on the porch staring out across the vast, dark plains with his two brothers and father by his side. Muscles sore from hours working the land in the heat, they sat in silence, drinking cool water, and letting their bodies rest.

But in the worst of the heat, Clifford, just short of seventeen, couldn't help but turn to his father and ask him again about the Wormley farms.

Butted up against their farm, the old Wormley land hadn't seen use in fourteen years. It was still owned, they presumed, by someone in the family, but no one bothered to come out and make use of it, or sell it off to those who wanted to.

Clifford always thought the story itself mattered less than the way his father told it. Spoken with a slow, matter-of-fact sounding drawl, his father told how Zackary Wormley had lost large patches of crops three years in a row to animals and severe weather, until his financial situation grew so severe he took his wife and five children down to the pond near his home and drowned them all. Used a rock to weigh himself down and join them.

Only one of the children managed to survive. Seeing his father strike his siblings, the young boy had hidden beneath the house, seen his father drag the bodies away, and sat tight for forty-eight hours. Legend had it that for ten hours straight the father had searched for his boy, and the child had watched those boots moving around the house over and over again. Anyone who did set foot on the Wormley land, or worse yet, approached the house, was mistaken by the ghost of Zackary as the lost son, and Zackary would drag them to the dried-up pond and force them to join the rest of the family.

The elder Firth told the story that night as he'd done so many times before, the sun all but set and the horizon a glowing line when the tale ended. Clifford watched the darkening plains with honest fear, imagining Zackary's ghost forever walking through the dilapidated remains of his home, across dead grass and parched dirt toward the still-moist remains of the pond his family had died in.

Alex, the oldest of the sons, snorted, shook his head at the end of the story. "All true," his father said, eyeing the boy.

Clifford watched his much taller, lanky brother pull himself up and stop by the front door. "No it ain't true, least not the ghosts," he said, eyes narrowed, shaggy hair all but falling across them. "Nothing out there but the same damn land and people working it as there has been for years, and you know it."

He slammed the screen door behind him, left Clifford and Allen alone with their father. Both looked to their father, eyeing his frown and narrowed eyes. Alex's outburst had nothing to do with ghosts or the Wormley farm.

"He'll come around," their father whispered.

THEIR MOTHER HAD DIED TWO YEARS PRIOR FROM A SNAKEBITE they hadn't taken seriously enough until things had gone too far. Alex had always stuck closer to his mother than his father, the man quick to knock down any dreams his son had of breaking free from the farm. Their mother, however, had fed Alex a constant stream of books detailing grand and faraway places, confided to him, who had confided to Clifford and Allen, their mother's dream of seeing those places in person one day.

When she died, and after their father buried her on the far end of the backyard, Alex had spent the night crying, something Clifford had never witnessed before. "Now she'll never get away," he told his brothers beneath the black sky and sparkling stars. "She lived and died without ever breaking free."

All three brothers shared the same large attic in the house, and when the sun departed completely their father told them to go up and get some real rest. On some nights a few of the neighboring farmers drove around, had drinks or played poker, but on that night Clifford left his father alone on the porch sipping a beer and watching the land.

The attic was dark, Alex already asleep when the two boys took off their clothes and climbed into bed. Through an open window Clifford watched the bright moon, shivered once more at the idea of ghostly Zackary watching mournfully over his land, still fueled by whatever had led him to take so many lives.

Clifford had always wanted to read the same books their mother had given to Alex, but after his brother's work declined as his interest in the fiction rose, their father had made sure his other sons only learned to read just enough to get their work done.

Distracted by the bright moon, he almost didn't hear the movement, head jerking toward the right, almost seeing a malevolent being leaning down over him, and before he could scream strong fingers clasped over his mouth.

Alex leaned in closer, eyes narrowed as he whispered, "Now you better not say a word or do a thing, you understand? I'm going over to that farm. Ain't nothing to it, and I'm going to bring back a rock from the pond just to show Dad it's all a pack of lies. If he comes looking for me, and I find out you squealed, I'll get you good for it later. Got that?"

Clifford nodded and Alex brought his hand back. He went for the open window, the drop short and easy to make, but before he ducked out Clifford sat up and called out as quietly as he could, "Be careful."

Alex paused halfway out the window, and Clifford didn't know what he saw in his brother's eyes, but he thought it looked sad and kind of lonely. "I'll be fine," Alex said, and vanished. Deep down, something in Clifford told him this had nothing to do with Zackary. He wasn't ever going to see his brother again.

ALLEN HAD ALWAYS BEEN THEIR FATHER'S FAVORITE. HE DIDN'T outwardly express it, but both Clifford and Alex knew it all the same. Allen was just too much like their father, content doing the same things, working the same land, and never bothering himself with anything beyond it. Even in appearance he more closely resembled their thickly built, shaggy-haired father, the same bushy brown eyebrows developing more and more on Allen with each passing year.

He listened to the tales of the Wormley farm with only passing interest, certainly bored with it long before Clifford could ever be. Had Allen seen his brother leave through the window, he would've gone right down to tell their father, not to get Alex in trouble, but to let the old man know they'd be short a worker the next day.

Allen woke first, as he always did, and informed their dad about Alex.

"You know anything about this?" their father asked when Clifford came down to breakfast.

Clifford nodded and lowered his head. "Saw him leave last night. Said he was going out to the Wormley farm."

Their father looked past Clifford toward the open front door and the flat plains beyond it. "That all he said?"

"Yup. Said he wanted to bring back a rock from the pond. He hasn't come back?"

Their father pushed back from the table and grabbed his hat by the front door. "No. I'm going out there to look for him. You two stay here. Allen, you know what work needs to be done today. Shouldn't take more than two hours or so to drive there and back. I'll expect to see some progress."

"You got it," Allen said.

Clifford stood by the front door and watched his father get into his rusted truck and start up the engine. He kicked up a spray of dust as he drove away from the house.

"Better get something to eat," Allen called over. "Ain't a day off."

By noon the sun had seared away what few clouds lingered in the early morning and Clifford stood up among the rows of crops to wipe away the sweat and return to the house for lunch. Lost in his labor, part of him had honestly forgotten about Alex and their father, and he was surprised to see only Allen sitting at the kitchen table.

"Dad hasn't come back yet," Allen said, a hint of fear behind his attempt at acting like an adult. Clifford took up a seat across from him, silent. "Must've had trouble finding Alex," he added, looking down, another thought clear in his face.

Maybe there was a hint of truth to the Wormley legends, that downturned face said. Allen no longer looked like a man, but a boy given more authority than he could handle.

"What should we do?" Clifford asked, saw his brother fidget.

"We keep working. Dad'll be annoyed if he gets back and we wasted the day worrying about him. Sure he'll be back by dinner."

Clifford nodded and got up to make his own lunch. He avoided looking through the windows as he did.

Both boys sat on the porch at dusk, staring into the distance, waiting to see the glare of headlights on the horizon. Instead they listened to the insects.

They went up to their beds in silence. Normally they didn't bother locking much, but that night they closed everything. They suffered in the muggy, sealed attic, blankets pulled up and faces glistening. Each creak made them jump, and when Clifford did drift off, he walked across the parched ground toward a large house in the distance.

Allen woke him shortly after six in the morning, already dressed, eyes red from lack of sleep. "I'm walking to the Wormley farm," he said.

They grabbed some day-old bread from the cabinet, some bottles full of cool water, and set off with the rising sun to their backs.

They walked for well over two hours, some times running a bit, others slowing when their legs refused to go any faster. Twice they paused to drink, eat, and rest, but never for long. Fear twisted Clifford's stomach in a knot, made worse when the house really did appear before them, a few tall, healthy trees growing by its side, making the building look small in comparison.

It didn't appear as it did in Clifford's dreams. The roof was caved in, windows busted out, porch swing only attached by a single rusted chain, and shingles scattered about the dirt lawn.

The boys stopped in front of the structure. Allen pointed to the side of the building and they hurried up to their father's truck. "Tires are flat," Allen said.

Near the far side of the truck the land sloped downward, and Clifford saw the remnants of a pond at the base of it, only a bit of water blackening the mud in the middle of what had surely once been a much larger collection of water. He began to look away, wanting to look away, when something else caught his attention; he saw colors floating amid the murky water.

He pointed but couldn't speak. He could only hear the crunch of Allen's boots as he started down the incline toward the water that looked about waist deep, maybe twenty feet wide at most. Clifford knew what his brother would find, the outline clearer with every second, and he thought Allen must've known as well.

He saw his brother fall to his knees at the edge of the water. "Who is it?" Clifford called out, started moving closer.

Allen glanced back at him and immediately got to his feet. He hurried up the dirt, eyes glistening. "Don't go down and look," he said. "Won't do you any good."

"Is it just Dad?" Clifford whispered.

Allen nodded and lowered his head. "Looks like someone got him in the head bad."

"Where's Alex?"

Allen looked around, lingering on the truck. He stepped up to the driver's side door, closer to the house, and looked in. "Keys are in here," he said. "Whatever got Dad likely got Alex, and I don't care to find out what. We need to get out of here and report this."

Clifford nodded and ran toward the car, but he froze at the movement in the dark, open front door of the building. A man burst from the front door, something long and shining held above his head. Allen had no chance to turn toward him, too close to the building, body halfway in the truck when the axe came down across the back of his head and jolted his body forward. Clifford saw the red-tipped blade rise again, Allen's convulsing face briefly visible through the passenger side window.

Clifford turned and ran. He ran past the pond and across the open plains. He heard a shout behind him but he didn't stop or look back. He ran with the image of Zackary Wormley chasing after him.

JUDGING FROM THE SUN'S DESCENT, CLIFFORD FIGURED IT TO BE close to six. He saw the farmhouse in the distance where his family had died just as the Wormley family had. His initial flight had taken him farther away from his real home, rather than closer, and he honestly didn't think he had the strength to travel around the farm to get back. Lightheaded from exhaustion and dehydration, his face bright red, Clifford knew he needed the truck if he wanted to get anywhere or find help.

He stumbled more than walked past the pond; saw Allen's body with his father's, floating in the bloody water. As he approached the truck he hunched low, did his best to use the truck to hide him from the house. He inched his head up to see inside it, the keys gone, trapping him.

The sound of soft movement made him jerk downward, but there wasn't any urgency to the sound, and he inched his way around the front of the truck until he could see the home's front porch, and Alex sitting on the steps.

His brother had the axe lying across his knees, staring at the plains, fingers drumming on the blade's handle. Clifford emerged from his hiding place and approached his older brother with a smile. "You got him didn't you?" he asked.

The dead eyes that Alex brought up to stare at Clifford told him otherwise. "No one to get," Alex said.

"You killed them?"

Alex nodded, returned his gaze to the open plains. "I realized it didn't really matter where I went. I wasn't going to any of those places Mom dreamed about. Farm barely makes enough money as it is, and I don't have the education to do much else. Besides, figured Dad would come for me, get me back if only out of spite. He used to complain I took after our Mom too much, but no, problem was always I took after him in all the wrong ways."

He pulled himself up; let the axe's blade strike the dirt. "But why this?" Clifford asked.

Alex smiled at him. "Because of you," he said. "You and your belief in this place. Was never about just leaving the farm, going to places, it was about being something different, outside of everyday living. Dad just couldn't understand it. But each time I saw that look in your eyes when he told the story, one even he didn't really understand the importance of, I saw you escaping in a way I never could."

He moved past Clifford, past the car, and stood at the edge of the pond, and something about the way he moved bothered Clifford, no hint of his brother's normal walk, somehow more rigid and upright. Alex threw the axe at the base of the water. When he turned back to Clifford he had a small pistol in his hand, one their father had taught them all to use in case trouble did come along. Though he smiled with the same face Clifford had seen since childhood, the lips curled in a different way, an aged quality to the expression beyond Alex's years of life.

"Took it the night I left," Alex said. "Got to finish things."

"Are you going to kill me?" Clifford asked.

Alex shook his head. He pulled out the keys from his pocket and threw them toward Clifford. "Mom mostly gave me adventure stories, but I read a book once on haunted places, scared me badly, especially when Dad went on about Zackary. One thing it said, and I don't know if it was true or not, but the worst haunting and the best legends are when a lot of people die. Ain't just Dad talking about this farm, you know. He never took you into town much, but I joined him, and I heard the other kids repeating the same tale. What will they say when another family dies here? How much further will the legend grow? Each time a boy like you looks out across those plains and shivers at the thought of this place, they won't be captured by reality, and I will have helped give them that. Of course, for that a person needs to live to tell the tale, someone like you. Zackary realized that as well."

Clifford swore he saw a glow in Alex's eyes, another face lurking below the surface, but with the setting sun shining on them, it might've been a trick of the light. Alex couldn't have done these crimes, no matter how much he'd hated their father's control; Clifford had known his brother well.

"He took you, didn't he?" Clifford whispered. "You took my brother's body."

The smile split much wider on Alex's face. "That's good," he said. "That's very good."

"Please, don't," Clifford began, but Alex brought the gun to his temple before the younger son could finish. Clifford closed his eyes from the grisly scene, kept them closed as he heard the body tumble down the dirt pond and come to a halt near the axe. Only then did Clifford step up to the edge and stare down at his family.

The Church of Thunder and Lightning

Peter N. Dudar

"You haven't told me where we're going yet," Tony announced.

His big, hairy fingers clutched the van's steering wheel as tightly as possible as he drove, all the while trying not to take his eyes off the road. The rain was coming down in torrents now, and he no longer felt sure that he could keep the WRVT news van in control on these back roads out here in East Jerkwater, Nowhere. The van was a clunky old dinosaur, with its telescoping antenna that always threatened to topple the vehicle over on its side whenever it was extended. Tony always seemed to get stuck with it on remote tapings because, well, he'd been with the station way back when it was first purchased and was one of the few people who actually knew had to handle driving it. It was bad enough that the station wouldn't let him drive one of the newer vehicles, the SUVs with the pre-installed navigation units and the four-wheel drive, but having the little blonde tart with no credentials and big ambitions of one day becoming the lead anchor on the evening news giving him directions on the fly, well, that was just ridiculous.

Lindsey sighed and shoved the map she had unfolded on her lap onto the center console.

"I've already told you," she snapped at him, her thick-lens glasses sliding down her nose so that her eyes glowered over the rims. "This is part of the 'Strange Religions' special I'm working on."

Tony's eyes shifted briefly over to the passenger side of the van, sizing her up, then he rolled his eyes as he turned his gaze back to the road.

"I hope this ain't gonna be like them crazy fuckers down in Moultrie… You know, the ones that was shaking them goddamn rattlesnakes with their bare hands." Tony rolled his eyes again, and a hint of perspiration forming above his bushy black eyebrows glistened in the dim light of his dashboard panel.

Outside the window, a flash of lightning lit up the coal-black sky.

"Just keep your eyes on the road, okay?" Lindsey pushed her glasses back up her nose and brushed a lock of curly blond hair out of her face. "And try not to breathe so hard. You're fogging up the windows."

Jesus, she was a pain in the ass. She'd only been at the station for a few years, immediately jumping from college intern to on-screen reporter in the blink of her long, lovely eyelashes. There was speculation among the boys back at the station that she was blowing her way up through the ranks (with tongue planted firmly in cheek), but it wasn't like Tony to pay attention to petty gossip. The fact that she was eye candy was trumped by the fact that she was very good at the business, and would have rocketed up the corporate ladder anyway. And here she was, calling the shots like she owned him when he was old enough to be her father, and probably had worked for the station longer than she'd been alive.

Tony's hairy right hand left the wheel and switched on the defroster. Lindsey pulled the map over and began examining it for the umpteenth time.

"The rattlesnake people are small potatoes compared to these people," she confided. "These people *want* to die. They want to be touched by the Finger of God."

"Sounds crazy enough to me. Do I want to know how you found out about them?"

Lindsey glanced up again, and her glasses once again began to slide down her pert little nose.

"A good journalist never reveals her sources."

Lindsey reached into her purse, pulled out a small compact, and began applying makeup. Tony risked a glance at her, his eyes wide with incredulity.

"Finger of God? What does that mean?"

"You'll see ..." she said, now rubbing dark crimson lipstick across her bottom lip. Outside, lightning flashed, followed seconds later by the low rumble of thunder.

"Don't see why you're putting makeup on," Tony said shaking his head. "It ain't gonna last once you set foot out there in this rain." His hands had doubled their grip on the steering wheel. "How far we got until I turn off this road?"

"At least another five miles," she answered, putting her compact away and examining the map yet again. "Just keep looking for a sign that reads

'Crawford.' That's where we're heading." She threw an annoyed glance at him. "And for your information, I have an umbrella to keep me dry."

"These idiots really want to die?" Tony took one hand off the wheel and ran it through his greasy black hair, as if the thought gave him a headache. "Jeezum Crow, Lindsey, you'll never get that past the censors if we catch one of 'em dying on tape. You know that, right?"

"Oh, would you just relax? They aren't going to die. More than anything, they're just trying to prove their fanatical devotion to God. We're just going to interview a few people, and video some of their ceremony, and then we'll be on our way."

"But you said …"

"But nothing!" She sighed heartily. "There's the sign right up ahead. See it? It says to turn right onto route number 127."

Tony made the turn gingerly, then accelerated slowly up the road, eyeing the homes on either side of the street. The two sat in silence for a few moments as the van rocked and splashed its way into the storm. When the silence began to grow uncomfortable, Lindsey turned to him and spoke.

"Have you ever seen someone die?"

"I've seen a lot of people die."

"Anyone close to you?"

Tony sighed and watched as his breath steamed up the windshield. He took his hand off the wheel and wiped the fogged glass until it was clean again.

"My wife Renee passed away eight years ago."

Lindsey felt her cheeks grow flush. "Oh, I'm so sorry. I didn't know you were ever married."

"It's okay. She passed from breast cancer. I held her hand when she slipped away. She was on enough morphine that she never felt a thing. It was a good death, especially after all the pain she went through. She didn't struggle or anything. She just stopped breathing, and …"

He glanced at her and took a moment to run his hand through his hair. He couldn't decide whether she really gave a damn or not, or if she was just in journalist mode, conducting some kind of facetious little interview with him just to pass the time. He gave her the benefit of the doubt.

"It wasn't like it is in the movies or anything, if that's what you think you're going to see," he said. "Her soul didn't come out of her mouth and float off toward the heavens or anything. No angels hovering over her bed waiting for her. Renee was alive one moment, and then she was gone. She

The Church of Thunder and Lightning

shit and pissed all over her deathbed. The nurses call it 'voiding,' as if that somehow gave her back her dignity or something."

Tony paused for a moment, and Lindsey could tell by the quiver in his voice that he was close to tears. She waited for him to speak again.

"If these idiots really, actually, honest-to-goodness want to drop dead, then chances are it's going to be violent and terrible. I'm not sure why you're so excited to see it, but I can guarantee you it won't be like you think it's going to be. I'm not sure if it's just a morbid curiosity for you, or if you just think this is a 'neat' story to cut your teeth on as a journalist ..."

"Nobody's going to die!" she repeated. "These are just a bunch of religious kooks. People love hearing about shit like this. It makes their own lives somehow seem normal. It's a compelling story. No different than that Jim Jones guy ... you know, the jerk that got his worshippers to drink the poisoned Kool-Aid?"

"Or David Koresh, or those bozos who were waiting for the comet's trail. Yeah, I get it. You're a bright girl, Lin ... It just seems like you should have more class than this."

Lindsey smiled. "You've been in this business long enough. You should know that if you want to get ahead, you've gotta give the people what they want."

"Even if what they want is to watch people die in the name of their God ..."

The town of Crawford looked like some sort of lonesome afterthought, carelessly dropped into an isolated valley miles from nowhere. Tony drove the van past a sparse row of farms and cottages that, had it not been for the telephone and power lines, would have resembled nineteenth century rural America.

"Not even a single satellite dish in sight," Tony marveled. "I doubt they can even pick up our station way out here."

Lindsey had already put the map away and was consulting a small piece of paper with hastily scribbled directions on it under the cab's overhead lamp.

"No wonder they're all anxious to die," she said, keeping her eyes down on her directions. "Without cable TV, what is there to look forward to in life? I mean, out here in the sticks. Religion is probably their only form of entertainment or something."

Tony chuckled nervously and ran his hand through his hair once again.

And then, without warning, he threw his hand back on the steering wheel and slammed on the brakes. The van hydroplaned for a few seconds, and he felt his heart actually skip a beat as he mentally prepared for the van to lose control and careen off the road, sending them tumbling blind into whatever waited out in the darkness beyond the road. The tires finally found traction, and the van skidded to a halt, sending Lindsey crashing forward until her seatbelt went taut and jerked her backward.

"What the hell are you doing?" she shouted.

"This town is deserted!" he shot back. "Look out there … There ain't a goddamn set of lights on in any of these homes."

Lindsey looked out her window at the row of houses on her side of the street. Indeed, all the lights were out.

"Maybe there's a blackout. Maybe they just lost a power line or something, or they're worried about the storm," she offered weakly, staring out her rain-beaded window.

"Lindsey, these homes are all pitch-black! They don't even have any candles burning or anything. If there was a blackout, they'd at least make an effort to light up one room of their houses. Don't you think somebody would be at home at seven o'clock on a Sunday night?"

She looked down at her watch in disbelief, then slapped his arm.

"Dammit, we're going to be late!" she shouted, and Tony shifted back into drive.

The parking lot to the church was nothing more than a patch of grass, but as they pulled in off the road, there was scarcely any place to park. Rows and rows of silent automobiles were being ambushed by the pelting raindrops. It was as if the entire town had come out to attend church service. And as if that wasn't enough, the church itself left them both gasping.

There was a solitary exterior light hanging over the front doors of the building, casting a dim puddle of light over all the parked cars, but when the lightning flashed again, they saw everything.

The building itself was an enormous slate-gray monstrosity, looming like a thunderhead waiting to explode in the darkness. Its dilapidated clapboard sides were adorned with sets of tall stained glass windows, each of which were eerily lit up from the inside of the church. The focal point of each of these windows was a long, yellow-tinted lightning bolt, twisting down from the top of the sash to the bottom. From their view inside the van, it looked more like some giant lunatic funhouse than a church. From the van it looked like a stone demon, or a sleeping god with the rows of cars bowing before it.

The Church of Thunder and Lightning

"What do you suppose they do in there when the weather is nice?" she whispered, just a tad louder than the pouring rain.

"I dunno," Tony responded, his eyes still fixed on the church. "Maybe they have bean suppers or play bingo or something." He glanced over at Lindsey. "Do they even know we're coming to film them?"

"Yeah, yeah. C'mon. Let's get the gear and get in before their service begins."

The church was deserted. The two passed down the center aisle, glancing at the rows and rows of pews where jackets and purses and umbrellas and other miscellaneous personal items were casually abandoned. At the foot of the altar lay a handful of long, thin metal poles that curiously resembled six-foot long fencing epees. Lindsey, with her wireless microphone in one soaked fist and her umbrella in the other, stared uneasily at the metal rods, then back down at the items in her hands.

Tony stared up at the altar, contemplating the mural painted across the back of the pulpit. It depicted a crucifix planted on the top of a mountain, with the image of Jesus painted on the wooden slats. All around him were dark, ominous storm clouds with bolts of lightning erupting in the direction of the cross. Long yellow lines of electrical current were arcing out until they touched his crown of thorns, and the tips of his fingers. It made Tony think of the famous Michelangelo painting of Adam on the ceiling of the Sistine Chapel, only with lightning bolts where God's hand should have been. The thought made him shiver. He took the lens cap off his High-Def digital camera, flipped the record button on, and began to shoot the painting.

"Where do you think they went?" he asked, his voice echoing off the great empty walls around them.

"Oh, shit, we're missing it," Lindsey cried. "C'mon, keep the camera rolling and follow me ..."

Lindsey darted toward a door at the rear of the building and burst through into the pouring rain. Tony followed, the camera bouncing up and down on his shoulder as his short legs trotted to keep up. He kept the camera on her as she sprinted, all the while trying to paw her umbrella open and get it over her head. Within seconds, they were both standing in the rain out behind the church, and immediately the two could hear the sound of people singing hymns somewhere out in the darkened distance.

Thunder roared and lightning crashed, and the field behind the church lit up like a nightmare.

The churchgoers were dancing and parading around the storm-ravaged field, each of them brandishing one of the six-foot metal poles they'd seen inside the church. The elderly, the middle-aged, thirty and twenty-somethings ... even the children were parading about with their metal poles pointed toward the heavens, waiting for the lightning to strike, waiting to be touched by the Finger of God. Many were speaking in tongues, so that their gibberish sounded like a ward of psychiatric patients rather than a congregation of worshippers. Tony stopped and gawked at them, his heart racing in his chest as he prepared himself to probably witness one of these lunatics get struck by lightning.

"Are you getting all this?" Lindsey screamed above the storm. She'd been expecting something like this all along, but the shock of actually seeing it happening left her almost dumbfounded.

"Yeah, but I'll get it better when I get the floodlight on."

"No!" she screeched at him. "Leave the light off. They don't even know we're here. Let's keep it that way for as long as we can."

"The video copy won't be any good without it. You won't be able to see anybody unless the sky lights up when the lightning ..."

"No lights!" she repeated, struggling against the cold rain with her umbrella drawn above her. "Let's just keep this as natural as possible."

"You didn't tell them we were coming, did you?" Tony stopped dead in his tracks. The lightning flashed, turning the stormy night sky into day again, and a roaring bolt from the heavens connected with one of the parishioner's poles. The bolt arced as it contacted the metal, causing a shower of sparks to fly about the crowd. An accompanying boom shook the earth, crashing loud enough to wake the dead. The electrified man danced about for a moment or two before his muscles contracted and his figure went completely stiff. When the bolt passed through him into the ground his knees buckled, and the darkness came pouring in before his dead body could fall to the ground.

The hymns being sang in the darkness ceased momentarily, replaced with the sound of a loud voice preaching to the congregation.

"Praise God! Praise Brother Jesus! Let thy will be done, Oh Lord!"

"We need to get closer," Lindsey shouted over her shoulder. The adrenaline was coursing through her now. Fear was gone, replaced by an urgent need to not miss an instant of what was going on around her. This was her ticket to real journalism. This was her big break.

"Are you fucking crazy? Someone just died out there!" Soaking wet from head to toe, Tony had been out there long enough and had seen all he needed to see. He could smell the smoke now, and the scent of burning flesh floating all around him, followed by the odor of urine and feces as the fallen corpse began to void all over the field. And, never far from his wary subconscious, the realization that the camera on his shoulder was every bit as dangerous as them goddamn metal poles the parishioners were carrying. Everybody out behind the Church of Thunder and Lightning was in real, mortal danger, and that included Lindsey and himself. All of this was wrong, and a quick thought passed through his brain ...

I wish we were back with them goddamn rattlesnake shakers!

"Fine, give me the camera," she snapped, dropping her umbrella onto the ground. It bounced against the soggy earth once before a gust of wind snapped it up and blew it away.

Lightning struck again in the field, and another pole-carrying worshipper was snuffed out of existence in a blinding flash of light. His agonized scream pierced the night in spite of the roaring thunderclap that stripped his life away.

From the darkness, the sound of voices began to wail and call out in triumph, shouting "Alleluias" and "Amens" into the face of the storm. And then, the more haunting shouts of, "Please, God ..." and "Take me, Oh Lord, I'm ready!"

"Take the fucking camera!" Tony screamed at her, holding the equipment out to her in his wet, hairy fingers. "I'll be in the van waiting for you."

As she took the camera, the sky ripped open again and a bolt of lightning fell to the earth, and a little girl in a bright yellow dress was touched by the Finger of God.

Lindsey gave him a disgusted look, and then pushed ahead toward the field, the rain pouring down on her and the camera. In the darkness beyond her, Tony could see the silhouettes of the worshippers dancing around, poles waving about in the air. A few had set their poles down long enough to drag the dead bodies out of the way, and then returned to their ceremony in the hope that they should be the next to be touched by the Finger of God.

Tony never looked back as he ran toward the van in the front parking lot.

It was hours before the storm finally passed. Hours of Tony turning over the ignition and starting the van, planning to just drive away and leave Lindsey behind, then shutting the engine off again in a fit of anger. He found himself thinking of Renee on her deathbed; how he ran his fingers through her hair as he watched her chest rise and contract until her breathing ceased, and then watched the little green line on the EKG machine go flat. Then his thoughts drifted back to Lindsey, out behind the church running around with his Sony High-Def camera on her shoulder in the middle of a horribly lethal thunderstorm. Christ, she'd been gone for what felt like an eternity. And every bolt of lightning, every crash of thunder in the field behind the church made his heart race and his eyes wet with tears. Renee's death had been a blessing, one he'd prayed for after watching his partner in life suffering for so long. Now he was praying for Lindsey. He found himself trying to bargain with God—the way he'd tried to bargain for Renee, when she'd first been diagnosed—offering whatever promises came into his mind. Anything to keep the Finger of God away from her.

How she'd ever found about these freaks he couldn't imagine, but then he'd felt the same way about the rattlesnake shakers. Seeing them dancing around, shaking live copperheads with their bare hands, had given him an instant case of the willies. But at least they could take snakebite serum if they managed to mess up and get bit (and one or two *had* gotten bit before that ceremony was over). These jerks had no options once the lightning struck. There was no cure for death, that much was certain.

And no cure for stupid, either. Not just for these people, but for Lindsey as well. The little blond tart with her master's degree and lust for big-time journalism, she didn't even care one bit if any of these people died tonight, so long as it bettered her career. Tony made a mental note to tell their producer that he was all done working with her after this little escapade.

If she managed to make it through tonight alive, that was.

There wasn't enough alcohol to in the world to make him forget about this assignment. This was the one he'd be carrying with him to his grave.

Tony watched as the congregation (what was left of them) exited the church. They were smiling and laughing under the dim light from above the building's doors as they made their way to their cars and drove off into the darkness. None of them seemed to acknowledge his presence, or give a hint that they had perhaps run into his colleague out behind the church. As the parking lot emptied, Tony finally worked up the nerve to go out and look for her.

The smell of death and electricity was immediate, and shades beyond terrible. It seemed to linger in the warm, humid air, as if the clouds above had trapped the malodorous stench and pressed it back down against the earth. He felt himself holding his breath as he sidled his way around the building and into the darkness. The dread of panicked anticipation crept over him as he found the row of laid-out bodies, waiting to be buried by the light of day as the storm drifted off to wherever storms go when their hearts have emptied and died. There were so many … far more than he'd have dared to believe.

He had no problem finding Lindsey, as the video camera's LED light continued to blink on standby mode on the ground next to her. Its red flash winked like a serpent's eye in the darkness. Tony wondered in terror what he would see if he picked up the camera and switched it to playback mode. He thought he might see exactly what she had seen before the lightning burned the life out of her body. How the camera could still be working was a mystery, but then, didn't the Lord work in mysterious ways?

Tony wrestled the camera from her cold, dead grip and made his way back down to the van, weeping as he struggled to decide whether or not he'd watch the video footage. The video would now be considered evidence, and legal authorities (as well as the company insurance department) would want to view it to make whatever determinations needed to be made about Lindsey's death. There was a brief moment where Tony considered just smashing the camera on the ground and destroying the footage, but decided against it. Who was he to piss off a God of such terrible vengeance?

He opened the van's door and set the camera on the passenger seat where Lindsey had been sitting. He closed the door, sighed, and took out his cell phone. His fingers trembled as he dialed 911. He took a breath and waited to speak to whoever might be waiting on the other side to respond to his emergency call. The air around him felt warm and humid and made him shiver. There was an awful second where he was sure the sky would rip open once more, even though the storm had passed, and a bolt of lightning would find him. It filled him with terror, and made him wonder what the Finger of God might feel like.

Contributors

MICHAEL ARRUDA published his first short story back in 1998. Since then, he's published short stories in anthologies, magazines, and websites. He also cowrites the movie column *Cinema Knife Fight* with L. L. Soares. Michael also served as one of the first cochairs of the New England Chapter of the HWA.

DAVID BERNARD is a native Bay Stater who now lives in southern Florida but still writes primarily of New England. His most recent work can be found in the Harrow Press anthology *Mortis Operandi* and the Pill Hill Press anthologies *Daily Frights 2012* and *Daily Bites of Flesh 2011*.

TRACY L. CARBONE (*www.tracylcarbone.com*) is a New England native who lives with her daughter and a houseful of pets. She has published several horror and literary short stories in magazines and anthologies in the U.S. and Canada. Her YA horror novel, *The Soul Collector*, will be released by Shadowfall Publications in late fall 2011. She is Cochair of the New England Horror Writers (NEHW) and a member of the Horror Writers Association (HWA).

GLENN CHADBOURNE's artwork has appeared in over thirty books, as well as numerous comics and magazines. His trademark pen-and-ink drawings accompany the work of today's hottest horror authors. His story "Deep Six," coauthored with Holly Newstein, appeared in *Cemetery Dance Magazine*. Glenn lives in coastal Maine with his wife, Sheila, and pug, Rocket.

CONTRIBUTORS

ROXANNE DENT has sold eight novels and four shorts. She also cowrote two plays put on by the Firehouse Theater in Newburyport, MA, and won first prize from *Fade In Magazine* for her screenplay, "The Pied Piper." She is currently working on a full-length Victorian mystery.

STEPHEN DORATO is a native Bostonian whose work has appeared in *Gothic.net*, *Feral Fiction*, and *Blood Lite III: Aftertaste*. He lives in a small coastal town with his lovely wife and a capricious labradoodle.

PETER N. DUDAR is a proud alumnus of the State University of New York at Albany. Aside from writing scary fiction, Peter is cohost of *Radical Static*, an 80s music radio program on 97.1 WJZF out of Standish, Maine (*www.WJZF.org* to listen online), and writes erotica under the pseudonym Manlius Latham. He lives in Lisbon Falls, Maine with his wife Amy and their daughter Vivian.

DANNY EVARTS (*www.dannyevarts.net*) is an illustrator, editor and graphic designer who lives with his partner in the wilds of the Maine woods. While his primary work is for Shroud Publishing, a freelance stable keeps him busy. His illustrations can be found in *SHROUD Magazine* and the *Hiram Grange* Series, among many other places. His Unchildren's Book with Nathaniel Lambert, *It's Okay to be a Zombie*, was released in 2010.

CHRISTOPHER GOLDEN (*www.christophergolden.com*) is an award-winning, bestselling author of novels for adults and teens, as well as an editor, screenwriter, and comic book creator. His original novels have been published in more than fourteen languages in countries around the world.

P. GARDNER GOLDSMITH is a television scriptwriter and author who has worked on *Star Trek: Voyager* and *The Outer Limits*. His short stories have been published in the US and UK, and his recent book, *Live Free or Die*, was named Book of the Month by the Freedom Book Club.

JOHN GOODRICH lives in the haunted Green Mountains of Vermont, the last refuge of true Lovecraft country. Every story he has published, including this one, reflects some aspect of his unsavory lifestyle. When not writing, he is studying to become a lab technician in order to better practice his haruspicy.

CONTRIBUTORS

SCOTT T. GOUDSWARD lives and writes in New England. His short fiction has appeared in Pill Hill's *How the West was Wicked* and *2011 Daily Bites of Flesh*. Scott's Non-fiction has been nominated for the Rondo Award and been on the HWA's Stoker preliminary ballot; *Shadows Over Florida* and *Shadows Over New England* (Foreword by NEHW's Christopher Golden), both from Bear manor media. Scott also has a Novel, *Trailer Trash*, and an anthology, *Traps*, from Dark Hart Press.

JOHN GROVER (*www.shadowtales.com*) is a horror/ dark fantasy author residing in Boston. He has been published in *Flesh and Blood Magazine, Morpheus Tales, The Willows, Wrong World, Silver Blade, Screaming Dreams, Best New Zombie Tales, Northern Haunts* anthology from Shroud Publishing, and the *Zombology* series by Library of the Living Dead Press. He has also authored several collections and chapbooks.

RICK HAUTALA (*www.rickhautala.com*) has more than thirty published books to his credit, including the million copy, international best seller *Nightstone*. He has also published four novels under the name A. J. Matthews. His more than sixty published short stories have appeared in national and international anthologies and magazines. He lives in southern Maine with author Holly Newstein.

STACEY LONGO's (*www.staceylongo.com*) stories have appeared in *Shroud Magazine* and *The Litchfield Literary Review*, as well as the anthologies *Malicious Deviance, Hell Hath No Fury,* and *Zombidays: Festivities of the Flesheaters*, among others. She lives in Connecticut with her husband, Jason, and two cats, Wednesday and Pugsley.

JOHN M. McILVEEN lives is Massachusetts and works at MIT's Lincoln Laboratory. He is, or has been: a father, son; electrician, pipe-fitter, carpenter; bookseller, writer, editor, publisher; facility, electrical and mechanical engineer; winner, loser; student, teacher; beginner, pro; on top, and on bottom. He likes being a father the best … the rest he'll figure out someday.

PAUL McMAHON sits amid the clutter and chaos of four kids and tries to write monster stories while dodging Nerf darts and jump ropes and holding still while the youngest sings Barney tunes and braids his hair. He's still in

CONTRIBUTORS

there, somewhere, searching for an escape through his fiction. His work appears periodically in the wild, making a chaos all its own.

HOLLY NEWSTEIN's short fiction has appeared in *Cemetery Dance Magazine* and the anthologies *Borderlands 5*, *The New Dead*, and the forthcoming *In Laymon's Terms*. She is coauthor of the novels *Ashes* and *The Epicure* under the pen name H. R. Howland. She lives in Maine with the author Rick Hautala and her fur kids, Keira and Remy.

KURT NEWTON's poetry has appeared in *Weird Tales*, *Strange Horizons*, *Chizine*, *Star*Line*, *Dreams and Nightmares*, and *Mythic Delirium*. His eighth poetry collection, *The Ultimate perVERSEities*, was published in 2010 by Naked Snake Press. He lives in Connecticut.

DAVID NORTH-MARTINO's fiction has appeared in *Dark Recesses Press*, *Afterburn SF*, *The Swamp*, and the *Extinct Doesn't Mean Forever* Anthology. He is hard at work on his first novel. When he's not writing he loves to study martial arts. He lives with his wife in a small town in Massachusetts.

JEFFREY C. PETTENGILL is a New England native who by day is a financial analyst for a hospital, writing when he can find time. He is a member of HWA, NEHW and EWAG. His horror has appeared in *Bits of the Dead*, *Love Kills: My Bloody Valentine*, and *Daily Bites of Flesh 2011: 365 Days of Flash Fiction*.

PHILIP ROBERTS (*www.philipmroberts.com*) lives in Nashua, New Hampshire and holds a degree in Creative Writing with a minor in Film from the University of Kansas. As a beginner in the publishing world, he's a member of both the Horror Writer's Association and the New England Horror Writers, and has had numerous short stories published in a variety of publications, such as the *Beneath the Surface* anthology, *Midnight Echo*, and *The Absent Willow Review*.

L. L. SOARES (*www.llsoares.com*) is a Stoker-nominated writer whose fiction has appeared in many places, such as *Cemetery Dance*, *Bare Bone*, and *Horror Garage*. His story collection *In Sickness* (with Laura Cooney) is available now from Skullvines Press. He also writes film reviews at Cinema Knife Fight (*cinemaknifefight.com*).

MICHAEL TODD is a writer and a shredder guitarist with over 3000 live performances in North America with such "horror" acts as Wretched Asylum, Big Top Charlie, The Dead and the Damned, and American Hellbilly–the Rob Zombie Tribute. His original songs have been heard worldwide, most notably "3:15," his song about the real murders that occurred in Amityville. Michael is also working on a novel, a screenplay and several short stories which he hopes to publish once the gigs run out.

B. ADRIAN WHITE lives among the secluded forests and mist-covered fields of central Massachusetts. He has written the sinister Faustian novel, *The Soulless*, and is working on his second novel, *The Industries*. Besides crafting dark supernatural fiction, he writes technical documentation for the sustainability website, ECOMII.

STEVEN WITHROW is a Rhode Island poet, storyteller, and author of six books for visual artists. He is the producer of *Library of the Early Mind*, a documentary exploring children's literature. He studied at Roger Williams University and Emerson College and has taught at Rhode Island School of Design and Suffolk University.

K. ALLEN WOOD (*www.kallenwood.com*) is a former musician and music journalist. His fiction has appeared in *52 Stitches, Vol. 2* and *The Zombie Feed, Vol. 1*. He is also the editor/publisher of *Shock Totem*, a biannual horror fiction magazine. He lives and plots in Massachusetts.

TRISHA J. WOOLDRIDGE is the readings and events coordinator of Broad Universe, an international non-profit supporting women in speculative fiction. She's published in the EPIC award-winning (2010) *Bad-Ass Faeries 2: Just Plain Bad*, EPIC award-nominated (2011) *Bad-Ass Faeries 3: In all Their Glory*, and several poetry and non-fiction venues. Visit her at *www.anovelfriend.com*.

T. T. ZUMA (ANTHONY H. TREMBLAY) lives in New Hampshire and reviews dark fiction for *Horror World* and *Cemetery Dance Magazine* under the pen name T. T. Zuma. "The Burial Board" is his second published work of horror fiction.

Shroud Publishing

Shroud Publishing LLC is an independent publisher of speculative fiction with a dark focus.

In addition, *Shroud Magazine*, a journal of dark fiction and art, features original art, film, music reviews, and articles that illuminate the thin veil between reality and fantasy.

Shroud's Anthology *Beneath the Surface: 13 Shocking Tales of Terror* was a Bram Stoker Award nominee, and many of its other collections and novellas have gained acclaim throughout the horror industry.

For more on Shroud, visit
www.shroudmagazine.com

SHROUD PUBLISHING
MILTON, NH